D0829034

THE FLEET
BOOK 6: CRISIS

Including . . .

Christopher Stasheff
ORPHANS

Khalian pirates discover that revenge is possible when
victory is not.

Poul Anderson
KINETIC KILL

The weapon was unthinkable, the defense unbearable.

Chelsea Quinn Yarbro
TARNHELMS

Invisible aliens make perfect assassins—but can the
Syndicate keep them under control?

Mike Resnick
PAWNS

War is a game with living pieces—and some are
expendable.

AND MANY OTHERS!

CRISIS

THE FLEET

BOOK 6

Edited by
David Drake *and* Bill Fawcett

ACE BOOKS, NEW YORK

This book is an Ace original edition,
and has never been previously published.

THE FLEET
BOOK 6: CRISIS

An Ace Book / published by arrangement with
Bill Fawcett & Associates.

PRINTING HISTORY
Ace edition / February 1991

ISBN: 0-441-24106-9

Ace Books are published by The Berkley Publishing Group,
200 Madison Avenue, New York, New York 10016.
The name "ACE" and the "A" logo
are trademarks belonging to Charter Communications, Inc.

PRINTED IN THE UNITED STATES OF AMERICA

10 9 8 7 6 5 4 3 2 1

CONTENTS
Book 6: Crisis

INTERLUDE

With thousands of ships spread over an area across which it can take months for a courier to deliver any message, any fleet needs rules to guide the conduct of its officers when acting independently. Traditionally these rules cover virtually every aspect of command decision and are referred to as the Articles of War.

Article VII
Every person subject to this act who shall- (1) Traitorously hold Correspondence with or shall give Intelligence to the Enemy;
   (2) Or fail to make known to the proper authorities any information received from the Enemy;
   (3) Or shall relieve the Enemy with any supplies, shall suffer Death, or such other Punishment as is herein-after mentioned.

A year after one of the elite brainship decoys confirmed the existence of a massive Syndicate fleet, it had still not appeared to contest the Alliance occupation of Khalia. During this time thousands of intelligence officers, clerks, analysts, and scouts worked to locate the home worlds of the Syndicate of Families. Slowly, carefully, data were sifted and patterns analyzed. Even as they worked, everyone knew the peace was deceptive and there would come a battle that would determine the fate of both human empires.

The Fleet used this year to build and train. Thousands of ships were commissioned. Often they were manned by new recruits leavened with a few experienced officers. Slowly, frustratingly slowly, for Duane and his staff, these ships began to arrive at their forward bases on Target and nearby Khalia. Located only a few light-years apart, the planets were an almost-ideal base from which to strike out at the cluster suspected to contain the Syndicate.

For many months tensions between the still-proud Khalian warriors and Fleet personnel erupted into sporadic violence. Neither side was ready to forget or forgive the atrocities perpetrated by the other. Even as a grudging mutual respect developed, some incident was needed to jell the union of former foes. Fleet propagandists waited, hoping for some event they could make into a symbol of unity between the races. When the incident did occur, it involved two most unexpected participants.

ORPHANS
by Christopher Stasheff

IN THE DARKNESS of space two ships fought against a dozen. The two were cruisers—one of the Fleet, one a Khalian pirate—captained by two old enemies, Commander Sales and Captain Goodheart, who had finally found a foe greater than their own hatred—the Merchants, they who had suborned the barbarian Khalia, armed them with modern weapons, and given them spaceships for chariots. Now, the Khalian pirates fought with savage glee, able at last to strike at the humans who had betrayed their kind—and the human Fleet ship fought with the zeal reserved for traitors to their species.

But in the midst of all that zeal, a cold stab of reason came through to the Fleet signalman, who realized that this was his final battle, that there was almost no chance of his surviving. Though he could think of no finer way to die, he knew with an even more desperate longing that the people on the Terran planets must learn of the Syndicate nest they'd blundered into, and the merciless, instant tactics of the Merchants. So, even as

3

he routed signals between ships, he opened a transmission channel, locked a dish to stay pointed toward Target no matter how the ship maneuvered, and stabbed a tachyon beam at the forward base, carrying the ship-to-ship signals, audio and video, on both Fleet and Khalian frequencies. If he had known the Merchants' band, he would have fed their signals through, too—but the Fleet, as yet, could not even hear their enemies. He even redirected a few precious launches to send message torps speeding off in reserve.

Then a Syndicate torpedo holed her defenses, and Good-heart's ship became an expanding globe of light. Minutes later, Sales's Fleet cruiser exploded, scattering debris thousands of miles around a globe of plasma, sending a furious wash of energy over the tachyon channel to Terra.

One piece of that debris was a cigar-shaped cocoon, two meters long and a meter wide. It shot spinning end over end for a thousand miles and more, and surely would have convulsed its lone inhabitant with nausea, if needles had not stabbed into him just before the explosion, releasing chemicals that slowed his metabolism and sent him into the deepest of sleeps as a cryogenic unit froze him in seconds. On the pod floated, into darkness, bearing a wounded crewman who had been slapped into a freezing pod by the medics, to be thawed out when a hospital ship picked him up. But he was far from Terra now, far from the routes of Fleet ships, where none but Merchantmen came. His pod sailed on through the unending night, alone, unknown, unknowing.

On the station orbiting Target, a bored signalman sipped coffee and eyed the girlie cube that was waiting for the end of his shift. Nothing ever happened in an automated station. Why did they bother having a human on duty?

The alarm sang.

The signalman jarred upright in his chair, searching his banks of monitors and tallies. There—red flashing on Vertical Four! The system didn't know what to do with a rogue signal, whether to waste permanent memory on it or not. The signalman hacked at his keyboard, finished the sequence, and pressed "execute" just before the buffer filled. The jewel on the tally glowed, showing that it was cutting, just in time. The signalman heaved a sigh of relief and settled back, keying in a stepped-down relay of the signal, and turned to his monitor to see just what kind of tachyon "fish" his energy net had caught.

"Cannon Three is out!"

"Screens overloading!"

"Cut life-support to minimum and route power to screens!"

Behind all the Terran words were the shrilling whistles of Khalian speech, but the signalman couldn't comprehend them. He could understand, though, the huge explosion of light as the screen flickered to scale down sensitivity to cope with the glare—and he saw the silhouette of a corvette in front of the light ball. The signalman didn't need a book to know it was a shape he'd never seen before, ever—and he didn't need a translator to tell him what it meant when the Weasel whistles cut off as the light globe exploded. For a moment reverence for a gallant enemy touched his heart, shoving aside the hatred of Khalians brought by generations of war—then a pang of loss as he realized that whoever was fighting those Khalians was also fighting the Fleet ship that was sending the images.

"Commander Sales!" a voice yelled from the screen, "they got Goodheart!"

"Get *them*," a deeper voice snarled.

"Torpedo away!" a nasal voice snapped.

The signalman hung on to the edge of his chair, watching, waiting, forgetting that this signal was at least hours, probably days, old, and the battle long ended.

Then the silhouette of the corvette blew apart into debris, and the expanding light ball dimmed where it had been, while shouts of victory rattled around it.

Then the whole screen erupted in a wash of light, dimmed instantly but cut by a hash of snow, and white noise roared with it.

The signalman realized he was dripping with sweat. He watched the tally on the cube cutter, the jewel on Vertical Four . . .

Both were out.

The signalman sat back with a sigh. Whatever it was, it was

over—and two gallant ships had died. He sat still for a moment in silent respect.

Then he leaned forward, keyed the signal for HQ on Target, and said, "This is Station Two. Emergency. Route me to the adjutant."

Another sentry received the signal, another sensor operator on a lonely vigil—but this one had fur and sharp teeth and was planetbound, on Barataria, the Khalian pirates' nest. He was a Khalian communications operator, who knew which buttons to push but very little of what happened inside his console. He only knew that an unscheduled signal triggered the alarm, so he did as his detail prescribed—keyed in the recorder. As the light beam engraved the signal on the cube, the operator frowned at its trace on his screen, at the warble-and-hash it made on his speaker. He pressed the call button for the officer of the watch and said, "Alert. Unscheduled transmission being received. It is scrambled—encoded with an unknown cipher. What shall I do?"

"It is what?" the officer barked, astonished.

"Scrambled. Shall I continue to record?"

"Of course!" his superior snapped. "If it is scrambled, it is very likely to contain important information! Be sure it records completely . . ."

A huge burst of static rasped through the speakers. The operator's ears fairly rang with it—then seemed to echo in the sudden silence. "Transmission complete," he informed the watch officer. "Procedure?"

"Take the cube to the new Bards," the watch officer said immediately. "They should have it on the screen within the hour."

But they didn't—not for many an hour to come.

"It is Sales's cipher," the Intelligence officer informed Throb, the Castellan—the ranking Khalian officer in Captain Goodheart's absence. "We recognize its progressions—but we have not yet been able to assign it meanings."

"Not yet!" Throb screeched, exasperated. "That parasite has been plaguing us for two years! Why can you never break his code?"

"We have, several times—but though he keeps the same encoding of the signal, he is continually changing the meaning assigned to any given wave form. By the time we break one, he has shifted to another. And in this instance, the majority of the signal is video—we cannot even say with certainty which mathematical structures are for scanning, and which for color vectors. He keeps shifting video systems."

"Then isolate the audio portion and break *that* code! But I must know what he spoke of, and quickly!"

"We shall do it as promptly as we may, Lieutenant."

But the Alliance did it quicker. They already knew Sales's code, of course—they had the computer-enhanced image on the screen in minutes. The adjutant listened and watched for ninety seconds, then woke up the admiral. The admiral watched the whole recording, and woke up the CEO on Terra, sending the whole sequence as a squeezed signal. The CEO watched it, then called in the Cabinet, who watched in awed silence.

The final burst of white noise accompanied the flare; the screen went dark; and the CEO turned to them all, seeking out each one's gaze, one by one, as the impact of what they had seen diminished.

"It will have to be edited down, of course," the minister of internal policy said at last. "The broadcast nets will cut it themselves, if we don't."

"No, they won't," the minister of communications said softly. "I'll invoke the Public Safety Clause. They'll show it intact. I think they would, anyway."

The CEO nodded. "Show it just the way it is. It speaks for itself."

The commentators couldn't allow that, of course—but they did keep the introduction brief. Everyone who was watching the news that night, on all the Terran and Khalian planets, sat silent in awe, feeling grief well up, as they watched the gallant Terran and Khalian ships, enemies turning against a greater enemy, fighting to the last without the slightest inclination to flee, from a foe who fought in deadly silence, with no warning, no demand for surrender, no slightest offer of mercy. They watched, and saw a human come to the aid of a Khalian, fighting other humans . . . .

Merchant humans.

The screen went blank, then lit again with the image of the two commentators.

"But they were enemies, Dave!" said Chester. "Sworn enemies! Captain Goodheart, sworn to destroy every Terran ship he could—and Commander Sales, sworn to destroy Goodheart!"

"They died forsworn." Chester nodded, frowning. "In the end, they realized who the real enemy was—and humans and Khalians joined forces against him."

"It is a lie!" Throb leaped up, naked claws poised over the man's image on the screen. "All humans are enemies to all Khalians! The Merchants swore to aid us, and betrayed us! The Fleet slew us wholesale, gutted our planets!"

"You have heard for yourself," Serum said. He was older, beginning to gray around the muzzle. "We all heard the captain's voice. The Merchants are the true enemy."

"It was altered!" Throb lifted his head as an even better explanation hit, widening his eyes. "It was a complete fabrication! It never happened, none of it! The captain still lives! It is only that the Terrans wish to make us think he is dead!"

"What is, is." Serum's sorrow deepened to sternness. "Do not seek to deny what is real, or you will lead yourself and all your warriors into disaster."

"I deny nothing but a lie! I state only what is true, what must be true! Must it not, Globin? . . . Globin!"

The pirate colony's only human sat immobile, back bent, shoulders sagging, hands between his legs, head bowed.

"Globin!" Throb shrilled. "Are you senseless? Do you not hear? Tell them it is a lie!"

Slowly Globin lifted his head. His eyes were red; his face was gray; tears streamed down his cheeks.

Throb stared at him as though he were seeing a ghost.

"Let him be," Serum said softly. "His god is dead."

• • •

Globin—torso long, legs short and bowed, head two sizes too large for his ill-proportioned body. Eyes too huge through his bottle-glass spectacles, face a doughy mass, hair a black thatch, mouth almost lipless. Globin, the genius.

Globin, the outcast.

His fellow humans had heard his new name, given him by Goodheart's Khalian pirates, and had twisted it to express their new hate. To them he became—

Globin, the traitor.

A traitor to all his race, to all that is right and good, for he helped the Khalian pirate prey upon human ships, helped the bloody Weasels shoot down Fleet ships.

Georgie Desrick, the outcast.

His playmates mocked his ugliness, his schoolmates parodied his clumsiness. His classmates scorned him for his bookishness, hated him for his exalting of the mind and complete disregard of the body.

But what friends could he have, except books? When none would teach him the use of his body, because it was too great an effort for so slow a learner?

"I swear, Georgie Desrick, I don't know what you bother living for!"

"Why don't you just drop dead, Georgie Desrick?"

The question was well asked—and its only answer was faith. Faith in his God, faith in humankind. Georgie Desrick clung to life by religion.

Finally, his fellow junior officers, in spite and hatred, manufactured excuses, made him a scapegoat, and set him adrift in a lifeboat.

And in the darkness and despair, faith at last wore out, and Georgie Desrick cursed both his race and his God.

Then Goodheart saved him—Goodheart, seeking to cultivate a human traitor, though Globin couldn't know that until it no longer mattered—for Goodheart was his friend, Goodheart was his teacher, Goodheart was his protector.

Goodheart was his god.

Saved by Goodheart, nurtured by Goodheart, given a name by Goodheart, accepted by the pirates on Goodheart's orders,

Globin lived by Goodheart and for Goodheart, all for
Goodheart . . .

And Goodheart was dead.

"No, Globin, no!"

It was a furred paw that caught his hand, clawed fingers that
twisted the knife from his grasp, a Khalian doctor that pressed
the anesthetic spray against his arm . . .

No, not Khalian, he thought with groggy insight as he sank
down into the depths of sedation. Not Khalian. Pirate. Goodheart's pirate . . .

"What use, Throb? The captain is dead! How can you aid his
revenge?"

"By finding his slayers!" Throb snarled as he stepped into
the shuttle. "I cannot sit idle when my captain is dead, and his
killers boasting in their guilt! You are Castellan in my absence,
Serum!" And he slammed the hatch shut.

Serum watched the little shuttle lift off, his spirit ascending
to the battlecruiser with Throb, knowing well how intolerable
it was to sit and do nothing when every cell of his being cried
out for vengeance.

Light-years away Throb's ship broke out of hyperspace and
began to snoop, lying quietly while its sensors scanned the
whole area and searched for stars that moved. When it found
none, and no signals other than the background static of stars,
it winked into hyperspace again and was gone, to emerge a few
light-years farther along the course, moving steadily in toward
that part of the sky from which the final transmission had
come. Again it scanned the sky, lying still for an hour and
receiving—nothing. So it jumped again, and again . . .

"It will take us months," the helmsman estimated.

"Assuming what?"

"The top cruising speed of the captain's ship, multiplied by
the time elapsed since he left port."

Throb nodded. "Then months it will be."

But it was only a day. Finally, when they broke out, there
was radiation—the sub-light transmission of ships in conflict.
Throb listened and recognized the battle as the one he had
already watched, too many times. "Laggard light speed only

now carries word of his doom! How long since the transmission was received on Barataria?"

"Five days, Lieutenant."

"Then we are five light-days from the scene of the ambush, or less! Helm . . ."

"Object in movement!" cried the sensor operator.

Throb swung to the screen, staring. A pinpoint of light moved, only a little, but moved. "Bearing!"

"Toward us—two degrees to starboard. Velocity is half Tau!"

"Half of light speed? It will approach us in minutes! Match velocity! Ready an intercept!"

Throb himself longed to be suited and jetting, but it was two lesser crewmen who drifted in space, waiting as the silvery pod approached them. It swam beneath them slowly; they dropped down to it and attached the grapple. "Haul in!"

The winch sang, and the mile-long cable began to pull in, bringing the pod with it.

"It is not a lifeboat," the crewman reported. "Can it be a coffin?"

"Perhaps; the Fleet honor their . . ."

"Ship appears!"

Throb spun about. On the display a spot of light moved where none had been before. "Battle stations! It cannot be a friend!"

It was not. It approached rapidly, dot swelling to a discernible oblong. Magnification showed them a foreshortened view of . . .

"The same silhouette as the murderer of our captain! Attack!"

"The cable will snap, Captain. We will lose the pod."

Throb cursed, then said, "We must wait for him—but fire as soon as he is within range."

Fire blossomed from the Merchantman's nose.

"Shields up!" Throb shrilled. "Can you crank that winch no faster?"

"It comes at top speed, Lieutenant."

"So does the Merchant! Forward batteries! Fire!"

The screen went lurid as their own shields drank up the

attacker's energy bolt. It cleared, to show the enemy adazzle as their bolt struck his defenses—but the next bolt did not strike at them, but a little to the side.

"He shoots at the pod!" Throb screamed. "It must be of vast importance! Toward it, maximum thrust!"

Their ship surged to the side; the screen went scarlet as Throb shielded the pod with his own ship. Then he felt a slight shudder, and a crewman shouted, "Pod aboard! Expedition recovered!"

The sensor op howled, "Two more ships appear! They accelerate toward us!"

"The coward has called for help!" Throb spat. "But we shall not leave without wounding him, at the least! Evasive action! All batteries fire when clear! Torpedoes away—fire one! Fire two! Fire three!"

The ship rocked, shot forward, dived, rolled, shot on again, leaving a trail of energy bolts speeding toward the Merchant-man. His screens glowed red, then orange, yellow, white . . .

A new star lit the night.

"He is dead!" Throb crowed. "My captain, savor this first sip of the draft of vengeance!"

"We must live to bear him a full cup," the helmsman snapped.

"Jump!" Throb shouted. "Set course for Barataria!"

The whole ship seemed to turn itself inside out, then right side in. The crew sagged in their seats, the pitch of battle ebbing.

Then Throb loosed his webbing and rose, turning toward the aft hatch. "Let us see what fish we have caught."

The medic stood by, hypos ready, as the mechanics cracked the seal. Air hissed into vacuum, and they lifted the top half of the pod. Motors hummed as hidden machinery began to revive the occupant.

"A human!" Throb spat.

"With the uniform of the Fleet," the doctor reminded him. "He is badly wounded."

"Heal him then! He must talk!"

The medic bent over the pod, striving to recall what little he knew of human medicine.

Throb waited, the minutes dragging, cursing the slowness of revival.

Finally, the human's eyelids fluttered, then opened. He looked around him, frowning, not understanding . . .

Then his eyes widened in recognition, and he screamed.

The doctor jammed the hypo bulb against the inside of his elbow and squeezed. The sedative shot into his bloodstream, and his eyes closed, returning to sleep.

"When he wakes," Throb hissed, "assure him he is among friends. Nay, we will even swear to return him to his own kind—for he is a survivor of the ship that fought against our captain's enemy. And call me—I shall want to ask him questions. With warmth, with respect—but with insistence."

"Globin."

The voice pulled him up from the depths of nonexistence; a strong grip hauled him out of the dear darkness he longed for. "The Council has need of your knowledge. You must meet with them, Globin."

"Why?" he muttered through a mouth that felt as though it were made of cotton. "Why should I?"

"For Goodheart's sake."

The lieutenants looked up, six of them, as Globin came in, ashen-faced, glary-eyed, leaning on a cane and the doctor's arm. They were six.

Globin made seven.

"What need have we of this intruder?" Hemo said with a contemptuous twist of his head.

"Well asked," Globin croaked, glowering. "What need? Why pull me out of the death I crave?"

Even Hemo stared, shocked.

It was Throb, strangely, who spoke to him gently. "Our captain is dead, Globin. You must help us find the slime-sheet who slew him."

"To what purpose?" Globin looked up, almost indignant. "Why must I? For what?"

"Why," said Hemo contemptuously, "to slay them, of course."

"Revenge?" Globin sat bolt-still, eyes widening. "Do you speak of revenge?"

"Of course!" Hemo spat. "Is your species so bovine that I must speak it aloud for you? Certainly, revenge!"

And the cause burst white-hot within Globin, bringing him upright in his chair, returning a beat to his heart and heat to his blood. He would not die, but live—for revenge!

They told him the way of it—their signalmen had broken Sales's code, and Throb had been wrong—the Alliance had broadcast the entire event, even as it had happened, as much of it as they had seen. Still, Throb had not believed. He had demanded Goodheart's last known course, had saturated that sector with calls to his captain—encoded, of course, and relayed through the network of satellite repeaters that Globin had designed to prevent any Fleet ship from tracing Barataria by its emissions. Failing to receive answer, he had dredged the vector of Sales's transmission from the signal records and filled space with calls to his captain—but there had been no answer. Even then, unsatisfied, he had taken a ship and gone to search—

"No answer?" Globin exclaimed. "To so much effort? How long have I been unconscious then?"

"Two days, Globin," Throb said softly.

"Two days!" Globin bowed his head. "Two days I lazed in that soft darkness while my captain's killers escaped!"

"Two days while I wasted time proving the signal's truth," Throb corrected. "But I found a medical pod, with a crewman of the Fleet who had been wounded, and frozen till he could come to hospital. We could not save him, but he lived long enough to tell us the truth of what he saw. I am convinced. The captain is dead, Globin."

Globin bowed his head, grief upwelling again.

"He is dead." Then Throb hissed his indictment: "But you are alive. Globin, find me his killers."

"You must come, Globin."

Globin didn't even take his eyes from the display. "Leave

me. I have almost determined where the captain met
his . . . his last enemy."

The crewman was silent a moment out of respect, then
pressed, "I greatly dislike to intrude on so vital a moment—but
if you do not come, there may be another death. Many."

Globin sat still, eyes on the display.

Then, slowly, he turned. "Whose ship is at hazard?"

"Hemo's," said the courier. "Come quickly, Lieutenant."

Globin came into the central communications hall one pace
behind the courier. He saw Throb, Serum, and the other three
gathered around the main display screen, gazing up at the
image of Hemo.

"I will not!" the giant face raged. "If his killers will come
anywhere, they will come here!"

"The captain would not have wished . . ."

"The captain would wish to be avenged! You cannot tell me
where his slayers lie, Globin cannot tell me where they lie!
Here I stay, till they come, or death does!"

Globin stepped up behind Throb. "How has he done this?"

Throb whirled, and there was the faintest ghost of relief in
his eyes before pride masked it. But he did not say, "Thank the
gods," or "You have come!"—all he said was, "He is a
captain, and one of the lieutenants. Who could say him nay if
he took his own ship and sped? The captain is gone."

Globin could have said something about the Council, but it
would have been worthless—the Khalia were fiercely indepen-
dent; only their personal loyalty to Goodheart had kept them
disciplined. They were feudal; the liegeman's bond was
everything. Without it, there was no cohesion.

So Globin said none of that; he only asked, "Where is he?"

"On a line between Khalia and the coordinates from which
the captain's death signal came." Throb took a breath, then
said, "I have persuaded, I have worked upon his fellow-
feelings, his duty to his crew, to us! He will not be moved."

Globin nodded. "You have appealed to his emotions. You
wish me to appeal to his reason."

"Yes, such of it as he has left! Globin, make him see his
folly!"

Globin frowned, and moved slightly to the side, into the video's pickup field. "Why, Hemo?"

Aboard the pirate ship Hemo saw Globin's form behind Throb's, and his lips pulled back from his teeth in a snarl. "You ask me this, *human*? You, whose race slew my captain?"

"I denounce them as cowards," Globin said without hesitation. "Hemo, why?"

The Khalian glared at him, then growled, "There were Merchant agents among the Khalia, were there not? And ships must have come to bring new ones among them, to contact them, to take them away for reassignment."

"True. But they are gone. The Merchants called all their agents back when Khalia fell."

"Fool!" Hemo raged. "Can you truly believe that? Can you think that the vile traitors did not leave a few of their kind, to infiltrate your own bloody Fleet and suborn whom they could?"

Globin was still, eyes glazing in that look Hemo knew so well, the look of sudden, total concentration on an idea. He nearly spat with contempt—any warrior who let his mind wander so would die in an instant.

Throb saw that, too. On the screen he urged, "It is nonsense, Globin. How could they hope to succeed?"

"By deception," the human answered slowly. "In this much, Hemo makes sense."

Hemo felt a surge of glee that Globin supported his idea—and hated himself for it.

But the human was stepping closer to the camera, frowning. "Yet those who would have stayed would have been volunteers for death. They would have known that their Merchant leaders could not come to fetch them—it would be death, with the Fleet convoy around Khalia. Hemo, the idea is well founded, and we will find a way to lead the Fleet to examine their own, to discover the traitors—but the Merchants will not come again to Khalia. You waste time, you waste fuel and air. Come back."

"You would deter me from our only chance at revenge?" Hemo screamed. "Do not speak to me, traitor! Do not seek to weaken the resolve of a . . ."

Off the screen an alarm hooted.

Hemo whirled about. His sentry was pointing at the display and shrilling, "Enemies! They come!"

"Accelerate toward them! Battle stations, all! Prepare to launch torpedoes, prepare laser cannon!" Then Hemo turned to the signalman. "Route all sensor output into the transmission link to Barataria!"

The signalman hesitated. "The enemy will trace us by them, Lieutenant—and Barataria with us."

"They cannot—we have the new communications system that the Merchants cannot detect!" The signalman still hesitated, so Hemo said it, though it galled him: "Globin made it! Signals, use it!"

In Barataria the screen suddenly divided into quarters, one showing the view of space as seen from Hemo's bridge, one showing a polar projection of the area of space comprising the enemy ships and his own, a third showing an ecliptic projection, all four ships edge-on—and the largest showing Hemo's gloating face, spinning to grin at them. "Look and see! Will not come, will they? Wastrel, am I? Now comes revenge!" With a savage gesture he turned to howl commands. "Torpedoes, fire when we near maximum range! Battery one, fire at medium range!"

"There are three of them," the sentry reported.

On the screen Globin and Throb saw the single blip of the Merchantman divide into three. The space view jumped, and jumped again, until the ships were visible across the kilometers, reflecting starlight. The view jumped again, singling out one enemy as it sheered to the side, momentarily in profile . . .

"It is the same!" Hemo crowed. "Their silhouette, it is the same as that of the ships that slew the captain! They are Merchantmen indeed!"

"Record," Throb snapped to the signalman, suddenly remembering the values of propaganda.

"Recording already, since the alarm," the technician answered.

"They're surrounding him," Globin said, voice low and tense.

On the screen, two of the Merchantmen had shot out to the side. Disregarding them, Hemo hurtled head-on toward the central ship—and the other two pulled in behind and to either side.

"They surround you, Hemo!" Throb shouted.

"Battery one, fire at the nearest!" Hemo sang. "Battery two, fire to starboard!"

Beams of ruby light stabbed out from each side of the pirate ship, to coruscate against the Merchantmen's shields. A yellow ray lanced out from its nose, toward the central Merchant ship—yellow, to show a torpedo. But a red pencil from the central ship touched the yellow line, and fire burst where the two lines intersected.

"Torpedo destroyed," reported the forward fire control.

"Fire two!" Hemo answered.

Then the ruby beam from the forward ship lanced out past the explosion, to lick wildfire across Hemo's forward screens. Scarlet rays shot out from each of the flanking ships, englobing the pirate.

"Hemo, no!" Throb moaned. "They will overload your screens, they will roast you!"

But the pirate ship shot to the side, then upward, and the ruby beams winked out, for fear of hitting one another. They realigned instantly, catching Hemo again—then winked out again as he moved, then began to blink as the pirate ship danced in a wild and unpredictable dervish whirl, now here, now there—and always, always, lancing back at its enemies with fire and torpedo. Golden bursts showered the enemy's screens; lances of fire kept them glowing.

"He will explode his reactor, he will empty his batteries!" Throb groaned. "For he cannot keep up this mad dance forever! He will empty his arsenal, he will be void of torpedoes! He must withdraw!"

"He cannot," Serum said simply.

And the Merchantmen were beginning to close in. Closer and closer they came, tightening the circle in which Hemo's ship danced, desperate and maddening. The ruby beams became shorter, shorter . . .

But their screens glowed more brightly, for each of Hemo's bolts loaded them more heavily.

Then, suddenly, the central Merchantman shot forward in a ramming rush. At the same moment the two side ships stabbed simultaneous lances of light.

"Up!" Hemo barked. "Rotate!"

The cruiser spun end for end, and the ecliptic display showed it suddenly high above the plane in which the three Merchantmen tightened their noose—

And on the polar display, two ruby lances found each other.

"Well done!" Throb cried. "Oh, well done! He maneuvered them so that they were in line, and knew it not! Oh, well done!"

"How brave," Globin whispered. "How valiant." He felt humbled by Hemo's daring, his contempt of death—almost, his yearning for it.

Then scarlet spat from the remaining ship, scoring Hemo's vessel.

Pandemonium broke loose, shrills and screeches as two dozen Khalians all gave the alarm at once.

"Be still!" Hemo howled. "Batteries, fire at will! Keep him away! Damage control, what news?"

"Tail gone," the damage control officer snapped. "All leads and tubes blocked, and atmosphere is contained, but the rocket drive is gone."

"He cannot maneuver," Throb moaned.

On the screen Hemo's face composed itself into a mask of determination. "We will die, then—but we will take our enemy with us if we can. Batteries, at the slightest chance—fire!"

"He will not give them that chance," Serum breathed.

And it seemed the Merchantman would not. He fishtailed slowly about the disabled pirate in a long arc, always moving, never predictable, but taking his time, choosing the most vulnerable spot for his next, and final, bite. Even as he did, he spat torpedoes, compelling Hemo's cannoneers to use up energy licking at them with their lasers—and the Merchantman's own cannon streaked out, heating the weakened screens white-hot, breaking through to score Hemo's ship, to nibble at its hide.

"Can you not help him, Globin?" Throb demanded.

But Globin stood as though in a trance, eyes gazing far away, mind working. He knew that even though they could not receive the Merchant's signals, there was every chance that he could hear them. After all, it was the Merchants who had given the Khalia their communications apparatus—and might already have broken Globin's new transmission mode and deciphered his new code. They might be listening to every word the pirates said. He had to tell Hemo what to do, but in such a way that the Merchant would not understand . . .

"Hemo," Globin snapped, "jump! Half-degree cube!"

There was silence for a second; then Hemo shrilled, "Navigation! Jump! Half a degree, cubed!"

Globin stared at the screen, holding his breath, while Throb demanded, "What does he mean?"

Then the Merchantman spat its full charge, a column of red—but where it lanced, there was nothing but empty space. Hemo was gone.

"He cannot jump into hyperspace!" Throb realized what had happened. "Not for such a short distance! It is so hazardous as to be fatal!"

But Hemo's ship had already appeared at the edge of the screen, behind the Merchantman but in range. "Fire all!" Hemo screamed, and ruby light lanced out, seemingly from every inch of the pirate's hull, the yellow streaks of torpedoes among them. The Merchant turned ruddy, then orange, as his screens overloaded. Two feeble beams reached out toward the pirate, but winked out as, inside the yellow bubble, the Merchantman began to turn, to bring a broadside to bear on the pirate, but the globe of overloaded shield was growing lighter and lighter, hotter and hotter, almost white . . .

White, pure white, expanding, fountaining, an incredible skyrocket, silent in the endless night.

Then it faded, and Hemo's ship alone drifted in the screen. Its crew cheered. They howled. They sang.

Hemo screamed with triumph, as loudly as any of them. Then he spun to the screen, eyes alight, caroling, "Thank you, Globin! I never thought to say it to you—but, thank you! My rockets were disabled, but not my FTL drive! I humped half a degree toward the Merchantman, and half a degree to the side, half a degree up—half a degree, cubed! I might have died, but I was doomed if I did not! Yet I lived, we all lived—and he is dead! You are truly one of us, truly of the captain's men! You are a noble pirate indeed!"

"Not so noble as yourself," Globin returned, eyes aglow. "Your valor humbles me, Hemo. We cannot lose you. Endure, till we have sent a man to bring you home!"

"I shall endure! For my captain is avenged!"

"Yes, we have drunk of revenge." Throb's paw was firm on Globin's shoulder. "Is the taste sweet, Globin my friend? Does it satisfy your thirst?"

"It is a beginning," Globin answered.

INTERLUDE

Articles of War
Article II
Every Flag Officer, Captain, Commander, or Officer
commanding subject to this Act who upon Signal of
Battle, or on Sight of a Ship of an Enemy which it may
be his duty to engage, shall not,

(1) Use his utmost Exertion to bring his ship into
Action;

(2) Or shall not during such an Action, in his own
person and according to his Rank, encourage his
officers and Men to fight courageously;

(3) Or shall surrender his Ship to the Enemy when
capable of making a successful defence, or who
in Time of Action shall improperly withdraw from
the Fight,

shall, if he has acted traitorously, suffer Death; if
he acted from Cowardice shall suffer Death, or
such other Punishment as is herein-after mentioned; if he has acted from Negligence, or

through other Default; he shall be
dismissed . . . without Disgrace, or shall suffer
such other Punishment as is herein-after mentioned.

Heroes are an asset. It is one of the ironies of war that the
greatest heroes are often too valuable to risk in combat. A
modern war needs heroes, live ones, who can spread the word
to the taxpayers about the good work being done with their
credits. Even more than atrocities, heroes inspire the civilians
to produce, donate, and even enlist.

Roj and Minerva were heroes. They had survived in situa-
tions where they should have been destroyed. They had opened
the way onto Target by destroying its protective net of robot
satellites. Most importantly, they had blundered into the
combined Family fleets and survived. Therefore they suffered
the traditional fate of heroes. During their thirty-fifth omni
interview in two weeks Roj began to giggle. Even more
surprisingly Minerva, linked from orbit by a narrow tachyon
circuit, actually began encouraging his mirth with a string of
highly esoteric puns. Having handled heroes before, the Fleet
propaganda experts knew that it was time to get them off the air
and into some safe, isolated position.

In a moment of uncharacteristic shortsightedness, Minerva
agreed to do a calculation for Roj. At the top speed that the
functional, if almost obsolete, dreadnought they now flew
could fly, the Fleet Academy on Port was exactly two months,
four days, five hours flying time from the nearest point any
Syndicate ship had ever been seen. Roj often quoted this figure
after spending several hours numbing his frustration with
ethanol. They were in about as safe a location as was possible.

Unfortunately, in a modern war no place is really safe.

FINAL EXAMS
by Peter Morwood and Diane Duane

"SPEEDBIRD ONE-NINER TO Dock Control; requesting release clearance."

"Control to One-Niner, you are cleared for launch at this time."

"One-Niner confirms release. Switching to Launch Control, frequency two-zero-zero-decimal-three-zero. Speedbird One-Niner out."

"Have a nice one, Roj, Minerva. Dock Control out."

"One-Niner out. All right. Retract docking booms."

"Docking booms unlatched, retracting . . . Docking booms secured."

"Release umbilicals."

"Release. Ship is floating free."

"Mr. Peason?"

"Sir?"

"You have control. Take her out. On manual."

"Manual? Oh, shi— I mean, yes, sir. I have control, sir. Setting maneuvering thrusters to station-keeping."

"Mr. Peason?"

"Sir?"

"If the maneuvering thrusters are at station-keeping, why are my repeater screens showing a three-degree yaw to port?"

"Sir?"

"Correct it, mister."

"Sir!"

"Mr. Peason?"

"Sir?"

"I said correct, not overcorrect. My screens now show a seven-degree yaw to starboard. Tell me, Mr. Peason, why is the docking bay getting closer?"

"Warning, proximity alert, warning, proximity alert!"

"Oh, bugger. . . . Thrusters ahead one-third."

"No, asshole! Not yet . . . !"

"Warning, collision alert, impact imminent! Warning, collision alert!"

Olympus-class brainship RM-14376 hit one of the main support pylons on the orbital dock facility at a glancing, forty-degree angle. It was enough. Her hull began to buckle, and the brainship's twelve thousand tons of mass was still accelerating at four g right up to the instant that her main drive went critical. The frightful screech emitted by her onboard warning systems cut through even the rending sound of the collision, but by then it was far too late. Her main screen flared white in the instant before a rolling fireball of thermonuclear detonation consumed the ship, the dock, and everything else for six cubic kilometers of space around Port.

Senior Captain Roj Malin stared at the blank, sputtering repeater and then clenched his fists, hearing only the drumming of blood in his ears as he tried to put what he had just seen into some sort of perspective. There were a great many things that he might have said, and a great many others that he might have wanted to say, but knew he should not. Opening his mouth without due consideration had gotten Roj in trouble before, and would probably get him in trouble again when it was reported back. Even so—he drew a deep breath as he swiveled his seat around and stood up—there were some things that *had* to be said, and right now he was in just the mood to say them.

"God*dammit*! If you think that's the way to handle a brainship, mister, then you've got another think coming! I've seen better navigation from a crew of stoned-out Weasels! Suffering Christ on a crutch, how many times do you need to be told, you set the maneuvering thrusters first and stabilize the bloody things before you touch *anything else!* You may have broken this ship and you may have broken this docking facility and you may have broken your mother's heart, but by God you'll *not break mine!* Reset the simulator, Mr. Peason, and then the entire student group will do it again for *your* benefit, and you'll keep doing it until you get it *right*, and if you make just one more mistake like the last one, I'm gonna climb up the front of your tunic and I'm gonna pry your nostrils open with this datapad and I'm gonna crawl inside your pointy little head and I'm gonna *kick some fuckin' sense into it!*"

He glowered at the row of shocked baby faces staring at him from above the collars of their squeaky-clean new uniforms, and guessed from the expressions that at least some of his annoyance was finally sinking into whatever the Fleet Academy was passing as good brain material these days.

"Mr. Gillibrand," snapped Roj, "you have the conn. Repeat the exercise and remember this, I don't care if your father *is* a sodding general, you're in *my* class, not his! Carry on."

He flopped back into his command chair and kicked it back around to face the simulator repeaters, breathing hard. Though neither his students nor the rest of the Academy staff would have believed it for a minute, Roj really didn't like having to bawl his classes out for their mistakes; but there were times when only full-throated abuse could dispel the aura of hero worship that hung around the simulator tank and got in the way of education. Rank, so the saying went, hath its privileges. Roj hadn't seen any sign of it being true, either in his case or in Minerva's. Between the pair of them, they had picked up every decoration, commendation, and award that the Fleet could offer to a brain-brawn team, but not a single one of those awards had been enough to keep them on anything approaching active duty. "Too valuable," one staff officer had said. "Irreplaceable knowledge and experience," said another. "Invaluable assistance during training," from a third.

Even before their last mission Roj and Minerva had seen the way the wind was blowing. The Academy's principal combat simulator system had been outdated by the Khalian war, and now the tutors were pressing for something not only more up-to-date, but more realistic as well. Their choice had been live pilots, those who had survived a full tour of duty against the Weasels and who, for the most part, were only too glad to be pulled from front-line duty to confront nothing more dangerous than a class of inexperienced students.

In Roj Malin's view, there was definitely nothing more dangerous than a class of inexperienced students, especially those who couldn't see what they were studying because of the stars in their eyes through having an accredited Hero as a tutor, and since he and Minerva had taken up their duties at the Academy, his doubts had been confirmed a dozen times. And now they had just been confirmed all over again. At least where the Khalia had been concerned, he had known that they were actively trying to kill him. The students weren't so safely predictable.

Gillibrand, whose father was indeed a general, approached the command console at first as though it was made of eggshells and broken glass; but Roj had already seen him twiddling his fingers in the air like a virtuoso concert pianist, and had a sneaking suspicion that the simulator's reset button was going to be needed again. And again. And again. They should never have put a loud pedal on that thing.

"How much more of this have I got to put up with?" said a plaintive voice in his secure-circuit earpiece. "This class hasn't gotten beyond orbit yet and already I'm getting fed up with being crashed into things."

Oh, boy, thought Roj. Now Minerva's pennyworth as well. The brain-core's voder was capable of many sensitive nuances of speech, and right now it was managing to sound bored, irritated, put upon, and generally insulted all at once.

"Cheer up," said Roj. "It's only a model."

"Maybe. It feels more like a wax doll with pins stuck in it.

Why doesn't the simulator tank make up a model of *you* and let them wreck *it* just for a change?"

"Wouldn't look the same at all."

"Of course not. I've seen the ads on the omni. For a bigger bang, blow up a brainship." Minerva uttered an irritable little snort that more usually heralded incoming fire. "So when do we rotate classes and get some capable students for a change? Next week? Next semester? Next year?"

"Take it up with Colonel Fotherington-Thomas," said Roj, a little weary with the argument that had been going on ever since they were seconded to the Combat Training Faculty of the Academy. "If anybody knows stuff like that, it ought to be the principal of the Staff College."

"Ought to, maybe. But he won't tell me anything!"

"I don't know that— Wait one." Roj paused, staring narrowly at the repeater screen while Ensign Gillibrand actually succeeded in maneuvering the computer-generated brainship clear of drydock without hitting anything. He smiled hastily and punched in a couple of variables so that at some stage in the next five minutes, Gillibrand would end up confronted by a pukon-class dreadnought already well inside orbital traffic separation. There were a great many incorrect methods of handling a proximity alert—as recently demonstrated by Ensign Timothy Peason—and three that were correct and by the book. Roj was curious to see which Gillibrand would choose.

"Sorry, Minerva. You were saying?"

"The Honorable Colonel Basil Fotherington-Thomas would rather talk to the clouds or the sky than listen to what I have to say."

"Because he doesn't want to lose us."

"Because his views on what he terms artificial intelligence are, ah, somewhat archaic."

"Then he should get on nicely with this class."

"Very amusing."

Roj shook his head and glanced at the lens from which Minerva was watching him. "Too easy, Minerva. Baz F-T's no bigot. For one thing, he hasn't got the brains for it."

"And for another . . . ?"

"It's our old friends in Research and Development again. We may not be on active duty, but we're still testing things for them. That new maths coprocessor for one." There was a pause of several seconds, while both considered the problem.

"SIGISMUND? I know it—but not what the acronym stands for," Roj asked.

"Neither do I, Roj dear. As I told you, nobody in this damned faculty tells me anything."

"Including what's happening elsewhere?"

"Oh, now that they told me. 'Don't mention the war,' they said. I mentioned it once, but I think I got away with it."

"Yeah. You don't want to annoy the Weasels, not now that they're on our side."

"That," said Minerva, weighing her words carefully, "is a matter of opinion. There are times when I wonder if Project Firefrost wasn't a better idea than we thought at the time."

"*Unternehmung Endlosung*," said Roj, and there was a vicious edge to his voice. "No. It was never a good idea. And I'm glad it didn't work. We weren't dealing with Weasel civilians, but with their military—and the ones who supplied them."

"*Warning, proximity alert!*" yelled the verbal alarms, beginning to whoop as their simulator-slaved sensors were advised of a dreadnought closing fast. Roj gave his full attention to the repeater screens as he watched what happened next. Gillibrand hammered desperately at the manual-control console like an inebriated musician trying to play "Fairy Bells," so that the simulator cage lurched sideways and its screen image showed the million-ton mass of the pukon-class battlewagon slipping out of their path and out of danger.

"Not bad," said Minerva in Roj's ear. "He shows definite promise."

"Except that I've never been quite sure what he's promising," said Roj with a smile. "Intelligence—artificial, military, or otherwise—has never played a great part in the Gillibrand family."

"Or any family with a long military background," returned Minerva with a smile that was no less poison-sweet for being heard and not seen. "Like the Malins, the Martins, and the Moleswor—"

"Warning, general alert," said the bulkhead speaker, making Roj jump in his seat. Normally the damned thing said nothing unless he had programmed it for the students' benefit, but right now it was blaring a klaxon warning as though the sky was about to fall in on their heads. And perhaps it was. The computer-generated signal choked off with a sound like a cat drinking treacle through a straw, and was replaced by the voice of Colonel Basil Fotherington-Thomas. Which was, if anything, worse.

"Staff and students of the Fleet Academy!" he said. *"Perimeter sensors have picked up a contact that refuses all identification hails. We must therefore assume that this is an enemy sneak attack. It will enter weapon range in twenty-plus minutes. I am calling battle stations."* (Stations-stations-stations, said the PA system's internal reverb.)

Roj blinked once, twice, glanced at his students—who were acting with commendable restraint under the circumstances, Gillibrand having even remembered to flip the simulator over to standby hold—and then stared at Minerva's primary lens as he would have looked someone more human in the eye. "An enemy sneak attack I can accept," he said. "But which enemy?"

That, right now, was the problem. The Khalian Weasels had not only sued for peace and thrown themselves on the mercy of the Alliance and its Fleet, their High Council had gone further and declared that any foe strong enough to defeat them was strong enough to deserve their active support. So there were Weasel ships—at least, those who hadn't turned privateer rather than surrender—flying in formation with those of the Fleet nowadays, despite the misgivings of old campaigners like Roj and Minerva.

(And those misgivings might well have been another reason why they were pulled out of the first line of battle. A certain lack of selectivity in someone's fire-control could put the new Armistice alliance back to the beginning again. Something nobody wanted, not on either side. Not with the Syndicate to deal with.)

Minerva had been the first of any Fleet ship to encounter the Syndicate, and had it not been for another R&D experiment—fitting a scoutship's brain-core into the hull of a light cruiser—neither she nor Roj would ever have escaped with their information. And even despite the urgency of their mission, blowing a metallic planetoid apart to provide screening chaff was considered just a touch excessive . . .

"What say," Roj was smiling as he spoke, "we go to standby all by ourselves, just as a precaution?"

The irises deep within Minerva's primary lens contracted, and then expanded again. That was one reason why she had insisted that all her brainship manifestations have the primitive iris shutters, rather than a phototropic filter. So that she could wink. "Why not?" she said. "If it does nothing else, it should give the kids a thrill. And break the monotony of this goddamn training routine!"

Roj was too well mannered to ask aloud which reason had precedence in Minerva's mind. The brain's voder had a selection of voice tones that could cut like razors—he knew from experience—and Roj had no desire to provoke them again. For all that Minerva's preferred tones were those of an elderly maiden lady, she could slip into the coarsest Marine slang at a moment's notice. It worked particularly well on staff wallahs, the sort of people who hadn't heard a sharp word come their way since the day they put on their fancy red-and-gold tabs. They could jump very nicely when prodded the right way.

As, he hoped, could students.

"You all heard the colonel," he said to the repeater screen just an instant before rotating the command chair so that he could glare at his students from the proper angle. "Battle stations, the man said. *So why are you all sitting here?*"

The effect was something like dropping a firecracker into an ants' nest, or a long-delay sub-kiloton munition into a Weasel emplacement. There was an instant of disbelief, and then everybody was running every which way. At least on the valhalla-class hull shell that was Minerva's present incarnation, there was room to run about. Roj imagined the confusion that would have ensued had he issued the same order aboard the old olympus scout, and hid a smile behind his hand. "Intimate" was the kindest way to describe those ships, and he had heard several other descriptions that hadn't been kind at all.

"And what about us?" asked Minerva. She sounded eager, dubious, and testy all at once. "We're not supposed to involve ourselves in active duty."

"According to Rear-Admiral Agato. We're not to go looking for trouble. That doesn't mean we have to sit still if trouble comes looking for us . . ."

"And us with a shipful of cack-handed dunsels? We've got trouble enough, Roj."

"I know, I know. There isn't a service chief in history cretinous enough to send a vessel crewed by a boatload of children out on a mission of any importance, and I doubt that Agato means us to start the practice now." He slapped the bulkhead beside him and grinned full into the lens pickup. "But don't forget the firepower this thing has at its disposal. We can make quite a nuisance of ourselves before we get to hell out of harm's way."

The main screen flickered as Minerva speedscanned her fire-control data, and then she chuckled. "Everything short of a forty-centimeter bacterial cannon," she said. "And the way things have been going, they'll install that sometime next week."

"Just to see how it works?"

"Why else. After all, Roj dear, old vets like us won't be going back into combat again, now will we?"

"That's what they think. Take us out."

Running on full autonomous control, Minerva slipped from her holding bay with the sort of ease that the students would have given their eyeteeth to achieve. Roj wasted no time in watching; he was already studying the trajectory projections on the big secondary screen, and wondering, Who the hell are they . . . ?

That was the problem. The Big D and her task force were supposed to be guarding—of all places—Khalia and Target against intrusions by elements of the huge battlefleet that Roj and Minerva had almost run into during their last active mission. The Alliance had toyed briefly with reactivating Plan

Poseidon and blowing both planets apart to deny their rich resources and convenient locations to the enemy, but wiser heads had prevailed. Instead of a scorched-earth strategic withdrawal, there was likely to be—or for all Roj and Minerva knew, had already been—a full-scale fleet-level battle somewhere out in the depths of Khalian space. The incoming blips might be nothing more than message torps reporting on progress or lack of it; but equally, they might be a few Khalian freelance raiders like the Delta corvette Roj and Minerva had chased last time—or an opportunity attack by a lightweight flotilla while the bulk of the fleet was pinned down elsewhere.

Whatever they were, they hadn't counted on the presence of a valhalla-class cruiser, or they would have been a lot more circumspect in their approach.

"ECM is up and running," said Minerva briskly. "If they're scanning, I wish them joy at the attempt." A telltale on the primary console flipped from amber to green with a small, decorous chiming sound. "And the main drive is on line for one hundred percent thrust at your discretion."

"Or yours," said Roj. "Plot us an intercept course."

"Plotted."

"Then let the students know. Full alarm klaxons for Red Alert, Condition One, and then full military power. Let's go make trouble . . . !"

Roj promised himself that he wouldn't look into the student quarters for a while . . . at least for long enough to let the inevitable reaction wear off. He busied himself looking over the manual fire-control station, which Minerva obligingly popped out for him, and making sure of what they had handy. Bacterial cannons seemed unnecessary, in retrospect. Besides her plasma cannons, Minerva was carrying more than enough smart nuclear missiles in her rotating launchers to make things at least interesting.

"ETA to the base force's rendezvous with the blips is ten minutes," Minerva said. She had a slightly abstracted sound to her voice.

Roj glanced over at the closest of her sensor consoles. "Hmm?"

For a moment she was silent. "A lot of chatter back there," she said. "They're rattled."

"I'm not surprised. Not much like a simulator run, is it?"

"In that they've realized that they might accidentally get dead," Minerva said a little more sharply, "no."

Roj shrugged. "They're going to have to deal with the idea sooner or later," he said. "Better to do it with a valhalla-class craft wrapped around them. They have that much better a chance of getting home safe."

Minerva synthesized a sigh. "True. Still . . . they're so young."

"Seems I remember you wishing in the middle of the simulations that some of them shouldn't get any older," Roj said, teasing. "The way you were being crashed about."

"Ahem," Minerva said, sharp-voiced. Then, "Ah: better signal from the blips now," she said. And added, "Hmm."

Roj looked up from the fire-control board in alarm. "I wish you wouldn't say 'hmm' like that," he said. "It's like hearing someone go 'oops' in the control room of a fusion reactor. What is it?"

Her voice was flat. "Look at these."

The screen nearest him came alive with the blips that Fotherington-Thomas had mentioned. Minerva's packet-synched scanning was possibly better than even the base had—which now made Roj worry a bit as he saw the six blips heading for them, in open formation, at the vortices of a tetrahedron. "What's the scale on this?" Roj said, doubtful.

"The usual. Screen diameter equals a hundred and sixty klicks."

But on that screen the blips had appreciable size and shape. They were long, narrow lozenge-shaped, double-headed arrows. "Minerva," Roj said, "they *can't* be that big. Can they?"

"I rarely pray for equipment malfunctions," Minerva said, sounding rather unhappy, "but this time I might make exceptions. The mass readings on those things are what you look to see from small moons. Leaving their accelerations entirely out of the discussion for the moment."

Roj shook his head. "Suggestions?"

"Shoot first and ask questions later," Minerva said. Her

voice sounded tight. Lights began to flicker green on the arms-control console. "If I were you, I'd sit yourself down there and strap yourself in."

Roj did.

"All right, children," Minerva said, and her grim voice echoed through the hull, "pressure suits all. Then sit down and stop scrambling around as if you were being chased by Weasels with fleas! Increased acceleration in sixty seconds."

Roj wondered again what was going on back there, but the sight of the trajectories suddenly beginning to trace themselves out on the screen near him gave him something to be much more concerned about. The curves that the six ships were tracing were much too acute: they were flowering out from their original trajectory in tight hyperbolas that were almost curve-expressions of right angles. "Minerva . . ." he said.

"Not manned," she said, sounding grimmer than ever. "They're telerobotically controlled."

"Holy shit," Roj said softly. Such ships could carry oversize power plants whose unshielded radiations would fry any normal crew—because there was no crew to worry about frying. They could maneuver in ways that would kill anything made of flesh and blood. Their pilots—if that was the right word for them—were sitting somewhere comfortable, perhaps even somewhere planet-based, working the ship remotely, as if it were a gigantic toy.

Whereas brainships, and almost every other kind of ship the Fleet flew, had people (or at least Weasels) inside them. Compared to the telerobotic ships, Fleet vessels were fragile, overshielded, delicate contraptions, as full of breakables as a china shop, and as vulnerable as one when the bull came calling.

Roj felt the acceleration begin to push him back in his seat as Minerva poured the power on. "I take it," he said, "that Agato's little scruples about us not getting involved go out the window about now."

"You take it right, sonny boy. This is a time for doing as you would rather not be done by. Have you counted those ships? Have you counted the other blips on that screen? And did you compare their sizes? We have a problem here, and if we don't

stand up on our tailfins and do something, all these kids'
parents are going to be receiving condolence letters sometime
next week. The mails being what they are."

Roj swallowed. There were only four other ships responding
to the incursion at the moment. He had no idea of what else
might be handy, or getting ready to scramble. But the truth of
it was that none of the other ships were likely to be as well
armed, or as heavily engined, as Minerva was. Neither sitting
the encounter out nor turning tail was likely to save them.

He watched the Syndicate ships continue flowering out of
their original tetrahedral formation. Shortly they would pause
in their hyperbolas, and curve in again to catch Minerva, or
whatever other ship was in range, from all sides; at least, if
they had any grasp of tactics, they would.

"Looks as if your maths coprocessor is going to get a
workout," he said.

"Mmm," said Minerva, sounding momentarily abstracted
again. "Dammit. Roj, those kids back there are beginning to
sound like mice at the cat show. They haven't been adequately
prepared for combat yet, and there's no way they're going to
get used to it in the next twenty minutes or so."

Roj hit one of the controls on his panel and shifted the screen
to a view of the ready room. Their students had obediently
strapped themselves in and were trying to pass the time
chatting, but they were looking at the screens too, and reading
them correctly, and several of them, Peason in particular, were
almost frozen with fear.

Roj chewed his lip. "Are you thinking what I'm thinking?"
he said.

There was a longish pause. "Depends."

"Can you do Fotherington-Thomas's voice? Silly question.
Of course you can. Your voder can do any sound you've ever
heard."

There was a long silence. "Roj, you scoundrel," Minerva
said. "I'm not sure this is ethical."

"Screw ethics! If it works, they'll never know. If it doesn't
work, they'll die confused instead of terrified, and God can
explain it to them."

That camera iris blinked at him thoughtfully. "And what about after we take the heat off, so to speak?"

"Then we play it by ear as usual, lady."

Silence again. Then Minerva said, "You are a reprehensible and dishonest creature, Roj Malin, and it's a pleasure knowing you. But if I had fingers, I'd count them after shaking hands with you."

Roj snorted and started making adjustments to the fire-control board, keeping his eye on the screen that showed the back room.

"Now hear this," Minerva bellowed. Except that it was Fotherington-Thomas's fussy accent to the last consonant, and Roj almost jumped at the sound of it again. *"This has been a drill. I repeat. This has been a drill. All vessels stand down from alert and return to assigned courses. Response time for this drill showed only fifty-three percent of optimum. We will expect much better next time. Commanders will assemble in four standard hours for debriefing and evaluations. Out."*

On the screen, the faces in the back room went through more expressions in the matter of a few seconds than Roj could ever remember having seen from them. "All right," Minerva said. "I'll cut accel for about two minutes—that's all I can spare you: I'm trying to work up maneuvering speed. You get on back there and bawl them out, and make it about half an hour's worth, because you won't be able to go back there again until afterward."

Assuming there is *an afterward—*

Roj headed back to the ready room and paused, framed in the doorway as its heavy blast shielding retracted in front of him. He braced clenched fists on his hips and swept a slow, simmering gaze across the students, back and forth until every one of them had tried to meet his glare and failed. "Fifty-three percent," he said. "Is that the best you can do? Is that as fast as you can move? I doubt it, because I've watched you clear the room at the end of my classes. Would you move faster if I clapped a laser cutter to your well-upholstered little backsides? Because if that's what it takes, I'll *do* it!"

The entire student contingent jumped at his roar, but Roj was just getting warmed up. "Mr. *Peason!* Wipe that smile *off*! This isn't any bloody laughing matter, because what you lot have shown me is that as combat personnel you're *crap!* Yes, Gillibrand, Mr. Flying Fingers, that means *you too!* And what the hell are you all doing sitting down? You're on board my ship and that means when I come in you *stand up!* Get those straps released! Squaaad . . . Wait for it, Grabber, wait for it. Squad, ten-*shun!* Oh, Jesus ever-lovin' Christ, *Mr.* Grabber, what do you call that? Standing for the ladies? I don't care if you *are* wearing a pressure suit, I want to hear those heels *smack!* You lot are officer cadets, not a bunch of old women! Again—squad, atten-*shun!*" Roj stalked along the ranks, glowering and breathing audibly through his nose.

"That's more bloody well *like* it. But fifty-three percent," he said again. "And who do you think gets to explain *that* shitty performance to the colonel? Minerva? No way! Me! I'll get the flak—unless I can come up with something that shows I'm commanding something more than this *shower!* I've got four hours before I make my report, and in that four hours you lot are going to put in some *work,* and you are going to do it *well,* or by God somebody's going to be walking home and it won't be *me!* You can't handle a cruiser any better than *my old granny* and you can't respond to an alert at any speed worth *shit,* but we'll see how you can deal with target practice at *combat level!* That's right, Mr. Peason. I said combat speed, and I *fucking mean it! Stations!*"

He slapped the com installation beside the door without taking his fiery stare from the students. "Minerva, release those drones. Wide dispersion. Then unlock the number two gunnery rigs. Let's see if this lot can save my hide."

"You mean, save their own," said Minerva's own voice.

"Something like that. Guns to active status." The multiple firing yokes popped from their recesses along either side of the ready room, and without needing another word from the appalling martinet their tutor had become, the students strapped themselves back into their seats. Even the scary speed of the blips displayed on each installation's targeting screen was better than the expression on Captain Malin's face.

"Good," he said as the blast door slid open behind him. "Just remember, it's not my ass anymore. It's *yours!*"

"Ah, but you've got us," Roj said, trying desperately to sound cheerful.

"Te morituri salutamus," Minerva groaned, and launched another three torpedoes.

The little ships were arrowing in closer, in a swarm at first, then dividing as their parent ships had. They turned even more quickly, curved even more tightly—tight hyperbolas that looked terribly wrong, but worked nonetheless. Like a swarm of bees they began circling Minerva, looking for a weakness in the ablative hull—

—and not without reaction. Fire lanced out from six different places in her hull, tracking with the little ships. One of them blew in a wild burst of fuel and air and reaction mass, a brief sun that Minerva swiftly left behind her. The other ships backed off slightly, but still matched her course and buzzed around threateningly, firing lances of blue fire, probing for a weakness.

"How much of that can you take?" Roj said softly, bringing one of the missile launchers on line at his console and considering each of several of the big ships as a possible target.

"Not very bloody much," Minerva said. Her hull shuddered once more as another spread of torpedoes left.

"Still working on the countermeasures. You want to steer these?"

"Will do." Roj stared at the projected trajectories of the big Syndicate ships on his fire-control screen, let his eyes go a little unfocused, tried to feel which way they were going rather than to reason it out. One of his instructors had once spent quite a while trying to explain to him that this was an effective way to hyperprocess data. It had seemed iffy at the time, but it was worth a try, since there was no way in hell that he was going to be able to match Minerva's computers in plain old reasoning power.

"There," he said, slapping one course in, and "There," adding another, and a third—

The ship rocked. Minerva cried out.

"What is it?"

"Nuke," she gasped after a moment. "Just a little too close.

A few eyes burned out. Still working on their countermeasures."

Roj began to sweat bullets. He had only heard Minerva make a sound like that once or twice before: it sorted ill with her usual acerbic invulnerability. While hammering on the fire-control console with one hand, he slammed the other down on the com control and roared, *"Who the fuck let that one by? Peason, was that you?* Never mind, I don't care *who* it was, but do you realize that would have burned out Minerva's eyes? Do you know how much those optics *cost?* Do you know how long you would have to work as the deck-scrubbers you're all equipped to be before you replaced even *one* of them? And do you realize that the colonel is going to look at the tapes of this little party, and the odds of you lot *ever* sitting in the front seat of anything more advanced than a spacescooter are getting fairly dim? Seven saints in a sidecar, I can't even give you dimwits a *motherfucking videogame* to play without you shafting it every way from Sunday—"

On the fire-control screen there was a bloom of green fire. "Got one," Minerva said, sounding a little breathless.

"Keep at it, boyo, you're doing better than I've been. God damn this miserable electronic abacus straight to—"

There was a screech of delight from the ready room as another of the little attack ships ran through one of the waist-mounted plasma beams and sliced itself in two like an abruptly explosive cheese. And then another howl as a second beam stitched its way across the hull of yet another of the small frigates, catching it right in the engines. The detonation was silent but impressive.

Roj unloaded another three torpedoes, felt them fire, studied the screen, went unfocused, adjusted their trajectories again, not quite toward where he thought the next two of the big Syndies were going to be—just a little off, that seemed to be the way—

"Got the algorithm of their countermeasures," Minerva said. "I think—"

Another terrible shudder of the ship. "That's the first layer of ablative," Minerva said, sounding worried. "Another one in that spot will not be good."

"How not good?"

"How long can you breathe vacuum?"

"Noted. Peason, that *was* you," Roj shouted. "I *saw* you, mister, don't deny it! Can you please, if it's not too much fucking trouble, not crash your used enemy vessels into the one you're riding in? Thank you ever so much." He put an extra little turn on one of the torpedoes he was steering as it flew. The big Syndie ship it was aiming for twisted impossibly, twisted past it, then back onto course again. And blew up.

"Holy shit, how did that happen?" Roj muttered.

"You forgot your other torpedo. I think. Almost, almost ready. Aha! So that's how they've been doing it, the clever little swine! How dare they wave-shift my own tachyar! We'll see about that. Roj, for all sweet sakes cover my back, here come another two—!"

"Heads up now, you assholes, this is it," Roj shouted, "don't blow it! Get those little guys off our case! Now, Gillibrand, goddammit"—and he grabbed at the fire-control console as the hull shuddered and boomed again, the worst yet—"get your thumb out of whatever orifice it's in at the moment and onto the firing button, yes, you too, Grabber, come on, shoot at something even if you can't uncross your eyes long enough to hit it, come on, come on—!" He was loading every torp that Minerva had not already declared dedicated, there were only three of those ships left now, the terrible sharp double-arrow shapes coming at them two and one, two of them arcing apart from each other to be the pincers, the third coming down from "above" like the sting in the scorpion's tail, and he saw how the sting was curving slightly up and away to make him think it was going to abort the run, but he could clearly see where it was going instead. "Come on, come on!" he shouted to the kids in the ready room, and slapped the last course corrections into his torps and let them go free—

—and all the images in the screen changed, blipped suddenly a degree or more in one direction or another—all the *wrong* directions—

"True enemy positions displayed," Minerva said dispassionately. "Correcting weapon assignments—"

—and there was one bloom of expanding signal on the screen.

And another.

The third kept coming.

"Clean miss," said Minerva, but this time she sounded almost cheerful. "Doesn't matter, Roj, I've got their number—"

There was whooping and screaming coming through the com circuit from the ready room. "All right, you lot, knock it off," Roj said, glancing at his screen, "you still have one of them lef—"

The motion caught his attention out of the corner of his eye. The one screen that mimicked "the windshield" was showing a needle-nosed shape, lozenge-sectioned, getting bigger and bigger and—

A line of blue fire hit it. It blew up.

The whole ship felt as if it had been kicked up and backward. The lights went out. There was a sound that Roj could *feel* all through his body, like a bass drum being beaten one hard stroke. He held his breath, wondering if he would ever get another chance at one. Then he let it out and yelled, "Minerva!"

No answer.

"Minerva!!"

And the lights came back on.

"You needn't shout," she said.

Roj looked at his screen. It was clear, blessedly clear and empty, except for the bloom of one more large explosion.

He hit the com switch again.

"Peason," he said. "I may just let you live. Check with me in five minutes."

"Another two weeks in overhaul," Minerva grumbled. "For half an hour's pleasure. I don't know how I keep letting you get me in to these things."

"Me!!"

"At least," Minerva said, "the combined forces now have the countermeasures to the Syndicate's 'dislocation' countermeasure. They'll be shooting at the actual positions of the attacking ships—rather than the fake ones manufactured from Fleet tachyar signals."

"Thanks to SIGISMUND."

"That piece of crap," Minerva said with a sniff.

"Yes," Roj said, "the one you ordered six more of. I heard you talking to the Quartermasters' office this morning."

Minerva laughed softly. "And I heard you saying good-bye to 'your boys,' " she said. "You old softie."

Roj blushed profoundly. "Well, after all," he said, "they did the job."

"And they only fainted and screamed and cracked up a little," said Minerva dryly, "when they found out."

Roj blushed harder. "Well, what was I supposed to do? Lie to them?"

Minerva burst out laughing.

"Oh, no," she said. "Not to them. And not to the class who are waiting for us . . . I believe right about now. You'd better go let them in."

"But the overhaul—!!"

"About the only thing that was not broken during that run," Minerva said with infinite regret, "was the simulator."

Roj got up and headed for the airlock. "We must have a nuke left over here somewhere," he said, "just a small one . . ."

Minerva's laughter followed him all the way down to the door.

INTERLUDE

Articles of War
Article LXXXVII
Every Person in or Belonging to . . . Navy, and borne
on the books of any Ships in Commission, shall be
subject to this Act; and all other Persons hereby made
liable shall be triable and punishable under the Provi-
sions of this Act.

Article LXXXIX
All other persons ordered to be received or being
Passengers on board any . . . ships shall be deemed
to be persons subject to this Act, under such regula-
tions as the Admiralty may from Time to Time direct.

Eventually the Fleet gathered its strength in the salient tipped
by the two major Khalian worlds. Almost a million spacemen
and Marines soon swarmed over or hovered above the home
worlds of their former foe. Khalia itself proved a surprise to
most of the personnel arriving. These new recruits, most

unblooded in battle, expected to find a defeated and broken population. In assuming this they had overlooked the unique Khalian sense of warriors' honor. To be defeated by a capable foe bore no disgrace; dishonor would have been to have not fought well. In every battle, every war, one side had to be the loser. To have fought well and lost had no stigma and affected Khalia's population much less than it would have a human world.

Many Khalians offered their services to the Fleet. Most were assigned auxiliary posts, ones that didn't require them to be armed. A few of their most experienced fighters were posted to ships, though never in command or in key positions. The memory of the Weasels' savage raids was too fresh to allow that level of trust. Only a very few were allowed to man ships of their own. Even these ships held a Fleet observer, who had a veto over the captain's decision and control of a large bomb planted inaccessibly inside the ship's engines.

When Khalia was occupied, hundreds of scientists and sociologists descended upon the planet. Their joint purpose was to determine how far the Fleet could trust the Khalian offer of service. Realizing that nothing except time would convince the Admiralty to trust their former foes, most of these scientists pursued "related" studies. It proved even more important that the Khalia were able to study these civilians. Unlike their tight-lipped military counterparts, the scientists were quite willing to discuss the expanse and strength found in the Alliance. Rather quickly the Khalia realized they had never really had a chance to defeat such a powerful enemy. Most then took the next step and came to the teeth-gnashing realization of how badly three generations of their race had been used.

The Khalian culture, seemingly inscrutable to the experts of the Fleet, was actually very similar to that of the pre-Roman Celts or the early Japanese. Both were heroic, bardic cultures whose members valued honor and reputation over even life itself. What confused the specialists was the high level of technology that had been grafted onto a basically primitive cultural pattern. While they looked for group psychosis and underlying gestalt awareness, the Khalia continued to hold a very straightforward grudge against humans that had set them up and left them in their time of greatest need.

The unrest caused by a baffling lack of trust by their new human allies confused and frustrated most Khalians. Veterans who had raided human colonies with near impunity failed to see why they were being left useless while the Alliance strained to import personnel from bases three months distant. Occasionally this resulted in violence. More often the casual, competitive violence inherent in a heroic culture exploded in the face of boys whose only other experience with physical danger was on the omni. Even after the Goodheart incident, the Fleet was slow to recognize the value of what they were being offered. As time passed some of these spurned warriors were unable to adjust to peace and joined those few remaining holdouts who had chosen piracy rather than surrender.

Occasionally rare individuals from both sides were able to find a degree of mutual understanding.

KYŌDAI
by Steve Perry

1.

ALONE AND IN THE WARM DARK, Stone walked along the wet, narrow street of the Khalian village. His flexboots made little sound on the damp cobblestones. It was late, and low, heavy clouds filled the sky, threatening more summer rain to expand the puddles. The only lights were ancient electric pole-lamps casting dim pools at sporadic intervals, and the infrequent glows that shone from windows in the moss-covered rock buildings.

Stone among the stones. The thought brought a smile to his lips, if only a small one. Who would have ever thought that he would be here on Khalia, of all places?

From a public house fifty meters ahead, more light spilled into the street as the door swung open to allow a trio of Khalian males into the night. The door closed, shutting off the inside lights, but a small neon sign in Khalian above the portal gave off a pale blue shine that attracted insects. The local equivalent of moths flittered against the neon, casting ghostly shadows onto the street.

Stone had never understood why his people called the Khalia "Weasels," for they had always reminded him more of tusked pigs, like boars he had seen once in a zoo on Earth. Upright, dangerous, wild boars.

The way the three moved told Stone they had indulged in whatever chemical they favored to alter their consciousnesses. Stoned or plashed, and likely to be more than a little surprised to see a lone human walking the streets of their little town. Surprised and, just as likely, unhappy.

The man crossed the road, seeking to avoid contact with the trio of Khalians as they turned and started up the street in his direction. The war was over, the Khalia had surrendered, but even in his brief stay Stone had felt the smoldering resentment a hundred times over. He had chosen to walk from the spaceport to his destination, more than two hundred kilometers. Walking was the best way to see the territory, to absorb the culture, and he had done much of both. He had learned that it was hard for a warrior race to accept defeat, and while the Khalia had done so, it had not always been with grace. Thus far, he had managed to turn away the wrath he had felt.

The three Khalians were laughing and joking among themselves as they moved, slapping each other with heavy paws, swaggering along the cobblestones and feeling little, if any, pain. All three wore gray cross-straps with the twin knives. Stone didn't recognize the clan from the color or insignia on the straps.

The largest of the trio, still only chest high to the Terran but wide in the body and probably almost as heavy as Stone, lifted his head and sniffed the night air. The wind was at Stone's back, what little of it there was, and he knew his scent would be carried on the humid air.

The three stopped as the larger Khalian uttered a short curse. Stone continued walking, across the street from them and nearly past. They could not see as well as he, but they were not blind.

"Hold!" the leader of the trio called in Khalian militaryspeak.

Stone sighed. He wore a dark synsilk coverall and a pack with a sleepsack holding that few belongings he owned. He carried no weapons. He stopped and stood staring at the three as they crossed the road toward him. Their movements were considerably more controlled than they had been only a moment earlier.

"What are you doing in our village, ape?"

"Just passing through, Bold Warrior."

The three came to a halt three meters away.

"Passing through? To where?"

"The eastern border of the Western Province, Warrior."

"Alone?"

Stone felt the danger that rested in his answer. He could have said that his party was just ahead, that he was expected, but he had given up lying long ago. He was but thirty, a young man, but he had learned that he could not master his Art dealing in anything but truth, no matter what the danger.

"I am alone, Warrior."

And not just now, but in totality. His family was dead and he was the last of his line. He had nothing but his Art left.

The leader glanced back and forth between his two companions and snapped his teeth together once in a hard click. The other two Khalians edged away from the leader and slowly began to move to encircle Stone.

"Not wise, ape. The night is full of dangers. One could slip on a wet cobblestone and fall, breaking bones. Or step into an unseen hole."

"I appreciate your concern, Warrior, and I will watch my steps carefully."

"No, you will not. We do not allow *animals* to roam the streets of our village."

The leader reached up and pulled one of his knives from its sheath. The steel whispered as it left the hard plastic. The blade glittered in the dim light, catching blue glints from the public house's neon sign. "Your piss-colored hair will look good on my wall."

No subtlety here.

Stone took a deep breath. He searched himself for fear. There was only a faint, distant fright. He might die here, carved by this drunken trio, but if that was his fate, then so be it. Death came when it would. They were armed, they were

warriors, he was outnumbered, but none of that meant anything. He had nothing left but technique. To fail in that would
be the one unforgivable sin.

Because he was close to a building next to the walk, the
other two could not get behind him. There was one in front,
one to the left, and one to his right. The one in front would lead
the attack. The Khalia were tough, they would give no quarter,
but only a fool would travel in the country of his enemies
without knowing their weak points.

"But I won't even dirty my claws, ape. My blade will sing
its song for you."

Stone decided to give it one more try.

"Do you not wonder why I am alone?"

The leader paused for a pair of heartbeats. Then, "Because
you are an ape and thus stupid." With that, he stepped in and
jabbed, a straight thrust at Stone's face.

He meant to mutilate before he killed. To inflict torture and
make his victim cry out in fear. To feed on the pain. This was
a bad mistake.

Stone lashed his arm out in the crossblock, left close, right
extended. His slightly bent wrist caught the Khalian at the
elbow and wrist, popping the knife loose from his paw. Stone
closed his left hand on the thick wrist, imprisoning the
attacker's arm. At the same instant the man snap-kicked, toes
bent back, so that the ball of his foot thumped solidly into the
nerve plexus just below the Khalian's sternum. The strike hit
just at the point where the clan straps crossed. For the next
thirty seconds the Khalian would not be able to breathe.

The man stiffened his body and dropped, concentrating his
weight on the Khalian's arm at the elbow, twisting to his left,
and the leader was thrown into the path of the attacker to
Stone's left. The second Khalian cursed and leaped back to
avoid his comrade.

A little under two seconds had passed.

The third attacker leaped at Stone's back, claws extended
instinctively to rend, but the man came up from his crouch and
thrust his right foot backward in a heel kick. The hard plastic
of his boot smashed into the Khalian's snout with enough force

to flip the attacker backward to land on his head. Stone heard the skull crack.

The leader was trying vainly to breathe. Stone still held him in the forearm lock, and the only way the second attacker could move in would be to step on his downed friend, a most unstable platform.

Stone released the leader, pulled the remaining strap knife from its hilt, and stabbed the fallen Khalian between the fourth and fifth ribs at an angle, skewering his heart. He jerked the knife out, stood, and threw it at the remaining attacker's open mouth.

Coming up on four seconds.

The final Khalian's reflexes were slowed by whatever he had drunk, but he was still able to bat the knife down. While he was doing that, Stone leaped over the dying leader, dropped to the cobblestones on his butt, and hooked his left foot behind the Khalian's ankle. He thrust with his right boot at the Khalian's thigh, jerked with his left foot, and the surprised Khalian went down backward.

Stone rolled up, snatched the knife from the ground, and shoved it into the stunned Khalian's throat. He buried the long weapon, stopping when the steel hit the cobblestones under the Khalian. The blade's tip grated against the rock and broke.

Stone danced away and spun, automatically scanning for more attackers.

Seven seconds. Eight—

Stone stared into the night. His heart was thumping too fast and adrenaline was coursing through him. He took two deep breaths and forced his tight shoulders to relax. The street was quiet, none other than the three attackers and himself visible.

He nodded to himself, once. His technique had been good. Not perfect, but good. Two of the three attackers were certainly dying, the other might survive, but this was not his concern. He had instigated nothing, his conscience was clean. The three had called their fates to themselves. It was karma. Theirs to die. His to live.

He took another deep breath, let it out slowly, and moved off into the night.

2.

Berq watched her quarry as he emerged from the ground-effect car in front of the brothel, bracketed by his two guards. The quarry was old, sheathed in fat under his graying fur, with platinum dental inlays shining from his upper tusks. He was a rich Khalian merchant, a dealer in poisons, a seducer of kits, a pervert, and, as such, probably no worse than hundreds like him. It was the quarry's misfortune, however, to have plied his drug trade on Berq's home world. On Aerie, the planet of the Nedge—called Target by the ruling human off-worlders—the quarry had incurred the notice of one with enough anger and money to engage the Guild With No Nest to do something about him. Unwise in the extreme. It had been three years and some since the contract had been drawn, but the Guild dealt in nothing if not patience.

The slowing GE fans continued to stir the dust next to the outdoor restaurant where Berq sat, thin clouds shining in the early morning light. She was aware of being noticed by the other patrons of the place, for though there were Nedge on many worlds, the bird-folk were still relatively rare on Khalia. Such a thing made her work more difficult, of course, but such things were also part of the job.

The fat Khalian entered the brothel with his guards. Inside, Berq knew, the quarry intended to engage in perverted sex with either an alien female or an immature Khalian kit, those being his two favorites. Berq had paid well for this information. The more an assassin knew about her quarry, the better. Berq was the best off-world operative the Guild could field, her father had been the Master of Assassins until his death, and her mother, dead also, the first female Nedge ever admitted to the Guild With No Nest. She bore her mother's name and, as such, could not allow herself to dishonor that name, no matter how difficult the assignment. She had no siblings to blot away the stains of failure, no children who would come to finish her task.

And this, she reflected as she sipped at the warm *yiba* in its cheap plastic cup, was not the most difficult assignment she had ever been given. The quarry was armed and guarded, though that was of no great importance in itself. He was a Panya—her race's name for the Khalia, it meant "rat"—but she had killed more than a dozen aliens, apes, rats, it did not matter. The special circumstances around this assignment required that the quarry's end look like an accident, and that was a bit more difficult. Killing was easy with a wand or dart or one's hands, but making certain that it seemed an accident or natural death sometimes complicated things.

Berq finished the drink and stood. The madam of the brothel was about to offer her new arrival a special treat. Would he care to lie with a female Nedge? And a virgin in the bargain? Certainly he would, for he had acquired the perverse taste for her kind, Berq knew.

Berq went around to the back of the brothel and opened the unguarded locked door with the code provided her by the madam. She waited in the empty office as had been prearranged.

After a few moments the madam arrived, a Panya herself, retired from active sexual service long ago.

"He is ready," the madam said.

"Good." She paused, then said, "You have been to my world." It was not a question.

"Yes. I, ah, worked there when it was occupied by my kind some years ago."

"And when you were on my world, you heard of the Guild With No Nest."

"Yes, of course."

Berq knew these things, but it was important to make certain the Panyan female was sure beyond any doubt. Careless assassins had short careers.

"Then you know there is no place the Guild cannot reach, no nest deep enough, no perch high enough to escape them should they want to . . . touch you."

"I—I have heard it so, y-yes."

"You have been well paid for your efforts here. The humans would not allow you to remain in business if certain information should reach their pale ears. The Khalian in the room waiting for me also has clan who would take it badly if they knew you had aided me. But more importantly, if ever word should get out as to what happened here this day, the Guild With No Nest would make it a priority to find you and all connected with you. Father, mother, sons, daughters. Do you understand what this means?"

"Y-y-yes."

"Then take me to the pervert."

The madam led Berq down a narrow hall. The floor was an overlay of wood strips, polished and slick, and Berq allowed her eyes to go wide in mock-fear as the madam took her to a doorway flanked by the quarry's two guards.

"Hold," one of them ordered.

The two females stopped, and the guards moved to search Berq for weapons. They stripped away her shift, made her remove her boots, and then leered at her nakedness. They slid their paws up and down her body, lingering over her genitals and breasts, laughing softly to each other as they fondled her.

"Nice, the soft feathery skin?"

"It's all pink on the inside, eh?"

Berq pretended fear. She could easily kill these two while wrapped in the Amaji trance, without having to use a major *kata*. But killing the guards would convince anyone with half a brain that their employer had met an unnatural end.

"She's unarmed. Send her in."

The quarry lay upon a flat cushion, his normally retracted and hidden sexual member revealed, though it was still flaccid, and his clan straps and knives were tossed onto the floor. He was not a Panya expecting trouble.

The door closed behind Berq.

"Ah, bird-woman! Come to me and let me show you what a real mate can do! Feel the power of a Khalian male!"

"P-p-please, Lord Warrior, d-d-do not make me do this! I have never been with a male and you are s-so huge!" She pointed at his organ with one hand and pressed the other to her breast.

As she had intended, the fear in her voice and her pose inflamed the quarry. His member went turgid and he rolled from the pad and up, and swaggered toward her. Tell a male of any species his organ was large and he would practically explode with pride.

"I won't hurt you, bird-woman. I know your kind. Come, I'll teach you pleasure—!"

She lashed out with her foot and connected with his now-rigid member. He opened his mouth and grunted with the pain. Normally protected, the Panyan sexual member was exquisitely tender when exposed, Berq knew. She had made it her business to know.

She danced behind the injured quarry, wrapped her arm around his thick neck, and applied a choke hold. Her arms looked thin and weak next to his flesh, but that was deceptive. A trained Nedge assassin had great strength.

Before the quarry could do more than blink in fear and wonder, Berq had shut off the oxygenated blood flowing to his brain. He realized his danger and reached for the encircling arm, claws extended, but Berq hooked one foot around his leg and heel-kicked his scrotum, smashing again the now-limp sexual member.

He tried to reach for himself and to retract the injured part, but his time was up. He fell, unconscious.

Berq continued the choke hold.

Presently, the quarry died.

She dragged the corpse to the pad, lay on her back, and pulled him on top of her. She wrapped her bare legs around his fat hips, took a deep breath, and screamed, a high, fearful sound.

Nothing happened.

No doubt the guards had heard such things before.

"Help! He's hurt! Help!"

That brought them.

Both guards ran to their master. They rolled him off of Berq, cursing all the while. It took only a moment for them to determine that he was dead. There were no marks of violence, save the battered sexual organ, at which both guards carefully avoided staring, since peering at another male's unsheathed member was an ingrained racial taboo among the Panya. Berq knew this, too.

"What happened?" one of them demanded, grabbing her arm.

"He—he was—we were—he stopped and moaned and grabbed at his chest!"

The guards looked at each other.

"Damn," one of them said. "Shit."

"There are worse ways to go. He was old. Let's get him out of here. He has clan in the city, better that he died there, at home, than here."

"What about her?"

"She's an off-world bird-whore. She won't say anything, will you?"

"N-n-no!"

"I didn't think so. Come on. Let's move him."

As they dragged the dead quarry out of the room, Berq allowed herself a small smile.

3.

In the temple Imani sat cross-footed, back straight, meditating. Thoughts kept intruding, the sense of impending *something* beating at his calm with frantic wings. Dark days had come to Khalia, and darker days lay ahead. It took no master of *ladju kasi* to know this.

The stone under him had warmed from his fur, but the temple itself was cool under the pounding summer sun, cool and quiet and dark. The students were in the courtyard, practicing attack-and-defense set patterns or formal dances under the senior student's watchful eyes and nostrils. All was calm and as it should be to the casual observer, but Imani knew that was not so. He was old, had seen many things in his life, and had finally achieved a kind of self-peace that allowed him to be content. In his youth he had been a firebrand, burning with desire to prove himself, to utilize the rare and arcane fighting arts he had learned. He had killed with his paws, many times, over real or imagined insults. He had gone to war and used his skills with weapons to good effect there. As a young and swaggering Khalian, he had been one to fear, one whose path it was better not to cross.

It had taken age and wisdom before he had finally understood that the best martial artist never had to use his skills. Simply by being in a place, he could diffuse anger, could thwart an attack by no more than his presence. Not an easy task, but not one to shirk because it was difficult. In the learning of it, he had outlived all his old enemies. And his friends, as well. The surviving members of his clan were mostly great-grandkits, most of whom he had never even met. He had survived much longer than even he had expected.

Imani sighed. His meditation was not going well. He could not keep his mind clear. Whatever disaster buzzing around before it lit was causing a ripple in the Flow that could not be ignored.

The old Khalian stood. His cold joints protested, but obeyed as always. He came up in a single, smooth motion, so that in one instant he was seated, in the next he was standing, and there seemed to be no transition. Naturally, he was no longer as fast as he had been as a young Khalian. He had compensated for this by honing himself so that he was efficient, that he wasted no energy on any move. The term *ladju kasi* meant literally "fast paws," but he had learned that there were different kinds of speed. No matter how quickly a Khalian could snap a death swipe, it was useless if it did not hit the target.

Time for practice.

In the spring-chamber, Imani touched the controls that cocked the attack mechanisms. The room was small, as it must be, and the fourteen attacks when reset were invisible once they withdrew into the wooden walls, floor, and ceiling. Essentially no more than thick blocks of polished wood on springs with timers, the attacks were a test reserved for instructors. The timers and sequences scrambled each time, and the order of the fourteen was therefore almost random. There was no place safe in the chamber, at least two of the strikers could reach every part. The trick was to block or dodge the attacks in the right sequence. A miss was worth a bad bruise, a broken limb, or, when set at full power, death itself.

Imani took a deep breath and stepped on the trigger plate. He would have from three to nine seconds before the first striker.

He expanded his awareness, listening for the telltale hum of the striker about to release. Whoever had polished the scratches from the hardwood had done a good job, the strikers blended perfectly into the patterned wood, making it almost impossible to see exactly where they were. Imani had spent long hours as a student polishing the damned things himself, and after years of that and further years of defending the chamber, he knew exactly where the fourteen were even if he could not see them—

Hum!

Imani dodged left and whipped his left arm up, batting the polished block aside—

Hum!

He dropped low and fired his right arm up, wrist bent, to block the second striker—

Hum! Hum!

A hook kick and a swipe saved him from the next two—

Hum!

His left paw's claws snapped out and he raked the next striker hard, deflecting it, leaving deep grooves in the wood. Some poor junior student would curse over having to smooth that out—

Hum—!

Fifty heartbeats later, Imani, sixth master of the temple, stood back in the center of the chamber, breathing a little harder, but finished with the exercise. The thirteenth attack had brushed his left hip, only a glancing touch, hardly more than a ruffling of his gray fur. Still, Imani was perturbed. Either he was truly getting old, or the unseen disturbance he felt had bothered him more than he realized. He hadn't been touched by a striker in the last fifty defenses.

It was a bad sign.

4.

Once he was past the outposts of civilization, Stone walked easier. This part of Khalia was dressed in summer colors, it was almost pastoral, broken by large swatches of forestland here and there. The Khalia were carnivores to a large extent;

they raised meat animals much like cows, but wild game was still a large part of their diet. Now and again he would pass keeps, low, rambling structures built of local stone, and he stayed well clear of these. The days were warm and sometimes rainy, the nights a little cooler but still humid, and it was a bearable climate for a man. Stone lived mostly on concentrates, tasteless but nourishing, and he had been trained to recognize several edible plants with which he supplemented his diet.

He had been walking for nearly thirty kilometers since last seeing any signs of Khalian civilization when he reached his destination. Night had fallen and the stars had come out to dot the sky with their strange constellations. He knew the local names of some of them: The Goat, Long Tooth, The Hand of the Giver. They gave much more light than did the stars shining down on Earth, strewn thickly here as they were. In places the stars seemed clumped together to form bright splotches that would rival the light of a small moon.

The temple lay ahead another two kilometers, the largest group of structures he had seen since leaving the last village nearly a week past.

Stone continued to walk. He was uncertain of his welcome, but he had come a long way to see if the stories of the temple's teacher were true. A Khalian who had achieved real mastery, so it was said, who had fought and won a hundred battles to the death and who had along the way become one with the universe. The fighting arts had grown watery on Earth; Stone had reached the pinnacle of what he could learn from his own kind. But if the stories were true, this Khalian master might have something to teach him.

It was not as though he had anywhere else to go.

It was worth crossing the galaxy to find out. His uncle's name had eased the trip. Not every man had a genuine war hero, an admiral, for a blood relative. And his uncle had made many friends before he'd died in battle, some of whom gladly offered a hand to the nephew of the famous Ernest Stone, and the last of his distinguished line.

Through the Khalian night, Stone walked. A freshening breeze brought the smell of rain, and distant lightning and thunder confirmed the approaching storm. If he hurried, he might be there before the skies opened up.

5.

Berq piloted the rented flitter through the rough air. The storm was getting worse, and while she would have circled around it, the flitter's sensors indicated that the pod was only one of a string of such, extending for fifty kilometers in an angular line.

The short-winged little craft was an old one, and Berq knew enough about flying to know that it would fare badly in the roiling clouds. She dropped her altitude so that she was a few hundred meters above the ground, under the overcast ceiling, and nursed the flitter along slowly. It was no worse than driving a ground car in a heavy rain, and she was high enough to avoid the tallest trees. The country here offered rolling hills, none of them large, and at her present altitude she could pass over the tops of them with only a slight upward nudge.

Nedge were natural fliers; few felt any qualms in the air. It had been millions of years since they had come down from the trees, but the old senses lingered. Personal wingsuits were big recreation items on her home world, and on any planet where a sizable collection of Nedge could find the room to fly. Even half-blinded by the sheets of rain, Berq enjoyed soaring in the little craft.

Lightning flared, flashing through the flitter's plastic windows and strobing the interior. Berq was pleased with herself. The assignment had gone well. The quarry had been eliminated, and she was winging her way toward the Western Spaceport with only a little over two hundred kilometers to go. Another hour and she would be there, and a few hours after that, she'd be on a ship home.

More lightning, closer now as she reached the center of the storm pod, and the thunder booms were enough to rattle the flitter. Berq adjusted her controls and brought the aircraft a little higher. The wind was gusting and she had no desire to fly into a shear and find herself impaled on the tops of the trees only a hundred meters below.

The thunder began a continuous rumble of a moment, and the white flashes seemed to shade to a darker reddish-orange glow. Some of these worlds had strange weather happenings, ball-lightnings and such, but that growing roar and fiery light did not seem natural. To her left the dark clouds reflected what looked to be a fire in the sky.

What *was* that?

Berq checked her sensors and spotted the source on her doppler. A ship. Big one, at least big enough to hold a hundred Nedge, if her sensors were calibrated right. And that glow meant it was coming down on rockets! Talk about antiques.

Or maybe the ship's repellors had gone out. Maybe it was some kind of emergency—that had to be it, otherwise why the hell would it be landing way out here past the edge of nowhere, and in the middle of an electrical storm? No pilot with any sense would risk going through the eye of a storm this bad, not if she had a choice.

Well. It was not her business. Let the rats splash themselves all over the countryside if they wished. She had accomplished her task and she was leaving.

The landing ship vanished behind a distant hillside, probably ten or fifteen klicks away. The glow died, along with the rumble, and Berq felt a certain curiosity. Didn't seem to have crashed. What the dervish, she could divert a couple of minutes out of her way to check it out.

She pulled a slight turn in the flitter and headed toward the little hill her sensors showed was there. She couldn't see shit in the pouring rain, but she was low enough to see a hundred-passenger ship if she flew over it.

Berq dropped the flitter lower, to get a better view. She followed the contour of the hill, still fifty meters above the trees.

Half a klick, maybe, just ahead, it should be—

The flitter's main engines died. The entire control panel went blank, all the screens wiped. Even the running lights on the ends of the stubby wings blinked out. The flitter's power was gone, as if it had been cut with a sharp blade.

Fuck! The flitter was dead in the air and gliding like a thrown brick!

Frantically Berq looked for a clear spot. She had only a few seconds to find a perch for this bird or she was going to be joining her ancestors.

6.

Resting in his private cell, Imani heard the sound in the storm, and he searched his memory for its match. He had not always been a teacher a week's walk from the nearest village of any size. He had done his duty as a soldier, had been off-world a dozen times, and the noise that cut through the rain was one he recalled. He had not heart such a thing in many years, but he knew it for what it was: a ship's landing rockets. Such rocket engines were only used rarely, such as in the event of an emergency that somehow stopped the use of repellors, or when the commander did not wish for repellor energies to be detected. Khalian pirates had long ago learned how to sneak onto a planet. Repellors generated vast, double-butterfly-shaped fields that would show on spysat or ground-based sensors for hundreds, even thousands of kilometers. Like a bright fire in a dark night, repellor fields were hard to miss and impossible to mistake for anything else. On the other paw, dropping from space without power and waiting until the last minute to kick the engines into life was effective, if risky. True, rocket engines made loud noises and bright visible lights, but neither would be heard or seen far in the middle of a thunderstorm.

This was the ripple in the Flow, Imani had no doubt.

Why was a ship landing here?

The senior student tapped lightly at the open entrance to Imani's cell. "Master?"

"I heard it," Imani said. "A ship has landed, not far from here. Take three third-levels and go and find it. Report back when you have done so. Do not allow those on the ship to see you."

"At once, Master!"

The student departed, eager to be off to see the surprising phenomenon. Imani took a deep breath and allowed it to escape. His stomach fluttered once before he forced it to calmness. This event was the problem he had felt. How large a problem and what must be done to resolve it remained to be known. Perhaps it would be minor.

There came a sudden tension in the air, an itch-behind-the-eyes kind of feeling. What—?

The dim electric lamp next to his pallet winked out.

Imani stood and moved easily in the darkness to the doorway. All the hall lamps were out, too. The generator had gone down. It was not new, but it had been repaired and overhauled only a few months back.

Imani went back into his cell and picked up the com unit next to his pallet. Dead. The com was powered by batteries, automatically recharged when low.

The master of the temple padded through the well-known dark halls to the computer room. Most of the instrumentation was powered by the generator, but there were also battery- and solar-driven units. The old air-defense sensors were not used anymore, but had been kept operative as a matter of course. They were self-contained and held lithium cells good for at least ten more years.

The sensors were inoperative, but the old-style mechanical needle on the battery pack showed that the cells were still more than half-charged.

All the electronic gear was out, but in some of it, the power sources were still good.

Imani sighed. The temple had been pulsed. Somebody had swatted them with an EMP energy field, fusing even the shielded electronics and effectively killing power and communications.

Such a thing had to have come from the unexpected ship. Who? Why? It made no sense to spend that kind of energy on a poor temple with no value. They were kilometers away from anything here, and Imani could think of no reason for such an attack. There was a possibility it could be an accident, but he did not think it so.

The something wrong had just gotten worse.

7.

Stone had managed to reach one of the small outbuildings before the storm split the skies and hurled its heavy rain and lightning at him. The building had seen better years, and had, from its smell, once been the home of livestock. The floor was dirt, covered in patches with moldy hay, but the roof was sound. Wind howled through the open windows and rotted door, but there were corners kept dry. Stone found one of these corners and sat in it. He would wait until the rain slackened or stopped before he tried for the main building. He had come this far, there was no hurry now.

A few minutes after he arrived, a roar began. Stone went to one of the windows and peered out into the downpour. What he saw in the darkness were the triple tongues of rocket engines, lowering a fair-sized craft in the distance. He couldn't judge how far away it was, but it was not close. The rocket's flames were no more than pencils of fire, and he could block them out with one hand at arm's length.

Odd. He hadn't known there was a port anywhere around here. According to his information, the one he'd arrived at was the only extee port for five hundred klicks. And surely even the Khalia didn't use *rockets*?

A heavy gust of wind drove the rain into the window and it struck him like tiny wet hammers. Stone moved back into the shelter of the stable. He was not concerned with ships, only with his Art. It was not important.

8.

With the power gone, the flitter's controls responded sluggishly on the hydraulic backups, the dead craft nosed down, and it took most of Berq's strength to hold the little ship steady. The glide was more a controlled fall, and she aimed as best she could for a patch of bare rock down the hillside. It looked in the lightning flashes as if a landslide had cleared a path through the trees sometime back. The ground seemed more gravel than foliage, though some undergrowth had come up since the slide.

Ho, Mother and Father, prepare to welcome your only child
to the Cold Skies—

A less skilled pilot would have missed it. As it was, Berq
barely managed it, landing on the flitter's belly. The craft
bounced back into the air, came down, bounced again, and hit
a final time. The nose of the flitter dug into the gravel and
struck a rock, the ship did a half flip, twisted into the beginning
of an Immelmann, and hit on one wing, breaking it off. Half of
the plastic windows shattered, but the craft spun back onto its
belly again. After what seemed forever, the destroyed flitter
skidded to a stop.

Rain splattered on Berq's head and ran down into her eyes,
and it was the nicest rain she had ever felt.

Perhaps not just yet, my parents.

All power was still out, the com dead, and she was a long
way from anywhere. Nobody would be coming to find her,
either, since she had filed a false flight plan and was traveling
at 180 degrees different from what she had claimed.

Well. Aside from a sore shoulder and an ache in one hip, she
seemed to be uninjured. Nothing wrong with her feet.

She unstrapped from the seat, collected her bag, and paused
to assemble a small spring-dart pistol from components dis-
guised to look harmless. The darts were stacked-carbon needles loaded with anaphylactic nerve poison and while the little
gun only had an effective range of about fifty meters, it would
stop anything smaller than a curl-nose stonewall dead in its
tracks. Even a curl-nose would be unhappy about being shot.
The magazine in the pistol's butt held ten darts, and Berq had
two spare loaded mags. No point in wandering around a
strange countryside naked. She was alive and armed and could
walk. Somewhere.

9.

Stone heard the sound of running footsteps splashing
through puddles. The rain had slackened some, the brunt of the
storm passed, and the time between lightning flashes and
thunder had grown longer.

At first he thought the footsteps were coming for him, but he held still and they passed, moving off into the distance. After a moment he stood and moved to the window. The distant lightning flashes were enough to reveal four figures in the distance, Khalians running in the direction of the ship he'd seen landing earlier.

That made sense, he supposed. Maybe they hadn't been expecting company.

As the rain slowed to a stop, Stone saw that the lights of the main building had gone out. Storm must have caused a power failure.

Well. Time to go and see if anybody was home.

10.

Imani felt the alien presence before the knocking on the temple's outer door. He was already there, waiting, holding a bright blue biolume stick when the visitor announced himself. Was this one from the ship? It hardly seemed likely, given the EMP attack, but Imani had not survived this long by acting thoughtlessly. He had collected his old personal sidearm, an antique rocket auto. The pulse wouldn't have hurt the solid-fuel rockets or simple mechanical operating system. He strapped the launcher around his waist and loosened it in its holster.

The scanners were out, but there was a preelectronic peephole lens built into the thick wooden door, and Imani looked through this to see the visitor.

A human stood there. He was tall, had light fur on his head, wore a coverall, and carried a small bag upon his back. He bore no visible weapons.

Imani opened the door. "Yes?"

"I am called Stone," the man said, his militaryspeak flat and without accent. His head fur looked green in the blue light of the biolume. "I have come to see the master of this temple."

Imani had seen a few humans in his time. They were brash, usually undisciplined, and generally soft. Not this one. He carried himself in balance, no small accomplishment, and from his stance and moves—or rather, his lack of movement—Imani knew him for what he was almost instantly: here was a swimmer in the Flow.

"I am Imani. Enter."

The Khalian moved back to give the human plenty of room. He did not doubt that this one—Stone, where had he heard that name?—also knew him for what he was. The *wa* was unmistakable in the entryway, and one swimmer usually could recognize another.

"Why have you come seeking me?"

"To learn."

"Ah. This way."

"You keep your temple dark."

"A problem with the power source." He produced another biolume, squeezed it, and the light around them doubled. He handed the stick to Stone. They continued to walk.

"What is your system called?"

"Chan-gen," Stone said.

"And you are adept at it?"

"Yes."

"In here. The biolume will give you sufficient light for you to see what you need to see."

With that, Imani opened the door to the spring-chamber and motioned for Stone to enter.

The man looked at the Khalian, eyes unblinking. He nodded, once, and Imani felt the thrill of recognizing another who was a near equal. Stone knew he was about to be tested, knew that it was dangerous, and knew that if he refused, he had wasted his time in coming here. All this was apparent in the simple nod to Imani, and the Khalian returned the nod with full courtesy.

Stone entered the room. Imani shut the door and used the outside controls to set the strikers. He kept the setting at full, potentially lethal power; to do less would be to show disrespect for one who was obviously in control of himself. He might fail and die, but he would want to be tested fully. Certainly Imani would in his place.

Even through the closed door, Imani could hear the hum of the first striker as it drew near its release.

Whatever else the human was, he was brave. In a strange test chamber with only the light of a single biolume, no doubt on the floor by this time, even the slightest mistake would

prove fatal. Imani hoped that whatever gods the man spoke to
would take an interest in him. Or that his skill was very sharp
indeed.

11.

The first thing Berq did was climb to the top of the hill upon
which she had crashed. This was natural to her, to go up to see
what she could, and as the rain dropped off, the going became
a lot easier. A half hour's slippery hike brought her to the hill's
peak, and from there she could see things under the thick
starlight.

First and most obvious was the ship. This was a squat craft,
the grayish hull rainbowed with annealing friction marks from
dozens of atmospheric entries. Wisps of steam still rose from
the cooked ground. The ship was dark, no running lights or
hull lamps lit. She didn't recognize the configuration. It
seemed like a military hopper, company-sized, but there were
no navy markings on it she could see. No markings at all.

There seemed to be glimmerings and movement on the far
side of the ship, but she couldn't see who was there from her
perch.

The damned thing was partly responsible for her being here.
The least they could do was give her some help.

One did not get to be a top assassin, however, by putting
one's hand into an occupied *detz* nest. Better she should check
this out a little before she went tromping down the hill waving
her arms at whoever was rattling around in the dark. Maybe
they had lost power, but surely there'd be some kind of
emergency backup for lights? They should have flashlamps, at
least.

Berq circled her way down, angling across the wet hillside
until she was well aslant to the ship and able to move in the
cover of a copse of evergreen trees. It took maybe another half
hour, and along the way she began to be able to hear the
passengers. They spoke in a language she was not familiar
with, and while she didn't understand the words, the tone
sounded military. A deep voice would cut into the chatter every

now and then, and it sure sounded like a non-com's "Shut the fuck up!" to her.

Finally, she managed to creep along a ragged line of dark bushes. The bushes still held a lot of water that fell on her at every slight touch against the damned things. She put her bag down, and crawled under one of the bushes until she could see the gathered passengers.

Under the starlight, things were not as clear as they would be in daylight, of course, but there was enough illumination to reveal creatures unlike any Berq had ever seen.

They were quadrupeds. The front legs were relatively thick, almost like a big Nedge's or a skinny Terran's in size. Looked to be three toes, big pads on each. The rear legs were curved, resembling a springbok's or maybe a craftdeer's. But where a deer would have a neck, these things had an extension of the torso, widening to another set of shoulders and thick arms. Their necks were short, almost invisible, and the heads were heavy, roundish blocks. The skin color was hard to determine in the starlight, it looked dark gray or black, and the skin itself was loose, hung in a number of folds that effectively hid facial features, save for beady eyes and a thin slash of a mouth. Whatever they were, they weren't native to any world about which Berq knew. Some of them were obviously male. Some seemed to be female.

And she was right about them being soldiers, too.

All of the things wore a long knife or a short sword on a strap around the upright torso. Some of them had laser rifles on shoulder slings. A few wore packs over the horizontal body section. Some carried handguns in holsters. There were patches of cloth or paint-bearing insignia on some of them. There were thirty or so trampling around in the mud, and from the way they sank into the ground in the one g, Berq estimated that the larger ones would probably go about two hundred kilos, maybe a little less. She couldn't tell if there were more on the ship.

Whoever—*what*ever—they were, she was pretty certain they didn't belong here. Invited company generally didn't come down hidden in a storm and bearing arms.

Berq didn't think she'd be asking these creatures for a ride to the spaceport. In fact, it was a good idea for her to leave before maybe one of them saw or smelled her or whatever.

Using great care, Berq slid back from the scene. If they were military—and sure as dungbirds ate shit they were—then they would put out some kind of perimeter guards. Maybe she was outside the sentries, maybe not. She could deal with them if need be, but better they never knew she was here. Whatever they wanted, it was not her business, and the sooner she could get to the port and off-planet, the better.

She worked her way back to the trees cautiously, using all her stealth techniques. When she was two hundred meters away, she relaxed a little. Probably outside their guards, if they'd had time to post any.

She was nearing a large boulder when she heard something behind her. She spun. There was a Khalian, he was nearly on top of her, moving in fast. And he had friends, too, three of them.

"Get him!" one of them yelled.

She'd never get her gun out fast enough.

Suddenly out of time, Berq did the only thing possible: she wrapped herself in the Amaji trance.

Named after the mythical raptor, the Amaji fighting flight was designed to bypass the slowness of conscious thought. The twelve major *katas* combined covered virtually every possible attack, ranging from a single opponent to six; unarmed, armed with knives or sticks or swords or spears. Once wrapped in the trance, a fully fledged expert would not return to ordinary consciousness until the fight was won—or the master was dead. There was no in-between. The power of the response was dictated by the force of the attack. A killing strike upon one in Amaji would draw a like response.

Not all higher consciousness fled. Berq saw, as if from a great distance, that the Weasel leading the charge had not extruded his claws or drawn a weapon, which he certainly would have done had he intended to maim or kill her. Lucky for him.

Berq twirled, laid a hand almost gently on the back of the charging attacker's head as she danced from his path, and gave him the Eagle at Sunrise.

The Khalian did a half flip and hit the boulder.

She cast Wren-in-Nest, and sent the second one flying.

She dropped to Low Perch, and the third one tripped over her outstretched leg and pinwheeled into startled unconsciousness against the unyielding rock.

She spun once again, in the classic helicopter strike Dying Dervish. The impact of her hammer fist against the last one's skull was most satisfying. He hit the wet ground with a great splash.

The Amaji scanned the skies for danger. Seeing none, the raptor took wing. The trance was broken.

Berq regarded her work. Not bad, especially considering that these particular Weasels, given their moves, were passing adept at some fighting art.

She drew her small pistol and approached the first attacker, who was conscious and moaning. Probably would have a sore back for a few days, that one.

Berq spoke upward of twenty languages and all three of the common militaryspeaks. "Let's talk, you and I," she said to the groaning Panya.

12.

When Stone pushed the chamber door open, the old Khalian stood there, wrinkles gathered at the corners of his eyes and nostrils dilated. It was what passed for a broad smile among the Khalia.

"Surprised?"

Imani said, "No. I did not hear your body thump the floor, nor any major impacts from the strikers. How did you fare?"

"The fourth one hit me here"—he touched his right shoulder with a finger—"but only a glancing blow. The twelfth brushed me here." He touched his hip.

Imani smiled again. "Very good."

"How often do you engage the chamber?"

"Daily."

"And how do you fare?"

"One touch in the last fifty tests."

Stone was impressed. It had taken all his skill to keep from getting beaten to pieces in there. He offered Imani a bow of respect. This old Khalian had powerful *ki*, a blind man could not fail to see it.

Imani returned the gesture. "I currently have no students able to train in the spring-chamber."

"You have now."

Wrinkle. Dilate. "Ah. I am honored."

"The honor is mine, Master."

"Let us call each other 'Teacher.' I can see that you have things to show me, as well. Can I assume you had nothing to do with the ship that has recently put down near here?"

"I watched it from the stables. It landed on rocket power and the configuration of the engines did not look like one with which I am familiar."

"Have you any personal electronic devices?"

"A timer. A musical tone generator."

"Would you see if they remain operative?"

Stone picked up his pack and removed the two items. The blue glow of the biolumes was more than enough to show that both devices *were* inoperative. He looked at Imani, puzzled.

"Our friends in the ship have laid an EMP upon us."

"Why?"

"I do not know. It is an interesting puzzle. But I am afraid it is also a bad omen."

Stone thought about it for a moment. "Are you at war with anyone?"

"Not to my knowledge."

"I heard rumors . . ."

"Explain."

"On my way to Khalia I sometimes traveled with the military. Before he died, my uncle was highly regarded among our Fleet. There were rumblings of some kind of action around Khalia, of battleships being moved to this sector. Nothing official."

"Ah. There is nothing of military value around here, but such a place would be ideal to land a small force for fifth-column activities. The nearest village is some distance away. Our two vehicles will have been damaged by the pulse and our communications have been wiped out. I have sent some of my students to check on the ship, but this was before I knew about the EMP strike. They could be in danger. I must go and see to them."

"I'll go with you."

"It is not your problem."

"It has just become mine, *Sensei*."

"I have an old hunting rifle somewhere. I'll get it for you. *Sensei*."

Stone followed his new teacher down the dark hall.

13.

The night skies had cleared almost completely, and there was more than enough light to see as Imani and his new friend Stone moved through the grounds in the direction of the distant ship. They were armed, Imani with his rocket pistol and Stone with the air rifle, but they would hardly be a match for troops, if indeed there were any such.

And whose troops would they be?

As they walked over the familiar grounds, Imani stopped suddenly near the outbuildings. Someone was coming.

"Take cover," he said quietly to Stone. "We have company. Shoot only if I do."

The human nodded and moved quickly and silently to a tartfruit bush, where he slid into the dark foliage.

Imani drew his pistol and flattened himself against the toolshed.

Several sets of footsteps. Slogging across the muddy ground. He recognized the sounds of his students and started to relax. No. Wait. They were accompanied by another, one with a lighter tread. Not a Khalian. Nor a human. Imani felt something else, some strength in the Flow, emanating from this unseen presence. Another swimmer? He sniffed the air, caught the scents of his students, but did not recognize the ginger-spice odor of the alien. It seemed almost familiar, but he could not put a name to it.

The first of the four students came into view, passing Imani where he pressed against the wood of the shed. He let his tension flow out with his exhalation, and shifted his weapon slightly.

"Hold up," came a command from the still-unseen alien.

The two students stopped. Because Imani had willed himself into the technique of no-mind, neither had seen him, though he was plainly in view were they only to look.

"I've got a dartgun pointed at these four," came the alien voice. "Unless you want to see them drop like cut wheat, best you come out and act peacefully."

Imani grinned, in spite of the problem. She—it was definitely a female of some kind, he felt—knew he and Stone were here in hiding. Yes. Another swimmer for certain. Imani did not believe in coincidence. She, like Stone, had been sent for some purpose. He holstered his weapon. If this alien meant his students fatal harm, they'd already be dead. So she might be dangerous, but she was reasonable. Besides, the Flow had sent her.

Imani said, "Stone."

The two Khalian students jumped.

"Master!" one of them said, relieved.

Stone emerged from the bush, airgun still held ready, until he saw Imani wave it down. He lowered the weapon.

Imani moved into view.

It was one of the Nedge. He hadn't seen one in years, not since his liberty at the Circleworld station, and only briefly then. And this one was another equal. The Flow must have major reasons for this.

His students looked as if they had been in a battle, holding themselves stiffly, but obviously wearing new bruises and maybe even a fracture or two.

"I am Imani, master of this place. This is Stone. I see you have already met my four students."

The female Nedge nodded. "You should teach them to think before they move."

Imani shrugged. "They are young. We were all young, once."

The Nedge chuckled. "You're right. I forget that sometimes." With that, she tucked the small gun into her belt.

"I'm called Berq," she said.

14.

Berq followed the old Khalian and the Terran to the main building. At first she had wondered what a human was doing out here, but when she drew closer, she understood. These were adepts, anybody with her own skills could hardly miss the way they moved and stood. She had spent more than two thirds of her life training to learn the moves that would allow the Amaji to function properly, and she understood well the desire to attain perfection. They worked in different systems, but past a certain point, all systems flew to the same end. These two were like her.

Inside the temple Imani turned to his students. "What of the ship?"

The first one who had attacked Berq lowered his gaze and spoke softly. "We did not get to it, Master."

Imani looked at Berq.

"Sorry," she said.

"It is my fault," Imani said. "I am a poor teacher."

"I can tell you about the ship. I was leaving the area next to it when I—ah—met your students."

"And taught them a humility I have failed to teach them, honored lady."

"Female?" the senior student said. "She is *female*?"

"You are dismissed," Imani said to the four. "Go and find a way to lessen the darkness in here. Rig torches or biolumes."

The four scurried away quickly.

"Our electronics have been disrupted by an EMP."

"Damn! That must be why my flitter went dead. Those ugly quads blew me out of the air!"

"Quads?" Imani said.

Berq described the ship and its occupants. It was obvious that Imani did not recognize the creatures from her description, but the man's reaction said that he did. Imani noticed this, as well.

"Stone?"

"When I was on the last leg of my journey here, I heard stories about such creatures. An officer got drunk and said maybe more than he should. They sound like the Kosantzu. A young race involved with the Syndicate, according to my source."

"Why would they be here?"

Stone shook his head. "I don't know. But if the Syndicate has anything to do with it, it's grief. And if the other rumors I heard have anything to them, then Khalia may be in trouble."

Berq said, "How so?"

"It sounds to me like the planet is about to be attacked. And maybe the invasion has already started."

15.

Daybreak was still more than three hours away when Berq had arrived with her news. Stone knew that she was made of the same stuff as he and Imani; more, she had an edge sharper than his own. He had recently been forced to kill three Khalian attackers; she had defeated four of the same opponents—but without seriously damaging them, a much more difficult task. Killing was easier by far than controlling.

Stone and Berq sat at a table in a small room alone, Imani having gone to speak to his students. Shortly, he returned; by the light of several biolumes, the Nedge drew them pictures. It was obvious she did not want to be here, that this was not her business. But as she sketched the layout of the ship's landing site, and then the Kosantzu—if that's who they were—Stone realized too that she had a grasp of military strategy and tactics at least equal to his own. The temple was isolated, without communications, and a too-obvious target for the invaders. Certainly Berq could escape on her own in the dark, but she did not know what kind of sensor equipment the Kosantzu could field, and come sunrise, she would be in strange country, at a decided disadvantage against an unknown number of faster, probably stronger, and certainly better armed enemies.

That they were enemies none of them doubted for a moment.

Berq pointed at the drawing of the Kosantzu. It was well rendered, using the tight lines of a skilled draftsman. The Kosantzu were ugly brutes.

"The legs are thick, and the upper body appears to be fairly powerful. Here is the scale."

Quickly she sketched in a line drawing of a Nedge next to the quadruped. Hmm. About man-height in front, sloping to shorter hindlegs.

"The skin appears to be thick, they are sort of a dark gray color. I didn't see the teeth. All of them I saw carried edged weapons, some had sidearms, others laser rifles. There were heavier weaponry, broken down for transport. No armor. I'd say this is light infantry, probably some kind of covert force rather than a stand-and-fight unit."

"Horse ninja," Stone said.

"Would that we had one to dissect," Imani offered.

Stone nodded. Yes. Knowing what was apparent was important; knowing your enemy's invisible secrets was also important. Did they have heart and lungs in the main torso? Or were there organs in the upper body? Nerve plexes? Where was the brain? Where best to strike or shoot to bring one down? Offhand, the rear end seemed to be the weak point, it would be easier to break its back, perhaps, than it would be to snap a man's or a Khalian's, but would that do you any good? Maybe they could operate just as well on two as four. They seemed descended from herd animals. Would they move in formation, or could they function just as well alone? How fast were they? How high could they jump? A lot of questions and very few answers.

Well. This kind of information would come as it would. There was nothing to be done for it.

"What do you think?" Imani asked.

"We don't know what they want," Stone said, "but if they have any kind of military skill at all, they'll have to secure the temple, it's the only civilization around here. They had sense enough to hit us with a pulse to take out power and communications. I'd have to assume they'll come here pretty quickly before we can figure out what is going on or maybe get some kind of com back online."

Imani nodded. "Berq?"

"I agree with Stone. Were I leading the quads, I would already be halfway here. They can camouflage the ship so routine spysats won't pick it up, and nobody is apt to stumble across it on foot. If we assume they didn't land just to waste their time, there is somewhere else they want to get to, and they'll need a place to hide that many troops. The temple would be a good base."

Imani said, "That is also how I see it. I have sent my students away. They number a dozen and they know the terrain, so I expect one or more of them will manage to reach the nearest village, about five hard days on foot. They will inform the proper authorities."

"You could have sent fewer and kept some here," Berq said.

"They are enthusiastic, but more likely to get in the way than help. We have no projectile weapons with which to outfit them."

"We could just fade into the woods and wait for help," Berq said.

"I am Khalian and these serve those who exploited us. I cannot run and hide and do nothing. Would you, if it were your world?"

Berq offered a shrug. "Probably."

Imani fixed her with a cool stare. "Loyalties are different," he said. "What if someone attacked the Guild With No Nest."

Berq blinked once, and then regarded the Khalian with a piercing look.

Stone was aware that something important was being said. But he had never heard of something called the Guild With No Nest. Some kind of clan?

"I am not so poor a teacher that my best students could be defeated so soundly by any but a very skilled fighter. I have heard of the Amaji and the few who can fly with it."

Berq nodded. "Your point is well taken."

"You are certainly free to leave if you wish."

"Maybe not," Berq said. "I do owe them for knocking my flitter down."

16.

Quickly Imani took stock of their weapons and of their plan. The airgun was accurate and effective on deer to a hundred meters. His rocket pistol would throw a missile farther, but it would take a steady hand to hit anything past that same hundred meters. Berq said that her dartgun had half that range. They were therefore somewhat limited in their options. There remained less than two hours of darkness, and they had better make the best use of the night that they could. Once the invaders reached the temple and the sun came up, things would be much more difficult. The only real advantages they had were that he knew the terrain better than the invaders and that for a time, at least, they had surprise on their side. Plus maybe one other: Berq had said that each of the invaders carried an edged weapon. Perhaps they had some kind of personal honor. That might be worth something. He said as much to Berq and Stone.

"I have Khalian fighting knives. You would honor me if you would carry them."

"Of course," Stone said.

"My pleasure," Berq said.

"I think we can find some straps to fit you. And let us move quickly. There is a gully through which any sizable force must pass to reach here. If we get there first, it would be to our advantage."

17.

Berq was uncertain as to her motives. Somehow, the old Khalian had challenged her honor, in a way in which she could not quite determine. It was not her problem, this business, and yet she found she could not simply walk away. Was it because these two were like her? They had the feel of warriors, and if not her equal, then they were close to it. Outside of a few inside the Guild, Berq had never met another, Nedge or alien, who could fly with her. And even in the Guild, she was the best. What would it be like to go into battle with equals at her side? Even against such odds?

Well. The odds were bad, but that was the way of it. All life was a risk. One made do. And she had no one waiting for her at home. If she did not return, the Guild would elect a new Master of Assassins. She would not be missed by fledglings or a mate.

They took fifteen minutes to move supplies from the temple to a nearby patch of forest, then set off for the gully. She remembered passing through it earlier, and it was a perfect place for an ambush. There was a narrow path next to a rain-swollen stream, and the sides rose perhaps seven or eight armspans to high ground. Fifteen meters with the dartgun was too far for tack-driving accuracy, but she could hit a target the size of the Kosantzu all night long. Whether the needles would drive far enough into that thick skin to allow the poison to work, or whether the poison would affect the creatures, was another matter. There was only one way to find out. She had survived death once this night. The muggy air was especially sweet because of that. And she had been living on borrowed time since the guard's gun had jammed on her third assignment a dozen years past. She had accomplished her last assignment. She had nothing to lose but her life, and the first thing an assassin learned was just how fragile life could be.

She certainly could do worse than Stone and Imani for fighting companions. What the gods will, happens. She would soon see what the gods had in mind.

18.

Stone wished he'd had time to practice with the air rifle. Imani told him it was sighted dead on for fifty meters, center hold with the three-dot iridium glowsights, and good for five shots before the motorized pump had to be worked. The weapon held five rounds and he had a packet of forty-five more after the first loading was gone.

Whatever scenarios he had imagined on his trip across space to come here, this had not been one of them.

Still, he was committed. Death would come when it would. Technique was all.

19.

They were an hour from false dawn when they arrived at the gully and set up. Imani and Stone took the east side, Berq the west. All the years since last Imani had done killing battle seemed to drop away, and the feelings he remembered came back. Different, in that he was not afraid to die in quite the same way, he had made his peace with the Taker, but the same in the anticipation.

Five minutes passed, and he smelled them before he saw them. They had an oily, musky scent, and it was heavy on the night air. Imani raised one paw and gestured to Berq across the gully. The three of them had agreed on several signals beforehand, simple things. Here they come, this one said.

There they were. Given their size and numbers, they moved fairly quietly through the gully. Nothing rattled or clinked. Thirty or more, Imani guessed. He did not have time for a certain count before they were almost directly below.

As agreed, he tracked the second five. Berq would shoot at the first five, Stone the third group. Since the Nedge had the shortest-range weapon, her shot would be first.

Imani heard the quiet *twang!* of the dartgun and without waiting to see the effect, he began firing.

The rocket launcher's *whoosh* was joined by the *whump* of Stone's airgun.

Below, somebody screamed orders as several of the Ko-santzu fell, dead or wounded. A few flashes of hard orange light bounced from the gully's upper edges, tearing chunks of rock away and boiling the wet dirt where they hit.

Imani's rocket pistol was very visible in the dark. He managed four shots before the laser fire steadied and found his position. He slid back from the edge as the beams of half a dozen weapons baked black the spot where he had been a second before.

Stone also rolled back as other beams found his position.

Across the gully several hot laser claws raked at the Nedge's perch. Her weapon did not give off any telltale flashes, but those below had set up a field of fire and were taking no chances. Imani saw Berq scoot away from the edge as the coherent light bounced all around her.

"Go!" Imani said. "To the rendezvous!"

20.

A kilometer away the trio met. Berq arrived first, Stone and Imani shortly thereafter.

"I shot all five," Berq said, "but only three went down. I think maybe the needles didn't dig deep enough on the other two. I don't think I missed."

"I shot four, four fell," Imani said. "I sought to hit where a deer's heart would be."

"I only shot three. I think the brain is in the head, though. I hit the first one there and he collapsed fast. The second one I hit in the upper body and he fell, but got up. The third one I hit on the lower body, right at the shoulder. I didn't have time to see what he did."

Berq said, "So we killed or wounded ten. I made it thirty-five of them."

"You have a sharp eye," Imani said.

"That leaves more than two dozen, even if all the ones we hit are out of action," Stone said. "And we will play hell sneaking up on them again."

"Back to the wheat field?" Berq said.

Imani nodded. "I have six high-explosive rockets. If they cross after daylight, we might get a couple more."

"And if they hurry and get there in the dark?" Stone said.

Imani shrugged. "We will have to try something else."

21.

The Kosantzu were not altogether stupid. They had made a bad mistake going into the gully, but they did not repeat it by moving their remaining force across an open field of knee-deep wheat. Even though they didn't arrive at the edge of the field until well after the sun rose, they stayed in the cover of the trees.

"What do you think?" Stone asked.

"They'll probably flank the field. Or set up one of the heavier weapons and blast away at the first sign of fire," Berq said.

"We can't form much of line with just us three," Stone said.

"We fall back," Imani said.

22.

The man, the Nedge, and the Khalian watched from the woods as the Kosantzu cautiously approached the temple. The quads were prepared for resistance, though there would be none.

Berq's vision was the clearest, and she could see well enough to tell that two of the Kosantzu carried large-bore charged-particle spitters, to judge by the large capacitor packs attached, and several others waved directional sensors back and forth, probably sweeping for signs of life-heat.

There were no signs of the dead or wounded.

"They have to believe that whoever jumped them will run for help, so they won't be waiting around very long."

"Yes," Imani said. "We'll have to take them out before they leave and maybe spread out."

"A difficult chore," Berq observed.

"Perhaps not, if those swords they carry mean anything."

Berq and Stone both looked at Imani.

"You are an assassin," he said. "You know what the surest way to take out a target is."

Berq nodded, understanding.

Stone didn't pick it up so fast. "You know of a method to take out more than a score of heavily armed soldiers with what weapons we have?"

"If I can get one of their laser rifles."

"Looks to me as if a laser pulse would glance right off those things unless you hit it solid. Our own weapons are as effective."

"Not quite."

He explained.

23.

The sentry was understandably nervous. He paced back and forth in the open, next to the nearest outbuilding. If the sentry had a sensor—and they had to assume he did—he would have it tuned to Khalian body mass. Since both Berq and Stone were larger, he'd spot them, too. The thing probably had a range of at least fifty meters. Even if they could sneak up on him somehow, he'd know they were coming if they got too close. Too, the Kosantz had picked a fairly clear spot, and he would see anybody trying to come across the open ground between the woods and himself. It was a distance of two hundred meters between the woods and where he stood, too far to use the airgun.

The trick was to get close enough to shoot him without being seen.

Berq claimed to be an expert with a rifle, so she would be the shooter. It would be up to Stone and Imani to distract the sentry long enough for her to get a clear shot.

The plan was simple.

Stone worked his way around the far side of the sentry. They would offer the Kosantz one target—Stone insisted that he be allowed to provide it—and when he was drawn to it, Berq would move within range.

Stone crept and crawled through the still-muddy grounds, Imani watching for other guards. When he was thirty or so meters away from the guard, Stone stood and offered a fully erect heat shadow.

The guard's sensor *cheeped*, and he spun surefootedly, unslinging the laser rifle and snapping it up to his upper shoulder.

Stone dropped like his namesake.

Having his target disappear, the Kosantz trotted forward a few steps, weapon held ready.

Berq left the cover of the trees and sprinted toward the guard.

Stone leaped up and dropped flat again.

The Kosantz guard whipped his rifle into position and fired.

The silent pulse scorched over Stone's prostrate form, sizzling the air and missing him by maybe ten centimeters. He could feel the heat, or imagined he could. Too close.

The Kosantz moved toward Stone, ready to blast anything that moved. Come on, Berq—!

Berq realized that the guard would reach a place where he could see and hit Stone before she would get to optimum range. She was twenty meters out. She stopped, dropped prone, and held her aim high, over the Kosantz's head. She caught her breath, sharpened the sights, and squeezed the firing lever. The *whump* kicked the weapon back against her shoulder. She looked at the target. He was raising his weapon again—

The Kosantz's shoulders jerked back and he clawed at the middle of his back with one hand, dropping the laser rifle. A good twenty-five centimeters below her point of aim, that hit. If she'd held on the middle of his back, she'd have put one right up his ass. Amazing what one thinks of during moments of great stress.

Stone came up and ran toward the wounded Kosantz, firing the borrowed dartgun. One of the needles got through. The sentry drooped over, quivering.

Stone snatched up the laser rifle and ran toward her. Imani angled in behind the man, moving fast for an old Khalian. Berq turned and moved back toward the woods.

24.

The laser rifle was coded. Any hand that pulled the firing lever other than the one to which the weapon had been custom-mated would disappear when the laser's nuclear battery went up. The unfortunate shooter would leave no more than a slightly radioactive crater twenty meters across and as much as two meters deep behind when he went, depending on how hard the surface was, of course.

The battery could be removed, but not without the trigger mechanism, since they were of a piece. There were tales of stolen coded weapons with the original owner's severed hand stuck in place under a new owner's grip, but that would not be needed here.

Imani removed the battery and firing mechanism and tucked it into his belt pouch, out of sight.

"No point in delaying," he said.

He started off, with Berq and Stone a few paces behind him.

Stone said, "That's what he meant when he was talking about the best way to assassinate somebody."

"Yes. Killing another is fairly easy if you don't mind dying when you do it."

Stone shook his head. "He had things to teach me."

"Is he not teaching you even now?"

Stone thought about it a moment. "Yes. I suppose you're right."

25.

When they were within shouting distance of the main building, Imani yelled out.

"Are you a species with any honor?"

Kosantzu emerged, assorted weapons held ready.

"They'd be foolish to go for this," Stone said.

"They are already foolish to be owned by others," Berq said.

"It's a big risk."

"Not so big," Imani said. "I know them, because I know my own people. We were thralls to the same masters."

A rough voice answered in Khalian militaryspeak. "Who challenges the honor of the Kosantzu?"

"I am Imani of Khalia, and I have already killed several of your stupid breed."

Some of them would have shot him then, but the speaker waved them down. "And you have come to give yourself up to our mercy?"

"No. I offer to fight the bravest of you in single combat. Or are those swords you carry merely for picking the dung from between your toes?"

"You have some point to this stupidity?"

"If I win, you withdraw from our world."

"And if you lose?"

"Then I am dead and it will not matter to me what you do."

"And what of your alien friends?"

Imani shrugged. "They are not my concern."

"You don't think they would actually withdraw, do you?" Stone said softly.

"Of course not," Imani answered. "Would you? No, this allows them to carve me to pieces for attacking them. Certainly *I* would find that more satisfying than shooting someone who slew my comrades. They might suspect some kind of trap, but they want to use those blades. I know."

"Put down your weapons," the leader called.

The three of them dropped their guns.

"Are there others besides you three?"

"No."

"Then come and prepare to meet your end, fool. I will cut you down myself!"

Imani started to take a step. Stone reached out and laid a soft hand on the furry shoulder. "May your gods be with you, *Kyōdai*."

"I do not recognize the term."

"It is from an old Terran language. It means 'brother.'" He looked at Berq. "It also means 'sister.'"

Both Imani and Berq nodded, short, military bows.

The Kosantzu had no greater beauty up close, Stone saw, and they smelled like old boots left too long in a damp locker.

"Will you have a blade?" the Kosantz leader said, drawing his own and limbering his shoulders by swinging it back and forth.

"I'll use these," Imani said, pulling his knives. He showed his teeth as he backed away from the Kosantzu.

"Form a circle," the Kosantz ordered his troops.

How had Imani know they would do that? Just because they were herd animals?

"Watch those two." He nodded at Stone and Berq. "And keep a sharp eye to make certain no one else is out there."

It was eerie, how right Imani had been. "They will all be watching me fight their champion," Imani had said as he disassembled the laser rifle. "No matter what they are supposed to do, they'll be watching, especially after I draw blood. Be ready. Ten seconds after I cut him. No more."

Berq and Stone were bracketed by a pair of the soldiers, but all eyes were on the combatants.

They circled, and Stone saw that the Kosantz moved well, almost gliding, his footing sure. From the way he handled the sword, a slightly curved weapon about a meter long, he knew how to use it.

The Kosantz leaped in and slashed. He was fast, but no faster than a man—or a Khalian.

Imani dodged and blocked with one of his knives. Steel clanged on steel.

An excited rumble went up from the crowd.

The Kosantz jumped back and recovered his guard position. "Good!" he said. "It will not be mere slaughter!"

"Oh, but you are wrong," Imani said. He darted in, blocked the downward slash with one knife, and stabbed lightly with his other blade.

His technique was, Stone saw, flawless. It was only a nick, he could have easily buried the blade to its hilt in the Kosantz, but knowing he could, there was no point.

The crowd of soldiers rumbled louder.

"Ten," Berq said softly. "Nine. Eight. Seven."

The angry Kosantz leader charged. Stone saw that the two guards were watching the fight intently.

"Go," he said.

They moved back a hair, failed to draw any notice, then turned and sprinted. Stone ran as fast as he could. Behind them, one of the guards reacted, saying something Stone could not make out.

"Three . . . two . . . one," Berq called as she ran, easily three meters ahead of Stone.

"Farewell, *Kyōdai*," Stone said.

The world went black before he heard the sound and Stone lost consciousness. Too close—

When he awoke, it was to Berq's birdlike gaze. His head hurt and he was nauseated.

"You were hit by a piece of debris," she said, pointing.

The severed, pulped head of a Kosantz lay on the ground a few meters away.

"It worked," Stone said.

"Yes. Several of them survived the blast." She tapped the knife in the strap on her chest. "I finished them."

"He was dedicated to his art, our brother," Stone said. "I could have learned much from him."

"You have learned how to die. What is more important?"

She was right. "What now?" he said.

"I return to my home world. I have responsibilities. And you?"

Stone shook his head. "I have nowhere I must be."

She sat silently for a moment, gazing at the still-smoking crater behind them. "I have been thinking about expanding our Guild," she said. "As my father did when he admitted females to it. He recognized that change was needed, that talent lies where you find it.

"There have never been any aliens in the Guild With No Nest.

"Would," she said, "you like a job, *Kyōdai*?"

"Sure. What exactly is that you do, Sister?"

Why, he wondered, did she find that so funny?

INTERLUDE

The navy of the Families didn't have the Articles of War. In its
stead they had several hundred years of traditional behavior
that was every bit as rigid and unforgiving. The extreme
concentration of authority in the senior family members also
meant that summary execution was the rule and it was
necessary for a senior officer to merely make his case for the
record. A record he controlled and presented.

As the full strength of the Alliance was being gathered near
Khalia, the family heads began to realize the need to make use
of every resource. Among the many options they chose was
the extensive use of those robotic sciences retained from the
collapse of the empire. While immensely costly, many of the
robot warriors proved devastatingly effective. Another option
was to attempt to recruit allies from other nearby clusters. This
ploy failed due to a combination of annoyance at occasional
Khalian raids and a lack of desire by potential allies to become
embroiled in a war on a side that was far from assured of
victory.

Controlling an entire cluster, one of the most important

sources of reinforcements for the Family Navy and Marine units were the numerous nonhuman races already under their sway. Many of these were found to have been too badly repressed to serve in any combat capacity. Other races' physiologies were too dissimilar to be effectively included in the Syndicated forces.

The success of the Fleish family in developing the primitive Kozantzu pressured the more established families to emulate their efforts. The result of the Schline family attempt to prepare the Dashanks, a short, powerfully built race of humanoids, proved particularly disastrous, in an effort to counterbalance the success of other families in recruiting primitive warriors. The Dashanks were technologically more advanced than the other races recruited. This meant that the Shanks could be used to man much more sophisticated weapons and even service ships. While once restive, the entire race seemed to enthusiastically support the Schline family war effort. The Shanks' leaders produced highly qualified recruits in large numbers. Schline prestige was restored. When the great armada gathered for a "neutralizing" strike against Khalia, a Schline admiral was in command.

Unknown to the Families, the culture of the Dashanks was based upon honor and revenge. It was also a most practical race, whose heroes were the members who gained their revenge and lived to enjoy it. One of their most powerful myths was the tale of the Seventeen Rogiers. The Rogier family was displaced from their lands and nearly destroyed by another clan. Seventeen generations later, the Rogiers had recovered its strength. Then, and only when ready, it struck. The displacing clan was completely slaughtered. The ancestral lands were restored.

It had been, coincidentally, seventeen generations since the Schline family ships had first arrived on the Dashanks' world. Of the ships carrying Dashank Marines, less than fifty percent reappeared. Most of these were those which carried mixed detachments of Shanks and Kozantzu. In most cases what remained of both units was unfit for combat.

TARNHELMS
by Chelsea Quinn Yarbro

THREE MORE MONTHS, which here meant seventy-eight days. Then there would be no more class-4 Syndicate station with the amenities of a freight terminal, no terrible planet with disgusting natives that almost never ate human beings. Keane Travers stared out his station window at the landscape he had come to loathe; a featureless expanse of lichen-covered slate interrupted with sudden, close outcroppings of spiky things that looked like plants but were in reality colonies of symbiotic life-forms existing somewhere on the biological scale between animal and vegetable. In the distance there was a sawtooth range of mountains with the usual evening thunderstorm piling up behind them, hurling the first of night-long lightning bolts through the clouds. Travers sighed, and asked himself, as he had from the day he arrived two years and seven months ago, how he could stand it.

"You'll be back on Danegeld soon," said his proctor, who stood to be promoted to manager as soon as Travers was gone, yet was not too eager to see him go, since he was as fond of this place as Travers was.

"Good," said Travers, listening to the sound of a nearby Tarnhelm striking at one of the uglies, the creatures that constituted about half the Tarnhelms' diet: they looked something like a cross between a porcupine and a stag beetle, and were about half the size of adult humans. Uglies usually had the sense to stay under cover, especially in the late afternoon when the Tarnhelms were most active.

"I suppose you'll be glad to go home," said his proctor, trying not to sound too anticipatory. "Who wouldn't."

"I'll be glad not to be here," Travers corrected him.

No one liked Siggirt's Blunder: the name said it all. It was a small, miserable excuse for a planet out at the edge of the Cluster, a minor addition from the days when Haakon Siggirt had been trying to pretend the Syndicate was an interstellar Hanseatic League. Everyone on the Board of Directors said Siggirt's Blunder was generally useless, having few minable concentrations of minerals and almost no other significant exports to speak of, nor any position of trading advantage.

Except, of course, there were the Tarnhelms.

"We've got a meeting with the head of the Waxy Tarnhelms set for tonight," said Regan Keir, the programmer for the station. "The senior Waxy Tarnhelm agreed to it yesterday. At least you'll have that to your credit."

"Well, if they actually show up, it'll be a first," said Travers, folding his arms over his chest. He looked at his proctor. "Waxy Tarnhelms would be the best, though, wouldn't they? If they arrive for the meeting, it will be a feather in all our caps. What do you think the chances are, Croydon?"

"Who knows?" replied the proctor. "Waxy Five and Waxy Nine have made pacts with us, and Waxy Six and Fourteen are considering it, which might turn the tide in our favor; that would account for half of the squadron leaders—if they call their rabble squadrons. They know about our dealing with the Sandy Tarnhelms, and the Dusties, too, and for the most part, I've been informed that they are satisfied that we have fulfilled our part of the bargain, at least to the satisfaction of four of the

Waxies, who think themselves superior to the Sandies and the Dusties. So we can figure the officers are in our favor, but I don't know about the senior Waxy Tarnhelm."

"I hope we find out," said Travers, and stared out the window.

Of the twenty identifiable independently mobile life-forms on the planet, the Tarnhelms had proven themselves the only ones of interest or value. They were solitary predators, looking—when you could see them—something like the mantas from the seas of Old Earth, but much bigger, nearly the height of an average man when their fans were down and not extended, with a double array of spines on either side of their dorsal crest. Their small faces, nestled in a ruff of hooked tusks, were soft and puckered like rotting apples. They possessed a complex language composed almost entirely of adjectival phrases and subscribed to a rigid code of conduct that appeared to be: kill everything but your blood, your boss, and your boss's blood, and eat it if you can. They stank of burned lentils.

"It's promising, their interest," said Keir.

Travers turned back toward the window and squinted at the sky. "Do you think they're watching us?"

"Who knows? Why bother to look?" asked Croydon. "Even if they are, it doesn't mean much. You only have to worry about Tarnhelms when you can see them." He sat down with his back to the window. "Come on. It's almost time for supper. Staring at shimmering spots in the air—if you can find them—won't help."

"I don't trust them," said Travers, as he had since he had first accepted his post on Siggirt's Blunder. "They make me nervous."

"They probably feel the same way about you; most primitives are like that," said Croydon, punching in an order for high tea. "Scones or cakes?" he asked.

Regan Keir shoved her springy deep-red hair back. "Cakes, the little ones without the frosting." She drew up a chair and sat down next to Croydon.

The manager allowed himself to be persuaded. "Why not?" he asked the air, and hoped that some of the snoop systems would not be set off by his remark. Discontent was regarded with suspicion back home, where no one had seen the mind-numbing desolation of Siggirt's Blunder. Travers chose one of the deeper chairs and moved it near the table in the entertainment grotto. "High tea. Think of the tradition." He gave them a negotiating smile. "Do you ever wonder what these high teas used to taste like?" he asked the other two. Station etiquette required that he have at least one meal a day with them as they were his closest assistants; the other fifty-three residents of the station had less call on his attention.

"Like this," said Keir, dismissing the question.

"How do you know?" Travers asked. "Those high teas were back on Old Earth, and they weren't the same all over then. So this might be entirely different from the real high teas." He rarely got into arguments, and now he wondered why he was bothering. It was something to take his mind off the Tarnhelms, he reckoned.

"There is no way to find out," said Croydon. "And probably the taste was different, because the substances were not the same as what we have now. They speak of milk and cream, but do they mean mares or cows or camels? They don't bother to tell us that." He tapped a few more buttons. "We will have to trap a few more uglies for the Tarnhelms; they'll want a snack."

"I hate those things," said Keir with a shudder.

"I hate them," Croydon said with sudden passion. "Deadly, stinking, hideous, appalling things. Sometimes I think I'd do anything to get away from them and this place. Why don't we just load them into ships, seal them, and send them on dead courses for their sun—or any sun."

"The Tarnhelms?" Travers asked, turning his head as the chief butler of the station appeared with his enormous rolling cart. He did not want gossip going around the station about Keir's or Croydon's attitude, though he supposed it was too late to stop all speculation. It was not possible for him to change how they felt, and it would be a mistake to try it.

"No; the uglies. And the crawlies. And the wigglies." She touched her hair again, which was a sure indication of nervousness. She glanced once over her shoulder toward the window, then resolutely put her attention on the tea cart. "I think I'll have lemon with mine, Harrington," she said, as she always did. "And ask Chambulo to bring his reports to my office before the change of shift."

"Very good, Programmer."

"This is the worst place for wildlife," said Travers, trying to make a joke of it and failing. "Uglies, crawlies, wigglies, nasties, scurries, ookies, horrids—what a zoo of unpleasantness."

"Let me have some of that Sinquet-Kway coffee, Harrington," said Croydon. "With sweet Immeric cheese." He had a decided preference for the produce of the gaudy and hedonistic planet that grew almost a third of the groceries for the Syndicate. "I think the Sinquet-Kway coffee is better than any other, don't you?"

"Of course, Proctor," said Harrington, setting about serving their tea.

"We're having Tarnhelms in later," Travers informed Harrington, although the chief butler obviously knew this already. "We'll need some uglies for them to devour and perhaps a scurry or two, if they're not too ferocious. It won't do having a scurry tear this place up before we get the cooperation of the Tarnhelms. They don't eat ookies, do they?"

"I don't believe so, sir," said Harrington. "More's the pity."

Travers sighed. "Yes."

Keir was handed her tea first, served in a cup the size of a soup plate. "How do you want to conduct the discussion?" she asked Travers, her voice faltering only once.

"That will be up to the Tarnhelms, I should think," said Travers, his tone quite level. He had to fight an impulse to laugh, keeping up this ancient tradition so far away and under conditions like these. If the Syndicate did not put so much store by forms, he would have abandoned high tea as a waste of time. "I'd like a few of those nut-crusted milk balls," he said to Harrington. He had a weakness for nut-crusted milk balls.

"Three or four, Manager?" asked Harrington.

"Four, if you will," said Travers. "And while we're dealing with the matter of this evening, I think Kasagio ought to be warned that his security crew will have their hands full. We don't know how many Tarnhelms will be here, and how many we will be able to see most of the time." The day before Kasagio had warned him about protecting against a covert Tarnhelm attack, but Travers had not listened. Now he was having second thoughts.

"We can put the mass detectors into operation," suggested Croydon. "They use a lot of power, but we'll know for sure how many Tarnhelms are here, and where they are."

"But they'd know we doubted them," Travers replied, attacking the first of his nut-crusted milk balls. "According to everything we know about them, doubting their word is about the worst thing you can do."

"And believing them is the stupidest," said Keir. The three of them sat in silence for a short while, each mulling over their shared predicament.

"They're vital, or so the head office says," Travers reminded them at last as if they had been holding a conversation. "According to the report, the Tarnhelms will make all the difference for us, now that we're having to deal with the Alliance. They should have stuck to their systems instead of coming pirating into ours." He said this last petulantly, annoyed that he was expected to deal with Alliance treachery.

"But suppose their Fleet finds and makes their own deal with the Tarnhelms—they could do, you know—or comes up with something that can see them when they're out of phase," said Croydon. "It's bound to happen sometime."

"Do you want to tell the First Son he's wrong?" Travers asked.

Croydon shook his head. "Put it that way, and the answer is no."

Goro Kasagio folded his massive arms across his broad chest and glowered at Travers. "It's not a good idea," he said. "Letting them in here with none of the mass detectors set up. Might as well throw all the security out and send the squad home if we don't have mass detectors. Letting them in at all is pretty risky. You're proposing something to make it worse."

"But they will be offended by the mass detectors," said Travers, finding it hard going to convince Kasagio of this since he did not believe it himself. "If we offend them, they won't make any pacts with us."

"We have pacts with the Dusties and the Sandies already. There isn't so much risk with them, or so it appears. We can't handle the Waxies very well, but someone's decided this is good. They want those killers off-planet. And you know once one he/he, one he/she, and one she/she leave Siggirt's Blunder, there will be no way in creation we can stop their spread. Why do we need the Waxies as well? You think we need all of them cooperating—all three tribes—or we won't have a chance with any of them off-planet: I know the theory, and I think it's fried." He was more resistant than ever. "We have a very small force here, and our security is pretty chancy as it is. If we start making changes because watching our backs might not go along with the Tarnhelms, there's no point to any of it. If the Tarnhelms come in here at full strength and only a few of them visible, I can't guarantee the safety of anyone here. They eat humans, remember."

"Not very often; and if they give loyalty, they keep their word." Travers lowered his head, sighing as he did. "Goro, it's never easy. If the First Son himself had not demanded this, I might have refused." This was not quite the truth, for Travers was too much a part of the bureaucracy and too much a diplomat to consider acting against the family's interests, no matter what the instigation. "I considered refusing. I want you to know that. I gave it serious thought. But I didn't think that it would be wise for me or anyone on Siggirt's Blunder to tell the First Son that his strategy was wrong. Unless you'd like to make the attempt."

"Not me," said Goro Kasagio. He put his hand on the three energy weapons strapped to his belt. "If we've got to do this, I can order my men to set their stunners on wide. That way if there are invisible Tarnhelms around, we'll be able to knock them out. They can't stay invisible when they're unconscious—hell, if they stay invisible too long it knocks them out, takes too much energy—and we're bound to hit some of them." He held up the palm-sized stunner. "Is that acceptable?"

"I suppose so," said Travers, not looking forward to the evening at all.

"While they're invisible, that's all they can do: stay invisible," Kasagio reminded him. "And they aren't really invisible. We could put up some supra-light scanners: they might show us something."

"No scanners," said Travers, wishing he could get about thirty hours' sleep. "Nothing like that."

Kasagio shrugged. "Has anyone thought about the problems of turning loose invisible carnivores in the Syndicate? Has anyone read any of my reports? Is anybody explaining this to the board? Do they know what they're playing with? Are they that blind?" He flung his hands in the air to disown the whole senseless mess. "And they want the Waxies, the ones you can't get ahold of. Sandies and Dusties provide a little purchase—why aren't they sending them instead?" He slapped his big hands together. "I'll report to you when the Tarnhelms arrive then," he said. "With my men, in uniform, ready for action if it comes."

"But not too obvious about it, if you please," said Travers, hoping that no one in the Syndicate would question his decisions. "If the Tarnhelms think we've acted against their honor, we'd never get anywhere with them, and the Sandies and the Dusties might withdraw from their contracts with us, as well. The top managers would not want that."

"And none of us wants to serve here forever, do we? Or on Wasteland Two. All right. We'll be careful. Whatever that means. Worry about the Tarnhelms, watch out for the obvious. What's obvious to a Tarnhelm?" Kasagio asked, chortling. "You answer me that one, Manager."

Travers shook his head. "Sorry."

At a distance and visible the Tarnhelms looked like enormous horned helmets drifting toward the station. In the dusk they remained near the ground instead of spreading their fans and drifting overhead. The largest of them was in the lead, and this was the one who identified him/himself to Kasagio when they arrived at the station perimeter.

Travers and Croydon had changed into their formal robes,

each of them wearing the wide collars designating their ranks. Keir had donned a magnificent gown that glittered with jewels from four different planets. Her nose wrinkled as the Tarnhelms entered the atmosphere of the station.

"I hate lentils," she whispered.

"Quiet," said Croydon, trying to keep from sneering.

The senior Tarnhelm floated into the room, fans still held low. He/he admitted several nerve-jarring squalks that were translated by the wall monitor as, "The gods of your home protect you on your travels, hideous outlanders."

"And a gracious good evening to you as well, Senior Tarnhelm," said Travers at his smoothest. "Please accept our hospitality, and know you are welcome." This was dutifully rendered as quacks and squeals, which seemed acceptable to the Tarnhelms.

"I am senior Tarnhelm, famed for decades of battle and deception," he/he announced. "We of the Waxy Tarnhelms, the most accomplished and feared of our race, will listen to your proposition if it is not too boring."

"We will endeavor not to bore you," Travers said. "But we do not wish to insult you with nothing more than discussion. It is our intention to provide you with food and entertainment first." With a sigh he clapped his hands and looked around as Harrington, in full regalia from lace shirt to kilt, came into the reception area. "Where are the uglies? Our guests do not wish to be bored."

"I will bring them at once," said Harrington with a bow to Travers and the Tarnhelms.

"Is that he/he or he/she or—" asked the senior Tarnhelm.

"We have only he/he and she/she," said Travers, knowing how shocking that notion was to the three-sexed Tarnhelms.

"So that is true, and not a tale? Very dangerous, only having two," said the senior Tarnhelm as the rest of his/his company yipped in response.

"No doubt you're right," said Travers, wishing now he had ordered a scent enhance and the hell with protocol. He knew from past experience that it would take days to get the burned lentil stench out of the station.

"We do not do wrong things." There were more yelps of

agreement. "We are honorable Tarnhelms. You summoned us to speak with us," said the senior Waxy Tarnhelm.

"Yes, of matters to our mutual benefit and honor, and will do much for our mutual accord. But first amuse yourselves with a short ugly hunt. When you have . . . dined, then we will speak together." He bowed, hoping the senior Waxy Tarnhelm had been told what the bow meant.

"Uglies," said the senior Waxy Tarnhelm, and Travers did not need the even, metallic voice of the translator to know how much hunt-lust was in that word. "Excellent."

Travers sighed as he gestured to Harrington to release the uglies.

Thirty or so of the spiny, beetlelike creatures rushed through the reception room, and at once the Tarnhelms rose just far enough into the air to be able to pounce on their prey. As they hovered, most of them disappeared, then became visible once again as they dropped on the uglies, the double row of barbs on the underside of their fans extended to hold the uglies once they were caught. There were twenty-three Waxy Tarnhelms in the reception hall.

After about twenty minutes of this grisly sport, the senior Waxy Tarnhelm floated toward Travers, sucking at the last bit of ugly caught in his/his facial tusks. "A pleasant beginning," he said to Travers.

"Kind of you to say, Waxy Tarnhelm," Travers replied, feeling that the first hurdle had been cleared.

"You want to make pacts with us, as you have with the lesser Tarnhelms," said the senior Tarnhelm. "It is not our practice to do what Dusties and Sandies do." He/he drifted over toward the largest window where he/he spread out his/his fans to the fullest extent.

Travers did his best not to be impressed, though the Tarnhelm was more than twice his height across. "We are aware of that. But we know also that you Tarnhelms have remained here on this planet, and you have not been"—he almost said "allowed," but changed his mind—"asked to leave this place for other planets."

"It is true," said the senior Tarnhelm.

"We can make that happen; we can place you on other

worlds. In fact, this is what we want to do: we want to offer you positions with our security forces, in your capacity as guards who can become invisible."

"We are not invisible," said the senior Tarnhelm. "We have perfect camouflage."

"It amounts to the same thing," said Travers, going on, "few other species we have found have your remarkable abilities." He did not add that of those who had good camouflage, none were intelligent enough or large enough to serve the Syndicate's purpose.

"No others can do what we do," the senior Tarnhelm corrected with pride.

"Quite likely," agreed Travers at once. "That is why we wish to deal with you, don't you see? We know that we can find your talents nowhere but with you." He saw that Croydon was looking pale, and so gestured to him. "This is my second-in-command, my proctor. This is Croydon," he said, knowing that the Tarnhelms were not comfortable with the concept of names and wanted to keep them as simple as possible.

The proctor set his teeth and bowed. "An honor, Senior Tarnhelm."

"His name is not the same as yours," the senior Tarnhelm accused.

Travers cursed inwardly, but did what he did best: faked it. "We are cousins," he lied, jabbing Croydon in the arm to cue him. "But we are of the same blood." If you stretched a point, he thought, it might be remotely true, for both of them were descended from English-speaking colonists.

"A poor arrangement," said the senior Tarnhelm. "It is what comes of having only two sexes."

"No doubt you are right," said Travers, then with determination got back on the subject. "We wish to enter into an agreement with you. You, we are aware, wish to be able to travel beyond this planet. We of the Syndicate need dependable security . . . uh, beings. You have the capacity to imitate invisibility, and that invisibility extends to those inside your fans. With practice, two Tarnhelms can provide almost complete protection for a human, covering everything but the eyes, if that is necessary." The thought of having those fans with their curved hooks all around him made Travers feel nauseated, but he went on gamely, "We are empowered to make such a bargain with you, if you are willing to do this for us."

"As senior Tarnhelm, what I tell them is law," he/he declared.

"I, too, am so empowered," said Travers, trying not to wince as he held out his hand to the senior Tarnhelm's fan.

Apparently the senior Tarnhelm shared his distaste. He/he puckered the row of tusks around his face as he/he brushed his/his fan over the edge of Travers's knuckles. "We will send teams of two to protect you with our capacity for mimicry, and you in turn will aid us in moving about the territory known as the galaxy. Given the troubles we have experienced in the past, we are going to have to detain one of you as token of your bargain."

"Token!" Travers burst out, knowing beyond doubt that he would be the one selected. That was the way the family did things. It was not possible. Not when he was almost off this abysmal rock in the middle of nowhere. "I only have three more months."

"Then they will send another," said the senior Tarnhelm, though Travers knew the manager, and was certain he would not.

"I do not think so, Senior Tarnhelm," he said heavily.

"The greater the honor for you, then," countered the senior Tarnhelm.

Keir and Croydon listened to this in silence, Keir showing almost nothing of her emotions, but Croydon doing his best to conceal the little smile that hooked the corners of his mouth upward.

"We will notify the Syndicate that we have achieved the first level of accord," said Travers, his eyes growing slightly glazed as the prospect of years spent on Siggirt's Blunder.

"You will do that, of course," said the senior Tarnhelm, one of his/his sounds transformed into language sounding like metal dragged along smooth metal, raising sparks as it went.

"We will need your . . . fan impact impression to settle the dealings," Travers said uncertainly, confident that he would encounter resistance on that point.

"I do not think so," said the senior Tarnhelm, his/his expression very thoughtful. "Perhaps later but not now."

"I see," said Travers, hoping he had not entirely destroyed the first level of accord. "For our kind, we need some sort of endorsement."

"You may take Waxy Eight," said the senior Waxy Tarnhelm.

This was just the confrontation Travers had hoped to avoid. "But we cannot do that, not until we have some endorsement of the accords."

"Waxy Eight will be sufficient," said the senior Tarnhelm, his/his voice rising to a jumble of hisses and squeaks.

"But he must remain on the surface until the accords are met," said Travers, feeling he had fallen into the most ludicrous farce. "We must have an endorsement—not an actual Waxy Tarnhelm—to present before we can proceed with accepting your terms."

"If not Eight, then Five," said the senior Waxy Tarnhelm.

Travers decided it would be enjoyable to throttle the senior Waxy Tarnhelm, but could not make himself do it. He stifled a cough—who knew what that might mean to the Tarnhelms—and made another game try. "We don't want to ask you questions you might find offensive, but you see, our accords have been established over hundreds of years and thousands of agreements. I have an obligation to my senior, or first cousin, to make these arrangements in a particular way. This is the agreement we advocate everywhere, so that all dealings are the same and no one can question our contracts. Before any goods change hands, before any services are performed, it is our tradition, the very core of the Syndicate, to have our accords set out so that everyone may be clear of what we are doing and how it is valued. Do you understand that?" He suspected that the senior Waxy Tarnhelm had no comprehension of it at all. "I am not permitted to do it any other way. If I do it another way, then I fail."

"We comprehend failure," said the senior Waxy Tarnhelm. "We have executions for all sorts of failures."

Travers swallowed. "Yes. I rather thought you would."

It took very nearly five hours, but at last the Waxy

Tarnhelms agreed to leave the impression of their first and second fan claws as tokens of acceptance of the terms. The senior Waxy Tarnhelm was the last to put his impression on the document, and pronounced himself satisfied, which made Travers more worried than ever.

Travers's continuing assignment, which came just as soon as confirmation of the agreement with the Waxy Tarnhelm reached the family headquarters and was returned to Siggirt's Blunder, was no surprise; everyone expressed sympathies to Travers and three station staffers asked almost at once for a transfer form: Croydon was one of them.

"I'm sorry you're stuck with this place, of course. Anyone would be. But you know how these things are. Well, you can't want me to stay here forever. I know you've been here a long time and it's really your turn to rotate out, but you're used to this, aren't you? It doesn't get to you the way it does to me. You handle it better. Leave me here another year and I'd have to be kept in a mental protection unit for a good long time," said Croydon with ill grace. "It's bad enough one of us getting marooned on this god-awful rock, but more than one, well, it simply isn't realistic. Is it." He gave a gesture of mollification to Travers. "No need to tell you that, is there, old son? You're the one being shafted, after all. Still, at least you'll have double salary for every day you stay here after your official tour is up. A pity you don't get the double salary while you're here. Still, it's a gesture. You'll be able to enjoy yourself when this is over. That's better than nothing."

"What am I going to do with it here on Siggirt's Blunder?" Travers asked unhappily, then squared his shoulders. "On the other hand, they can't extend my time here more than ten years"—the very thought was enough to make him gibber—"and on this place, that's only . . . Christ! Eleven months of twenty-six days, that's two hundred eighty-six days per year, and in ten years, that means two thousand eight hundred sixty days. Almost eight years Old Earth time." Saying the last made Travers lower his voice to a whisper.

"Well, but you're an old hand at these outposts, aren't you?" Croydon asked with a tone of voice that was almost malicious, though his eyes were pleading with Travers to understand. "You know how to make do. I can't manage that, never could. You're able to accept the way things are. You don't let that stop you."

Meaning, thought Travers, that both he and Croydon knew he had been passed over for promotion and was likely never to advance much higher than he was at present. He chose his words with great care, for he wanted his fiction to be convincing. "Sometimes a man isn't sent to these places because he has disappointed his family. Sometimes he is sent there because he is good at doing this job." This was not the case with him, but he could see he now had Croydon's attention. "I am an old hand at these outposts, yes. Which means that I have dealt with more strange forms of life and more difficult customs than you can think of. So before you set yourself up as a person who knows more about these things than anyone here, remember that I have already served nine years on Limbo." His smile was more wintery than that despised planet.

"You don't like Tarnhelms," said Croydon with complete certainty. "But you see, I despise them. Worse than despise. They're repulsive."

"No, I don't like them, you're right about that," said Travers, doing his best to look well steeled. "I didn't like the bratcyclers on Limbo either." He waited while Croydon digested this unwelcome bit of partial information.

While Croydon was not convinced, he was curious enough to be willing to give Travers the benefit of the doubt while he ran down his records in the company access files. "You could have mentioned it."

"Why?" Travers said softly. "Were you going to stay here?" He nodded to his second-in-command.

"There are Tarnhelms in this station, Manager," said Goro Kasagio with an air of gloomy satisfaction. "I've had reports for days."

"You've seen them?" Travers asked.

"Ha-ha," said Kasagio. "You said no mass detectors. How could I see them?"

"Then how can you know?" Travers asked.

"I feel them. I can sense them. There are three, maybe four of them drifting around the station. Sometimes you can feel them when they cut through the purified air stream. There's a slowdown in the system, but it's not the system, it's Tarnhelms."

Travers did his best not to be critical. "What makes you think that the Tarnhelms are doing this? Do you think there's any risk?"

"An unknown number of invisible predators on the loose in this station who eat human beings is risky," Goro said testily. "What would you expect? Don't you want something done about this?"

It had always been Travers's greatest gift to dither without showing his dithering. He put the tips of his fingers together and though his expression was vacant and studious, his thoughts were a frenzied shambles. What if Goro Kasagio was right, and there were Tarnhelm spies in the station? There was nothing he could do to find them that would not turn them against him. He said "Ummm" once or twice, then looked at Goro. "If you will be good enough to come to my quarters after supper, I think we had best assemble a worst-possible scenario before I contact the Tarnhelms and see what I can find out about their doings."

"Another wait-and-see?" Goro jeered. "Are you serious?"

Travers gave Goro a hard look. "Consider what's at stake here."

"That's what I am doing," Goro insisted, exasperated.

Travers did not dignify his outburst with comment. "We've just completed a very difficult security contract with the Tarnhelms, and for the first time the safety and security of the family heads can be guaranteed in a way they never have before. The Tarnhelms have said they are loyal, and their honor is of the greatest importance to them." He rubbed his palms once. "I don't want this to turn out to be a disaster."

"If you let those things off-planet, you'll have all the disaster you'll ever know." Goro lifted his fists. "There are Tarnhelms here, Travers. Don't say I didn't warn you."

"And if you're wrong?" Travers asked. "If we investigate,

then the Tarnhelms will say we have broken their code—which is accurate—and will have an excuse to move against us and make war on the station. Being the Waxy Tarnhelms, they will command the Sandies and Dusties to join with them, because of the Waxies' position in their . . . uh . . . culture." He pursed his lips to keep from continuing so that his voice would not shriek.

"You are ten kinds of a fool, Travers. You're a sensible manager, and right now we need a troop of armed Kosantz berserkers with someone like General Shanks Rogers to lead them." He started down the hall. "I'm sending an emergency signal to Heimlend about the possible danger here. On my own. I'll say that it's against your orders."

"I wish you wouldn't," said Travers softly. "Really, Kasagio, I know you think you must, but please reconsider."

"Why? So you can delay until we are unable to defend this station at all?"

Travers shuddered to give his answer. "Listen to me. I have thought about what you've said. I read your preliminary reports, and I am aware of the danger we're in. And I will tell you what has me the most concerned now: that if you are right, then the Tarnhelms may have already decided to war with us. If there are Tarnhelms in the station, let us hope they remain invisible and relatively helpless. If we start seeing them, then we'll be in the shit, no doubt about it."

"Then why aren't we sending for reinforcements?" Goro asked, desperately puzzled, his eyes angry and resigned.

"Because I'd like it to appear that what we are doing is standard procedure. If we behave as if there is nothing odd about our circumstances, the Tarnhelms may be convinced." It was whistling in the dark and he knew it, but he said it with his usual forthrightness, and Goro Kasagio narrowed his eyes, considering.

"I'm going to increase security patrols and I want to put the housekeeping staff on alert. If there is anything, the most minor thing, out of the ordinary, I want to know about it at once." He put his hands on his hips and stared at Travers, painfully trying to believe him.

"You're doing superior work under difficult circumstances,"

said Travers, in the hope that Goro was not too cynical to be
swayed by the compliment.

Goro shrugged and turned away, returning to his control
area.

Travers was congratulating himself for squeaking through
that one when he felt a flutter of air pass his face. He stopped
still, his hand on the wall. Something—he could not *see*
what—something had touched him.

"The cousin is not pleased at the reports he has been receiving," said the family proctor, a tall, prosperous fellow with a
beak of a nose and hair so very pale that at first glance he
seemed completely bald. His name was Hylander and he had
married well three times.

Travers studied the receiving screen, trying to gauge the
wanted response. He decided on a single, serious nod and a
soft answer. "Yes. There has been a disruption here at the
station. We're not in complete agreement here." He was
dressed in a houppe that was expertly cut and made of fabric
that would have cost Travers's annual salary. His grandeur was
the more impressive for being understated.

"Your security team is adamant about the Tarnhelms. He
says that the previous interdicts were sound and ought not to be
lifted now, or at any time." He pulled at his lower lip, a gesture
designed to strike terror into his underlings.

"The Father himself lifted the interdict and requested that
the Tarnhelms be brought in under Syndicate aegis. He said
that there was not reason enough to continue the interdict when
the other family heads were so eager to bring in the Tarnhelms
as contract security teams. It was the family's thinking that it
would be more appropriate for us to have the Tarnhelms
guarding us instead of bodyguarding the Fleet's admirals once
they are found." He saw disapproval on the proctor's face. "I
don't intend anything facetious. As I recall, you supported the
idea at the time they lifted the interdict, though our recommen-
dation was for caution." All that was on record, he thought
with relief, so that if there was a review now no one could say
that Travers had been in favor of the Tarnhelm interdict—or
against it.

"I am familiar with the records. I am not asking to review these decisions in quite that way. I have had extensive reports on the usefulness of the Tarnhelms as espionage personnel, along with his recommendations for their larger applications. A very forward-thinking fellow, your proctor. I think his potential is enormous if he isn't so ambitious that he cannot make his way to the goal sensibly. The Syndicate can offer a great deal to someone like Croydon. Now your security man is something else again. Not much of a risk-taker, is he? Oh, I don't say he isn't well enough in his way. He is one who prefers the safest path and there may be some excuse, given your situation there. What is most troubling is your security man is adamant about the danger these Waxy Tarnhelms present. He claims they are more warlike than the others of their kind, and that they have plans of their own." He shook his head. "This isn't satisfactory."

"Oh, no, of course not," said Travers. He was thinking as fast as he could. "It is true that of the three sorts of Tarnhelms, the Waxies are the most capable of mimicry. They do not have the same texture of surf . . . skin, and their invisibility is the most complete. A man wrapped in one of them is nothing more than a pair of floating eyes. It's a great disguise, no doubt about that." He could not entirely conceal his shudder, for the thought of letting one of those creatures wrap around him seemed worse than living entombment.

"What is it?" The proctor's keen eyes had not missed Travers's aversion.

Travers made a muddle of self-deprecatory chuckles. "A touch of claustrophobia, I'm afraid. Surface sleeping cocoons do it to me, as well." He thought that was rather neatly handled. "And I'm not fond of the scent of burned lentils."

"Burned lentils?" Proctor Hylander asked, and Travers had the pleasure of seeing that august fellow bewildered.

"Burned lentils," he said more emphatically, taking full advantage of what little credibility he had. "You see, they smell of burned lentils."

The proctor's wince was eloquent. "Strongly?"

"Yes." Travers straightened, mustering himself for the task of getting off the proctor's hook. "Well, what would you want

me to do in this situation? If the Syndicate wishes the
Tarnhelms contained again, I'm afraid that will be awkward,
especially since we have already shipped a dozen Sandies off to
Christiania. The Syndicate is making progress there, and it is
one of the places the First Son believes the Tarnhelms will be
useful. He said that it could mean the difference of losing
control of Christiania or keeping it."

"I am aware of the stakes," the proctor snapped. "And my
information is certainly more current and complete than your
own." He patted his wide, bejeweled collar. "The First Son has
not yet changed his mind about the Tarnhelms. He has said he
wants someone to give him a reassessment of the situation."

More than anything Travers wanted to scream, to tell
Hylander that the whole Tarnhelm idea was crazy from the
start, that the Tarnhelms were the worst and most dangerous
carnivores in Syndicate space, that once they got loose no one
would be safe. But that would be the same thing as calling the
First Son an irresponsible idiot, which would put him on
Wasteland Two for sure. Siggirt's Blunder was dreadful, as all
class-4s were, but Wasteland Two was class-6, and that was
worse than class-5's Limbo or Far Outback. He had to use
every discipline he knew to maintain his dignity. "Let me
recommend," he said, as if making a necessary sacrifice for the
good of the station, "that an outside observer be sent. I believe
that some of our station staff have become polarized in their
thinking, and it has made a difference in their assessment of the
situation."

"It would take three weeks to arrange such an observer,"
said Hylander, dismissing the entire suggestion. "You will
have to be more diligent, do your best to present a mix of
opinions and assessments." Travers was once again back on
the hook.

He made one last attempt. "What about a series of inter-
views—perhaps by one of your staff?—who would do as we're
doing now, with everyone on the station, to get a better
picture?"

Proctor Hylander was an old master at this game. "If your
report indicates that's necessary, then we'll do it. In the
meantime, we'll continue to make the usual supply runs, but

will keep cargo to essentials until all this is cleared up. The Danegeld ships will not make planetfall there while the crisis is going on. No need making this any more dangerous than it need be, is there?" He made the appropriate gestures and remarks and rang off with barely polite haste.

Travers sat in the receiving room and wondered if perhaps there were such things as curses, after all, and he was the victim of one. He could not rid himself of the notion that he was trapped no matter which alternative he chose and that none of the alternatives was correct.

Regan Keir found him still there sometime later. "It's almost teatime," she said, then saw that he was upset. "What's wrong, Keane?" She almost never used his first name, and so it caught his attention at once.

"The First Son wants another station report. About the Tarnhelms." He was sitting with his elbows braced on his knees, his chin in his hand. "I can't think. I've been trying to for the last hour, but I can't." With his free hand he slapped his head. "Nothing."

"You'll figure it out. You always do." She took the seat opposite him. "I've got to change for tea—so should you—but if there's anything I can do . . . ?"

He gave her a wan smile. "I hope so, but I can't guess what it would be." He looked up as a breeze slid around the room. Breeze? he asked himself. Or Waxy Tarnhelm? Was Goro right, and the Tarnhelms were truly here? "I'll be in for tea shortly. Have Croydon take care of the ordering this time."

"If that's what you want," she said uncertainly. She was almost on her feet when she added, "There might be something I can do with the program for the station: you know, change something, or set up a few closed registers, so we can keep things . . . well, very private."

"From the Tarnhelms?" he asked, knowing he was grasping at straws, but unable to resist.

"Possibly. But not just them. There might be another connection?" Her smile was so tentative as not to be a smile at all. "But if they had help, in here . . ."

Travers frowned. "Someone from here? Do you honestly

think any member of this station staff could . . . help the
Tarnhelms?"

Her face was somber. "Well, we all hate it enough, don't
we?"

Two days later Travers received an urgent summons from Goro
Kasagio to join him in the sports hall, adding that they had to
meet alone.

"Alone?" Travers asked with heavy skepticism. "Here?"

"Sure. I found something. Well, actually Nugunda found it.
An hour ago."

"All right." With a sinking feeling at the base of his spine,
Travers got to his feet and tried to think which of his various
outfits would be the correct one for this interview. Certain
standards were required on stations even in emergencies. At
last he selected his least impressive mid-length working
houppe and tugged it over his head without bothering to wear
his wide collar. As he hurried off toward the sports hall, he
tried to imagine what it was that so troubled Goro that he would
demand Travers come alone. Was it Tarnhelms or station
staffers who troubled him more?

"Come here. Housekeeping's coming to take care of it, but
I want you to see it just as I found it." He had dressed hastily
and had not bothered to add ornaments or insignia to his
clothes. He took Travers by the arm and tugged him toward the
far corner of the sports hall where most of the various kinds of
equipment were stored. "It's back of the spickle-ball nets," he
said urgently.

Behind the snarl of nets, there were drained and desiccated
carcasses of three ookies and two horrids.

"They haven't been dead long," said Goro, breathing
shallowly. "Chambulo came in for a morning training, and got
a whiff. He notified me. I notified you." He got a little closer
to the dead creatures. "The mandibles are still in place, and
you know how fast those things fall off once a Tarnhelm gets
its hooks into them."

"A day at most," said Travers, trying to think of a way not
to be sick on the shiny sports-hall floor. "Which of them has
that sulfur stench?"

"Horrids." Goro stepped back and took a deep breath. "I tell you, Travers, we've got Tarnhelms here." He looked up at the ceiling. "They could be hovering just over our heads, and we wouldn't know it, not without mass detectors."

"But—" Travers began.

"But that would endanger the treaty and everything else. The Family Father would be angry because he wouldn't get his troop of invisible assassins." He saw something in Travers's face and shook his head in disbelief. "You don't believe that crap, do you? You don't really think that the use is purely for defense and protection? Travers, don't be an idiot!" Goro slapped his legs as he took a single, long stride away from the manager of the station as he tried to find a response to Travers. "The family has lost three rich planets to other families since he came to control. There is too much to be lost. You do understand that much, don't you?"

"Our family has never resorted to aggression, not as you mean it." Travers appeared to be steady and confident as this jolt ricocheted through him.

"They want the Tarnhelms for two purposes: to get their assassins to their targets and to be assassins themselves. If the Tarnhelms could do anything other than invisibility while they're invisible, the Family Father would give them the whole job. But they can't attack unless they're visible. So they have to smuggle in people." He rubbed at his forehead. "And now you know that the Tarnhelms are here."

"Are you sure they were killed in the station, and not brought here?" Travers asked. He could not help but be distracted by the evil, sliding odor of the corpses.

"Who'd bring those things into the station?" Goro demanded. "And why? What would be the point?"

Travers sighed and nodded. "What would be the point," he echoed, having no answer to give to such a sensible question. "Well, let housekeeping attend to it. I suppose I ought to talk to the Waxy Tarnhelms." That meant girding up for the surface and arranging for transportation to the nearest Waxy Tarnhelm settlement. "Tell Chambulo that he'll have to be prepared to wire up a buggy for me with a translator, and have one of his best men come with me for the driving." He did not want to go out there. He did not want to go near a Tarnhelm again in his life.

"How soon?" Goro inquired, looking up as housekeeping arrived. "Over there. You'll need masks."

Only one of the three housekeeping staff pretended to be amused, though when Croydon arrived a few minutes later, he burst out in grating laughter.

The ride onto the Waxy Tarnhelm butte took most of the afternoon, ruined two complete sets of tires, and broke one of the fuel bars. By the time they arrived at the Waxy Tarnhelm settlement, Travers ached all over, he was so tired he had trouble extricating himself from the buggy, and he found it more trying than usual to be courteous with the Tarnhelms.

"Waxy Seventeen," he said to the first Tarnhelm to greet him, hoping he had read the fan markings correctly.

"He/he says 'What are you doing here, miserable smear of offal,' " said Bingham, the translator.

"How pleasant to see you, too," Travers murmured, then did his best to be diplomatic. "Is the senior Waxy Tarnhelm willing to speak with me?"

"He/he is at his/his fourth meal," Bingham translated.

"I will wait until he/he has finished," said Travers, glad that he was traditionally excluded from dining with the Tarnhelms. It was bad enough watching them make a snack of uglies. He signaled to Bingham to follow him. "Keep your eyes open; I'll want a report later."

They had completed three circuits of the camp when the senior Waxy Tarnhelm came from his/his slag heap of a dwelling, cleaning his facial tusks. "It is a surprising thing to see you here," he/he said through Bingham, who added, "and I don't think he/he likes surprises."

"Naturally," said Travers. "Senior Tarnhelm," he said, hoping his voice would not crack with fear, "tell me: have any of your number remained behind at my station?"

"Why would you want to know this?" demanded the senior Waxy Tarnhelm, clearly offended.

"Curiosity," said Travers, trying to be nonchalant in his

style. "You might have wanted to learn more about us. We must appear strange to you."

"Some he/shes are there, of course," said the senior Waxy Tarnhelm, clearly unconcerned with so obvious an answer.

"Will you tell me how many, and—" Travers began, only to be stopped short.

"Nothing is revealed."

That was the most obvious truth to Travers, who made another sally but with plummeting nerve. "Just some he/shes?"

"The he/shes have been." Again the same unpleasant sound, but no indication of shock or insult.

"They have," said Travers with a steadiness that amazed himself. "I was not aware of them. Had I known they were to be our guests—"

"They were not guests. They were in readiness." He/he indicated the sky where the nighttime thunderstorm was charging up. "All is in readiness."

The fragile hope Travers had clung to all the way up the butte failed him. He lowered his head, trying to think of something he could say without giving way to defeat. "What do you mean?" He had read a theory that the Waxy Tarnhelms migrated, though no one had been able to prove it in spite of many attempts at it. He said a forlorn little prayer to something out in the darkness to let this be about Tarnhelm migrations, nothing worse. "How in readiness?" he asked, as offhandedly as he could.

"For departure." The senior Waxy Tarnhelm made a gesture that Travers was certain was rude, then issued several short, determined orders.

"I think we're expected to go now, Manager Travers," said Bingham, who was definitely frightened. "Right now."

"Is it that drastic?" asked Travers, wanting to flee, to fling himself off the butte just to get away.

"Yes." He was already levering himself into the buggy, struggling with the harness as Travers clambered in beside him. "I can't bear those things," he said as soon as the buggy doors were secure. "I hate them."

"So do I," said Travers wearily, leaning his head against the body harness. He glanced back to see over two dozen of the

Waxy Tarnhelms hovering around the place where the buggy had been only seconds ago. He frowned as he watched them. "Did you notice any he/shes or she/shes?"

"I don't know the difference," said Bingham. "It has something to do with the color of the spines, doesn't it?"

"Yes," said Travers.

"They could have been . . . somewhere else? Indoors maybe, or at another one of the settlements?" He was not driving as well as when they had come up the mountain: the buggy rattled and shook and jolted its way toward the valley where the station waited.

"Yes." Travers knew he had to notify his superiors at once, though he shrank from the task.

They rode in silence for a while. Then Bingham said what had been on his mind. "They've already got out, haven't they, sir."

Travers sighed. "Yes."

"I don't know how I can tell you how dangerous it is," said Travers uncertainly as he stared at Hylander's enormous face. "Having the Tarnhelms out, that is."

"Ungoverned, savage killers, you mean? Without blood contracts to hold them? Oh, I have some notion, yes I do," said Hylander, his voice cutting more than his posture of outrage. "Is it too much to ask how many are gone?"

"Yes, and too much to ask where," said Travers. "But I know they went on the supply ships, which means they have some way to get past the mass detectors as well as our other inspections." There was another alternative, but he could not bring himself to suggest it.

"And what if someone at the station is doing it, what then?" asked Hylander. "Or hasn't that crossed your mind?"

Travers did not answer at once. "No, it didn't cross my mind, not at first. I thought about the Syndicate and the Tarnhelms themselves. I thought about possible rivals whom we haven't identified. I thought about the people here last because they are part of the family. I don't like to think that any member of another family would be so foolish as to unleash the

Tarnhelms on the Syndicate. That is why I was reluctant to think about the staff here." He met the ferocious eyes in the screen as directly as he could. "I wanted to think that we were a little bit better than the rest of them. Then it wouldn't be so bad that I wasn't quite as good. It would average out." He got up from the couch and walked away from the screen, apparently unaware of how very rude he was being.

Hylander stood stupefied by what Travers said. "The strain has been too much for you," he said at last, his head shaking with disbelief.

"Yes, I think it probably has been too much," said Travers. "This planet, this station, is too much." He wandered over to the port and looked out at the lurid reflections in the clouds as lightning clawed through them. He remained silent, then said, "You know, they have shadows, the Tarnhelms. You can't see them, but they do cast shadows. You ought to remember that."

"Travers?" Hylander's voice was no longer able to inspire fear in Travers. He came back to the screen. "What are you doing?"

"Arranging my evening. We're having a going away party for Croydon. He said once he'd do anything to get out of here. It seems he was telling the truth when he said it." He came and stood before Hylander. "Better warn the Family Father that he's got a problem he's going to have the devil's own time getting rid of."

Hylander was beginning to look worried. "Listen to me, Travers. You've been there a long time, and you know a great deal about the Tarnhelms. It might be best if we bring you here and—"

"I don't think so," said Travers, feeling absurdly calm. Well, he thought, I am either completely sane or completely mad for the first time in my life. "You've had me for decades and now it's over." He sighed. "I am going to dress for high tea, I am going to congratulate my treasonous proctor, and then, when I've got good and drunk, I'm going outside for a midnight stroll."

"You can't be serious," Hylander protested, his features

going plum color with distress and making his pale hair visible. "Why, you can't do that. You're not allowed to do that."

"Yes, I can. I've done my time with the Tarnhelms. Now you can do yours." He gave a last gesture of farewell, doing it gracefully for the first time, and turned off the receiver screen.

INTERLUDE

During the period of relative calm between the fall of Khalia and the titanic space battle that marked the real beginning of the war between the Alliance and the Syndicate of Families, both sides prepared feverishly. The Alliance knew only that they were facing a major human power of unknown strength. As always Fleet strategists planned for the worst. The Families had spent years studying the Alliance, and were only too aware of the Fleet's strength.

During this time the Syndicate devoted most of its intelligence efforts to delaying the Fleet buildup at Target and to sabotage. Thousands of humans were arrested on the suspicion that they were Syndicate agents. A frightening number were actually guilty, making those responsible for counterintelligence wonder just how badly the Alliance had been infiltrated. During this same period, much effort was expended locating and confirming the Syndicate worlds.

Among the more heroic actions set in this period was the defense of Monitor Post D3487, a small base that had the misfortune to be on the most commonly used route used by

Syndicate ships for clandestine entry into Alliance space. The saga of their three-day holdout against overwhelming attack was retold on every omni station for days. Four members of the staff received posthumous Spiral Galaxies, the Fleet's highest award for valor under fire.

No one could have ordered the personnel of Monitor Post D3487 to make their suicidal stand; in the final reckoning such a decision must be made by the individuals involved.

And in every war, there are many individual decisions with wide-ranging effects. . . .

KINETIC KILL

by Poul Anderson

AFTERWARD WE LEARNED that it had been a feint. The Syndicate command hoped it would make Admiral Duane concentrate his attention on Target, leaving the way to Khalia relatively clear when their real task force arrived. The naval histories record how she declined the gambit. They say little about how we who were at Target beat off that initial attack. Our detachment was small, the enemy's no larger. It became a minor battle, remembered mostly because the Syndics, withdrawing, joined the main fray at a critical moment and very nearly brought victory to their side.

Well, be it major or incidental, after an engagement the wounds hurt equally and the dead are down in the same darkness. We must keep station, pending new orders, but since there was no further imminent danger, we went about the grim business of cleanup. I was in our flagship, the light cruiser *Aubourg*. Her screenfields and interceptors had worked perfectly, saving her from all damage. Casualties elsewhere

124

necessitated redistribution of officers among auxiliary units. Still amazed at being alive and whole, I found myself in charge of a frigate sent forth to search around.

From the pilot cabin, I could at first see no trace left by war. Even a single planetary system is too big. At its distance the sun was hardly more than a blue-white spark, brightest of the stars that thronged the black. Silence enclosed me, inhuman peace.

The intercom broke it: "Large metallic object detected" and figures for position and velocity. "Probable ship section, likeliest off one of theirs."

My heart banged. "Close in," I directed. "Try to establish communication. Be prepared for possible hostile action. In that case, respond initially with solid missiles." Bulkheads and self-sealing hull might well contain air, living personnel, and some working armament.

"Question, sir," came from another post. "Lieutenant Holland speaking. Shouldn't we go after men of ours first? Let those bastards wait."

I heard my own words as cold as the thought behind them. "In principle, an excellent idea. In practice, though, that may after all be a piece of a Fleet vessel. Besides, let me remind everybody that I am an officer of Intelligence. We know much less about the enemy than we should, prisoners are still our major source of information, and we do have other units conducting salvage. That's why I don't want any survivors who resist simply nuked. We'll take them alive if we can, and bring them back to *Aubourg* before resuming operations." I paused. "You need not be unreasonably gentle with them."

"Yes, sir. I understand now." I realized that what had surprised Holland, and maybe the rest, was less the instruction than the source. I made no bones about my hatred of the foe. It had caused arguments in my mess. The general feeling was that the Syndics were, at least, human, not Khalian. Commander Fujikawa actually maintained that by their lights they were warring in a just cause, for their society and its values.

To hell with such bleat.

We boosted cautiously toward rendezvous. Presently we made contact. Yes, it was a fragment of a cruiser that our fire had reached. Twenty-five men and several corpses were inside. Their senior officer gave surrender. He was fluent in our language, though his accent made it a trifle hard to follow. However, exhaustion and grief speak a universal tongue.

Good, I thought. That can be taken advantage of. "You outnumber us," I said. "Therefore you will do precisely as you are told. Be warned, at the slightest suspicion of treachery we will blast the lot of you."

"I swear we are helpless—"

"That is as it should be. Stand by for further orders." I cut him off and let him think about my tone of voice.

The objective hove in sight, a great curving shell, wanly agleam in starlight except where the metal lay bubbled and blackened. When the ship burst asunder, this compartment had separated cleanly; but scraps tumbled everywhere around, broken and twisted. Some had been alive a few hours earlier. The part that remained more or less intact was indeed unarmed; with a thrill along my spine, I recognized it as the central control section. Oh, our tech boys would be busy dissecting! It was not unscathed, of course. Blobs of sealer marked where shards had sleeted through. This, and the shock wave from the explosion, accounted for the dead inboard. Without treatment for radiation, their comrades would soon join them.

It tasted foul, that Fleet people might float too long in space and die that wretched death because I ferried a clot of Syndics to sickbay. But what we could learn from them might in the long run save more Fleet lives, and cost more enemy. Duty is duty.

Our boat matched velocities. Two men suited up and secured a gang tube between airlocks. At our end waited a squad with firearms, nightsticks, and lengths of cord. As each foeman entered, they seized him, bound his wrists, and hustled him off to the hold. Only then did they allow the next one to proceed. After they finished, I sent three in full armor, bearing rapid-fire weapons and grenades, to ransack the shell and make sure.

Not that I really awaited trouble. Most of the newcomers moved like ill-made robots, empty-eyed, dazed. Dried blood smeared faces. A few got roughed up when they didn't respond to commands that should have been obvious whether or not they knew the language—till an old hand among us said quietly, "Sir, they're deaf. Ruptured eardrums." I heard later that what he saw caused the youngest member of my search party to vomit in his helmet.

The last man out was the senior, tall, gaunt, gray-haired. Somehow he kept his shoulders straight, and he had thrown a dress tunic over his combat fatigues. At sight of that forlorn dignity, my pulse leaped. He bore vice admiral's insignia and a triple row of service ribbons. We'd caught us a big fish.

I signed my squad to hold off. "Don't tie him," I said, and, hypocritically, "he rates respect."

His lips quirked, a gallows smile. "I do rank you, Lieutenant Commander—"

"McClellan," I supplied. "You shall have the honors of war, provided you conduct yourself as befits your status." Make clear immediately who was boss.

"My men?"

"Confining them is a necessary precaution, but they will not be mistreated. *We* observe the rules of civilization." I turned to my second officer. "Take over, Mr. Srinavasan. While the prize is being checked out, have its orbit determined precisely and beam a report to Captain Yuan. Then, if I haven't returned, start back to *Aubourg*. I will be in my office with Admiral Godolphin."

My orderly followed the two of us, a pistol at his hip. It wasn't needful. I could readily subdue my Syndic, after what he'd been through. Nevertheless he walked firmly. "You know the family emblems," he remarked.

I nodded. The symbol shone proud on his breast. "It's my business, that sort of thing."

"Interrogation already? You might allow me rest, if not a wash and a change of clothes." I heard neither self-pity nor appeal, but scorn, and felt an irrational need to explain.

"Not much available on a boat, and when we get to the ship shortly, you and your men will go straight under medical care. Since you are capable of coherent speech, I'm taking the opportunity while it lasts."

"I am not required to give you more than my name, rank, and serial number."

"Don't be afraid. I have no intention of torturing you." Only of leaning hard into your weariness. "Wouldn't you like refreshment and conversation?" I can play the good cop, too. "Here we are."

We seated ourselves in the bleak little room, on opposite sides of my desk, staring at each other across the computer terminal. The boat throbbed and murmured around us. Now and then a shout penetrated the door. Olson brought coffee and sandwiches. The aroma was like a benediction. "We have stronger stimulants," I offered.

Godolphin shook his head. "No, thank you."

"Why not? You'll feel much better."

The dulled voice sharpened. "I do not know what else may be in the tablet."

Anger tore the smoothness off me. "We have no psycho-drugs aboard. I told you, the Fleet abides by civilized canons. Is that too hard for the Syndicate to understand?"

A flush stained his pallor. "That was a gratuitous insult. It belies your claim."

Clearly, the soft approach would gain me nothing. Very well, go tough. Shake him in any way that comes to hand. "Frankly, you deserve worse. We thought the Khalia were monsters, and they turned out to be your cat's paws."

It struck home, but he responded gamely, "We needed that first line of defense while we prepared ourselves. Shall your Alliance swallow us up? We have our own society. We will remain what our forebears were."

"Not if I can help it. Considering what that precious society is capable of doing."

"I tell you, the Khalia—"

With more strength behind them, my words trampled his down. "I know what some of those campaign ribbons on you stand for. You've been in what your people call the New Sirius theater. It overlaps our sector thirty-seven. Need I say more?"

He blinked, then squinted, as if puzzled.

"Adzeta-37," I pursued. "Or, in Fleet officialese, Advanced Star Base Zeta in the sector. One habitable planet, Verdea. Ten years ago now, though the business goes back twenty-five. Does that refresh your memory?"

Again the gray head shook. "There is none in me. I do not know which of your bases thereabouts you refer to. Our designations are different. And my time in the region, three years past, was brief."

"Still, ranking high, you should have heard— No?" Deliberately dubious-sounding: "Maybe you didn't." I tossed off my coffee, wished it had held a stiff slug of brandy, but postponed ringing for more. "All right, I'll give you the story."

I kept my gaze locked on his while I talked.

"You must recall that twenty-five or more years ago the sector was peaceful, the Khalia and the war against them far off. Or so the Fleet believed. However, they'd struck from unexpected quarters before. A base out in that direction was a wise precaution. It wouldn't cost much. Adzeta was a G-type sun, Verdea wonderfully Earth-like. That was the name for it, as nearly as humans can pronounce, in the language of the principal nation. For it had sapient natives, friendly, beautiful, creative. Their most advanced countries had gotten to the point of industry powered by fossil fuels, ingenious machinery, and yet not fouling their world much. They were delighted to cooperate with the Fleet, getting knowledge and technology in return for raw materials, labor, eventually supplies and equipment they produced themselves and sold to the humans. Naturally, we couldn't allow immigration, it wasn't our real estate, but Fleet personnel and their families made a small permanent settlement, made their homes there.

"The project was still at an early stage when a Khalian squadron arrived. The Fleet hadn't tried to keep the work secret, that would have been impossible, but it hadn't expected attack in those remote parts. Remember, back then we knew little about the Khalia, most analysts thought they were more like pirates than imperialists, encounters were relatively infrequent and seldom large. This incident changed a number of opinions.

"The Fleet had maintained a guard, just in case, which proved barely adequate to beat the raiders off. If they'd succeeded, they'd have blown us and our installations out of existence. As it was, the survivors of the guard must wait for reinforcements before they could scout the neighbor stars. On a planet of ten light-years off, they found the base from which the assault must have been staged. It had pretty clearly been set up for the purpose after we commenced on Verdea, though it was astonishingly well equipped. The Fleet commander felt constrained by prudence. He allowed only a quick examination before he had it nuked. Too bad; but at the time, how could he have known?

"Afterward we kept a stronger force at Adzeta and patrolled the region. For the next fifteen years, nothing else untoward happened. On Verdea, I mean; elsewhere, you know, the war grew like an infection. The colony flourished. The natives began producing a surplus of matériel for the fighting fronts. They were dreaming great dreams. A new generation was growing up, trained in the new knowledge, looking outward into the universe. Our human enclave was happy too, also full of hopes for their lives after the war ended, as surely someday it must.

"Until—"

Luck alone had reigned. A patrol craft chanced to go out of hyperdrive and examine ambient space, in purely routine fashion, at a moment and a place where detection was possible. A few hundred astronomical units farther away, the radio input would have been too feeble to identify against cosmic background and the hurrying light-spot would have gone unnoticed. As it was, the receivers found an anomaly. Since the assignment of the craft was to investigate anything unusual that she might come upon, lest the Khalia spring a new surprise, she drew near. After fifteen years of blessedly boring rounds, her crew was doubly eager.

She had to use hyperdrive to approach, for the source was traveling near the speed of light. Though small, it rammed a tunnel through the interstellar medium; excited atoms left a wake of long-wave radiation, while X rays and visible photons blazed from the bow shock.

It was headed for Adzeta. The passage would be close, as such events go, less than two hundred million kilometers. While this posed no obvious hazard, it should have considerable scientific interest—how might such a thing originate?—

and in any event, fortune had also decreed that the skipper be a cautious man. He abandoned his circuit and went straight back to Verdea to report. Headquarters sent a large ship, properly equipped, to investigate in detail.

But our luck wasn't good enough, thought Rear Admiral Simon Berling.

Viewscreens in the primary control center, the bridge, surrounded him with stars. Adzeta still dominated them, but only as a point of brilliance in their midst, hard by the frosty shore of the galactic river. The dreadnought *Celestia* swung almost thirty billion kilometers distant, out in the comet cloud; and nothing of that was visible.

Silence loomed. The breath in Berling's nostrils, the blood beat in his head, were a tiny clamor beneath it. Slowly, as if his fingers had gone reluctant, he turned a knob on the scanner before him. The scene that it covered expanded.

First he discerned the brightness, a mere spark. Some fifteen megaklicks away, it crawled from constellation to constellation while he watched. Magnification increased. Beyond a certain point, optics blurred the image, but he saw it through the haze of its shining as clearly as he cared to, an ovoid about sixty meters thick, glow-hot forward, iron-dark aft, where the remains of intricate tubes, frames, and cables still clung.

Rest mass on the order of a million tons. His mind repeated the estimates his technical staff had given him. *Present mass, due to velocity, more than three times as much.*

"Yes," he said into the hush, "undoubtedly artificial. A weapon."

The image crept off the screen. He hadn't set the scanner to track. Instead, his look traveled the opposite way. The red glint that was Bitch brought it to a halt.

"Launched from there," his throat went on. "Where else?"

Memory flew a half score light-years to the dwarf sun and a planet that circled it. In younger days, with lower rank, he had visited yonder world several times, checking up. Nothing greeted him and his mates but lifelessness, thin winds whining across rock and sand, craters gouged by meteorites and three new ones that were human work. Memory spiraled back through time, to the day when the Fleet ships first arrived.

found the vacated Khalian base, and destroyed it. For a minute
hellflower radiances had overwhelmed the sullen sunlight. . . .
*Our men were wiser than they knew, nicknaming that star. If only
we'd gone through the place thoroughly before we loosed our
missiles. Then maybe, maybe—*

Too late.

Berling turned from the screen, a big man, grizzled, face
furrowed, but with an ursine strength in him yet. "And no
doubt, either, who did the job," he finished. "After the Khalia
were repulsed, the remnants of them went back to Bitch. They
knew they couldn't hold it, but they'd have a spell there,
unmolested, till our reinforcements arrived and we could go
after them. So they built this thing and set it on its course."

Captain Matthew McClellan, his executive officer, stood
beside him. The man's lean frame stiffened, fists knotted at
sides. Anguish spoke: "How, sir? How could they?"

"Quite an engineering feat," Berling said. His technies had
newly briefed him on their findings and ideas. "Put a reactor
on an asteroid that converts most of it to energy and thrust
mass. Have sensors and control systems inside the body,
protected from radiation. They do course corrections in the first
years of flight, while acceleration is low. It increases, naturally, as mass is shed, and gets fairly high at the end. The best
guess at a mean value is about one-tenth g. That implies some
ten years under boost. At the end, when the reaction drive has
used up everything it can, what's left is on trajectory with a
speed just under c. It takes another five years to complete the
crossing." He sighed. "A fantastic weapon. A one-shot affair,
to be sure. After it struck, the Fleet would soon deduce what
had happened, and could never again be caught by this
particular trick. It must have been the inspiration of some
Khalian genius; and maybe another Weasel became the chief
who got the job done. I wonder if they're alive now, either of
them, enjoying the thought of their revenge at last."

McClellan shook his head, violently, like an animal beset by
venomous insects. "Sir, I don't believe any Khalian could.
They don't have that kind of brains. This would be cutting-
edge technology for us. We'd need to assemble all kinds of

specialized workers and apparatus. Would a squadron planning a raid carry that along?"

"I wouldn't have expected so myself," Berling answered. Bleakly: "Nevertheless, it moves."

McClellan unclenched his fists and raised the hands, a fending gesture, a final protest. "Sir, *nobody* could aim a missile that exactly—across ten light-years!"

"They did," Berling rumbled. "Navigation even more astounding than the flight itself; but possible, yes, possible. You'd have to know this region very well, true, the exact proper motions of all your local reference stars, variations in gas and dust density, everything. But given that, your onboard computers could fine-tune the vectors under acceleration, till by the time your weapon was falling free—" His gullet seized up on him. He could only add, "Evidently the Khalia were hereabouts, exploring, surveying, unsuspected by us, for a long while before we came. That doesn't seem like them, either, but—" The terror surged forth. "But we've got the fact here staring at us. We've carried out our microfine measurements, we've run our computations, and we know. In a little over twenty-four hours, that thing will hit Verdea."

White serenity, the snowpeak of Holy Mountain, seems to float in a heaven alive with wings and song. Below, forest crowns ripple, golden-green leaves, shadowy deeps, asough under a wind that they make fragrant. A spring bubbles up in a dell, its water sparkling and chuckling off as a rivulet that tastes of cold and cleanness. A beast whose many-tined horns rake high aloft comes to drink. He does not fear nor disturb the pair who sit moveless among the flowers, a native and a human. They have become such friends, those two, that the first of them is guiding the second toward understanding of the Triple Way whereby the spirit may momentarily become one with beauty.

"Where?" croaked McClellan.

Berling shrugged. "Someplace in the northern hemisphere, that being the direction of Bitch. We can't determine it exactly. No matter. We're certain of an impact, which'll be equivalent to collision with a large asteroid. The kind of catastrophe that ends a geological era. Tsunamis, quakes, volcanoes, fires, ash, storms, clouds, unbroken worldwide winter for years on end. Last time on Earth, it did in the dinosaurs and a majority of other life-forms." He spoke flatly because he was afraid that if he didn't, he would scream.

"The Verdeans—"

"They may or may not survive as a species. Nearly all are bound to die, but maybe not quite everyone. Any that don't, though, will be starving savages. No agriculture, no civilization. And so, no support for our base. Its buildings and machines ought to last, unless the strike is nearby. But we'll have to evacuate. I don't suppose we'll ever come back. Conditions will be too hard, too expensive to cope with, for it to be worthwhile."

"Christ! In one more day."

"That's how fast the missile is traveling. On the heels of its own light, lurid but weak, as small as the mass is. They cannot see it from the target world until minutes before it is upon them."

Night, perhaps. Violet overhead, few stars, for the full moon is up, Ysatha Bay bridged and besparked with silver. The luminance washes the plumage of the Verdeans, turns its daytime azure to a mysterious opalescence, fills their great eyes, where they walk by twos and threes along the shore or in the village lanes. Some humans are among them, also savoring peace. A flute twitters low. Phosphorescent lichenoids growing on shingles outline the gracefulness of roofs. Softened by distance, the windows of homes in the Fleet community shine from their hilltop, by now a part of this landscape and beloved.

A sudden spark in the sky.

"Global defenses—" McClellan almost pleaded.

"You know as well as I do," Berling told him, "nothing we've got will stop so much momentum. Or you should know. Only recall the parameters."

"But, sir, this is a capital ship here. Firepower to wipe civilization off a planet by itself, if it can get through. That thing hasn't any screens or guns. Can't we vaporize it?"

"Everybody's first thought. If we were properly prepared, as we surely will be in future, yes, I can think of several possibilities. But right now—we'd have to go hyperspatial, emerge far enough ahead of it that we'd have time to get out of the way, send a barrage—and the warheads wouldn't go off. At that speed, impact would derange the triggers before they could function. We might, with luck, manage a blast close by. But then most of it would be wasted in space, directed charge or no, and the object would outrun nearly all the gas that was headed its way." Berling scowled. "The technical section has considered quite a few ideas, to no avail. They're still working on the problem. We can only hope they'll come up with something practical."

"Before it's too late."

"Stop whimpering!"

McClellan swallowed. "S-sorry, sir. I have a family on Verdea." *And you're a widower, your children grown and gone elsewhere.*

Berling softened slightly. "I know. Please understand, I'm on edge same as you. But our people's chances look pretty good. Immediate direct effects won't likely be too bad in their neighborhood, and the Fleet will take them off well before the ecology crumbles."

"We can pray for that, can't we?"

"If it makes you feel better. You might mention the natives."

Both men went mute.

In the background a fusion powerplant and a semiautomated factory stand incongruously sleek amid high old houses and little shops where handicraft brings forth exquisiteness. In the park singing kites cast their melodies on the wind and a poet weaves gold wire into lines that will charm the eye as well as the heart. Two mothers watch their young at play beneath a blossoming tree. "I think," says Jane, "when they are grown, sharing like this, they will do things and dream things we can't imagine." Selana rests quiet awhile before she replies, in her own rippling language, "I think we will understand them. Have we not already begun it ourselves?"

"Captain's attention, please." The intercom voice was jagged. "Technical report."

"Seal your circuit." Berling stepped to the terminal and sat down. McClellan stayed on his feet.

The nightscape of space burned above the face that appeared

in the screen, Commander Picavea's. "We . . . have our evaluations for you, sir."

"Well?" Berling snapped, though the haggardness he confronted was easy to read. "Spit it out."

"Not a chance, sir." Picavea ran tongue over lips that stayed just as dry. "None of our weapons can help. For a while the lasers seemed hopeful, but the math shows that they couldn't pump in more energy, in the time we'd have available, than might partially melt the thing; and the fused material wouldn't blow off, it'd cling and resolidify. Masses left in its path—all our boats, one after the next, wouldn't suffice. It'd go through them like a . . . a straw in a hurricane through a plank, scatter them in bits without losing enough velocity to miss Verdea. If we had time to bring out a really big mass, like an asteroid— But we don't. Everything my team thought of— Does the captain want the full report?"

"Never mind." Berling's tone had again gone hard and flat. "You and your computers know your business. What about the extreme tactic I suggested?"

Picavea drew a breath, a gasp. "Yes, sir. That ought to work. If we can do it within—" He forced eyes down toward his watch. "Within about ninety minutes of this instant. But it requires . . . our entire mass. Boats and everything. Plus a contact velocity of at least thirty kps."

"And absolutely precise aim," Berling said. "Have you developed a flight plan?"

Picavea jerked a nod.

Berling looked straight at him. "That's an honest computation? We wouldn't miss because of an irreducible margin of error?"

Picavea stiffened. "Sir, this team is Fleet."

"And you're ready to go through with it."

"Yes, sir." A grisly grin. "I can't say we're happy about it, but we accept the necessity."

"Very well. Give me a readout and printout. Meanwhile put the program into Navigation."

"Should I explain to them there?"

"I think not."

"I don't know. That doesn't seem right."

"We can argue during the ninety minutes. Move!"

"Aye, sir." Picavea's image vanished. Words, diagrams, and numbers began to unroll in the screen, a strip of paper from the slot beneath. Berling watched them a minute, then leaned toward his intercom.

"Captain to Navigation," he said. "Emergency. We're going on full automatic for the next hour or two. Acknowledge."

"Full automatic, aye, sir."

"Switch over and stand by."

"Sir—" quavered at Berling's back.

"Now hear this," boomed through the tunnels and caverns of the ship. "Now hear this. Prepare for acceleration followed by hyperspace maneuver. All hands off duty, to your quarters."

"Sir, what's going on?" McClellan cried.

Feet sped down corridors. Men and women tautened at machines. A deep tremor passed through metal and bones, power awakening. Invisible and unfelt, interior fields wove their mesh to take the added thrust off material and living matter. Like one huge organism, *Celestia* glided curvingly forward.

There was little tension aboard. Since everyone had not been summoned to stations, this could not be a battle alert or the like. Crew who were free speculated among each other what the Old Man did have in mind. Back to base, maybe? Except for the tech gang, they had received only vague information about their mission, for until a short while ago nobody had clearly known.

A shriek: "You mean to ram, don't you?"

Berling swiveled his chair around and regarded horror. "What else?" he said.

"But that's insane! We'll be destroyed—won't we?"

"Yes." Berling rose. "Sorry. No choice. It'll happen in a flash. We won't feel a thing."

McClellan gaped, shivered, drew his jaws shut.

Before he could speak, Berling continued: "We'll get up the right speed, then pass into hyperspace, overtake the missile, and reenter three-space at the calculated point to hit it with the proper intrinsic velocity, normal to its trajectory. The component of momentum we transfer will be a few parts in ten

million, but it'll deflect the missile enough. Barely enough; it
ought to miss Verdea by about one planetary diameter. That's
if we act promptly. The deflection is so little, it'll need a whole
light-day to bring the object even that much off target, and
naturally we want a safety factor."

"Safety!" McClellan groaned.

Berling laid a hand on the exec's shoulder. "Men have died
before that others might live." He couldn't force warmth into
his tone, it remained mechanical.

"But you said—they should be all right at the base—"

"I meant 'probably.' Besides, the Fleet would lose the base
itself."

McClellan's features congealed. He spoke harshly but lev-
elly. "A marginal value. No hostiles have come anywhere near
for fifteen years."

Berling nodded. "I've often wondered why they bothered to
try taking us out, back then."

"And no operations on our part, aside from patrols and—and
a trivial war production. Is it worth it? A dreadnought, capable
of deciding a battle all by herself, equipment not replaceable
for years, skilled crew that can never be replaced. What will
the High Command think?"

"Unfortunately," Berling said, "we can't take time to
consult the High Command."

"Nor our own people?" McClellan blazed. "I heard you.
You're condemning them to death without the honesty to let
them know."

"My feeling is that that would be no kindness."

"Or that they won't go along with it?"

"I am in command here, mister."

McClellan stood rigid against the stars. The ship sang
louder, stronger.

"I believe they have the right," he said after some heartbeats.

"Maybe," Berling said. "I have the question under advise-
ment."

"The right to—to refuse an unlawful order."

"We're not off to commit any atrocity. We'll stop one."

"If the commanding officer is obviously incompetent, insane, the duty of his juniors is to relieve him." McClellan turned on his heel and set off across the deck.

"Halt!" Berling shouted.

McClellan looked back. Tears started forth and glistened down the gaunt cheeks. "Sir, sir, I hate this," he stammered. "But I've got to. Let the court-martial decide between us."

"Halt, I told you. That's a direct order."

McClellan reached the door.

Berling bounded after him, caught his shoulder, whirled him about. "Are you afraid for your life?"

"Yes. Aren't you? Francie, Tommy, Alice— But more for the ship. I do believe it's more for the ship and what she means to . . . the Fleet, the Alliance. Please, sir, please."

Berling's powerful arm yanked. McClellan staggered. Berling released him and grated, "You'll stay here with me. Or must I call the guard?"

McClellan reached into his pocket. He pulled out a clasp knife and tugged the blade down. It shimmered broad and sharp, a tool for hard uses. "Do you dare?" he challenged. "I'm leaving. Unless you cancel that navigation program." As the ship changed more and more her direction, stars wheeled over the viewscreen like the march of seasons and years. "No?" he murmured wearily. "Well, my brother and sister officers may support you." He glanced at the knife, shook his head, and moved again to the door. "I hope they won't. Good-bye. I was happy serving under you, till now."

The door opened for him. He strode through.

Berling sprang. He flung his left arm around McClellan's neck. His right hand clamped fast on the wrist where the weapon was. McClellan choked. He lunged against the grip. Berling tightened it.

An odd small cracking noise sounded through the beat of energies. Blood ran from McClellan's mouth. He dropped the knife. Berling let go. McClellan fell to the deck. He struggled. Berling stooped over him, knelt, put palm on chest, brought lips near lips. McClellan's flailing ceased. He sprawled, mouth and eyes wide, breast still. A sharp stench lifted. A fractured larynx can be fatal, sometimes very quickly.

Berling climbed to his feet. He stood hunched, arms

dangling loose, and stared down. "I'm sorry," he mumbled. "I didn't intend that. Although—no big difference, is it?" He dragged the body back inside, gestured the door to shut, and plodded to his chair.

"Captain to Technical Section," he said at the intercom. "Sealed communication."

Picavea's face came into the screen. "You and I are pretty much running the ship, it seems," Berling said. "Arrange me a beam to Verdea. Before we go hyperspatial, I must report what's been happening and what we intend."

"Y-yes, sir."

"When you've closed the circuit for me, cut yourself out. I'll be describing everything, every last detail I can. Who knows what information may prove useful someday? But certain things ought to stay confidential."

"Even from us, sir?"

"Yes. However, if you fellows want to give me a short message—to your families or whoever—I think I can include that."

"Thank you." Picavea chuckled wryly. "Will do. *Morituri te salutamus.*"

"How's your team taking this?" Berling asked.

"Quite well," Picavea said. "We did get advance warning, after all, conferring with you, that desperate action might likely prove necessary. We're keeping to ourselves, here in the lab, and—talking, thinking, praying—an acey-deucey game starting over in the corner."

Berling smiled a bit. "Good lads. I wish I could join you."

Picavea tensed. "Sir, I do feel, most of us, the others deserve to know."

"I'll think about that," Berling said. "You may well be right. I can make the announcement later." Too late.

Picavea understood. "Thank you, sir. Uh, one thing—"

"Go ahead, son."

"It'd be . . . helpful to us . . . if you'd give us a few words."

Berling sighed. "I'm no orator. But, for whatever it's worth, put me on the big screen."

Picavea made an adjustment. Berling looked across a room

crowded with apparatus and faces. Young faces, mostly. He drew breath.

"Gentlemen," he said, no longer coldly, though it came out as a growl, "we're going to die, but it will be a good death in a good cause. I honor you for your courage and devotion. The Fleet will when it learns. A whole world will, for thousands and maybe millions of years to come. Because that's what we're mainly saving, a thinking race and its future, everything it may give the universe— No, goddammit, that's just abstract. Forget it. Think this way. *We* came to Verdea. It's in this danger because of us. For the honor of the Fleet, we will discharge the responsibility we have assumed.

"Thank you.

"Establish my contact, Mr. Picavea, decide on a few personal words for me to include in my dispatch, and call me back."

"Aye, sir."

The screen blanked. Berling settled down to compose, in his head, what he should tell them on the planet before *Celestia* went into the lightlessness of hyperspace and came forth again, for a moment, to the stars.

"—by sheer luck, a vessel of ours detected a missile that had been launched from the other sun after the raid failed, fifteen years earlier," I proceeded. "A relatively minor body, solid, but accelerated almost to light speed and aimed with incredible precision. It would have hit Verdea with force equivalent to an asteroid. Afterward our scientists ran computer models and verified that the effects would have been similar. Climate disruption, mass extinction, quite possibly including the native race, certainly the vast majority of it—hundreds of millions— and every civilization. We have no doubt the designers of the thing knew this. They didn't care.

"Does that jog your memory?"

Godolphin shuddered. "No." I could barely hear him. "No, I have never been informed."

Well, I admitted to myself, Verdea is an obscure planet, and the Fleet didn't want the incident publicized more than was unavoidable, and it chanced to occur when the attention of the whole Alliance was on the Battle of Ebo. However, within the Syndicate—

"What happened?" Godolphin whispered.

"A major vessel of ours sacrificed herself, crashing into the object and diverting it."

"That was heroic."

"My father was aboard."

"Then you have a glorious heritage."

As an officer of Intelligence, I have studied Berling's last communication in detail. The Fleet has never released more than a few carefully chosen lines of it. We claim security considerations. I daresay a certain amount of calculation went on at headquarters. Deliverance Day is a sacred festival on Verdea, inspiring, binding us closer to the autochthons, bringing us new recruits every year. And I—get quietly on in my life.

"You should not be this bitter," Godolphin said. "It was war."

I tasted that first reading of the report again. But what I spat out was: "So we assumed till recently. The Khalia, what else could you expect? Questions did nag us. They had the ruthlessness, but did they ever have that kind of determination, or that fine a technology? We supposed some among them must have had, and dismissed the matter in our minds except for adding precautions. Now it's become clear, given what we've discovered since. No Khalian planned that genocide. Humans did. Syndics. Adzeta was uncomfortably near a border of their space. Fleet scouts might have come on the truth prematurely that the Syndicate was behind the Khalia. So you arranged the raid, and when it failed, you set your longer-range scheme in motion."

"I swear I never heard—"

I begrudged every syllable. "All right. Not you personally. But your government. It would do Genghis Khan proud, Tamerlane, Stalin, Mao, El Brujo—no, I don't imagine the history means anything to you. But does common decency?"

Godolphin's countenance firmed. He straightened in his chair. "You accuse our leaders," he said quite softly.

"Or their immediate predecessors. And yours haven't disowned them."

"The Fleet has used extremely destructive weapons from time to time."

"Not against planets where sentient beings make their homes."

"Granted, to the best of my knowledge. I can sympathize with your attitude. Then you want me to turn on my nation and give you all the information I possess?"

"Think about it," I said. "You might redeem yourself."

Godolphin drew breath. "I will tell you this much, Commander McClellan," he stated. "I am reasonably familiar with the politics and the practical ethics of Syndicate society. I am also rather widely acquainted with naval officers, important civilians, and records, including secret files. You have my word of honor that no such thing as you describe was ever seriously proposed." He paused. "I do recall glancing at a theoretical study of near-c kinetic kill weapons, conducted many years ago. The conclusion was that they would not be worth the cost. Including the cost to our consciences."

"Apart from this case," I slapped at him.

He took it stonily. "An extraordinary situation with a possible net gain. But I repeat, it was never ordered from above. The raid, yes, no doubt. That is war. A surgical strike, which, unfortunately for us, failed. However, the genocide to follow, no, I repeat, no. It must have been the decision, the work, of a few fanatical officers on the scene. They cannot have asked for authorization, because they must have known it would be refused them. An accomplished fact, after they were safely retired—" Now he slashed. "Dare you claim that no one in the Fleet, in the Alliance, has never attempted anything comparable? Or done it?"

I had no answer.

"These things happen," he said. "It is also war."

We fell silent, there in our metal cage.

INTERLUDE

Articles of War
Article X
Where mutiny is accompanied by Violence, every Person subject to this act who shall join therein shall suffer Death, or such other Punishment as is herein-after mentioned; and such Mutiny shall, if he has acted traitorously, suffer Death, or such other Punishment as is herein-after mentioned; if he has acted from Cowardice, shall suffer Penal servitude or such other Punishment as is herein-after mentioned; if he has acted from Negligence he shall be dismissed from the Service, with Disgrace, or suffer such other Punishment as is herein-after mentioned.

During the closing year of the Khalian War, losses often outpaced production. This was especially true of transport ships, being both laden with loot and comparatively unarmed. These losses were compounded by the fact that every naval yard in the Alliance was mandated to produce only warships.

By the time Target was invaded and the majority of raiding stopped, the Alliance had lost almost twenty-five percent of its capacity to transport goods. At the time such losses concerned most the ship's owners, insurers, and crews.

As the focus of the Khalian war shifted from the edge of the Alliance into the surprisingly large area dominated by the Khalia, this changed. Suddenly there was a need to support a massive armada weeks away from the nearest Fleet support facilities. Simply impressing the ships and spacemen into a Fleet-controlled merchant marine force was not the solution. These ships were needed in commercial service if the economy supporting the Fleet was to continue to do so. Only a small number could be taken out of service, and politics being what it is, these were often those deemed least cost effective by the companies they were taken from. It was these rusted rejects that then Commodore Meier led successfully against the Khalian reinforcement in the space battle off Target.

Responsibility for maintaining the supply lines was quickly relegated to the Quartermaster's Corps. Many solutions were attempted. Among them was to have those planets normally considered too rural or lacking the manufacturing infrastructure to complete an entire ship manufacture large hulls that could be completed elsewhere. Enthusiastically competing to produce the biggest and best hulls, many of these worlds created transport ships more than a kilometer long. Outfitting these large hulls was often a challenge. The best electronic and propulsion components were reserved for warship production. This led to a number of experimental systems being field-tested far before they were ready. A few were surprisingly successful— some of those in a way never expected by their designers.

DISTRESS SIGNALS
by Scott MacMillan and Katherine Kurtz

FOUL WAS JUST about the only word to describe the mood that
Commander Talley was in as the Fleet evacuation shuttle
prepared to dock with the cargo ship now looming on starboard. After nearly twenty years of active—make that *very*
active—service, he was being transferred from a front-line
battlecruiser to take command of a massive but low-priority
supply ship whose skipper recently had been killed. With Fleet
massing to meet the combined forces of the Syndicate, Talley
should have been given command of a fighting ship. Instead,
he got this—all because some senator's dumb jerk of a son had
been stupid enough to step through an open hatch. . . .

And then, adding injury to insult, they had tried to foist a
vegetarian meal on him in the shuttle, probably knowing what
the bulk inherent in most plant foods would do to Talley's
sensitive digestive system. Dammit, it was enough to make a
man's guts boil.

And boil they did.

Talley could feel the pressure begin to build up somewhere between his belt buckle and back pocket. He wondered whether this was the real reason for his transfer. Other men in Fleet had scars to show for their battles fought and won; Talley had a grumbling gut—one that allowed him to eat only a few select, bland foods and that reacted explosively to anything else, particularly vegetables. He only hoped that things would stay quiet until they docked, or that in the ensuing commotion his malady would pass unnoticed. It didn't; and only his rank and reputation kept the crewmen from passing comments of their own.

If it wasn't bad enough being bumped from cruiser command to baby-sitting nonessentials, the usual snafu had seen that his personal effects were on the far side of the star system. The only kit that he had was the change of uniform he habitually carried anytime he left ship, and the sword that had been in the family for more generations than he could remember.

Avoiding the eyes of the deck crew, Talley glanced at the sword he was now carrying. His ancestor had worn it pacing the decks of the square-rigger he commanded in 1804, as he chased pirates along the southern shore of the Mediterranean Sea. He had been a legendary figure, a real swashbuckler. Single-handed, he had captured a pirate barque, and with this very sword had lopped off the head of the pirate captain.

At least that was the family legend. So from one generation to the next, from father to son, the sword had been passed down as each new generation of Talleys took up an officer's commission.

Things began to move again. Talley was in agony, and prayed that he'd be able to leave the deck before it happened again. His prayers were answered. Docking was completed, and Talley was able to leave the transfer deck without fanfare.

Trumpets didn't herald his arrival on his new command station either. Rather, he was met by the solitary figure of the ship's medical officer.

"Hi. Commander Talley? I'm Edna Purvis, your M.O." Dr. Purvis stuck out her hand in greeting. "Went over your medical records soon as they arrived. Saw you've got, er, excessive methane levels." She handed him a small bottle. "Just in case you're in any distress."

"Thanks," growled Talley, looking at the label and the pills inside. "How many, how often, and how fast do they work?"

"Well, by the sound of your voice I'd say take three now, and then cut back to one every couple of hours. You should feel better in about twenty minutes." Purvis smiled. "I can't say that they'll cure you, but at least they'll make you more comfortable."

Talley shook three of the small blue pills into the palm of his hand and gulped them down. They had no taste, and their dry coating liquefied almost as soon as he started to swallow. He was too glad for the almost-instant relief to wonder how an M.O. on an obsolescent freighter had access to such pills and the best physicians on Port did not. He grumped his thanks at her and shifted his small bag to his left hand.

"Point me at my cabin, Purvis, and then spread the word that I'll want to see the officers in the wardroom in . . ."

Purvis interrupted him. "In about thirty minutes. Aye-aye, sir. Follow me."

On the way to his cabin, Purvis pointed out the chow hall, ratings lounge, command bridge, and "Bear Country," the officers' wardroom. After leaving the commander at his cabin, Purvis went back to Bear Country.

"Well, chums, we've got a real winner." Purvis took a sip of her coffee. "This guy's seen lots of action, and my guess is he won't stand for any sloppiness. We can all kiss our pleasure cruise good-bye."

"A real by-the-books type, huh?" It was Executive Officer Huntley, as usual peering out from under his tousled blond hair through a pair of red-framed glasses, their oversize lenses reflecting the sodium lights in the bulkhead.

"Yup."

The cargo officer spoke up. "You don't suppose that he's going to want to inventory the ship, do you?"

"Ask him yourself." Purvis set down her cup. "He wants all of us here in Bear Country in half an hour."

"Does that include the galley slave?" someone asked.

"Sure, why not? He's got to meet her eventually." Purvis

stood up and stretched. "See you in half an hour. I'm going for a soak."

Talley still wasn't in the best of moods as he stepped from the shower, but at least the pills that Dr. Purvis had given him seemed to be working. Still dripping, he looked around for a towel and, not finding one, dried off as best he could with the shirt he'd worn on the shuttle. Nearly dry, he padded out of his bathroom and started a random search through the drawers in his cabin.

There was an ample supply of socks and underwear, along with some personal items that had been overlooked when the late—what was his name? there was a name tag that said Ivanoff—skipper's personal effects had been packed up and sent back to Port, but no towels. Well, thought Talley as he finished dressing and ran a comb through his hair, maybe the laundry just hasn't come back yet.

Bear Country was nearly full when Commander Talley arrived. Executive Officer Huntley managed to sound almost military as he called the assembled officers to attention when their C.O. entered the room. Most of them managed to find their feet and stand nearly to attention until Talley gave them, "As you were," and they collapsed back in their seats.

Talley looked around the room with a growing sense of distaste. He was used to commanding a small battlecruiser—nothing impressive: just three hundred or so men who took their orders from fifty or sixty officers who thought of themselves as the pride of the Fleet, the best in the universe. Looking around him now, he saw that he had twenty-five officers, and none of them, not one, looked as if he or she was worthy of commanding troops, let alone the respect of each other. He could feel the familiar pain as his guts tightened.

Talley had two choices; he could play it hard, or friendly. Although it ran against the grain, he decided to try friendly first.

"You people look as if you just heard orders to abandon ship. You look, in fact, like you have already abandoned ship. Well, ladies and gentlemen, we aren't abandoning *this* ship, so I expect to see all of you back in ten minutes, looking like Fleet officers. Atten-shun!" Talley turned to Huntley. "Dismiss these people."

Before Huntley could react to Talley's order, a commotion broke out in the back of the room as a large, almost heavyset, woman pushed her way into Bear Country. Talley could only stare, goggle-eyed, as six feet two inches and 210 pounds of flour-dusted femininity bulled her way through the assembled officers and came to a halt in front of him, standing at rigid attention. A stalk of broccoli jutted upward from a pocket that was filled from behind by the large cook's obvious femininity. Talley hadn't even liked broccoli as a child.

"What the . . ."

But Talley didn't get a chance to finish. Dr. Purvis stepped up and said, "Commander Talley, this is Chief Commissary Officer Thelma Ruel."

The galley slave saluted. Commander Talley blanched, and the methane level of the room rose by several points.

The second meeting in Bear Country went much smoother than the first, and Talley was glad that he had taken the "nice guy" approach with his command team. Huntley, his X.O., had sounded more military in calling the officers to attention, and Purvis had been persuaded to keep Chief Commissary Officer Ruel busy elsewhere. The cargo officer was busy preparing an onboard inventory, and in a few minutes he'd begin an inspection of the ship. In the meantime, two things bothered him: first, that he had forgotten to ask about towels; and second, he had the horrible feeling that he had met the galley slave before.

Executive Officer Huntley, clipboard tucked into the crook of his arm, knocked on Talley's door before he could brood himself into gut-rumbling misery about where he and Thelma Ruel might have met in the past. Pulling on his cap, Talley started out on his inspection tour of the FCTV 621-J. As they walked down the gangway toward the forward crew quarters, he and Huntley fell into casual conversation.

"Tell me, Huntley," Talley began, "how long have you been in Fleet?"

"Oh, about two years, sir. Joined up at the tail end of the last

big war against the Khalia, although I didn't see any action.
I've been stuck in transport all along." Huntley sighed, and
Talley couldn't tell if his exec really was disappointed with his
career or was putting him on.

"Spent all your time with the 621-J?" Talley asked.

"The which, sir? —Oh, yeah. No, I was transferred to the
Veg-o-matic a little over a year ago."

Talley stopped and turned to Huntley. "What do you mean
'the Veg-o-matic'?"

"Well, sir"—Huntley's face began to redden slightly—
"that's what the crew and everybody calls this ship. The
Veg-o-matic, sir."

"Huntley, why is this ship called the Veg-o-matic?" Talley
could tell from the pained look on Huntley's face that he wasn't
sure that it hadn't been a mistake to let slip the ship's
nickname.

"Because, sir," Huntley's voice dropped, and he avoided the
commander's eyes, "it's got Veg-o-matic drive."

Instinctively Talley loosened his belt a notch to relieve the
pressure on his lower regions.

"Mr. Huntley," he began, "I've shipped out with Fleet for
nearly two decades, and in all that time I've never once heard
of 'Veg-o-matic drive.' So what I'm going to do"—he could
feel the pressure in his stomach beginning to build—"is take
one of these little blue pills, and ask you to tell me all about it.
Okay?"

Huntley gulped as Talley swallowed the pill.

"Sir, I'm not totally conversant with the entire process. I
think it might be better if you talked to Lieutenant Bermann.
She knows all about veg-o—er, ah—this stuff."

The agony in Talley's lower abdomen was reaching critical
mass, causing him to clench his teeth in an attempt to control
himself.

"Fine," he managed in a strained voice. "Let's go see the
lady."

Flight Information Monitoring Officer Nancy Bermann had
been on the FCTV 621-J since its launch at the peak of the
Khalian offensive.

"It's really simple, sir. During the last war we lost a lot of equipment to the Khalia. Supply ships were in especially short supply, as was almost everything else. The big holdup wasn't in getting them built, it was getting them outfitted. Excuse me." She turned to the computer screen in front of her, scanned it briefly, then tapped a short command into the system.

"Anyhow, I had a distant uncle in supply. Maybe you've heard of him—Admiral Abraham Meier? No? Well, he knew that the major delay in getting supply ships launched was in finding brains for the guidance/control systems. Those powerful enough to control a ship this size were needed in the combat ships. Oops, here we go again." She returned to her keyboard for a few seconds.

"There. So six years ago, Uncle Abe—um, I mean then-Commodore Meier—looked around for another source of artificial intelligence to utilize in Fleet cargo vessels. And guess what? He found one. Not for nothing my great-grandfather Isaac Meier, Admiral of the Red, had him assigned to Transport Logistics. Commodore Meier combined hydroponics with liquid computers, and voilà! he had it: an organic think-tank." Lieutenant Bermann beamed at her commanding officer.

"Excuse me if I seem a little dense, but I don't quite understand," Talley began. "He hooked up a bunch of plants to some sort of computer to run a ship?"

"That's right." Lieutenant Bermann smiled like a mother whose not-too-bright child had just learned to tell time. "Come with me, I'll show you how it works."

The three of them headed down a service corridor that led to the center of the ship. After passing through a security door, Lieutenant Bermann led them into a dimly lit room with a low, domed ceiling. In the center of the room, stretching nearly across the thirty meters of its width, lay an illuminated pool with islands of vegetation floating on its surface. Talley noticed several towels lying around the edge of the pool, made a mental note to check on his towels when he got back to his quarters, then took a closer look at what was in the pool—ten tons of green plants floated in a clear nutrient solution. The bubbling mass appeared to be a conglomeration of dozens of different plants, most of which the captain thought he recognized. The entire arrangement stretched nearly the length of the fifty-meter hold.

Talley let out a low whistle. "It's big. How does it work?"

"Actually," Lieutenant Bermann began, "it isn't that complicated. Throughout the ship are small containers, each filled with a special hydroponic fluid. These containers are linked to the pool, here, by fiber optic cables. That accounts for the glowing light that emanates up from the bottom of the pool.

"Growing in each of the containers are plants that have been taken from the donors floating in the pool. These are called satellite plants, and their purpose is to send messages back to the donor plants here in the pool."

"Wait a minute," Huntley interrupted. "Plants can't communicate."

"Oh, they communicate all right, but in a different, more basic way than people. Let's say that you took a cutting from that plant over there. If you placed it in another room, and then exposed it to heat, it would react in a specific way. Now, if you connect the satellite plant to the donor via fiber optics—I know, this is really ultra low tech—the donor will react in the same way." She smiled at Huntley, who grinned back sheepishly.

"All you have to do is monitor the surface tension of the pool to know what each plant is, well, thinking, and then feed that into a computer to determine what action needs to be taken."

"Question." It was Talley's turn. "With all those plants sending signals back and forth, how does the computer know what's going on?"

"That's easy. The plants are blind except to the signals from their individual satellites. It's like the nervous system feeding into the human brain, except in this instance we're dealing with organic, rather than biological input." She sounded like a fourth-grade teacher lecturing to a class of brighter-than-average children.

"But, can it think?" Huntley was still somewhere near the back of the class.

"No. But the computer can assemble the data input from the plants and reach a mathematically logical conclusion, which is as close to thinking as you can get, without having a human brain."

"Well, obviously it works," Talley said tentatively, "and it has to cost a whole lot less than a Fleet brainship, if we had the priority to get one—which we don't. Why aren't there more of them?"

Bermann was pleased with the captain's question, because it gave her another opportunity to quietly brag about her family.

"Originally there were six of these ships built; three were lost by enemy action, two were retrofitted with 'real' brains, and this one has been used as an ongoing test lab to further refine and expand the techniques developed by my uncle."

En route back to her office, after Talley had left them to return to Bear Country, Lieutenant Bermann was able to extract a promise from the executive officer to help her with some hydroponic experiments that same evening. Odd, how she had never really noticed him before. . . .

Meanwhile, back in Bear Country, Talley collected a copy of the ship's inventory from the cargo officer and headed down to his cabin to read it through. In the cabin he tossed his hat on his desk, kicked off his shoes, and settled back on his bunk with the cargo report. He felt his eyes getting heavy after a few routine pages, and just before he nodded off, he had the pleasant realization that, for the first time in weeks, he wasn't experiencing what Dr. Purvis had referred to as "some distress."

It was graduation day at Fleet Academy, and Cadet Andrew Stewart Talley was about to receive his commission along with several hundred other cadets. For five years he had worked like a galley slave to earn his commission, and . . .

Galley slave . . . Suddenly, in his dream, Chief Commissary Officer Thelma Ruel came forward to pin on his lieutenant's bars. But instead of pinning on his bars, she grabbed him in a bear hug, pinning his arms to his side and dragging him into some nearby bushes . . . He struggled, but to no avail. He tried to resist, but . . .

Talley awoke with a start, and the realization that the old feeling was back in his stomach—that, and the certain knowledge that Chief Commissary Officer Thelma Ruel, aka the galley slave, was a long-lost love from his past. He took one of Purvis's little blue pills, which relieved the pain in his gut but did nothing for the strange feeling in his heart.

As he lay in his bunk, he took stock of his situation. He was in command of a transporter that was run by a floating vegetable salad. His crew was undoubtedly one of the sloppiest he had ever come across, and his food, at this very minute, was being prepared by a demented Valkyrie who once had been his lover. Or more accurately, had had him as her paramour. On the positive side, the little blue pills seemed to be working wonders.

Someone knocked on the door to his cabin, then stuck her head in.

"Excuse me, sir, but the exec says you're needed on the bridge right away."

Oh, crud, thought Talley. What could it be now?

Tugging on his shoes and grabbing his cap from the desk, Talley double-timed his way to the command bridge. One look around the command center told him the crew was on the edge of panic. Something big had to be up.

Ensign Simon Rooney rushed up to the commander and saluted.

"Signals officer reporting, sir. Urgent message from Fleet Flotilla Command."

Talley returned the salute and quickly scanned the message that Rooney handed him.

To the Commanding Officer FCTV 621-J
Priority Reading: URGENT.
You are to immediately report to sector 87-WW-1350
rendezvous at zulu time 18:25:00. Disengagement
priority 3. Acknowledge receipt of orders.
Robert Wright, Captain
Fleet Flotilla Command

As a cruiser commander, Talley had received orders like this a dozen times before, but usually with a top priority disengagement code. Priority one authorized breaking off hostilities, if necessary, to make the rendezvous. Code two allowed for the abandonment of distressed or disabled ships, while code three only provided for completion of necessary repairs before departure for rendezvous.

It was obvious that something big was on at last in the war with the Syndicate, and that every available ship in Khalian space was being called in to help. Talley guessed from the low priority of his call-up that he would be part of some diversionary tactic, probably a feint at the Syndicate flanks. It was a little risky—strategic defense initiatives always were—especially if they blundered into the path of a Syndicate "Star Crusher," one of their ultra-heavy battleships.

Still, even the most experienced Syndicate commander might be expected to withdraw if an unexpected armada suddenly appeared on his screens. If they really were warships, then sticking around for sensor readings could be fatal—and the Veg-o-whatever was larger than the biggest dreadnought. Trouble was, they didn't have any weapons—but the Syndicate wouldn't necessarily know that.

Talley turned back to Rooney. "Acknowledge receipt of order, and signal our immediate compliance." Catching the eye of a communications rating, he gave another command as he headed out the door and back to his cabin.

"Find Mr. Huntley and have him report to my cabin at once."

The small beeper next to the pool buzzed quietly as Huntley's wet arm groped for it in the pile of his clothes. He found it and pressed the small red button on its top.

"Lieutenant Commander Huntley here."

The small screen lit up, and he recognized the chubby communications rating on the bridge. "Skipper wants to see you in his cabin right away. It's important."

"Roger that. Out."

Huntley tossed the beeper back onto the pile of his clothes and hoisted himself out of the pool. As he hunted for a towel, Lieutenant Bermann admired his slim swimmer's body, the indirect light of the pool casting the most seductive greenish glow across his lean thighs. As Huntley quickly dried off and dressed, she revised her impression of the executive officer earlier that day: cute, but dumb. To that, she idly thought, she could now add one other important attribute.

Huntley was dried, dressed, and at Talley's cabin within fifteen minutes. The corridors and gangways of the ship were strangely quiet, and twice he stuck his head in—once at the chow hall and again at Bear Country—to rooms only to find them totally deserted. Figuring that all hands were probably at stations, he hurried on to Talley's cabin.

"Come in," Talley replied to the knock at the door.

Huntley entered and saluted. Talley nodded back, and indicated that the executive officer should sit down.

"This is the situation, Mr. Huntley. We've been ordered to rendezvous with Fleet near the left flank of the Syndicate force."

The color drained from Huntley's face.

"What I want you to do," Talley went on, "is see to it that the crew doesn't panic. Keep 'em calm. There won't be any fighting, and in all probability we'll be in and out faster than a pickpocket at a convention. Got that?"

Huntley's "aye-aye" was a good deal less than enthusiastic.

"Good," said Talley. "Let's get back up on the bridge."

Talley settled into the command seat and punched up a visual scan of the sonar readouts. He immediately saw the small blip that hung in the wake of the 621-J. Pressing the button on his intercom, he asked Central Log for a readout on how long the mysterious "blip" had been following them.

On the hangar deck Dr. Purvis surveyed the main shuttle and decided that it would easily hold all of the crew. Getting them on board might be difficult, especially Commander Talley, but—well, that would just be too bad. If he didn't abandon ship with the rest of them, then he would just have to face the Syndicate raiding party alone. That really wasn't her worry. Her job was to get the crew on the shuttle, get them off the ship, and let the boarding party in. They would take care of any stragglers.

Up on the bridge, Talley didn't like the look of things. The "blip" had been shadowing his ship for nine days, ever since the "accident" that had taken out the previous commander. You didn't have to be a rocket scientist to suspect something was up. Just as he was about to make a crew announcement, the first explosion rocked the ship. Seconds later a second shock wave reverberated through the hull, and complete pandemonium broke out.

In the confusion caused by the two explosions, Dr. Purvis was able to hit the emergency override switch in the hangar deck and sound the Abandon Ship alarm. In a matter of minutes the hangar deck was packed with almost the entire crew, struggling to get aboard the crew shuttle. On the bridge Talley was knocked down by the wave of crewmen streaming through the exit, and only barely managed to avoid being trampled in the stampede.

Talley was furious. There had been no damage report, and he had not given anyone the order to sound Abandon Ship. A quick visual scan of the hull did not reveal any damage, and internally the only activity seemed to be on the main hangar deck.

Talley left the bridge, intending to cross to the hangar deck by way of the ship's hospital. As he entered the hospital's waiting room, he was confronted by Dr. Purvis stuffing last-minute supplies into her black bag. She glanced back at him and, without stopping, shouted, "Hurry up, or you'll miss the shuttle. Try to keep them from taking off without me."

Talley walked up to her and laid his hand on her shoulder. "They aren't taking off."

"Oh, yes, they are," said Purvis—and plunged a syringe into Talley's chest.

Before Talley could do more than gasp, everything went black and the floor rushed up to him. Purvis stepped over the crumpled form of her commanding officer and ran through the operating theater to the rear exit of the hospital complex. Below her, on the hangar deck, the last of the 215 members of the crew were fighting their way aboard the Veg-o-matic's shuttle. As she reached the top of the stairs leading to the gangway, the last of the crew climbed aboard.

Purvis had just made it to the airlock door when the shuttle banged down its hatch and the main hangar door opened in the side of the hull. Purvis watched in disbelief through the airlock porthole as the shuttle fired its thrusters, nosed out of the hangar deck, and silently vanished into space.

Two miles away, the commander of the Syndicate raider watched the shuttle as its pilot hit the main drive engines and the craft rocketed out into the void. Pressing a flashing green button on the bulkhead, he signaled his own men to climb into their sled and seize the abandoned cargo transport.

In the hangar bay of the Syndicate raider, eight mercenaries climbed into the tight confines of the sled that was to take them into the ship lying immediately off their port bow. The deck tilted down in front of them, and the electromagnetic catapult launched them into space.

The "pocket rocket," as it was referred to by the men on board, had small directional thrusters in the nose, and enough of a capacitive discharge drive unit to propel it back to the raider if anything went wrong. Usually, nothing did go wrong, and once the captured ship was secure and any stragglers killed, the raider would pull up alongside the captured vessel and simply dock in its hangar deck. The pilot would then take over command of the captured ship and bring it back to whichever of the Syndicate families had hired him. Piracy hadn't changed all that much; only the equipment had become more sophisticated.

Cadet Talley struggled in the bushes, desperately trying to escape from the fulsome embrace of Thelma Ruel. She seemed to smother him, demanding more than any man could be expected to perform, especially under the conditions of this particular tryst. He tried to push her away, but to no avail; she loomed over him, her moist red lips pressing down hard on his own. Somewhere in the distance he heard voices . . .

"Do you think he'll make it?" It was the executive officer speaking.

"Hell, yes, he'll make it. I've been giving him CPR since I found him, and he's started breathing on his own. . . ."

Chief Commissary Officer Ruel leaned back over the recumbent Commander Talley and reinflated his lungs with a mighty puff, then began compressing his chest once again.

Talley groaned as his dream swam blearily into his consciousness and then adjusted itself into sharp focus, revealing the chief commissary officer about to once again deliver the "kiss of life." Mustering all of his strength, Talley just managed to avoid Thelma's lips. Coughing, he pushed himself up into a sitting position and looked about the room. In addition to Chief Commissary Officer Ruel, Huntley and Bermann were also present.

"Where's Purvis?" Talley asked.

"She must have made it to the shuttle," Bermann volunteered.

"I don't think so," Huntley offered. "I was monitoring the operation from the control tower, and I didn't see her come in. In fact, I was looking for all of you when I heard the shuttle leave."

Talley tried to stand, but his knees buckled. Thelma scooped him up and propped him against the wall, holding him in place with one of her catcher's mitt-sized hands. Talley shook his head, trying to clear it from the effects of the syringe, and from the nagging feeling of affection that he was beginning to develop for Chief Commissary Officer Ruel.

"Okay, everybody, listen up. Here's what we've got to do . . ."

From her vantage point in the airlock above the hangar deck, Purvis watched as the pocket rocket skidded across the landing pad, its front thrusters on full. From the sides of the small sled, exploding darts were driven into the steel mesh of the decking, helping to anchor the slithering craft. As the carbon fiber line played out, the pocket rocket slowed, nearly coming to a full halt before it crashed into the side of the hangar.

Inside, there was a moment of stunned silence following the crash of the impact. The Khalian pilot spoke first, his tail twitching with annoyance.

"I hate short deck landings."

"Not as much as we do," someone said. Hoots of derision went up in the small cabin of the sled.

"Cut the crap and put on your helmets." The voice came from a badly scarred human. One eye socket was empty, and to judge from the blast scars, most of the teeth and jaw were military-issue plastics. He was thickset and heavily muscled. The silence his voice enforced left no doubt about who was in command of the raiding party.

"Okay, Geek," he spoke again, "open the friggin' door."

A young Thalmud opposite the disfigured human turned and manually levered open the hatch. Carefully, his carbine at the ready, he stepped out onto the deck. The nothingness of space seeped into the hangar through the open escape door, and the Thalmud could feel its chill through his thin life-support suit. He attached a carabiner to the side of his ship and carefully made his way around to the emergency control panel on the wall opposite from where Purvis watched.

"Ellis." The Thalmud's voice was dull in the disfigured man's ear. "I'm at the panel. What do I do?"

Ellis's remaining eye ached. "Look, Geek. Like I told ya. One: open the panel; two: pull the big blue lever; three: tell your mother to come to my bunk tonight. Now get it in gear, or I'll shoot it off."

Geek opened the panel and pulled the lever. The hangar-bay doors grated shut, and the room began to pressurize. Then the pirate trotted back to the sled and pulled off his helmet, a shower of golden droplets flying everywhere as he shook his head.

"All clear."

Inside, the others pulled off their helmets and Ellis gave the order to "hit the streets."

Up in the airlock, Purvis counted as six of them formed up in front of Ellis before heading out in twos and threes to clean up any loose ends. She shuddered slightly at the thought of what would happen to her if they found her here in the airlock. Her best move would be to stow away in the cargo hold until someone from one of the families arrived to confirm her identity. The option was to sit around and wait for the goons to find her, and hope that one of them had enough intelligence to hear her out instead of passing her around to his buddies before they killed her.

Picking up her black bag, she headed back into the ship toward the side cargo bay. On the way, she almost ran into Bermann and Ruel, only barely ducking back out of sight without being noticed. She briefly considered warning them about the raiders, but then decided that her own chances for survival were greater if no one else knew of her presence on the ship. In the freight elevator, she pushed Storage Facility 17, and sank to the floor as the gondola moved silently within the hull of the ship.

The door opened, and Purvis, lying flat on the floor, stuck her head out, peering both left and right before standing up and making her way down the aisle in front of her. A hundred yards down the aisle she came to exactly what she was looking for: a consignment of portable field loos.

Well, she thought, like the Marines say, the three most important things in life: comfortable boots, a cold beer, and a dry place to hide.

Opening her bag, Purvis pulled out a scalpel and jimmied the lock on the field toilet. Inside, she set her bag on the shelf and was about to close the door when she spotted a small cluster of violets growing next to one of the bulkheads.

She walked over to the flowers like a little girl in a park. She looked both ways to make sure no one was watching, and then she picked several of them and brought them back to her hideout. Climbing in, she closed and locked the door, confident that she and her flowers were perfectly safe from detection.

On the bridge Commander Talley carefully keyed in the last of a series of commands to the central computer, sealing all exits and locking all doors—standard procedure in abandoning ship, and something that should slow down the advance of the raiders, giving Talley a chance to deal with them on an individual basis. Then, picking up his sword, Talley left the bridge and began to work his way down to the hangar deck.

In the main corridor Huntley was busy lifting up the last few meters of rubber decking and stacking it neatly against the wall. Looking back, he was satisfied with the job. Eight meters of metal gridwork lay exposed, its rubber matting carefully stacked to one side. To complete the picture, Huntley carefully laid a metal wrench in the center of the corridor.

Belowdecks, the galley slave had rigged a massive deadfall consisting mostly of frozen broccoli and dehydrated eggs—and had covered the floor of the galley with rehydrogenized cooking oil.

Finally, in her office, Flight Information Monitoring Officer Nancy Bermann sat at the keyboard of her computer, crooning softly to a small hydroponic satellite as she transferred control of the onboard closed-circuit television to the Veg-o-matic down in the pond.

Ellis was leaning against the bulkhead, chewing on a blade of grass as the two men with him heaved and grunted, trying to open the locked door. Finally, it gave way and the three were able to scramble through and into the passageway on the other side.

As they moved down the passageway, Ellis carefully tried each door. Locked. All of them locked. Feral creature that he was, Ellis sensed that something wasn't right. After a few minutes' deliberation, he decided to go forward, and to try to reach the bridge before checking on anything else.

Two decks below Ellis, the Thalmud and a human named Barish were moving along a corridor that led from the flight deck to the forward crew quarters. As they occasionally stopped to try a door, always locked, they finally came to a recess in the wall where a hydroponic tank was overflowing with sweet, succulent clover. Barish stopped in his tracks.

"Hey, Geek. You ever have any of this stuff back on your planet?"

"No. What is it? Some sort of plant?"

The Thalmud made a face at his last remark. Their diet was fairly simple: lots of meat and not much more, washed down with a thick beer made from animal fats.

Barish pulled one of the flowers from the bunch.

"Look, see, you pull the petals off of the flower here, like this, and then you chew on them. They're sweet. Go on, try one."

As Barish munched on the clover, the closed-circuit camera zoomed in for a close-up, his features being digitized and stored in the memory banks of the computer. In the pond a clover plant sent out shock waves of pain, tinged with the horror of having one of its satellites shredded and eaten. This was recorded by the tremors running through the surface tension of the pond, and stored in the same memory bank that held Barish's picture.

A few yards farther down the corridor Geek and Barish heard the sound of one of the doors being unlocked. Carefully the two advanced down the hall, testing each door handle until they found one that yielded when the locking plate was pressed.

Crouching low, Geek kicked in the door with his foot while Barish covered him with his carbine. It was a small room, a broom closet really, and empty except for the things needed to clean up in quarters. On one wall was an opening nearly two feet square, and Geek motioned toward it.

Carefully Barish advanced and peered into the opening. It sloped downward and seemed to be some sort of access chute. Barish considered it for a moment, then reached into his pack and brought out a flashlight. Carefully he shone it in the chute, but as far as he could see there was nothing.

Maybe whoever went in there found another shaft leading up or across from this one, Barish thought. Aiming his carbine in front of him, he climbed into the access chute.

At the other end of the chute, a small hydroponic satellite detected the additional weight on the conveyer belt that formed the floor of the garbage chute Barish had entered. As soon as it sensed that the chute was in use, it automatically turned on the conveyer that would bring garbage down to the shredders and compactors in the very keel of the ship.

Barish tried to turn around, but the chute was too narrow. Crawling backward was impossible because the belt moved faster than he could crawl. He tried to stop the conveyer belt by bracing his hands against the walls, but only succeeded in ripping the flesh from his palms.

Looking forward, he could see the spinning blades of the shredder coming nearer. In desperation he shoved his carbine in front of him, firing wildly.

The barrel of the weapon caught in the blades of the shredder, and was jerked violently from Barish's bloody hands. The machine tried to shred the gun, but to no avail. It jammed between the blades, and the conveyer belt stopped.

Barish was on the verge of tears of joy when the barrel of the carbine snapped and the belt leaped forward, pitching him into the shredder. His scream dissolved into a spray of pink foam as the blades reduced him to mulch.

Geek, hearing the screams echoing up from the garbage chute, fired wildly down into the blackness, then leaped back out into the hall to reload. The magazine slipped in his fingers as he fumbled with the weapon. When he finally fitted it into its slot and slapped it home, Geek started to breathe easier.

Thick, viscous oil exuded from the tubes that covered his head like hair, and the slimy golden liquid ran down his shoulders and covered his clothes. Geek stood up, shook his head, and moved on down the corridor, checking doors. It was at the end of the corridor that he noticed the light seeping under one of the doors. Carefully he tried the push plate and the door swung open.

It was a locker room, with lockers along one wall, some benches in the center, and several shower cubicles along the other wall. Geek picked up a towel and wiped off his weapon, then tried to wipe his own secretions from his hands and clothes. Finding it impossible, he looked at one of the shower cubicles. Tentatively he tested the water for both pressure and temperature. Turning the water on full, he stepped into the shower.

The hanging basket of moss in the corner sensed the presence of someone in the room, and the video camera confirmed that it was one of the intruders. In the pond the plants began to move in a rhythmic Coriolis pattern, the soft ripples being detected by the computer, which immediately closed all drains and locked the shower valves *on*.

It was fully two minutes before Geek realized that the water level in the cabinet was halfway to his knees. After trying in vain to shut off the water, he tried to force the door open, to smash its translucent panel, but to no avail. As the hot water rose higher, Geek was seized with panic and his hair excreted even more of the oily amber liquid. He tried to scream, but his mouth filled with water, drowning out any sound.

Haan and Yrbetta were too pragmatic to worry about locked doors. A solid boot on the push plate usually did the trick—not that there was anything worth taking in this part of the ship. These were the transport quarters, used during the last war to ferry officers to the front-line action. They hadn't been used in a year, and all were empty.

As the two Gections rounded the corner, they came face-to-face with a treasure well beyond their limited imaginations. There, growing on the wall in a big silver tank, was mint, the rarest psychedelic-aphrodisiac they had ever known. Back on their home planet, that much mint would be worth enough to establish a family for five, maybe six generations. Even allowing for excessive personal use, they were set for life.

Dropping their rifles, the two of them began to scoop great handfuls of the mint out of the tank and stuff it into their packs, pausing occasionally to put a wad in their mouths and chew like mad. Soon the frenzied activity began to slow down as the Gections came under the influence of the drug. As the aphrodisiac took effect, they began to weave and sway, slowly making their way to the nearest door. Yrbetta began to pull off his clothes as Haan tried to open the door, and succeeded.

Like the transport quarters, the airlock on that level hadn't been used since they had carried that last big batch of Fleet officers at the end of the Khalian wars. But the computer, acting on instructions from Veg-o-matic down in the pond, had no trouble overriding the safety circuit. Haan and Yrbetta, locked in a drug-crazed embrace, were sucked out into space, along with a dubious fortune in mint leaves.

It had taken forty minutes, and Ellis and his remaining men had barely moved one hundred meters down the corridor. Ellis was fuming, and his eye was burning like the coals of hell.

"That's it!" he shouted. "This ain't right. How many raids have we been on? Fifteen, twenty? And did we ever board a ship that's as tight as this one? No. And you know why? Because this isn't a ship, it's a trap. Come on, we're going back to the sled."

They had come to the first bulkhead hatch, and Ellis had already ducked through it, when the current hit the men behind him.

At first they only felt a tingling sensation in their legs. But as the current built in power and amperage, the tingling turned to pain and the men started to scream, stuck to the deck and unable to escape. As it reached full power, the men were slowly incinerated before Ellis's glassy-eyed stare. He gaped at the charred corpses and fought back the bile that was rising in the back of his throat. Then, dropping his weapon, he turned and ran back toward the pocket rocket.

He pulled up short and ducked for cover as he reemerged on the flight deck, for Talley and Huntley were standing over the inert form of his Khalian pilot. The Weasel's tail was pointing stiffly overhead, and the end was badly charred.

Talley touched the Khalian with the point of his sword. "So tell me again what happened," he said. His voice was incredulous.

"Well," began Huntley, "I was working my way up alongside the hangar so that I could try to sneak in to the sled here, when this one comes out and walks around to the front of his ship and starts to relieve himself." Huntley was trying hard not to laugh. "Suddenly there's this big blue flash, and everything smells of singed cat hair. Must've shorted a wire or something."

Talley nodded. "Yeah, it must have been something, all right. Okay, get a tug and drive it over here. We've got to get this sled turned around."

Stunned, Ellis moved around to the other side of the deck and quietly climbed up to the airlock, slipping through the door and heading forward to the side cargo decks. The lift panel on the freight elevator indicated that the car was parked on the fourteenth cargo level. Playing a hunch, Ellis punched the call button and, when the elevator arrived, entered and sent it back down to level 14. On the ride down, he turned out the lights and reached into his boot for the thick-bladed knife that he always carried. When the car finally stopped, he was crouching low, ready to spring if anyone tried to enter the car.

The door opened to an empty corridor of the freight docks. Carefully Ellis stepped out of the elevator and surveyed his surroundings. If there was anyone here, they could be hiding anywhere. The best thing to do would be to look for obvious hiding places—the sort someone might run to, if in a panic. That meant straight ahead.

Quietly Ellis moved down the aisle between the rows of carefully stacked freight. Twice he paused, straining to catch even the slightest sound, but there was nothing except for the emptiness of the room.

As he moved farther along the corridor he felt his foot slip just a bit as he brought his full weight onto it. He glanced down and saw several large splashes of hydroponic fluid crossing the space between the two rows of freight. Looking more closely with his one remaining eye, he spotted the violets hanging in the basket next to the bulkhead. He put his hand into the basket and it came away wet. He turned and looked at the freight opposite the flowers.

Surveying the military field toilets, Ellis had to admit that they provided excellent cover and concealment. Shame about leaving the tracks though. Could have just as easily put up a neon sign. Standing outside Purvis's hideout, he considered his next move, finally bending close to tap softly. Inside, he felt rather than heard someone move.

"It's okay to come out now," he whispered, smiling. "It's over."

Inside, Purvis wasn't taking any chances. She remained motionless and said nothing.

"Come on, open up," the same voice again. "It's all right."

Purvis slowly let out her breath. The voice didn't belong to the skipper or any of the crew that had been left behind. That meant it had to belong to one of the raiders. And since the voice was reasoned, then it probably belonged to the Syndicate rep. In any event, the owner of the voice knew where she was, and if he wanted to be nasty—well the odds were in his favor, to a point. Gripping the scalpel tightly behind her, Purvis unlocked the door.

The door slowly started to open but then stopped.

"Wait. I think I hear someone coming."

Instinctively Purvis opened the door. "Quick, get in . . ."

Ellis needed no second invitation. Before Purvis could react, he was in the booth with her, one hand over her mouth, the other stabbing repeatedly into her abdomen.

With a look of wide-eyed innocence, Dr. Edna Purvis died almost before she realized that she had betrayed herself. The Syndicate spy slumped to the floor next to the violets that had been crushed during her last, brief struggle. Unseen, a video monitor in the far corner focused on the broken flowers.

Ellis reached out and closed the door of the field toilet, locking it behind him as he did. As he was looking at Purvis's body, contemplating his next move, he did not hear the silent hum of the electric gantry as it stopped above him.

Operated by a computer deep within the ship, two strong hydraulic arms descended from the machine and clamped tightly to the sides of the field toilet. Lifting the toilet clear of the ground, the gantry then hummed across the ceiling and moved to the far forward end of the ship. Inside, Ellis felt the movement and beat frantically on the door, but it was held closed by the unit's pincerlike grip.

Finally, the gantry had the high-tech outhouse in just the right position, not five meters from the barrel of an ARP Gatling gun. Capable of firing one hundred rounds per second, it too was a holdover from the last days of the Khalian wars, installed as a last-ditch measure to prevent boarders from entering the ship by the forward cargo hatch. Slowly the cargo doors behind the field toilet opened, and for an instant Ellis, trapped inside, could feel the pressure drop.

Then the ARP opened up.

What sound could be heard in the thinning air sounded like ripping sailcloth as the three-second burst pulped the sanitary sanctuary and everything that was in it. With mercifully uncanny accuracy, the first round smashed through Ellis's skull, just inches from where his missing eye had been. He never knew what hit him.

On the hangar deck Huntley had managed to turn the sled, and had the pocket rocket pointing at the hangar doors.

"Okay," said Talley, "get into the control tower and open the doors. I'll see how this puppy flies."

Huntley trotted off to the control tower, tipped the lever, and opened the hangar doors. Below him on the flight deck, he saw the thrusters on the pocket rocket ignite, and Talley shot gracefully out the door.

Inside the Syndicate raider, its pilot watched as the sled came up closer and, at the last moment, flipped over on its back to dock with the larger ship. A moment later he felt the gentle bump of the pocket rocket sliding into the hangar bay of the ship. He settled down to a quick preflight check, and didn't pay any attention to the man approaching from behind until he felt the sword prick the back of his neck.

He turned slightly, but the voice caused him to freeze where he was.

"Don't even think about it. Just put this ship down in the hold of my transporter." Talley added, almost as an after-thought, "I'd try for a very smooth landing if I were you."

Once the hangar-deck doors were closed and the deck pressurized, Huntley met Talley at the hatch of the Syndicate raider. The pilot was the first out, and stood by quietly as Talley crawled out the hatch behind him. He said nothing to either man, but rather waited for them to make the next move. Talley lost no time in making that move.

As soon as his feet hit the deck, Talley had his prisoner flat on his face on the ground. Using a nylon strap, he ziplocked the man's hands behind his back, then dragged him upright and shoved him toward Huntley.

"Lock him in one of the cabins. I'll want to talk to him before Fleet gets their hands on him."

An hour later Talley had discovered the remains of most of the pirates. He had also begun to develop a grudging respect for the Veg-o-matic and her unusual control system.

In the kitchen, Chief Commissary Officer Ruel was pouring Lieutenant Bermann a cup of coffee as Talley came in through the main companionway door. As he pushed the door open, he tripped the deadfall that Thelma had so carefully constructed. Before he could be warned, it was too late, and several hundred kilos of slightly thawed broccoli and dehydrated eggs came cascading down.

Talley hit the floor like he'd been pole-axed, sliding across the galley and coming to rest at the feet of the galley slave. Everything went hazy, and Talley found himself back in the dream where he was a cadet, and Thelma Ruel kept trying to force her attentions on him.

He didn't return to full consciousness for almost an entire day. When he did, the first thing he saw was the cook as she held out a spoonful of soup. In it floated large chunks of green and white.

"Eat," she encouraged him. "Vegetables can be good for you."

Talley found it hard to argue.

INTERLUDE

Articles of War
Article XII
Every Person, not otherwise subject to this Act, who, being on board any ship, shall endeavor to seduce from his Duty or Allegiance any Person subject to this Act, shall so far as respects such Offence be deemed to be a Person subject to this Act, and shall suffer Death or such other Punishment as is herein-after mentioned.

Article VIII
Every Person subject to this Act who shall, without any treacherous intention, hold any improper Communication with the Enemy, shall be dismissed with Disgrace, or shall suffer such other Punishment as is herein-after mentioned.

Admiral "Dynamite" Duane bent over a display of space within ten light-years of the Khalian/Target system. They were coming. Scoutships had hovered at the fringes of the Syndicate fleet for almost a year. The attrition rate among these observers had been over eighty percent. But their vigilance had paid off. A tachyon transmission from an approaching scout had brought the warning that the entire enemy fleet had jumped up to FTL and was less than a day behind it.

This left Duane with a decision he had been dreading for months. The glowing yellow blips representing Khalia and Target were inches apart in his tank. These two planets were the only places worth defending, or attacking, for a hundred light-years. They were also so close that until the Syndicate fleet dropped back into normal space, there was no way to determine which was its objective.

Both worlds were vital to any future Alliance effort to carry the war to the worlds of the Families. Target contained the largest spaceport outside of the home port of the Fleet itself circling Tau Ceti. It contained repair facilities capable of servicing a hundred ships and refining and storage capacity greater than those on Regulus IV. And the Syndicate's leaders had to be aware of this. They had built the port to support their then Khalian allies.

Six hours' flight time away from Target sat Khalia. On that planet sat half a billion "Weasels," once the pawns of the Syndicate and now sworn to serve the Alliance with equal fervor (an enthusiasm about which Duane was more than a little skeptical). Also on Khalia were dozens of automated small-arms factories capable of producing an impressive array of deadly Weasel- or man-carried weapons. Khalia's manpower and resources made it fully as valuable as the facilities on the much more thinly populated Target.

A space battle is often a game of numbers. Like every other major battle, victory went to those who fought the best with the most. Intelligence estimated that the Syndicate's fleet at least equaled that which Duane now commanded. That had *at least* in part given the prematurely graying admiral many sleepless nights. Duane simply could not afford to defend both planets. While they were too close to allow him to determine which the enemy would strike at, they were too far for any ships assigned to one to support the other. The two Khalian worlds were six hours' flying time apart. It was unusual for a space battle to last more than two. With virtually no basis to make it, he had less than twelve hours to decide which world to defend. If he guessed right, they would have their battle. If he was wrong, the undefended world would be a charred cinder by the time they could correct the mistake.

Staring at the tank, Duane hoped for a miracle. Trying by sheer force of desire to have a letter appear like on the temple wall in Babylon. "Mene, men defend Target, or may Khalia," he visualized them. Neither seemed correct, neither seemed wrong. Ready to act, Duane hesitated. He was still staring into the tank three hours later when he got his answer. Though from a source far less angelic than he had expected.

NO QUARTER
by Janny Wurts

THE LASER HIT burned through the *Kildare*'s shields and vaporized the aft attitude jets in an instantaneous burst of explosion. The ejection of debris and gaseous propellant created recoil that the damaged system failed to counter.

On the bridge, in the act of rising to visit the head, Commander Jensen was spun sideways into the com console. The impact left more than a bruise. Over the stabbing pain of cracked ribs, and through the high-pitched, excited curse from the pilot on helm duty, the officer assigned charge of the *Kildare* strove against a mind-whirling onrush of vertigo to muster the necessary attitude of command.

"Damages?" he gasped on an intake of air that was all he could manage, being winded.

Across a narrow aisle banked on either side with instrumentation, the ensign still strapped in his seat recovered from surprise. "Aft attitude thruster's gone, sir, portside. Also the rear screen sensor. Burnt clear out. Hull's intact, but we'll need the engineer's report to know if it's stable."

That explained the horrible dizziness: inertia, not pain. The *Kildare* tumbled from the hit, her guidance units unable to compensate with one quarter of the system blown out. Left gray and disoriented from his own hurts, Jensen fought the buck of the deck and crashed back into his command chair. "Find out if she's stable," he rapped out in reference to the hull. Then he glanced across the gloom of the V-shaped control bridge toward the silhouette of his still-swearing pilot. "Get this hulk back under control, fast."

The pilot, the fair-haired son of somebody's father in the Admiralty, was nowhere near as good as the rating sewn onto the starched sleeve of his coverall. Neat to the point of fussiness he might be, but his hands were slow, and his touch, far from unerring. Trembling, he fumbled the controls.

Whiplashed by a second round of inertial force all the more aggravating for being unnecessary, Jensen shut his eyes in forbearance. The last pilot he'd been assigned had been a sloppy son of a bitch when it came to appearance; but he could by God fly. *Kildare* rolled, bucketed, lurched, and finally wobbled out of her tumble.

By then the young ensign had recovered his curiosity enough to voice the obvious. "Damn, Commander, who would be firing on us out here?"

Jensen ignored the question until after he had queried his one competent bridge officer, a wary middle-aged woman named Beckett who'd been born without the instincts of motherhood. "Gun crews intact, sir, and your engineer gives the drive systems a tentative okay," she answered in her husky baritone. The sandy hair pulled back from her forehead emphasized bushy eyebrows, and square, oversize front teeth. If homely appearance had stifled her social life, Beckett poured her frustration into her work. She'd already confirmed the engineer's next check. "Dak's testing the coil regulator for signal overload, but adds it's an outside possibility."

The laser hit must have grazed them, Jensen determined, and concluded further that if their shields had been breached, the attack weapon was more powerful than any small vessel should pack. Still, reassured that the main drive systems of his vessel apparently remained intact, Commander Jensen stared across an undecorated expanse of grate flooring to the junior ensign who had questioned inopportunely; a boy so fresh from his Academy training that he still wore his *hat* on the bridge; hunched in earnest over his board, the kid had a clear, pudgy complexion that ran to acne, and ears that stuck out from under spikes of silvery fair hair. He was currently gazing, rapt, at the image of drifting fragments on the main analog screen.

"I thought I asked you to check on the status of our hull?" Jensen snapped, pained by more than his ribs. He resisted an impulse to blot sweat from his brow, then silently pondered the selfsame issue. His ship was a converted yacht, a rich man's toy hastily revamped for Fleet service in the face of threat from the Syndicate. She was armed more for scout duty than defense; and with her untried crew and recently promoted senior officer, Admiral Duane had stationed her as far from any probable site of action as possible. Why *had* the *Kildare* been fired upon? And by whom, when they were just a patrol sent out for observation, in case the battle that currently centered around Target proved to be a feint?

"Beckett," Jensen said belatedly, "initiate a scan."

The communications officer nodded her leathery face, eyes underlit by the scatter of lights on her board. She did not belabor the point that she had done so, long since, but the blown aft sensors left her blind to near half of the analog grid.

On the bridge of the *Marity*, by appearance a hard-run merchanter, and by trade a skip-runner ship, a bearish, blunt-featured man scratched at the mat of chest hair through the opened neck of his coverall. The flight deck of his vessel was too cramped with instrumentation for a man of his size to stretch. This did not seem to trouble him as he turned deceptively lazy eyes to the mate who worked the console beside him. "They found us yet?"

Slender, elegant as an antique rapier, *Marity*'s mate, Gibsen, turned his head with a half-raised brow. Framed by a vista of illegal electronics and signal lights of alien design, he said, "No. And their pilot's a kid who can't fly."

In the half gloom of *Marity*'s flight deck, MacKenzie James didn't speak. On the graying side of thirty-five and muscled like a wild beast, he made no move. But the corner of his mouth that lifted toward a smirk said "incompetent" more plainly than words. His scarred hands stopped their scratching, and his gravelly, basso voice phrased orders with a sparseness that hinted at exasperation. "Forget subtlety. Show them."

As if blowing the hell out of the ass end of any Fleet ship hadn't been questionably unsubtle, Gibsen set tapered fingers to the controls and tweaked.

The *Marity* changed position.

Which meant Beckett, bent yet over a console set for a fine-screen search, suddenly got an eyeful of side vanes and struts where a second ago her instruments had shown emptiness. The impossible happened. She got flapped, screeched a startled oath, and jerked back before she thought to step down the magnification. "Dammit to hell with a hangover!" she repeated, sounding more like her gender than she ever had. "We're being messed after by a goddamn merchanter."

"What!" Jensen half sprang from his command chair, then sank back with a grunt of pain. Plagued by echoes of his own startlement reflected back at him by bare, metallic bulkheads, he went suddenly cold to the core. The only "merchanter" he could imagine near the site of a major battle against the Syndicate would be the *Marity*, command of the skip-runner and criminal MacKenzie James. "Get me a registry number," Jensen snapped through stabbing discomfort. "Or lacking that, scan for specs."

Beckett read back the requested information in her usual sexless voice.

"*Marity*," Jensen confirmed. And his manner held an edge that his crew had never known.

On the dimly lit bridge of the *Marity*, the mate Gibsen raised baleful hazel eyes to his captain. "Mac, they aren't minded to be sportsmen, this morning. The portside plasma turret is rotating our way."

"Beats hell out of being overlooked," Mac James said laconically. "Now give 'em something to chase."

Gibsen's narrow features lit in a grin, red-tinged by the lights of his console. "Lead them on by the nose, you mean." His delight did not fade through the split-second interval as he played his controls with a touch his Fleet counterpart aboard *Kildare* would have sworn on his scrotum was wizardry.

Beckett patently refused the belief that the *Marity* was anything other than a hard-used private hauler; she argued loudly up to the point when her screens displayed a maneuver that should by *Marity*'s aged specs have destroyed the integrity of her hull. Caught midsentence in denial, the com officer paused, closed her heavy jaw, then recited the formula that outlined the effects of inertia upon the *Marity*'s supposed limitations. "Bits," she finished heatedly. "We should be looking at flying bits of wreckage."

Cracked ribs prevented Jensen from rounding on her in a fury. As a result, his instructions to his pilot came out with unintentional control. "Tail her. And set our coils charging for transit to FTL. If *Marity*'s going to jump, we jump with her, or blow our coil condensers trying."

"Bloody hells, Commander, whatever for!" interjected Beckett. "We've an assigned post, and despite the provocation, I see no reason to abandon our position."

Jensen moved a foot and swiveled his chair toward her. He glared the length of the bare, functional bridge compartment. "Are you questioning my direct order?" he demanded with a rage that burned entirely inward; his face stayed deadpan, and his eyes, unflinchingly level.

Beckett's rough complexion reddened. "I question unreasonable judgment." Nonplussed, her huge hand flicked the switch that assured her words would be monitored and incorporated into the ship's official course log.

The fresh-faced ensign beyond her followed the exchange with an interest that could damn, if the issue ever came to court-martial.

Frostily stiff, Jensen said to his pilot, "Carry on, Sarchev. Follow the *Marity*."

Later, when the craft of MacKenzie James initiated FTL, the *Kildare* followed suit.

"Hooked," murmured Gibsen when the queer hesitation in human time-sense passed, and the darkness of FTL settled like a hood over both of the *Marity*'s analog screens. "Your boy commander's taken the bait."

On the adjacent chair, which had a tendency to leak its stuffing out of several haphazardly stitched rips, Mac James turned his blunt-featured face. Red-lit by the array of the *Marity*'s instruments, he showed the smile of a sated predator. He flexed his coil-scarred fingers with the method of old habit and murmured, "After the tangle we made of Jensen's plot at Chalice station, did you ever think that he wouldn't?"

Gibsen lounged back in his crew chair, his long-lashed eyes deeply thoughtful. He did not say what he felt, that the more you messed with a man's obsessions, the more dangerous he was likely to become. The corollary required no emphasis: Jensen's hatred of MacKenzie James was no longer rooted in sanity.

On the control bridge of *Kildare*, Communications Officer Beckett whacked a ham fist against her thigh. "You're crazy, and a goddamned danger to all of us."

Jensen regarded her outburst with no other reaction beyond a blink. "Question my authority one more time, and I'll see you stripped of your rank."

His total absence of passion was all that made Beckett back down. Surrounded by taut stillness that gripped the two other crew members present, she looked down and fiddled a few adjustments on her board. The next instant the chime that signaled departure from FTL sounded across silence.

"Short hop," murmured *Kildare*'s pilot, and the next instant everybody on the flight deck had their hands full.

The engineer called in to report a power failure in the main drive. "Coil leakage," he said tersely. "No way of predicting the stress crack that caused it. But FTL's a closed option until the system's been drained and patched."

Even as Jensen drew a pained breath to express his annoyance, Beckett delivered worse news: their precipitous flight after *Marity* had landed them all but on top of the leading edge of a war fleet.

"Identify," Jensen snapped back.

The greenie ensign did so, in tones surprisingly steady. "Syndicate, sir. On a projected course toward Khalia." He would have added the pertinent facts, concerning numbers of dreadnoughts and formation, but Jensen's next order prevented it.

"Where's *Marity*?"

"Sir?" Now the ensign's voice did quaver. Naively inexperienced, and fearful of questioning a senior officer, he added, "We should inform Fleet Command, sir. The skip-runner's presence is secondary to the defense of Khalia."

"Mac James's presence indicates involvement with the enemy," Jensen replied with a patience he did not feel. "Now find me *Marity*, fast, because in case you've forgotten your notes, draining the coils means we'll be without shields. We're a sitting duck right now for a trigger-happy skip-runner, and *that's* our first concern."

Almost in defiance, Beckett stabbed at her board. The analog screen flashed in response and gave back an image of scuffed paint and rust-flaked vanes, and the faded letters of a registry code that the years had weathered unintelligible. "She's off our bow," Beckett added sardonically. "Close enough to be in bed with, and right where we have no weapon to bear, and where our attitude control systems are too perfectly crippled to maneuver. That's not luck. I'd say this was a prearranged trap."

She did not belabor the point that *Kildare* was well within range to be detected by the approaching fleet. Despite the fact that she was a conversion from the private sector, *Kildare*'s weaponry specs readily identified her as a Fleet vessel. In seconds rather than minutes the *Kildare* and her crew of seven would be nothing better than a target.

The particulars of that dilemma had scarcely registered when a voice horned in through the security net that should have kept *Kildare*'s com bands shielded from outside interference.

"Commander, I'd say your survival options are limited to

one," came an intrusive drawl that made the skin on Jensen's arms roughen to gooseflesh. He knew the inflection, would recognize that grainy timbre anywhere for the voice of Mac-Kenzie James. "Unless you'd rather get slagged by a plasma charge," the skip-runner captain continued, "I'd advise that you surrender your vessel unconditionally to me."

Jensen's jaw muscles knotted. The moment held clarity like a snapshot, preserved in time by preternatural awareness of the bridge compartment, with its gray drab walls flecked with lights thrown off by the controls, and set in that dance of shadow and reflection, the faces of his officers, all staring. The pilot wore a stupid expression of surprise; the set of Beckett's outsized jaw showed cynicism; but of them all the greenie ensign was worst, with his wide-eyed, choked-back fear that implied utmost faith in his commander's ability to produce a miracle.

Feeling the stabbing ache of his ribs and a gut-deep hatred that made him shake, Jensen licked white lips. When he did not immediately speak, the voice of MacKenzie James elaborated.

"Boy, you'd better decide fast."

"Damn you," Jensen cracked back, though with no channel open Mac James could not hear.

Beckett said nothing. The ensign looked near to panic, as his awe of his superior officer became shattered before his eyes. Only *Kildare*'s pilot managed the wits to speak. "The skip-runner could be bluffing. He's got no protection, either, and the whole Syndicate fleet is bearing down."

Which was not only naive, but stupid, Jensen raged inwardly. MacKenzie James never backed himself into corners, except by clearest design. This skip-runner had sold Fleet secrets to goddamn Syndicate spies, and since he was uncannily reliable when it came to trafficking classified material out of the Alliance, the enemy dreadnoughts bearing down on Khalia were unlikely to advertise their presence merely to take out a contact likely to be useful against the Fleet. Nor would they blink at a prize ship stolen from an adversary. Wise to the ways of the skip-runner and determined to stay alive to best him, Jensen gave the only answer that left him any opening.

"I surrender the *Kildare* and all her crew to the master of

Marity, without condition." Through the heat of his own humiliation, Jensen was aware of his ensign trying desperately not to cry, and a glare of vitriolic contempt from Communications Officer Beckett.

Mac James's pilot had the hands of a monkey when it came to dismantling a control board. His narrow, sensitive fingers could reach and unhitch and disconnect circuitry behind narrow, cramped panels that by rights should have invited curses. Gibsen whistled, oblivious.

The sound set Jensen's teeth on edge, as did the quiet, deliberate voice of Mac James as he commandeered a communications console as yet unmolested by Gibsen's tinkering. It did not matter to *Kildare*'s former commander that the skip-runner, of his own volition, was following through with the duty first urged by the baby-faced ensign now bound and gagged in the back bay of the flight deck. That the message torp bearing word of the Syndicate fleet's vector toward Khalia was fired away under Commander Jensen's own codes did not matter; that Admiral Duane would receive the communication in time to give Fleet forces the edge in the coming battle to preserve the Khalian planets did not matter.

Jensen's mind centered on one thought.

MacKenzie James was a criminal. He did not act out of heroism, but only callous self-interest. If he wanted Khalia defended, that could only be because the two-faced Weasels who'd surrendered made a healthy, lucrative market for traffic in illicit weapons. Gunrunning being second only to state and military secrets on the list of Mac James's transgressions, *Marity* would be involved to her top vanes. Jensen stared at the stubble of hair that furred the crown of the skip-runner captain's head, just visible over the com station. Hatred and rage had both given way to a patience unforgiving as stone.

Tied to his own command chair, unmoved by Beckett's grunts of discomfort from the corner where she lay bound alongside *Kildare*'s ensign and pilot, Jensen waited in motionless tension like a snake coiled before prey.

Gibsen muttered a query from behind an opened cowling.

"Gun turrets next," Mac James said in drawllessly succinct

reply. "We'll want the coil regulator and the magneto banks, but leave life-support intact." The salt-and-pepper crown of hair disappeared briefly as Mac James leaned forward to toggle a switch. His next instructions to his mate were buried under a drift of garble from the com, most likely cross-chat on a Syndicate command channel.

Jensen ground his teeth.

Gibsen straightened with his hands full of circuit boards; and the foreign speech paused in an inflection that framed a question. MacKenzie James answered in the same lingo, and the response that came back was mixed with laughter.

There followed an infuriating interval while Gibsen and his skip-runner captain stripped the *Kildare* with sure, no-nonsense efficiency. Jensen found the pain of cracked ribs less intrusive than the pain of humiliation. He sat, strapped helpless on his own flight deck, unable to face away from the analog screen somebody had carelessly left operational—the screen that showed the passage of the Syndicate fleet bound to attack the planet Khalia, dreadnoughts and their fighters arrayed in formation like some grand, silent procession.

A few of the behemoths winked their running lights in salute of the *Marity* and her latest act of sabotage against the Fleet.

Blackly murderous, Jensen chafed at the lashing on his wrists. He considered a thousand ways to kill the skip-runner captain MacKenzie James, all of them lingeringly bloody.

The Syndicate fleet departed, leaving the black of space on the analog screen. Hours passed. Jensen's hands were numb. His full bladder became a torment. His wrists stung and his shoulders ached, and his ears had long since stopped hearing the thump and bump, and the hiss of flushed air from the lock belowdecks as the *Kildare*'s heavier components were off-loaded to the hold on board *Marity*. The tap of footsteps coming and going ceased, replaced by one incongruously light tread recognizable as that of MacKenzie James.

At the entry to the bridge he paused, and called instructions to his mate and pilot. "Go back to *Marity* and power up the coils. Syndicate's about reached Khalia by now, and when they find Duane there to give a hot welcome, I want to be gone from this system."

Gibsen said something that rang with cheerful sarcasm.

Then MacKenzie James strode across the metal floor plates, rounded the central bulkhead that divided the rear half of the bridge into two compartments, and ended by looking down at the commander still strapped to the central crew chair. He studied Jensen with an intensity that unnerved. For once, Mac's coil-scarred hands were still. A faded, much creased coverall covered his muscled shoulders, the cuffs unhooked and turned back where they'd bound at sinewed wrists through the hours of hanging in the wreckage waiting to spring the trap. Although the only one of *Kildare*'s original crew without a gag, Jensen waited for the skip-runner to speak first.

"Boy, the message torp giving the Syndicate war fleet's vector to Khalia went out under your codes. For that, your brass might overlook the fact that you were careless enough to get your ship boarded and stripped. If you've got the guts and the glibness to lay your story right."

Jensen regarded the captain he reviled with every fiber of his being. His career standing did not trouble him. That concern would arise later. Now, only one question burned to be answered. Staring into an expression like chipped granite, Jensen asked, "Why should you send that message torp? You're not a man who does favors on principle."

Mac James gave back a rogue's grin that harbored little humor. "Who else could have done the job and been ignored through the passage of the entire Syndicate attack fleet?"

Unsatisfied, Jensen said nothing.

The coil-scarred fingers flexed, one by one in succession with the familiarity of long-established habit. Mac James qualified on a note of dubious sincerity. "Say I didn't want Khalia scragged."

"Did it have to do with your market for illicit weapons?" Jensen demanded, burningly fierce.

The most-wanted skip-runner captain in space awarded his adversary a half shrug of dismissal. "You have one outstanding asset, boy. Your thinking is simplistically accurate."

Since the comment was the last that Jensen might have anticipated, he was left without ready rejoinder.

Untouchable, untraceable, and infuriatingly confident, Mac-

Kenzie James turned on his heel. He stepped off the stripped bridge of the *Kildare* and departed through the lock for his transfer back to *Marity*. Moments later the same accursed analog screen showed the skip-runner ship's departure.

Yet the last word came over the com channel the captain had deliberately left open.

"You have no propulsion system, no firepower, and no communication or navigational equipment left aboard," observed the blunt tones of Mac James. "However, in the aft console where message torps are stored, you'll find one Gibsen left behind. That should be sufficient to see you rescued, when the fight winds down over Khalia." A moment later the skip-runner captain added an afterthought: "Oh, yes, and your engineer, is it Officer Dax? He's locked in the emergency escape capsule. You'll want to let him out. Apparently he pissed off my mate some, and the air supply in the capsule was left off. . . ."

It was Cael, one of the laser crew, who worked out of his bonds first. Lanky, sallow, and looking as if he'd worn the same coverall for a week, he arrived on the bridge in an excited gush of talk. "Can't find Dax," he said breathlessly as he cut Jensen's hands free. "Damned skip-runner must've abducted him, or killed him, or something, because he's not in any of the compartments. Jesus, you should see what's happened down there. Ship's got no guts left, I swear. Stripped down to her coils, which leak, and are useless anyway."

"Cael," said Jensen, standing stiffly due to discomfort and an icy vista of fury. "Kindly be silent and cut your fellow officers free."

The next thing Cael chose to cut was Beckett's gag, which from Jensen's point of view was a mistake. She never did keep her mouth shut.

"You won't get away with this, Commander," she said, between hawking sour spittle from her throat. "That message torp to Fleet won't bring you farts for a citation, because I'm going to see you burn. You surrendered a Fleet vessel to a goddamned *skip-runner*, saw her stripped to her pins without a fight, and now you think to profit by it? Guess again."

Slapped awake from his obsessive desire to see MacKenzie James dead and rotting, Jensen simply stared at her. He did not notice the looks given him by the ensign, nor the baffled curiosity of the gunman who paused in his ministrations to the pilot. In a tone of velvet quiet, the commander said, "Carry on with your duties. I'm going down to free Dax."

Jensen strode coolly from *Kildare*'s bridge. From the moment he rounded the bulkhead, his crew burst into excited talk, but he did not hear. Sprinting full tilt for the access hatch to the lower level, he thought only upon how to save his career. Beckett was an unanticipated problem. Damn her for having no ambition whatsoever. Damn her for being a stickler for protocol. Old for her post, she'd probably never been promoted because the officers she'd served under hated her.

But deep down, Jensen knew that Beckett was only a fraction of the problem. Even if the other five members of the crew went along with a falsified story, how long before that greenie ensign or that all-thumbs pilot talked over their beer?

Involved in furious thought, Jensen hurried on.

Around the bend, past the gutted remains of the drive compartment, Jensen nearly collided with the other member of his gun crew. "Rogers," he said, trying not to wince at the stab of pain from his cracked ribs. "The rest of the crew are on the bridge. Join them and wait for my return."

"Aye, sir," said Rogers, his corpulent, ruddy features showing no curiosity at all. Cael often said he only came alive under his headset, with a live target in front of him.

Just then, Jensen was grateful for one crewman who was content with a stolid outlook. He ducked down a side corridor that narrowed into a tube. The light panels were out, lending a gray, echoing ghostliness to a downward plunge into dark. *Kildare*'s conversion had been too hasty for aesthetics; her gratings were blessedly bare. Jensen found the access panel by feel and tapped out the security code. A panel hissed open. Striped black and yellow, and glinting with reflective tape, the last remaining message torp rested untouched in its cradle, exactly as MacKenzie James had said.

Jensen lifted it out, grunting at the pain as cracked ribs protested the exertion. He hefted the capsule to his sound side, but found the effort a waste. The strain on the muscles called on to hold his body erect against the off-balancing weight hurt him just as much.

Breathing with all the tenderness he could manage and hating the fact his eyes watered from the effort, Jensen inched his way back down the access tube. He'd have to cross the main bay, which was probably unlighted, and that was the moment he'd be vulnerable if any of his crew chanced to stray from the flight deck.

The lights proved to be on, which was infinitely worse; Jensen felt exposed as he crossed the open expanse. His hands shook, and his fingers left sweaty prints on the reflective strips of the message torp. He pressed on, toward the shadowed alcove with its reflective emergency emblem.

The escape ejection capsule's lock cracked open with a faint hiss and an escape of stale air. Grunting despite his best effort as he ducked, Jensen pushed his way inside, the message torp tucked across his knees. He elbowed the plate that would light the interior, and saw what looked like a bundle of rags in one corner. The seeping red stains in the cloth belied that assessment.

Jensen set down the torp, shifted, and light from the overhead flooded over his shoulder to reveal the engineer, Dak, bound, gagged, and rolled up in a shivering ball. The knuckles visible through the strapping on his hands and wrists were grazed, and he had a gash on one knee, an elbow, and the curve of one acne-dotted cheek. His eyes, which were blue and bugged out, swiveled in surprise at the sight of his commander. He moaned something that had the ring of obscenity into his gag and thrashed determinedly at his bonds.

Preternaturally aware of the access hatch gapped open at his back, Jensen whispered urgently for silence.

"Hostiles are still aboard," he lied as he stooped over the battered engineer. He began with the wrist bonds and whispered into the ear that poked over the edge of the gag. "We're in very deep trouble."

Dak flexed his freed hands and gave Jensen a wide-eyed

look of sarcasm. His first words, as his gag came loose, were "No kidding."

Jensen let some of the anger he felt toward MacKenzie James leak into his voice. "Crew's all dead. Without quarter."

That shut Dak up, fast. Sealed in the escape capsule, he'd had no clue as to what had befallen. He stared in shocked horror as his senior officer continued.

"They spared me so they could pump me for security codes and information," Jensen fabricated. He paused, made a show of staring at his hands, which were abraded and raw from his constant twisting at the ties that lashed him to the crew chair. "I talked some, mostly as a ploy. The skip-runners thought I was scared and didn't view me as a threat. They tied me less carefully than they might have, and I managed to work free." Now Jensen raised his eyes and stared ingenuously at his engineer. "We need to blow the ship," he confided. "Take out those skip-runners before they have a chance to use my codes against the Fleet, or to make off with *Kildare* as a prize."

"They were going to leave me to suffocate!" Dak burst out in a fury.

Nervelessly, Jensen played along. "No doubt." He allowed a moment for the unpleasantness of that concept to register, then gently prodded for what he wanted. "I need you, Dak. We're stripped of all energy sources but that cracked coil unit, and somehow we need to destroy *Kildare*."

Dak's face grew thoughtful, almost boyish as he considered the problem. "Shouldn't be too difficult," he surmised, his knobby fingers tapping his agitation. "The crack's making the unit unstable anyway. All we need to do is play a current through it. Should create a critical imbalance on short order." He ruminated for a moment, chewing his lip. "Trouble is, once I start the sequence, there won't be any fail-safe. *Kildare* will explode, and nothing we do could stop the process."

"You'd rather die at the hands of the skip-runners?" Jensen said brutally.

Dak shrugged. "Rather not die at all, truth to tell. But I guess this is our best chance."

Jensen settled back with a show of relief that was not entirely feigned. "I'll see you commended in my report, for courageous duty to the Fleet."

For a moment Dak looked wistful. "My mom would appreciate that. If we ever get through this alive."

Jensen nodded. As his back settled against the console of the escape capsule, he made a point of wincing over his cracked ribs. "I've brought a message torp," he said thinly. "When you get back from sabotaging the coils, we'll launch the capsule without engines. If we're lucky, drift will carry us clear before the skip-runner notices. When we know we're away, the torp will call in a rescue."

At the crucial moment Dak's childish face looked uncertain. "I hate to go out," he allowed. He dabbed at the gash on his knee and made a face. "That damned skip-runner's mate fights dirty."

Cloaked in the icy air of command, Jensen held back a sigh. "I won't remind you of the need to keep out of sight."

"I don't ever wake up their husbands," Dak admonished dryly. "Be sure of it, I'll be *damned* quiet." He folded his awkward assortment of limbs, slipped past, and sauntered off into the main bay with his lips curled in a nervous grimace.

Left alone in the stuffy confines of the capsule, Jensen readied the panel for takeoff. Mac James had left all the systems operational, which was well, for he had no intention of leaving the *Kildare* by drift. He'd go under power, and fast as he could manage, and he'd watch his command blow from space. That his crew were to die without quarter caused his hands to shake only slightly.

He'd weighed his options and decided without regret. The ghosts of a greenie ensign, and that dried-up bitch Beckett, a gun crew, and an incompetent pilot would not haunt him half so much as a career despoiled by court-martial.

That Dak had to be duped was a pity. The kid was a gifted engineer. . . .

In a cubicle office of Special Services, a thin man with a dry complexion thumbed through the report. The lines that described Jensen's story were straightforward enough—that *Kildare* had been commandeered by the skip-runner MacKenzie

James, her crew murdered without quarter, and only her commander kept alive, for purposes of interrogation. With his vessel taken in tow to rendezvous with the Syndicate fleet, Commander Jensen had contrived escape, fired off the warning message torp to Admiral Duane's fleet, then arranged to scuttle *Kildare*. He had been rescued from his escape capsule, forty-eight hours after the battle off Khalia, in battered condition with several cracked ribs.

Cloth rustled as a short man seated in the corner shifted his weight. "The boy's lying outright. Mac James never kills unnecessarily."

The thin man's silence offered agreement. He thumbed the corner of the report for a moment before shuffling the pages straight.

The short man felt moved to clarify. "The security codes on the warning torp were Jensen's, but Mac James's personal cipher was appended. I say he's still alive, and that Commander Jensen destroyed his ship to hide evidence detrimental to himself."

The thin man stirred at last. "MacKenzie James is undoubtedly still alive. But the promotion to captain that's coming to Jensen cannot be stopped without blowing Mac's cover. With the Syndicate families being the threat that they are, I'm reluctant to call down a public hero. The people need the morale boost. And Mac's far too valuable a contact to waste just to bring a murderer to trial."

"Let it pass, then?" the short man concluded.

"No." The word held the hardness of nails. "Give Jensen a file in our records. He might prove useful someday."

INTERLUDE

Articles of War
Article IX
Every Person subject to this Act who shall desert his
Post or sleep upon his Watch, or negligently perform
the Duty imposed upon him, shall be dismissed from
Service, with Disgrace, or shall suffer such other Pun-
ishment as is herein-after mentioned.

The Fleet dreadnought was the queen of space. Larger,
better shielded, and bristling with weapons, they were also
incredibly expensive. Manned by a crew of over five thousand,
the dreadnought took five years to complete. It was estimated
that each of the Fleet's ten dreadnoughts had required resources
greater than the total Planetary Economic Value that was
generated annually by almost a third of the Alliance's member
planets.

The Syndicate battle plan was simple. The Fleish family
fleet, consisting of a single dreadnought and its escorts, would
feint at Target approximately six hours before the actual attack

on Khalia. By committing one of their own dreadnoughts to the feint, they hoped to panic the defenders into calling for assistance. Then when Duane's fleet was at its farthest point from Khalia, their main body would strike.

If the feint didn't work, then the Fleish ships were to eliminate any defenders and return to join the main battle as soon as was possible. They would then form a hammer that would slam the Fleet formation against the anvil of the combined Family fleets. In this way the Syndicate would have a decisive advantage whatever option Duane chose.

That was the plan, which axiomatically never survives the start of the battle. It didn't.

PAWNS
by Mike Resnick

THERE WERE THREE of them aboard the assault boat.

The commander was the oldest and most experienced. He would be twenty-three next month. Some weeks earlier he had decided to grow a mustache so that he would look more mature, but all it really did was give him the appearance of a baby-faced young man with a dirty upper lip. He had a girl back home—a bona fide childhood sweetheart—and he spent most of his spare time writing long letters to her. He loved baseball, knew there was no better cook in the world than his mother, and hoped to take over his father's farm after the war was over.

The pilot had a sneaking fondness for the commander, despite what he believed to be the senior officer's naiveté. The pilot was in for the long haul, and from what he had seen, it was going to be a very long haul indeed. He didn't carry much emotional baggage, and he was too cynical by half, and he didn't have all that much confidence in Dynamite Duane—or in anyone else except himself, for that matter—but he was a damned good pilot, and he knew it. He spent most of his spare time studying military tactics, against the day that he might command a ship of his own, and the rest of it he spent playing dozens of ongoing chess games by radio against other friends in the Fleet.

The engineer didn't talk much, and thought less. He had spent most of his adolescence keeping one step ahead of the Khalia as they devastated one planet after another, and it had made a deep impression on him. The Fleet could fight the Syndicate or anyone else it chose; he knew who *his* enemy was.

The assault boat was in formation near Target, as it had been since the first minor attack almost two hours ago, when the order came through:

Hold your ground.

"What ground?" muttered the pilot. "We're twenty thousand miles off the surface, or hasn't anyone noticed?"

"Be quiet," said the commander, concentrating on an incoming message emanating from his ear implant. He frowned. "The Syndicate just showed up."

"Who were you expecting?" said the pilot sardonically.

"See if you can get them on the screen," said the commander.

The screen hummed to life, and the three men quickly studied it.

"Seven cruisers," said the commander. "Not much of a force."

"Pawn to King Four," said the pilot. "It's early in the game yet."

"Still, I wonder where the rest of them are," mused the commander.

"Probably heading for Khalia," offered the engineer. "As far as I'm concerned, we ought to pull back and let 'em have it."

"It's a possibility," conceded the commander. "We can't defend both worlds. If I was going to let the Syndicate blow one to pieces, it would be Khalia."

"I hate to break up this lovely idyll," said the pilot, "but the other side has just brought its queen into play."

"What are you talking about?" asked the engineer.

"A dreadnought just joined the cruisers."

"It's a feint," said the engineer confidently.

"You'd sure as hell better hope so," said the commander. "I'd hate to go up against a dreadnought with an assault boat. It'd be like attacking an elephant with a gnat."

"I don't know," said the pilot dubiously. "You don't risk that valuable a piece this early in the game."

"May I remind you that this is a war, not a game?" said the commander.

The pilot shrugged. "All wars are games, and all games are wars."

"Duane knows what's going on," offered the engineer. "If we can see them, he can see them, too."

"I wonder where he is?" said the commander.

"Probably doesn't want to move too soon and frighten them off," said the engineer. "He's probably got the whole Fleet in attack mode, and he's just waiting for the rest of the Syndicate's dreadnoughts to show up."

"The rest of them?" repeated the pilot. "If he doesn't show up pretty soon, one's all they'll need. We're a bunch of very expendable pawns facing one hell of a queen."

"Relax," said the engineer. "No one's going to let us die so they can defend *Khalia*." He practically spat the word out.

"It must be a comfort," murmured the pilot.

"What must be?"

"Having the absolute, unimpeachable knowledge that you're right."

"It keeps me warm on cold nights," agreed the engineer with a boyish smile.

"Keep it down," said the commander. "New orders are coming through."

"See?" said the engineer triumphantly. "Now we'll beat a quick retreat and the bulk of the Fleet will move in."

"Pawns can't move backward," said the pilot grimly.

"Shh!" The commander placed a finger to his lips.

He lowered his head and closed his eyes, concentrating intently for almost thirty seconds. Then he looked up.

"What's our new course?" asked the pilot.

The commander frowned. "There isn't one."

"What are you talking about?"

"When the dreadnought appeared, we torped Duane and asked for clarification of our orders." He paused, puzzled. "He told us to hold our formation."

"Don't retreat *or* attack?" queried the pilot.

"That's right."

"See?" said the engineer. "It's *got* to be a feint! He'd never leave us here like sitting ducks if there was any chance that we'd be under attack from a dreadnought." He nodded, as if confirming his initial reaction. "The Syndicate's got no more use for Khalia than we do."

The commander turned to him. "Do you realize what you're saying?"

"Sure," answered the engineer. "It's a feint, and the Syndicate is going after Khalia."

The commander shook his head impatiently. "If it's a feint and Duane doesn't respond, what does that imply to you?"

"That they're going after Khalia, like I said."

"It also means that the Fleet is *defending* Khalia."

"No," said the engineer adamantly. "He's just biding his time."

"For what?" demanded the commander. "For the dreadnought to blow us apart?" He frowned again. "If he was going to defend Target, he'd be here already—or he'd at least allow us to break formation and retreat."

"You're wrong," said the engineer. "No human commander is going to waste a single life defending Khalia—not while we're out here exposed to attack. He's just waiting for the proper moment to move."

"Well, he'd better not wait too much longer," interjected the pilot. "They'll be within range in another twenty minutes."

The commander waved them to silence again as another transmission came through.

"Jesus!" he whispered. "I can't believe it!"

"What?" demanded the engineer.

"We torped for permission to retreat when the dreadnought appeared, and *again* he ordered us not to break formation." His youthful face bore a puzzled expression.

"I told you," said the pilot. "Pawns are expendable."

"I'm not a pawn!" snapped the engineer. "I'm a man, and I'm not going to let him hang us out to dry while he's defending Khalia!"

"You can't pick up your pieces and go home," said the pilot sardonically. "We *are* the pieces."

"We're facing a dreadnought in an attack boat and you keep talking about chess!" exploded the engineer. "What are we going to do?"

"We're going to hold our position and defend Target," said the commander, struggling to put a note of authority into his youthful voice.

"That's crazy!" protested the engineer. "You could peel the hull of this ship with a can opener. How can we stand up to a dreadnought?"

"We're not totally alone," the commander reminded him. "We're in a defensive formation along with the rest of the ships."

"You talk about formations and he talks about chess games!" raged the engineer. "Look at the screen! We've got a dreadnought bearing down on us!"

"Shut up!" ordered the commander.

The engineer glared at the commander, but made no reply.

The three men watched the screen for another ten minutes. Then the commander asked if there had been any change in orders, and received a negative reply.

"What in hell is he thinking of?" he mused, staring at the screen. "If we can't get reinforcements, why can't we at least get out of range?"

"If we all get out of range," answered the pilot, "five minutes from now there will be one more enemy dreadnought on its way to Khalia. Our function in this battle," he added grimly, "seems to be not only to die, but to take our time doing it."

The commander stared at him, but made no comment.

"Come on, Duane, come on, Duane!" whispered the engineer, staring at the screen.

"He's not coming," said the pilot.

"He can't be defending Khalia!" said the engineer. "He *can't* be!"

"Well, he's sure as hell not defending Target," said the pilot. "Here they come."

The commander whispered into his mini-mike, waited for an answer, and then sighed deeply.

"Well?" asked the pilot.

"Same as before," answered the commander. "We're to hold our position."

"Are we at least allowed to defend ourselves?"

"I don't see how we can hold it without returning the enemy's fire," said the commander.

"Well, we might as well pick out a cruiser," said the pilot. "We'd just be wasting our ammunition against the dreadnought. Besides," he added wryly, "there's no sense in calling attention to ourselves."

"I'll make the decisions around here, mister," said the commander.

"So now it's 'mister,' is it?" said the pilot. He saluted. "Aye-aye, sir," he said, making no effort to keep the sarcasm out of his voice. "Would the commander care to select a target?"

The commander looked at the screen again.

"A cruiser," he said lamely.

"Excellent decision, sir," said the pilot with a smug smile.

"Shut up!" snapped the commander, listening intently to his earphone. Suddenly he looked up. "Jesus! We've lost eleven assault boats already!"

Suddenly the pilot's smile vanished. "Whatever he's planning, I hope to hell he thinks it's worth it."

"He's not coming," said the engineer dully. "He's really not coming."

"Give the man a cigar," said the pilot.

"We're going to die, and he makes jokes," said the engineer.

"Quiet!" said the commander. "New orders coming through."

The other two stared at him tensely as he concentrated on the message he was receiving.

"Well?" demanded the pilot after a full minute had passed.

"It wasn't an order at all," said the commander. "Just a status report: we've destroyed one cruiser and damaged a second."

"And what have they done to us?"

"Forty-three ships dead or disabled."

"There's no way we're going to be able to protect Target, not with that kind of loss ratio," said the pilot. "Can you request permission to break formation?"

"I already did," said the commander. "The order stands: hold our position."

"It doesn't make any sense!" snapped the engineer. "Even if he's not coming to support us, why the hell can't we cut and run and regroup with the rest of the Fleet?"

"*That's* why," said the pilot, indicating the screen.

"What are you talking about?"

"There's still only one dreadnought, and only seven cruisers," explained the pilot. "This was a feint to draw Duane to Target while the Syndicate attacks Khalia in force, and he didn't buy it." He grimaced. "If it's any comfort, the history books are going to say he did the right thing."

"Who cares about the history books?" demanded the engineer bitterly. "None of us will be alive to read them."

"Probably they won't even mention this action," said the commander. "We're just a sideshow now. The real battle's probably being fought around Khalia even as we're speaking."

"Well, let's hope he's winning."

"Who gives a damn?" muttered the engineer.

"*I* do," said the pilot. "I don't know about you, but if I'm going to be a pawn, I want to know that I wasn't sacrificed for nothing." He paused. "I want to be avenged."

"I just want to live," shot back the engineer.

"You can't always have what you want," said the pilot. "Settle for making them pay for what they're going to do to us."

"Four cruisers have been disabled," announced the commander suddenly. He looked at the pilot. "Maybe we've got a chance after all."

"Disable the dreadnought and maybe I'll believe you."

"It's not impervious to firepower," said the commander with more confidence than he felt.

"It's impervious to *our* firepower."

"If enough of us can concentrate our fire on a few vital areas," suggested the commander, "if we can coordinate our attack, if the dreadnought will—"

"And if my aunt had balls, she'd be my uncle," interrupted the pilot sardonically.

The assault boat shuddered as the commander was about to answer him.

"Check our structural integrity!" he ordered the engineer.

"It seems to have been a glancing blow," announced the engineer as he read his instrument panel. "We're still airtight, and we still have power." He checked the panel again. "But our weaponry is inoperative."

"Then maybe it's finally time to get the hell out of here," suggested the pilot.

"We've got our orders," said the commander stubbornly.

"Our orders were to hold our position," said the pilot. "We can't possibly do that with no weaponry."

"*You're* the one who explained it all so logically," said the commander. "We're here to be sacrificed. I can't see that it makes any difference whether we've got operative weaponry or not."

"At least we had a chance, however slim, to defend ourselves before," the pilot pointed out.

"Do you think I *like* the thought of sitting here waiting to be blown to pieces!" demanded the commander. "I've got a family and a home I'm probably never going to see again. I'm twenty-two years old, for Christ's sake!" He paused, trying to control his emotions. "But I'm a serving officer in the Fleet, and I've got my orders."

"Check with Command again," said the pilot. "Tell them our situation. Maybe they'll give us permission to retreat."

The commander closed his eyes and concentrated on his earphone.

"The command vessel has been destroyed," he announced.

"Who's in charge now?" asked the pilot.

"No one. We've taken massive losses. The chain of command has been broken."

"Then we're on our own!" said the engineer.

"So is everyone else, and no one's breaking formation," said the commander.

"To hell with them!"

"If we try to retreat, our own men will destroy us," explained the commander. "They've already shot an assault boat that cut and ran."

"But this is crazy! We can't take another hit! It doesn't even have to be a direct hit—anything at all will rip us apart!"

"I know," said the commander.

"Then explain it to somebody!"

"There's no need to. It wouldn't make any difference." The commander leaned back in his chair. "We're not here to win; we're here to be sacrificed."

"But what's the point?" persisted the engineer.

The commander sighed. "If you can find a point to this whole stupid conflict, I'd love to know what it is."

"The point is destroying the Syndicate, not sitting here waiting for them to blow us out of space!"

"And six months ago, the point was destroying Khalia," said the commander. "And now we're being sacrificed to save their home planet." He paused. "I'm not a betting man, but I'd be willing to wager that in a year or two, or maybe five at the most, we're fighting side by side with the Syndicate against some new enemy, real or perceived."

"What are you getting at?" asked the pilot.

"Just this," said the commander: "I can accept being a pawn in the grand strategy of the battle. I can even accept the fact that pawns get sacrificed." He paused. "But there's one thing that's driving me crazy."

"What?"

The commander looked at the screen, where a Syndicate cruiser had just appeared. "Here we are, about to be wiped out by a human enemy so that Duane can save Khalia." He paused.

"I just wish I knew," he said wistfully, "whether I was a white piece or a black piece."

The three pawns watched in silence as the opposing pieces bore down on them.

INTERLUDE

Articles of War
Article V
Every Person subject to this Act, and not being a Commanding Officer, who shall not use his utmost Exertions to carry the orders of his Superior Officers into execution when ordered to prepare for Action, or during the Action shall, if he acted traitorously, suffer Death; if he has acted from Cowardice shall suffer Death or such other Punishment as is herein-after mentioned; and if he has acted from Negligence, or through other Default, be Dismissed, with Disgrace, or suffer such other Punishment as is herein-after mentioned.

The battle began almost an hour before the first shots flared across space. The Syndicate fleet dropped back into normal space just beyond the outermost planet in the Khalian system. This allowed them time to scurry into formation. Seeing the Fleet ships in a globe, indicating defense, the Syndicate ships formed themselves into a loose cylinder whose open end pointed at the smaller Fleet formation.

Reacting to the cylindrical formation, and an analysis that gave the two fleets near equality in numbers, Duane reacted by opening the globe out into a tightly formed pancake shape that would allow him to overwhelm each section of the attacking cylinder as it passed through.

Passing into the system proper the Syndicate ships reacted by maneuvering a similarly flat formation. Now minutes apart Duane ordered the dreadnoughts in the center of his formation to pull ahead of the edges, turning the formation into a cone whose point was aimed at the opposing flagship.

When the main forces were still several AUs apart, each side released a swarm consisting of hundreds of smaller ships. The goal of these fighters was to harass and disrupt the other fleet's formation while protecting their own from receiving the same treatment.

THE MOSQUITO
by Jody Lynn Nye

"IF I DON'T come back, you can have my stuff," Pilot Patrick
Otlind said, mining through his small personal goods locker for
the padded collar that fit into the neck of his flight suit. He
sealed the coverall seams, feeling to make sure that the circuit
conduits and medical monitors were in place.

"Good luck," Dr. Mack Dalle offered, his voice full of
concern. He stood propped against the door of Pat's shared
quarters, watching his friend suit up. "At least you've got
something to do. We'll be back here sitting on our butts waiting
for news."

With a critical eye, Otlind regarded his friend, a long, lean
figure in a white medical tunic. "You can fly a scooter. Why
don't you come along, too? I'm sure Meier would be glad to
have another one of his scooter pilots volunteer, even if you
will have to bend over to fit in the cockpit. You med staff aren't
going to have any action until it's all over." The day before
both men had taken a ribbing from two fighter pilots who had

stopped in to have Mack give them their annual flight physicals. The men had made a big thing about the three kill ribbons one was wearing, inferring any pilot who hadn't taken on another fighter and won wasn't in their class. The memory still irked Otlind and he added, "Wouldn't you love to see the faces of the next pilots you examine with you wearing your own kill ribbon?"

Dalle groaned. "I'm not that good. The action at the end would likely be me. I'd never hear the end of it if I came back wounded, kill ribbon or no."

"Whatzamatter, you can't get professional courtesy around here?" Pat slapped Mack on the shoulder and edged past him into the hall. "C'mon, I've got to report. You can walk with me down to the shuttle bay."

He was acting with more bravado than he felt. Admiral Abe Meier himself had addressed the assembly of medical corps pilots. For the big battle they needed every pilot who could handle a one-man ship. The number of converted Khalian fighters brought up the total to more ships than there were qualified men to fly. The Fleet couldn't fall back on its nonhumanoid complement: there wasn't time to refit all the units to anything but quadrupedal operation. Without hesitation, every medical courier had stepped forward to volunteer to do their part. They hadn't needed much convincing.

Besides, Pat wanted a crack at flying a real fighter. He didn't mind being on the behind-the-scenes courier squad, picking up after the fighting was over, but he had originally trained with the combat pilots. He envied them their repertoire of adventure stories with themselves as the heroes. Silently he shook hands with Mack, and turned away, leaving the medic at the hatchway.

He joined his fellows in the shuttle bay. There was a lot of slapping on the back and false cheer, but they all knew that this was the Fleet's biggest test, and they were an integral part of its defense. Most of the men and women assembled had already seen years of war service. By all rights, they should have been back on their home worlds and stations with their families, enjoying their mustering-out bonuses. They were tired. Otlind knew he was comparatively fresh, and it made him feel a little guilty.

A small squad of Khalia huddled by themselves in one corner of the bay. Otlind found it hard to call the rabid Weasels brothers-in-arms, but there was no choice. Orders came from above. Too many of his friends had died fighting them, and he'd picked up too many dismembered Alliance corpses where the Khalia had passed. It seemed an unbelievable about-face for any reasonable mind to have to make, but then, this was the military.

The flight deck sergeant signaled "scramble," and the pilots ran for their assigned craft.

"Otlind? You're my wingman," a burly woman in a dark green flight suit informed him. Her dark brown hair had red highlights in it that looked yellow under the harsh spots in the bay. She had tiny, slim-fingered hands and capable wrists at the end of her massive arms: power to back up superior small motor control. She clasped his right hand in hers.

"Right, Lieutenant Marsden. Nice flying with you," he said, following her toward their row. As soon as Otlind leaped for the cockpit of his craft, the lights in the bay darkened from white to red. He settled his muscular frame into the impact padding of the pilot's chair, fitting the webbing across his chest and adjusting the headrest against his neck.

As many times as he had practiced the takeoff and fan-out in the combat simulator, nothing equaled the feeling Pat got from actually powering up the fighter. It was immediately evident how much more oomph it had than his shuttle did. The fighters flew by attracting or repelling against the magnetic fields of larger bodies: planets, stars, and, in a pinch, other ships. They also featured repulsor fields that prevented the attraction from becoming fatal, sometimes providing the pilot with that one moment's grace to respond and swerve aside, with the help of tiny impulse jets, to avoid becoming a space-going hood ornament. You couldn't do anything with terminal velocity except loop around, and that took some skill. Otlind hoped that his was sufficient.

Marsden was wingleader for Charlie squadron, a regular fighting unit. She had offered to pair with Otlind instead of

sloughing him off on a flank unit with the other medical
couriers because she was impressed by his training record, and
thought that his instincts were good enough to keep him alive.
In the three days they had to train, Otlind had picked up on the
tricks needed to fly the Khalian hot rods faster than most of the
other medflies. At the moment, surrounded by ace fighters
swimming alongside him like guppies out into the vast ocean of
black, he didn't see that as much of an advantage. The job of
the fighter units was to provide a screen for the Fleet's
dreadnoughts. One by one the tiny craft left the protective
shadow of the *Elizabeth Blackwell*, and joined the warships
looming across the void over the glowing disk of Khalia.

"Count off, Charlie," Marsden barked into her com unit as
she shepherded her squadron into position. "Charlie One!"

"Charlie Two!" Otlind said, concentrating on staying dead
level on the plane with his wingleader. His armament consisted
of laser cannons and two missiles, one on either side of his
undercarriage. The tiny holotank showed a handful of minute
blips moving out into space before the larger dots that
represented the Fleet's transports and destroyers. Voices of the
other four pilots of Charlie squadron registered on his ears, but
his mind was pinned to the controls in front of him. As little as
he liked to admit it, he was scared. He was the least
experienced of the six, and he wondered where it would show.

"There is nothing out here but me and my voice and your
targets. Got that?" Marsden growled into her pickup. "Never
mind what the brass are thinking, or what the Syndic scum
throw at you. Acknowledge!"

"Yes, Lieutenant!" the pilots chorused.

What the hell, Otlind thought, it was better than sitting on
the *Blackwell* twiddling his thumbs. The medflies worked
twelve hours a day shuttling bodies back and forth, including
under fire, and they had yet to receive any of the credit or glory
for helping the Fleet keep running. Still, he kept thinking of
coming back a hero, an individual in a small ship, lauded for
beating the odds against the evil Syndicate, blowing hell out of
the bastards. . . .

The enemy ships showed up on his small holotank long
before they would have become visible to the naked eye.

Immediately Marsden started arraying her small squadron, matching the moves made by her opposite number, still halfway across the solar system. In his earpiece Otlind could hear the squadron leader replying to unheard chatter from other units strung out across the face of the Fleet's planetward flank.

We look like gnats, he thought, catching a glimpse of the activity in the holotank. Red blips indicated the Syndicate; white, blue, or yellow were classes of Fleet ships. He was flying a blue blip.

The enemy closed quickly. There was no element of surprise possible except, he hoped, that there were a lot more Fleet fighters in space than they expected. After all, where could the Fleet raise trained pilots in the middle of nowhere? Thousands of light-years from their main planets and on the edge of a sector they had occupied for less than a year. He grinned ferally, feeling that he had put one over on them already.

Immediately Marsden gave the order to engage. Indicators glowed around the red blips that she wanted them to take. The blinking one forward of Otlind's position was his. He altered course slightly as he flew toward it, computer-matching its moves for his best advantage, like a 3-D game of chess.

After all the hurrying up to wait, the action came quickly. The holotank revealed the laser shots flashed from the enemy craft. Otlind veered back and forth, dropping toward the planet with an impulse thrust to avoid a dead-shot that might have drilled him right between the eyes. He threw more power to his forward shields just in time for his computer to inform him that it had deflected a hit.

His suit suddenly felt too tight, as if it would constrict his arms, grappling them away from crucial controls. He was going to die, in the lousy first five minutes of battle.

"Dammit, Charlie Two, what are you doing? Peel left!" Marsden's voice barked in his ear.

That broke his mood of self-pity and woke up the pilot in his head. His hands moved before his mouth could make the acknowledgment, and the tank showed laser traces lancing from behind him and impacting on the Syndic's shields. He looped under and up, planting his sights straight into the belly of the enemy craft, peppering it along with Marsden until he saw its shield give. His craft flew onward, through the shower of hot white sparks it left as it exploded. Otlind could hear the rain of particles bounding off his hull. One down, a million others to go. He veered around to rejoin Charlie.

"That's my kill, Charlie Two," said the squadron leader matter-of-factly. "Wake up over there! That could have been you!" The holotank showed another red dot blinking, and he set his craft's nose toward it.

All at once Otlind's muscles settled. He'd already made his mistake, so the suspense was over. There was something about a pressured situation that brought out the best performance he could give. He flew high, left, and behind Marsden as she engaged a distant fighter in a firefight. It launched a missile toward her that he picked out of midspace with a lucky shot. It imploded in a cloud, which was shortly swelled by the remains of the craft from which it came.

More fighters swarmed in to counter them, attempting to cut them off from the rest of the flank. Their shields glowed white where his bolts hit them, but none of the sparks was a killing shot. The other Fleet gnats seemed parsecs away in his tank. Otlind got separated from Marsden briefly, pursued by two Syndic fighters.

"This way, Charlie Two," crowed a voice in his commset. It was Charlie Five, an older man who had been flying a fighter longer than Otlind had been alive. "Bring 'em to Daddy . . ."

Tri-vid games were in some ways more satisfying than real-life combat. He couldn't tell if the two bogeys had been blown up by Five and Six until he turned around to look. No *kabooms*, no triumphant electronic music, just a little encouraging chatter among the flyers on his squadron's frequency.

"Nice work!" he called to Five as he sailed below the others, seeking to reposition himself near Marsden. "That's some good flyswatting."

"Thanks, Two. Hey, look out, we've got more company!"

"Radio silence!" Marsden growled. "Watch your tanks for assignment!"

Three Syndic fighters had peeled off from the main force and committed to his position. There were more fighters coming this way than were attacking the spaceward flank. His three followed him as he flew an irregular serpentine pattern that sent their laser shots at his tail lancing harmlessly out into space, away from the bulk of the Fleet flotilla. Friendly fire was a problem, too. He didn't want to cream one of his wingmen.

More Syndics came out of the planetary glare and showed up big and bright in his tank. It was all he could do to elude their targeting mechanisms with fancy footwork. Their ships were nearly as fast as his was, and far more heavily armed.

He began to congratulate himself on his near-miraculous reaction time. The bad guys were missing him. There should have been at least one hit, but the computer insisted he'd evaded them all. He was invisible, passing without trace. Suddenly Otlind heard the Death Knell, the warning alarm in the system that alerted him that a missile had acquired him. It was coming in on his starboard flank. As long as it read his telltale trace, it would pursue him. He couldn't turn and blow it into dust with his three new buddies so close behind. The rest of Charlie squadron was involved in the thick of fighting. Flying straight to make it to them in time to knock out the pursuing missile was to leave himself vulnerable to a killing bolt.

Twisting and swerving, Otlind dove over the heads of two of the Syndic fighters, looped between the second and third, and slingshotted around Khalia's second moon. His tank told him that the Syndics had considerably blown up the missile that came hurtling toward them in Otlind's wake. Then he plummeted into the Khalian atmosphere.

"You Weasel bastards have never done me any good in your life. Now's your chance to change my opinion of you," Otlind mumbled through gritted teeth. His small ship bucketed as friction caught it in the magnetic/stratospheric envelope of the planet. The skin monitor whined as the outer temperature of his craft zoomed. But if anyone could handle dropping from vacuum to atmosphere and out again, it was one Patrick Otlind, ace scooter pilot. His subterfuge had worked. The Syndic fighters were nowhere in sight. They must have veered off when their ships began to buck against the friction, picturing him as a falling cinder. The radio exploded into life, blaring unmodulated atmospheric interference into his earpiece. He barked an order at the computer controller, and the noise died to a crackling hiss. There was no point in trying to break through the static to contact Marsden; she'd ordered radio silence, and the interruption might distract her from her job.

He blew through the upper atmosphere, trusting his instruments rather than squinting through the condensation frosting his cooling canopy. If he took a sharp right toward planetary south, he could come out of the corona on that side of Khalia and surprise the fighters attacking the rest of Charlie squadron.

Halfway around the world, Otlind saw a handful of big dots appear in his tank approaching atmosphere. They were red. Enemy craft, on this side of the planet? Khalian pirates? No, the computer said they were Syndicate troop transports. In his opinion, they had emerged from warp pretty close to Khalia. On the other hand, they had owned this world for fifty years and knew every wrinkle of space. It was a one-in-a-million chance that he had discovered them in the air before they made landfall. Those six ships probably held as many as two thousand troops.

Landing had to be prevented at all costs. If the Syndicate was allowed to return to Khalia, there wouldn't be enough survivors left to cheer the Fleet's victory parade. Besides, Meier had said that the Syndicate had left billions of credits worth of equipment that the Fleet wanted to claim for its own use. It would help extend the Alliance's war chest, they were finding clues about where the Syndicate systems lay, and the stuff helped support the attack on the Syndicate's home turf. He had also heard rumors of hidden bases and deeply planted atomic weapons just waiting to be detonated. Did anybody else know these ships were here?

He buzzed toward them, breaking right then left, while the computer controller dialed through the radio frequencies, searching for a Khalian ground station. The Syndic ships became aware of him, locking on telemetry sensors, which set off the Death Knell again.

Otlind could almost hear the belly laugh on the Syndic flagship's bridge when they figured out what he was. "Yeah," he agreed nastily, "I'm just a little fly. Nothing to worry about.

But you're going to have to come through me first before you land. Go ahead, try and swat me."

It occurred to him while the computer was trying to find him an open channel that it was stupid for him to take on six full-sized transports all by himself, but he was really too busy dodging to go away and think that one over. If one of those heavy guns managed to hit him, his shields would probably not be able to save him. He did not want to die. Fear kept his reflexes sharp, and adrenaline gave him speed.

A barrage of laser fire showed up as white lines in his tank. He eluded them, the last few by the thickness of the paint on his hull.

"You can't get me that easy," Otlind sneered, feeling cocky at his own skill. He punched the stud that armed the first missile, and peeled up and around to the right as the white contrail tore toward the flank of the lead ship. They had drifted down to the fringes of Khalia. Even in those wisps of atmosphere, the *boom!* of its impact was audible. So was the explosion that followed a split second later. The very air shook around his fighter. Otlind cheered. Telemetry indicated the lead ship was disabled. He must have struck it squarely in the engine room.

With glee, he circled around them and punched the second missile-arming button, eyeballing a target on the next transport. "See! This fly's got stingers, too. Take that!"

The missile thrust away and missed. It soared out of atmosphere and headed for space, neatly penning a line of white between two of the transports.

"Oh, frax!"

But his attack had achieved a purpose. The lead ship hung in orbit still at the edge of atmosphere. It was only a matter of time before something else blew it up, or gravity yanked it down. The other transports were forced to replot their approach. Otlind swooped between two of the ships, firing his laser cannons wildly. The big ships threw up heavier shields, which changed their reentry calculations yet again as the magnetic silhouette altered.

The edge of a laser bolt tipped Otlind's fighter as he passed the last transport, causing him to somersault over and over up toward space. He had seen it coming, but the maneuvering thrusters were unable to respond quickly enough to save him. That was the biggest disadvantage the fighters had over the medical scooters. The little medships were designed for superior mobility and agility in atmosphere, and more leisurely pace in vacuum. He kicked himself mentally for forgetting that, and vowed to compensate next time for the differences, if he lived.

The temperature rose uncomfortably in the cockpit until the whining life-support engines cooled it down again, but the shields held. Otlind fought the helm for control and gradually made the planet stop revolving over his canopy. He turned to make another pass, readying his laser cannons. The ships fired at him, but he had control of his ship, now. He was going to keep getting in their way if it was the last thing he'd ever do. His fighter zinged into atmosphere. Immediately the canopy clouded up again. He felt, rather than saw, the bulk of the new lead transport ship on his starboard wing. By the time his canopy cleared, he was well past the ships and coming around for another pass. They had changed position again. Every time he got in their way, it pushed back the seven-minute time frame they needed to land. Otlind grinned.

Voices came out of the radio pickup. He recognized the squeals, hisses, and growls of the Khalian tongue.

"I hope like hell this is a military comlink," Pat said, nudging his jaw control. "Breaker. Mayday. I am a Fleet single fighter, Charlie Two, at the following location," he read off the coordinates of his position from his heads-up display. "You have five, repeat five Syndicate transports attempting to make planetfall up here, and one more orbiting disabled. Can anybody hear me? I say there are troop transports entering your space one hundred eighty degrees out from the battle zone. I need help. Mayday. Over."

He let go of the control and listened. The voices, still speaking Khalian, became agitated. Otlind repeated his message distinctly and signed off, because he saw some old friends approaching. The three Syndic fighters he had left behind on the other side of the planet had finally caught up with him.

They had taken a safer descent angle into atmosphere than he had needed, and were firing laser cannons in his direction.

The shields' alarm went off as Charlie Two's shield was unable to completely protect the former Khalian fighter from two long-range laser hits. The little craft juddered and shook under him. The power indicator swan-dived. If the shields sustained more damage, he was in danger of losing power to his drives. He fired quickly at the three fighters, and then moved to evade their lasers.

That it had taken them so long to follow him into atmosphere made him think that perhaps the Syndic fighters were less resistant to friction than his craft, which Meier had made sure were coated with a newly developed Fleet-technology ceramic paint. It made them slightly less mobile and slower in atmosphere. With his long experience at dodging and weaving, their firepower, triple his, could serve a useful purpose.

He flung a barrage in their direction, and then turned tail and ran toward the troop transports. It took next to no time to vanish between two of the leviathan ships and into the clouds below. The large ships were so startled at his return, he met no incoming fire at all.

As soon as Otlind angled around the first massive hull, he shut off power to the shields. They were already hemorrhaging and would soon drain the drives that powered them, leaving him a sitting, or falling, duck. At the speed he was flying, he doubted the fighters could hit him anyhow. Losing the screens made him a smaller shadow and eliminated the danger of interacting explosively with the larger ship's more powerful screens, enabling him to slip in and out of places where another fighter could not pass.

The three fighters, seeing him drop shields on their heads-up displays, added more thrust. They closed in, following him between the transports with lasers firing. The transports scattered as the laser bolts impacted with sparks on their shields.

Making two quick left turns in midair, Otlind angled back upward through the clouds and into the midst of the transports. His tiny craft buzzed in front of the command blister of one mighty ship. He had time to blast the bubble into melted slag before the three small fighters rounded the fleet and were on his tail again.

The Death Knell went off this time with a double clang. He had been targeted by more than one craft, probably the fighters and perhaps one of the transports. There was no way to outrun the bolts. He slapped the shields back up just as explosions began to ring in the thin air outside his hull. He put everything he had into a repulse from the planet's gravity and his rear shields, and blasted toward the black canopy of space.

A split second passed. Otlind realized that he was still alive. His ship was more or less intact, and the transports were ignoring him. Two military corvettes, on a vector from the planet's surface, had appeared through the clouds and were pounding laser blasts into the transports' hulls. They appeared to be typically overgunned Khalian raiders, highly illegal after the surrender, but a most welcome sight to the lone pilot. The three fighters were nowhere to be seen. Otlind guessed that they had fled into space. No, his tank showed only two blips heading for outer space. One of them must have been destroyed.

The radio clamored for attention. "Charlie Two?" it inquired in a lisping voice.

"Who wants to know?" Otlind demanded, skimming safely in the blue-blackness above the planet's glow. Systems said that he was about ten minutes from drive shutdown. He turned off his shields and was rewarded with ten minutes grace more.

"I am the high priest of communications aboard the *Loyalty*. Khalia extends honor to its defender. We thank you for the warning. You bought us precious moments to stop our foe. If not for you, our ships would not have lifted. Your name will go down in our rolls of honor as a hero."

"So long as you spell it right, honorable Weasels," Otlind said, settling back in his seat with a sigh of satisfaction. The muscles of his lower back were unaccountably tight. He wiggled to ease them. "It's Otlind. O-T-L-I-N-D."

"Charlie Two, where the hell have you been?" Marsden's fury came over loud and clear through his headset. "We thought you were dead when you went down."

"Lieutenant, you're going to be really sore. I got lost, and then I had to break radio silence. I'm sorry," Otlind said, trying to sound contrite, but unable to wipe a justifiable grin off his face.

"Your power levels are too low. Damage report?"

"I'm missing a piece of wing, I've got burns in my tail and belly, and my shields are shot."

"If you don't take care of your toys, you can't have them," Marsden said, but her voice displayed no real irritation. "Get back to the *Blackwell*. You're in no shape to stay out here."

"Too bad I couldn't do more," Otlind said, hoping he didn't sound facetious.

"So that's how I saved Khalia," Otlind told Mack Dalle later that day when the brass had finished with him. "At least for that ten minutes I was a hero. But you know what really twists my tail? I blew up a transport and disabled two more, but the guys say they don't count. There was no confirmation and all the Fleet scanners were watching the big battle on the far side of the planet and the Khalians won't admit they had corvettes secreted on the planet. I *still* don't have any fighter kills on my record."

INTERLUDE

Articles of War
Article XXX
The Officers of all Ships Appointed for the Convoy and Protection of any Ships or Vessels shall diligently perform their Duty without Delay according to their Instructions on that Behalf . . . shall be Punished criminally according to the Nature of the Offence, by Death or such other Punishment as is herein-after mentioned.

Article XI
Where a mutiny is not accompanied by Violence, the Ringleader or Ringleaders of such mutiny shall suffer Death, or such other Punishment as is herein-after mentioned; and all other persons who shall join in such Mutiny, or shall not use their utmost Exertions to suppress the same, shall suffer Imprisonment or other such Punishment as is herein-after mentioned.

As the fighters' dogfight intensified overhead, contingencies that had been prepared long in advance were also put into motion. Many failed because they depended upon no-longer-willing Khalian warriors. Others were smashed by the efforts of the three hundred thousand militia and infantry left behind on Khalia. A few contingencies succeeded, including one that disrupted the entire orbital observation system protecting the planet itself. None of this affected the space battle immediately, a fact that confirmed the Syndicate's fear that they had lost control of the Khalia.

Like all good engineers, the Syndicate had in place one more backup system. Normally such a system is designed to ensure something happens. In this case the backup system was intended to ensure nothing ever happened on Khalia again. Originally meant to be activated from space, this particular backup was almost complete at the time of the unexpectedly rapid fall of the Khalia. As a result it was only partially successful. Which for many of those on the planet was quite enough.

MISSION
ACCOMPLISHED
by David Drake

NICK KOWACS LAUGHED to imagine it, him sitting at a booth in
the Red Shift Lounge and saying to Toby English, *"That last
mission, the one that was supposed to be a milk run? Let me
tell you what* really *went down!"*

"Come on, come on, come on," begged the logistics officer, a
naval lieutenant. "Your lot was supposed to be in the air thirty
minutes ago, and I got three more convoys behind it!"

"Keep your shirt on, sailor," said Sergeant Bradley. "We'll
be ready to move out as soon as Major Kowacs gets this last set
of voice orders—"

Bradley nodded toward the blacked-out limousine that
looked like a pearl in a muck heap as it idled in a yard of giant
excavating machinery. The limousine was waiting for the
Headhunters when they pulled into the depot. Bradley didn't

221

know what the major was hearing inside the vehicle, but he doubted it was anything as straightforward as verbal orders.

"That's faster than you'll have your equipment airborne even if you get on with your job," he concluded.

Bradley was acting first sergeant for the field element of the 121st Marine Reaction Company, Headhunters, while the real first sergeant was back with the base unit on Port Tau Ceti. Bradley knew that before the lieutenant could punish him for insubordination, the complaint would have to go up the naval chain of command and come back down the Marine side of the Fleet bureaucracy . . . which it might manage to do, a couple of lifetimes later.

As if in answer to Bradley's gibe, drivers started the engines of the paired air-cushion transporters that cradled a self-contained excavator on the lowboy between them. The yard had been scoured by earlier movements of heavy equipment, but the soil of Khalia was stony. As the transporters' drive fans wound up, they shot pebbles beneath the skirts to whang against the sides of other vehicles.

One stone hit a Khalian wearing maroon coveralls. He was one of thousands of Weasels hired to do scut work in the wake of the Fleet's huge logistics buildup on what had been the enemy home planet—when the Khalia were the enemy. The victim yelped and dropped to the ground.

Sergeant Bradley spat into the dust. If the Weasel was dead, then the universe was a better place by that much.

Drivers fired up the engines of the remainder of the vehicles the 121st was to escort. Four lowboys carried three-meter outside-diameter casing sections. The final piece of digging equipment was a heavy-lift crane to position the excavator initially, then feed casing down the shaft behind the excavator as it burned and burrowed toward the heart of the planet.

All of the transporters were ground effect. The noise of their intakes and the pressurized air wailing out beneath their skirts was deafening. The lieutenant shouted, but Bradley could barely hear him. "You won't be laughing if the planet-wrecker you're sitting on top of goes off because you were late to the site!"

Corporal Sienkiewicz, Kowacs's clerk/bodyguard, was female and almost two meters tall. This yard full of outsized equipment was the first place Bradley remembered Sie looking as though she was in scale with her surroundings. Now she bent close to the logistics officer and said, "*We* won't be doing anything, LT. It's you guys a hundred klicks away who'll have time to watch the crust crack open and the core spill out."

The Syndicate had mined Khalia. If the planet exploded at the crucial moment when Syndicate warships swept in to attack, the defenders would lose the communications and logistics base they needed to win.

But most of the Weasels in the universe would be gone as well. . . .

The door of the limousine opened. Bradley keyed the general-frequency override in his com helmet and ordered, "Five-six to all Headhunter elements. Mount up, troops, it's time to go play Marine." His voice was hoarse.

As Bradley spoke, his fingers checked combat gear with feather-light touches. His shotgun was slung muzzle-up for boarding the vehicle. The weapon's chamber was empty, but he would charge it from the box magazine as soon as the trucks were airborne.

Bandoliers of shotgun ammo crossed his back-and-breast armor. From each bandolier hung a container of ring-airfoil grenades, which Bradley could launch from around the shot-gun's barrel for long range and a high-explosive wallop.

Hand-flung grenade clusters were stuffed into the cargo pockets of either pant leg. Some gas grenades; some explosive, some incendiary, some to generate fluorescent smoke for marking. You never knew what you were going to need. You only knew that you were going to need more of *something* than you carried. . . .

A portable medicomp to diagnose, dispense drugs, and patch the screaming wounded. If you could reach them. If they weren't out there in the darkness being tortured by one Khalian while the rest of a Weasel platoon waited in ambush; and you still had to go, because she was your Marine and it didn't matter, you had to bring back whatever the Weasels had left of her.

Sergeant Bradley lifted the rim of his com helmet with one

hand and knuckled the pink scar tissue that covered his scalp. He didn't carry a fighting knife, but a powered metal-cutter dangled from his left hip where it balanced his canteen. He'd killed seven Weasels with the cutting bar one night.

Bradley was twenty-eight standard years old. His eyes were the age of the planet's molten core.

"Come on, Top," Sienkiewicz said, putting her big hand over the tension-mottled fingers with which the field first gripped his helmet. Major Kowacs sprinted toward them as the limousine accelerated out of the equipment yard. "We got a taxi to catch."

"Right," said Bradley in a husky voice. "Right, we gotta do that."

He prayed that the Headhunters would be redeployed *fast* to some planet where there weren't thousands of Weasels running around in Fleet uniforms. . . .

Sergeant Custis, a squad leader with three years service in the Headhunters, pulled Kowacs aboard the truck while Sie and Bradley hooked themselves onto seats on the opposite side of the vehicle's center spine.

"Cap'n?" said Custis as his head swung close to his commanding officer's helmet. "Is it true the Weasels are going to blow up their whole planet if we don't deactivate the mines first? Ah, I mean, Major?"

Kowacs grimaced. One of the problems with latrine rumors was that they were only half-right.

He checked to see that the flat box was secured firmly to his equipment belt. He'd clipped it there as soon as he received the device in the limousine.

Another problem with latrine rumors was that they *were* half-right.

"Don't sweat it, Buck," Corporal Sienkiewicz offered from the bench seat on which she sat with her back against Custis's back. "It's gonna be a milk run this time."

The lead truck was out of the gate with 1st Platoon aboard. A lowboy followed the Marines; the truck with Weapons Platoon and Kowacs's command team lifted into the number three slot.

There was enough crosswind to make the vehicles skittish. At least that prevented the gritty yellow dust that the fans lifted from coating everybody behind the leaders.

The Marine transporters had enough direct lift capacity to fly rather than skimming over a cushion of air the way the mining equipment had to do, but for this mission Kowacs had told the drivers to stay on the deck. After all, the Headhunters were supposed to be escorting the excavating machinery . . . or something.

"Six to all Headhunter elements," Kowacs said, letting the artificial intelligence in his helmet cut through the conversations buzzing through the company. Everybody was nervous. "Here's all the poop *I* know."

But not quite everything he was afraid of. He instinctively touched the special communicator attached to his belt. . . .

"A presumably hostile fleet is approaching Khalia," Kowacs resumed aloud.

"Weasels!" a nearby Marine snarled. The AI blocked radio chatter, but it couldn't prevent people from interrupting with unaided voice.

"The enemy is human," Kowacs said firmly. "Any of you replacements doubt that, just talk to a veteran. *This* outfit has met them before."

That ought to shut up the troops who were convinced the Khalia had broken their surrender terms. Kowacs's words told the Headhunter veterans *they* knew better, so they'd hold to the CO's line as a matter of status. And no replacement, even a Marine with years of service, would dare doubt the word of a full-fledged Headhunter.

It was only Nick Kowacs who still had to fear that the incoming warships were crewed by Khalians like the hundreds of millions of other bloodthirsty Weasels all around him on this planet. He looked out at the landscape.

The fast-moving convoy was three klicks out of the Fleet Logistics Base Ladybird—one of hundreds of depots that had sprung up within hours of the successful invasion of Khalia. The countryside was a wasteland.

The local foliage was brown and dun and maroon, never green. Even granting the difference in color, the vegetation was sparse and signs of habitation were limited to an occasional hut shaped like an oversize beehive.

How could the Alliance *ever* have believed a race as primitive as the Khalia was capable of sustaining an interstellar war—without someone else behind them, arming the Weasels and pointing them like a sword at the heart of the Alliance?

"FleetComSeventeen believes that the human enemy, the Syndicate . . ." Kowacs said as his eyes searched terrain that was already being scanned to the millimeter from orbit, ". . . has used its past association with the Weasels to plant a chain of thermonuclear devices at the planet's crustal discontinuity. If the weapons go off together, they'll crack Khalia like an egg and destroy everything and everyone the Fleet has landed here."

Corporal Sienkiewicz chuckled and said to Bradley in a barely audible rumble, "Including us."

The convoy was rolling at over one hundred kph. The lowboys accelerated slowly, but they could maintain a higher speed than Kowacs had expected. The Marine trucks had their side armor lowered so that the outward-facing troops could shoot or deploy instantly, but the wind buffeting was getting severe.

"*We're* not aboard a ship because we'd be as useless as tits on a boar in a space battle," Kowacs continued. "Anyway, the naval boys don't have near the lift capacity to get even Fleet personnel clear in the time available. Our engineering personnel are going to dig up the Syndicate mines instead."

Dig up the mines—or detonate them out of sequence, making the result a number of explosions rather than a single, crust-splitting surge. Asequential detonation was a perfectly satisfactory solution—for everyone except those directly on top of the bang.

"We're just along to protect the hardware," Kowacs concluded. "It's a milk run, but keep your eyes open."

A yellow light winked on Kowacs's raised visor, a glow at the frontier of his vision. One of his platoon leaders had a question, and the major's AI thought he ought to listen to it.

"Go ahead, Gamma Six," Kowacs said.

"Nick . . . ?" said Horstmann of 3d Platoon, aboard the

last vehicle in the convoy. "What are we s'posed to be protecting *against*?"

"Right, fair question," Kowacs agreed.

He'd asked the same thing when the orders came over the squawk box in the Headhunters' temporary barracks. The voice on the other end of the line said, "Any fucking thing! Get your asses moving!" and rang off.

Which was pretty standard for headquarters staff scrambling line Marines; but not the way Nick Kowacs liked to run his own outfit.

"I presume—"

"*I guess,*" spoken with an air of calm authority that impiied the CO knew what was going on, there was no need to panic.

"—that headquarters is concerned about Weasels who haven't gotten the word that they've surrendered. And maybe there's some locals who think we're planting mines instead of deactivating them. You know how rumors start."

Bradley laughed. Kowacs laughed also.

Another light winked: Sergeant Bynum, who was running Weapons Platoon until another lieutenant transferred in to replace Woking. Woking had died of anaphylactic shock on a Syndicate base that Fleet HQ swore the Headhunters had never seen.

"Go ahead, Delta Six."

"Capt—Major?" The veterans had trouble remembering the CO's promotion. Kowacs had trouble with it himself. "How did they locate these planet-wreckers, anyhow?"

Well, somebody was bound to ask that. Would've been nice if they hadn't, though. . . .

"They used A-Potential equipment," Kowacs answered flatly. The wind rush made his eyes water. "Toby English's Ninety-second is in orbit aboard the *Haig*. The destroyer's got the new hardware, and they've done subsurface mapping."

"APOT shit," said Bynum. "Like the stuff that left us swinging in the breeze on the last mission? The mission the brass said didn't happen—only we took fourteen casualties."

The only thing Nick Kowacs really understood about A-Potential equipment was that he never wanted to use it again. No grunt had any business tapping powers to which all points in time and space were equivalent. Maybe it wasn't such a bad idea if some other friendly used the technology, but . . .

The artificial intelligence in Bradley's helmet should not have been able to emulate Kowacs's unit and enter this discussion without the CO's stated approval . . . but it could. The field first broke in to state with brutal simplicity, "If savin' your ass is the only thing you're worried about, Bynum, you sure shouldn't've volunteered for the Headhunters."

Kowacs took his hand away from the special communicator. The plastic case felt cold.

Bynum muttered something apologetic.

"Alpha Six to Six," said the 1st Platoon leader laconically from the leading truck. "Hill One-Six-Fiver is in sight. Over."

"Right," said Kowacs. "Okay, Headhunters, we've arrived."

If anything, this landscape of pebble-strewn hills and wind-carved vegetation was more bleakly innocent than any of the countryside the convoy had passed through on its way here.

"Dig in, keep your eyes on your sensors, and be thankful we've got a cushy job for a change."

And while you're at it, pray that Fleet Vice Admiral Hannah Teitelbaum, whom Kowacs suspected to be a traitor in the pay of the Syndicate, hadn't gotten the Headhunters sent here for reasons of her own.

Corporal Sienkiewicz surveyed the landscape, flipping her helmet visor from straight visuals through infrared to ultraviolet, then back. Nothing she saw repaid her care—or explained her nervousness.

In addition to her massive pack and slung assault rifle, Sie cradled a three-shot plasma weapon lightly in her arms. She had no target as yet for its bolts of ravening hell, but *somewhere* out there . . .

"Gamma Six to Six," said the com helmet. "We're dug in. Over."

The rock in 3d Platoon's sector was a little more friable than that of the others, so they'd finished ahead of 1st and 2nd. Probably wasn't enough difference to make it worthwhile sending Horstmann's powered digging equipment over to help Lanier and Michie's men, though.

The excavation site, Hill 165, was one of a series of low pimples on a barren landscape. The crane was swinging the excavator into final position, nose down. Occasionally Sienkiewicz heard a bellowed curse as a variation in wind velocity rotated the machine out of alignment—again.

The Headhunters dug in by three Marine fire teams, just below the hillcrest so that they wouldn't be silhouetted against the sky. Each platoon, stiffened by two of Weapons Platoon's belt-fed plasma weapons, was responsible for a 120-degree wedge—

Of wasteland. There was absolutely no chance in the world that this empty terrain could support more than the Weasel equivalent of a goatherd. Sie had imagined a Khalian city from which furry waves might surge toward the humans; but not here.

And not from a tunnel complex, either. If the *Haig*'s A-Potential equipment had located planet-wreckers lying just above the asthenosphere, it would have spotted any large abnormality lying close enough to the surface to threaten the Headhunters.

So what the *hell* was wrong?

The self-contained excavator touched the ground. Its crew switched on their cutters with a scream that became a howl, then dropped into bowel-loosening subsonics.

The huge device disappeared into rock with the jerky suddenness of a land vehicle sinking into a pond. Just before the stern vanished from sight, a thirty-centimeter gout of magma spurted from it and spun ninety degrees in the magnetic deflector positioned above the pithead. The molten rock crossed a swale to splash and cool against a gravel slope three kilometers away.

Ten-second pulses of glowing waste continued to cross the 2nd Platoon sector every minute or so. Lanier's troops had left a corridor as the engineering officers directed, but they'd still be glad for their dugouts' overhead cover.

Nick and Top walked over from where they had been talking to the engineers. Bradley was carrying a communications screen of unfamiliar design in one hand. He looked okay again.

Sienkiewicz had to watch the field first pretty carefully nowadays, anytime there might be Weasels around.

"Anything out there, Sie?" the major asked, casual but obviously ready to react if his big bodyguard could put a name to her forebodings.

Sienkiewicz shrugged. "Not that I can find, anyway," she admitted. Her palms sweated against the twin grips of the plasma weapon.

The crane lowered the first section of casing to follow the excavator. Rock didn't simply go away because you heated it gaseous and slung it out the back of your equipment at high velocity. Pulses rising along the casing's magnetic field focused the waste in the center of the bore until it could be deflected to a tailings pile on the surface.

Kowacs must have been feeling the same thing Sienkiewicz did—whatever *that* was—because he touched the unfamiliar black object clipped to his equipment belt.

Sienkiewicz noted the gesture. "You know," she said, "it sorta looked like the guy who called you over to the car in the yard there . . . like he was Grant."

"Fucking spook," Bradley muttered. His fingers began to check his weapons and ammunition, as though he were telling the beads of a rosary.

"Yeah, that was Grant," Kowacs agreed. He started to say more, then closed his mouth.

The three members of the command team spoke over a com channel to which only they had access. The wind that scoured these hills also abraded words spoken by unaided voices.

Bradley touched the black monomer case of the object Kowacs had gotten in Grant's limousine. It was ten centimeters to a side and very thin. The outside was featureless except for a cross-hatched voiceplate and a small oval indentation just below it.

"I thought," the field first said, articulating the same assumption Sienkiewicz herself had made, "that all this A-Potential stuff was supposed to be turned in after the last mission?"

Kowacs's face worked. "It's a communicator," he said. "Grant says it is, anyhow. He thought . . . maybe we ought to have a way to get ahold of him if, if something happened out here."

He stared grimly at the stark hills around them. "Doesn't look like there's much to worry about, does there?"

Sie's right hand began to cramp. She spread it in the open air. The wind chilled and dried her callused palm.

"What's Grant expecting, then?" Bradley said, as though he were asking for a weather report. Wispy clouds at high altitude offered no promise of moisture to the sparse vegetation.

Kowacs shrugged. "We didn't have time to talk," the stocky, powerful officer said. His eyes were on the horizon. "Except, the other twelve excavators got sent out with Shore Police detachments for security. This is the only one that's being guarded by a reaction company."

"Anybody know who gave the orders?" Sienkiewicz heard herself ask.

"With a flap like this on, who the hell could tell?" Kowacs muttered. "Grant said he'd check, but it'll take a couple days . . . if there's anything left after the Syndicate fleet hits."

Then, as his fingers delicately brushed the APOT communicator, Kowacs added, "There's no reason to suppose somebody's trying to get rid of the Headhunters because of what we saw on that last mission."

"No reason at all," Sienkiewicz said, repeating the lie as she continued to scan the bleak horizon.

Bradley stared at the pattern on the flat-plate screen. He adjusted the focus, but the image didn't go away.

"Major!" he said sharply. "We got company coming!"

Bradley had borrowed the screen from the engineers so the Headhunter command team could eavesdrop on the excavator. A peg into rock fed seismic vibrations to the screen's microprocessor control for sorting.

Though the unit was small, it could discriminate between words vibrating from the sending unit on the excavator's hull and the roar of the cutters and impellers. Thus far, the only words that had appeared on the screen in block letters were laconic reports:

PASSING TWO KILOMETERS, IN THE GREEN.

PASSING FIVE KILOMETERS. REPLACING HEADS FIVE-THREE AND FIVE-FOUR WITH BACKUP UNITS.

PASSING EIGHT KILOMETERS . . .

When there were no words to decode from vibrations traveling at sound's swifter speed through rock, the screen mapped the surrounding hills. It had found a pattern there, also.

The command team's dugout was as tight and crude as those of the remaining fire teams: two meters on the long axis, a meter and a half in depth, and front-to-back width. The walls were stabilized by a bonding agent, while a back-filled sheet of beryllium monocrystal on thirty-centimeter risers provided top cover.

Kowacs bumped shoulders with the field first as he leaned toward the screen. Sie scraped the roof when she tried to get a view from the opposite end of the dugout.

"What is it?" Kowacs said. Then, "That's just Hill Two-Two-Four in front of us, isn't it? Vibration from the excavator makes the rock mass stand out."

"No, sir," Bradley said. "There was a pattern, and it's changed."

His lips were dry. He'd never used a screen like this before and he might be screwing up, the way a newbie shoots at every noise in the night. But . . . years of surviving had taught Bradley to trust his gut, to flatten *now* or to blast *that* patch of vegetation that was no different from the klicks of jungle all around it.

Something here was wrong.

PASSING TWELVE KILOMETERS, the screen said, blanking its map of the terrain. HEADS RUNNING EIGHTY PERCENT, STILL IN THE GREEN.

The quivering map display returned to the screen. It shifted, but the clouds changed overhead and the planet surely trembled to its own rhythms besides those imposed on it by human hardware. . . .

"The digger's getting deeper, so the vibrations don't look the same up here," Sienkiewicz muttered. She looked out the firing slit toward Hill 224 and manually adjusted her visor to high magnification.

"Headhunter Six to all elements," Kowacs ordered in a flat, decisive voice. "Full alert. Break. Alpha elements, watch Hill Two-Two-Four. Break. Delta Six, prepare to redeploy half your weapons to Alpha sector on command."

Metal glinted on the side of the hill a kilometer away. Bradley centered it in the sighting ring of his visor and shouted, "Support, target!" so that his AI would carat the object for every Headhunter within line of sight of it.

"Break," continued the major, his voice as bored but forceful as that of a roll-call sergeant. "Knifeswitch One-Three"—Regional Fire Control—"this is Headhunter S—"

The transmission dissolved into a momentary roar of jamming. Bradley's artificial intelligence cut the noise off to save his hearing and sanity.

The glint on Hill 224 vaporized in the sun-bright streak of a plasma weapon. A ball of gaseous metal rose, then cooled into a miniature mushroom cloud.   •   •

"—arget for you," Kowacs continued beside Bradley.

So long as he was transmitting out, the major couldn't know that his message was being turned to garbage by a very sophisticated jammer. Instead of a brute-force attempt to cover all frequencies, the enemy used an algorithm that mimicked that of the Headhunters' own spread-frequency transmitters. The low-level white noise destroyed communication more effectively than a high-amplitude hum that would itself have called regional headquarters' attention to what was going on.

"You're being jammed!" the field first said, slipping a RAG grenade over the barrel of his shotgun.

Airflow through the center of the grenade kept the cylinder on a flat trajectory, even though it was launched at low velocity. The warhead was hollow, but its twelve-cm diameter made it effective against considerable thicknesses of armor.

PASSING EIGHTEEN KILOMETERS, said the borrowed screen. Sound—through rock or in air—was unaffected by the jamming. Bradley heard the fire teams to either side shouting because their normal com had been cut off.

The side of Hill 224 erupted in glittering hostility. Bradley adjusted his visor to top magnification as Kowacs's rifle and Sie's plasma weapon joined the crackling thunder from all of the 1st Platoon positions.

The enemies were machines. Individually they were small, the size of a man's head—small enough to have been over-looked as crystalline anomalies in the rock when the *Haig* scanned for planet-wreckers.

There were thousands of them. They began to merge into larger constructs as they broke through the surface and crawled toward the Headhunters on Hill 165.

Bradley clapped Sie on the shoulder. Light shimmered across the track of ionized air from the muzzle of her weapon to the patch of molten rock across the swale. "Save your ammo!" Bradley shouted.

He pushed himself through the tight opening between the ground and the dugout's top cover, then reached back inside for his shotgun. RAG grenades had a maximum range of five hundred meters, and the aerofoil charges in the shotgun itself were probably useless against *this* enemy even at point-blank.

Bradley ran in a crouch toward the crew-served plasma weapon in the second dugout to the right. He expected bullets—bolts—*something*, but the enemy machines merely continued to roll down the slope like a metal-ceramic sludge.

Even at a thousand meters, bullets from Marine assault rifles seemed to have some effect on the individual machines. An object in a marksman's killing zone flashed for a moment within a curtain of rock dust cast up by deflected bullets. After the third or fourth sparkling hit, the machine slumped in on itself and stopped moving.

When two or more machines joined, the larger unit shrugged off bullets like a dog pacing stolidly through the rain. Only a direct hit from a plasma bolt could affect them—and Weapons Platoon had only a hundred rounds for each of its belt-fed plasma weapons.

Bradley knelt at the back of the gun pit. "Raush!" he ordered. "Blair!"

The crew triggered another short burst. Air hammered to fill the tracks burned through it, and ozone stripped the protecting mucus from Bradley's throat.

He reached through the opening and prodded the gunner between the shoulder blades with the shotgun's muzzle. "Raush, damn you!" he croaked.

The gunner and assistant gunner turned in surprise. Their eyes widened to see the gun and Bradley's face transfigured into a death's head by fear.

"Single shots!" the field first ordered. "And wait for three of the bloody things to join before you shoot! Don't waste ammo!"

Bradley rose to run to the other 1st Platoon gun pit, but Kowacs was already there, bellowing orders.

Nick understood. You could always count on the captain.

Raush resumed fire, splashing one and then a second of the aggregated creatures into fireballs with individual bolts.

Not every aimed shot hit. The machines moved faster than they seemed to. The survivors had covered half the distance to the Headhunter positions.

Bradley loped across the hilltop. His load of weapons and ammunition weighed him down as if he were trying to swim wrapped in log chain. Without radio, face-to-face contact was the only way to get plasma weapons from distant gun pits up to where they could support 1st Platoon.

Bradley thought of dropping the bandoliers of shotgun ammo he was sure were useless, but his hand stopped halfway to the quick-release catch.

This didn't seem like a good time to throw away any hope, however slim.

"Grant!" Kowacs shouted into the APOT communicator as a shining, five-ton creature lumbered up the slope toward the dugout. It was the last of the attacking machines, but it was already too close for either of the crew-served plasma weapons to bear on it. "We need support fast! Bring the *Haig* down! We need heavy weapons!"

Sienkiewicz fired three-shot bursts from her assault rifle. The bullets disintegrated as orange-white sparkles on the creature's magnetic shielding, a finger's breadth out from the metal surface.

Sie's plasma weapon lay on the floor of the dugout behind

her. The muzzle still glowed a dull red. She'd fired her last two plasma rounds an instant apart when a pair of low-slung creatures lunged suddenly from dead ground to either side.

Those targets now popped and bubbled, melting across the face of the rock from their internal energies; but there was one more, and Sienkiewicz was out of plasma charges.

Kowacs dropped the communicator and aimed his rifle. The creature was fifty meters away. It was shaped roughly like an earthworm, but it seemed to slide forward without quite touching the rock.

The dark patch just above the rounded nose might be a sensor window. Anyway, it was Sie's aiming point, and maybe two rifles firing simultaneously—

Kowacs squeezed the trigger, leaning into the recoil. He watched through the faint haze of powder gas as his bullets spattered vainly.

The fat black cylinder of a RAG grenade sailed toward the target in a flat arc. Kowacs and Sienkiewicz ducked beneath the dugout's rim. The hollow *whoomp!* of the armor-piercing charge rippled the ground and lifted the Marines a few millimeters.

Kowacs looked out. Wind had already torn to rags the black smoke of the explosion. There was a thumb-sized hole through the machine's skin. The cavity widened as the creature's snout collapsed inward like a time-lapse image of a rotting vegetable.

Bradley knelt beside the dugout, sliding another RAG grenade over his shotgun's barrel to the launching plate. It was the last of his four rounds: the ammo cans dangled empty from his bandoliers.

"Have you raised Grant?" the field first demanded. "Do we got some help coming?"

"I'll settle for an extraction," Sienkiewicz muttered. She looked down at the grenade stick she'd plucked from her equipment belt to throw if necessary. The grenade was a bunker buster, devastating in enclosed spaces but probably useless against an armored opponent in the open air.

"The trucks won't crank," Bradley said flatly. "The power-packs are still at seventy percent, but current won't flow through the control switches to the fans."

There was a moment of silence relieved only by the vibration of rock that spewed out of the pithead and hurtled across the sky. The stream cooled only to yellow-orange by the time it splashed on the tailings pile.

A plasma weapon began to thump single shots at a fresh target.

Fireballs flashed and lifted from Hill 224. Every time the residue of the bolt's impact drifted away, something fresh and metallic lifted from the same glassy crater. After the sixth bolt, the gun ceased firing.

"I don't know if I'm getting through," Kowacs said. He picked up the communicator and stared at it for a moment. Then he turned and shouted over to the next dugout on the right, "All plasma weapons to the First Platoon sector! Pass it on."

"All plasma weapons to First Platoon sector!" Sienkiewicz echoed toward their left-hand neighbors. "Pass it on!"

The dugouts were within voice range of one another. It was risky to strip the other sectors, but movement on Hill 224 proved there would be another attack here. The two plasma weapons that had not been engaged against the attack were the only ones in the unit that still had sufficient ammo to blunt a second thrust.

Kowacs's throat was swollen. He couldn't smell the foul smoke drifting from the creatures smashed just in front of the dugout, but he felt the tissues of his nose and mouth cringe at further punishment.

He put his thumb on the shallow depression beneath the communicator's voiceplate and said hoarsely, "Grant, this is Kowacs. Please respond. We need destroyer-class support *soonest*. We're being attacked by machines."

Part of Kowacs's mind wondered whether the creatures had their own internal AI programs or if some Syndicate operator controlled them through telerobotics. What did the operation look like from *that* bastard's point of view?

"We could use ammo resupply and a little extra firepower."

His voice broke. He cleared it and continued, "For God's sake, Grant, get Toby English and the *Haig* down here now!"

Kowacs lifted his thumb from the depression. Nothing

moved when he squeezed down. No sound—from Grant, of static, *nothing*—came from the voiceplate when he released the "key."

Maybe there wasn't a key. Maybe there wasn't even a communicator, just a plastic placebo that Grant had given Kowacs so the spook could be sure Headhunter Six would accept the mission that would mean the end of his whole company. . . .

"Bloody hell," Top muttered as he stared toward what was taking shape on the furrowed side of Hill 224.

A gun crew staggered over from 2nd Platoon with their plasma weapon on its tripod, ready to fire. They grounded beside the command dugout. The gunner slid behind his sights, while the assistant gunner helped the team's number three adjust the hundred-round belt of ammunition she carried while her fellows handled the gun.

Masses of shimmering metal oozed through the soil across the swale as if the hillside was sweating mercury. The blobs were larger than those that had appeared at the start of the first attack, and they merged again as soon as they reached the surface.

Clattering rifle fire had no affect on the creatures. None of the command team bothered to shoot.

Three plasma weapons, then a fourth, sent their dazzling radiance into the new threat. Blazing metal splashed a hundred meters skyward. The whole hillside glowed with an auroral lambency.

The ball of metal continued to grow. It was already the size of a cathedral's dome. Plasma bolts no longer touched the creature's shimmering skin.

It slid forward. The crater it left in the side of Hill 224 was the size a nuclear weapon would make.

Only two plasma weapons were still firing. The one nearest the command team had run almost through its belt of ammunition. The weapon's barrel glowed, and the rock a meter in front of its muzzle had been fused to glass.

Sergeant Bradley aimed his RAG grenade and waited. Sie arranged all her grenade clusters on the forward lip of the dugout so that she could throw them in quick succession as soon as the target rolled into range.

Kowacs emptied his assault rifle into the shining mass. It was halfway across the swale. Because of its size, the creature moved with deceptive speed.

As Kowacs slid a fresh magazine into his weapon, his eye caught the message on the excavator screen:

THIRTY-SEVEN KILOMETERS. TARGET RETRIEVED WITHOUT INCIDENT. A PIECE OF CAKE. BEGINNING ASCENT.

Top fired his RAG grenade. The shaped-charge explosion was a momentary smear against the monster's shielding, nothing more.

Heat waves shimmered from Kowacs's gun barrel. He fired the entire magazine in a single hammering burst and reloaded again. When the creature got within forty meters, he'd start throwing grenades.

And I'll say to Toby English, "Boy, you bastards cut it close! Ten seconds later and there wouldn't have been anything left of us but grease spots!"

Nick Kowacs laughed and aimed his rifle again at a towering monster framed by a sky that was empty of hope.

FRATRICIDE
by Janet Morris

"Toby?" Cleary's calm, sexy voice overrode Captain Tolliver English's all-com as if the two of them were in bed together. But they weren't. On his visor display, the purple privacy diode marking her transmission blinked: URGENT.

He fucking knew that. In the middle of a space battle for the very life of the Fleet, English's 92nd Marine Reaction Company was up to its collective ass in trouble. Special trouble because they'd become SERPA's "Special Electro-Research" outfit, complete with x-class equipment and untested mission parameters.

SERPA stood for Special Electromagnetic Research Projects Agency, and those SERPA parameters made the command-and-control (C&C) grid on his faceplate look like a bad dream. And Cleary, his female technical advisor, was as much responsible for that bad dream as anybody else.

"Toby?" came her voice again. "Delta Two, do you copy?"

In his electro-combatized personnel carrier, waiting to drop onto the skin of an enemy cruiser with his demicompany, English wasn't interested in a damned thing Cleary had to say.

His Associate AI took its cue from his spiking chemistries and wiped Cleary's purple bead off his com grid. Redhorse company's attenuated premission macho chatter filled his helmet. English toggled his visor back to real-time views of the men, equipment, weapons, and webbing in the back of the NOCM (Nocturnal Operations Clandestine Module) space-craft.

The dropmaster was floating over to his position by the door, pulling himself hand over hand like a spider, headed for a fly.

The bay door was going to open onto a near vacuum full of stars and enemy hardware and hostile telerobots and nothing much in the way of gravity. English's gut hated micro-gravity combat. His stomach was churning.

He self-tested the ELVIS/EVA pack he was humping into this battle: power-pack, jet-assist, and life-support for space combat, all in one SERPA special-issue package. Without it, he'd have died ten times already, doing these tweaky missions. But just because you had survived didn't mean you would survive. English's 92nd was writing the book on this kind of combat, as they went. And the survival-to-kill ratios, to boot. It wasn't confidence building.

Somehow the soft snoring of one of his veterans and the rhythmic gum-chewing of another steadied his nerves.

English turned and signaled Trask questioningly.

Trask, his Top, raised a fist and a thumb. They were in hush-time; you couldn't tell how much the Syndicate was capable of overhearing, SERPA countermeasures or not.

Sawyer, English's line lieutenant, caught his attention. Sawyer tapped his wrist and then his own helmet.

By then, English's helmet was showing him a yellow bead: dual-com.

"What, dammit, Sawyer? I got all these C&C parameters to soak up before we hit that hull." He was lying. He knew by heart what his SERPA team was supposed to do on that Syndicate hull. He just didn't have his heart in it. "You ready to jump, or what?"

Jump and drop were almost the same, these days. You didn't

get to fight anywhere but the space envelope when you were special electro-research. English's outfit had A-Potential experimental weaponry that made them all-Fleet choice for opening cans full of Syndicate robots, to see if there was anybody human inside, controlling the robots, or not.

English's dual-com diode pulsed: shielded. Sawyer said, "Query, Captain. Something wrong I should know about? TA Cleary just got off line with me. Said she couldn't raise you. Your coms self-test all right?"

"TA's a girl," English muttered, and then caught himself: "I'll talk to her when I have goddamned time, not going into a mission. Tell her to stay off the fucking internal privacy push, if she bothers you again."

Sawyer got up with the mastiff's grace that had made him English's first officer and sailed toward Toby slowly, gliding over APOT rifles and extended armored legs.

They put their helmets together. Sawyer said, off the com line: "Toby, you gotta relax. TA said—"

"Fuck TA," English snapped, but didn't break contact. His suit whirred as it ratched up his climate control. Cleary was going to kill him yet, getting him all hot and bothered before he— "Look, Sawyer, I got a bad feeling about this one, that's all."

Sawyer's helmet clicked against his as if the lieutenant had shaken his head inside it. "Anything happens to you, can I have your accumulated hazard pay?"

"Yeah, you bet. Take Manning on vacation to ASA-Zebra, on me." English dumped his visor scans and depolarized it, to look Sawyer straight in the eye. "We got about two minutes, I make it, before that door opens. You want to tell me something, Frank, you'd better tell me."

They'd known each other too long for English to miss all of Sawyer's signals: there was something more than a com status check on his blue-jawed lieutenant's mind.

Sawyer's faceplate cleared and he shifted to electronic privacy mode. At that moment English's AI decided that the captain needed a final scan of the drop zone and imported it to his visor display.

So English was looking at a synthesized schematic—a

real-time view of the Syndicate ship onto which his Marines were about to jump with the equivalent of blowtorches and can-openers—when Sawyer said, "TA wanted you to know that Nick Kowacs's One-Twenty-first was askin' for us by name before the *Haig* lost contact with them. The major wanted firepower and extraction, near as she could make out."

"Do I look like an air-taxi or a fairy godmother to you, Sawyer?" Despite himself, English's eyes defocused from the C&C graphic in front of him. If he had a friend anywhere in the Fleet outside the 92nd, it was Nick Kowacs. His mouth grew dry and needles seemed to be trying to sprout in his throat.

English pulled away from Sawyer and leaned his helmeted head back against the webbing draping the bulkhead, letting his eyes roam over his men. "Tell TA—" His words were a croak. He began again, "I'll talk to her. Get ready to rock and roll."

The dropmaster was reaching for the depressurizer. The red ready light started strobing.

And English's AI got him "TA," as soon as he thought about forming the sounds, while his hands were still automatically checking the seals on his gloves, his sensoring packages, and his hated A-Potential x-class weapons.

When she popped into his life again as a blinking red C&C bead, indicating she was safe on the *Haig* in the destroyer's war room, he'd already coaxed a test glow from the tip of his rifle. He popped the charge back into its native spacetime and half ported his weapon, pointing with his other hand to the dropmaster in an age-old "Go when ready" signal.

Sergeant Trask helped push the first of Toby's reaction Marines out the bay door as Cleary said, "Delta Two?"

English's Associate AI was, now and forever, "Delta One." The joke around the 92nd was that if any of the guys were killed inside their APOT suit-transducer/battle management systems, then the Associates would fight the rest of the battle using the powered exoskeletal suits to keep the corpses moving until the mission could be considered accomplished in terms that AIs recognized.

Whenever English heard Cleary's voice he wanted to quit this damned war, go somewhere and raise babies. He didn't touch her—not anymore. He couldn't touch her and do his damned job. But at least she was as safe as any soldier could be, in the belly of the highest-tech destroyer in the Fleet, Jay Padova's doubly retrofitted *Haig*.

"Delta Two to Ninety-two TA. Yeah, Cleary, what the fuck do you want from me? I ain't exactly goin' out to pick up diapers and a six-pack, here." She didn't know how he felt about her; she only knew he didn't want her in his outfit. He couldn't tell her why.

He could barely talk to her at all. When Sawyer and Manning had started sleeping together, English had bitched to all and sundry. So he couldn't sleep with Cleary. And he couldn't sleep without her, knowing she was a few bulkheads away. So he wasn't sleeping, and that didn't help his combat readiness one bit.

"Captain, Sawyer told you about Kowacs?"

"Yeah, yeah, TA. Did you hear me? I'm about to go soldier, here. You want me to bilocate, you got the wrong Marine. Otherwise, you and Manning can do any damn thing you think'll help the One-Twenty-first, and sign me off on your orders as you make 'em up." Better than that, nobody could do.

But Cleary's voice wanted better. Cleary always wanted better than you could do. He could see her so clearly—her dark hair, her pale intelligent eyes, her fine ass—that he couldn't see the bay door for a minute.

And when he could see it again, she was telling him that he ought to listen to what she had in mind and he was saying, "Just do it," because her transmission was overriding his audio of some problem at the bay door.

He got her out of his com and out of his head just in time to import the ongoing argument between Sawyer and the dropmaster.

"—can't take the risk," the dropmaster was yelling.

And Sawyer was growling, "My ass."

Then the NOCM shivered under English's feet as he moved toward the argument. Simultaneously the NOCM started to pull away from the Syndicate vessel under her.

English had men on that hull already—three of them!

He just kept moving, now that he'd started, toward the bay

door. He hardly saw his AI shift his coms as he said on open freqs, "Trask, flight deck. There's a little mistake here somewhere. Sawyer—"

Sawyer backed off, saying, "Navy says we can't—"

"Pilot's orders, Captain," said the dropmaster, an implacable growl in English's ears. "We've got to abort the drop. Too dangerous."

"You bet," said English, with a deep, regretful, understanding sigh, just before he bashed the dropmaster's helmet back against the bulkhead with the butt of his A-Potential rifle.

Sometimes you get lucky. The dropmaster slid bonelessly over the deck. English, tethering him to the webbing, said, "Everybody *go*! Guiness, drop 'em when ready."

No way they were leaving three of their guys on the skin of an enemy spacecraft.

Sawyer cut in to English's com: "Flight deck secure, slaved to your C&C circuit, sir."

Whatever Sawyer and Trask had done with, or to, the pilots, it didn't sound like they'd be flying anything, anywhere, anytime soon. The priorities of Marines in a naval fleet just weren't the same as your mission support's priorities.

As far as the Marines of the 92nd—the Fleet's badass electro-research specialists—were concerned, every Fleet machine and man were merely logistical support to their mission—whatever mission they were performing.

When English jumped down onto that enemy hull, he saw what the trouble was before his computer-assisted magnetic boots made hull contact: lots of Syndicate robots on the skin, defending their ship against the NOCM. They behaved like telerobots. But they couldn't be, because when you opened up the ships hauling them, there weren't any humans or life-support to suggest that humans had ever been inside.

Sawyer thought the Syndicate might be using some kind of A-Potential communicators, because A-Potential weapons ran on zero-delay, zero-point energy right out of Dirac's energy sea. But then, Sawyer was some kind of frigging rocket scientist, ever since he'd begun hanging out with Manning, the *Haig*'s Intel officer.

English didn't care if the robots were teleprompted by saints in East Jesus. He just wanted to blind their optical oscillators with ten to the tenth power neutrons per centimeter and about six million electron volts, the way his SERPA equipment was meant to do. That way, the eerie-looking metal men couldn't see him to shoot at him.

When he'd done that, starting with a flash to scramble the robots' incoming signals, he could use Transient Radiation Effects (TREs): any Syndicate robotic sensor or antenna was a pathway he could use to bombard a robotic combatant with TREs—as long as he could *see* it.

All this x-class SERPA antirobot gear depended on line of sight. You had to go one-on-one with the damned robots, to get them in your sights out in the open. Syndicate robots like these were shielded enough to be resistant to ionizing radiation to one hundred rads, so the power you were pushing out was in the gigawatt range and highly lethal to humans.

Which meant you really had to be careful about not shooting your own people with any of this gear while aiming invisible beams at a robot. Line of sight gave you huge fratricide problems, not just for Fleet communications gear, but for Marines.

The robots didn't care if they killed each other, as long as they killed Marines. So you went down real careful, and you shot real early. And you kept shooting, even if you couldn't see anything outside your black-polarized helmet.

Trask called these free-firing drops mad minutes. You shot all you could before you had Marines spread out along the hull among the enemy robots.

Once the 92nd was on the hull, your helmets ported in real-time field-of-fire grids. . . .

You played everything as close to the chest as you could, screaming and yelling yourself hoarse when the hull opened up by itself and more of the infernal things came climbing out to try overwhelming your fifty guys with sheer expendability.

English couldn't remember how many robots he'd personally shot. Or how many AI directives to move here or there or hit the deck or run like hell he'd obeyed. English's Delta Associate AI was better at commanding this mission than he

was. And they both knew it—if his Delta Associate knew
anything at all.

But it was English who had to talk to Trask, when Trask's
plot point orders brought him to direct intercept with five
telerobots trying to make off with Guiness's corpse in full
x-class armor.

The ported real-time view burst onto both of their visors at
once and English was shaking with suppressed combat reac-
tions: he wanted to shoot, but it was too dangerous; go over
there himself and help Trask.

But two of his three-teams were closer, and all he could do
was call them down.

No overhead fire from the NOCM was going to help them,
because anything that would take out these robots would take
out Redhorse's coms, life-support, weapons—and English's
Marines. Line of sight. All the enemy fiber optics terminated
in electronic hardware. To take out enemy hardware, you
risked taking out your own: fratricide.

Coms were dicey, by now. Hand signals and simulated
returns were replacing real-time field-of-fire grids on English's
screen because his AI had made some fucking command
decision. English had an override switch. He could pull his
Delta Associate's plugs and call his own plays without techno-
assist. But he was afraid to: his Delta Associate knew this
enemy better than he did.

He couldn't hear anything but his own breathing, so he
realized how ragged it was.

English pulled up a physio scan and blinked at what he saw:
his pulse rate was 140, his chemistries looked like they
belonged to a rapist on the rampage, and he'd lost three liters
of water from his body mass. All in fourteen and one-half
meters of combat. His oxygen-consumption rate was high, too,
but that was a blessing: otherwise, as spiked as he was, he
might wonder if he were still alive.

But, looking around him he saw, wonder of wonders, that
the skin of the Syndicate vessel was free of moving enemy
robots. One point for Redhorse.

He tried an all-com on a backup system and got a weak
response from Sawyer: "Headcount, Sawyer?"

"Captain . . . I make it one dead, two wounded but moving, and three down inside already."

"Let's finish it." He wanted to go down into that hive full of hostile robotics about as much as he'd want to sleep in a Weasels' den. Less, maybe. At least the Weasels hurt when they died.

He hated this fucking AI war. English had wanted to fight—and kill—Weasels, once: furry, vicious enemies with atrocious natures and a taste for human anatomy. He'd never wanted to fight electro-intelligences. Or humans.

Now the powers that were had decreed that the Fleet and its Marines fight side by side with Weasels against the Weasels' former oppressors. English didn't get it: humans should be siding with humans, the way he saw it.

Sometimes he wished he would find some guy from the Syndicate inside one of these space cans his ER company opened up for SERPA and OPSCOM and ISA and all the other acronymous spookish organizations, so he could ask a Syndicate human what the hell went wrong and why they were fighting each other.

But then at other times English remembered who and what he was: a Marine Reaction captain whose company was shoehorned into a Fleet destroyer.

Marine or no, Toby English had never wanted to kill people. He still didn't think it was any part of his job. The occasional personal enemy, such as a certain spook named Grant, maybe—but not humans in general. Killing men you didn't know and had no personal reason to kill was murder. Grant and his buddies from Eight Ball Command had made murderers out of English's 92nd, and then turned them into a special techno-commando outfit, and English couldn't do anything about that.

But if Toby ever got some Syndicate enemy in his sights, and the guy really was a human being, he was going to ask the megabuck question: How come we aren't negotiating some kind of settlement?

He couldn't figure why not, and nobody on his own side would tell him. If the Syndicate was a human society, you could trade with it. If you could trade with it, you didn't need to fight wars of extermination over turf and assets and raw materials.

It just didn't figure.

But this wasn't the day English was going to get an answer to his question. Once they'd cut through the Faraday-cage shielding, there was nothing inside the huge hull of the Syndicate vessel but more robots, in a dark, airless space that only infrared would illuminate well enough to suit English.

No people in here. Not a single Syndicate human. Just robots. Robots of every kind and some of no kind he'd ever seen, working in configurations he didn't understand.

But his AI did. Once they'd shot whatever attacked them, English's Associate directed what was left of the 92nd to take out particular stations and boxes and melt huge ropes of cabling as thick as a man, made up of a billion strands of hair.

During the search and destroy, English had to watch his C&C grid, trying to ensure that none of his guys disabled each other, shooting line-of-sight beams. And the whole while, somebody was humming in the emergency com, and somebody else was breathing too deeply, and coughing, a burbling cough full of far-too-much liquid.

During the entire sortie inside the Syndicate vessel, English couldn't raise a soul from the *Haig* or the NOCM that his AI insisted was still waiting above.

When they'd gutted the ship and English's Delta Associate had what it wanted, the AI in his helmet said, "Resume Command, Delta Two."

He hated his Associate every now and again. He'd programmed his not to talk to him except when absolutely necessary. Its voice added insult to injury.

And injuries they had. Not just fried equipment. Guys microwaved, irradiated, half-cooked—burned so badly through their suits that they sobbed or groaned when they moved. And two down from massive equipment failure.

But once you were out of the hull and under the stars, you could try telling yourselves it was worth it: the NOCM was going to be able to slave the Syndicate vessel and bring her in for study.

That was the mission, these days: acquire each other's

equipment, study enemy technology, try to reverse-engineer countermeasures—no matter how much hardware got fried or how many men lost their lives. . . .

English had to deal with Guiness's corpse. At least, now that the 92nd was in the personnel carrier, accelerating toward the *Haig*, they had gravity. Guiness's body wasn't floating around loose on its tether, nudging English's wounded and making them moan. He hadn't had First Sergeant Guiness under his command long enough to know, without pulling the dead guy's file, whether the poor bastard had a family for English to write some awkward letter to, tonight.

He knelt down over the body when they'd gotten it back aboard the NOCM and manually retracted the helmet visor.

The face in there, staring at him, had exploded eyes. Somehow, once Guiness's suit failed, a laser beam had hit him. In the human eye, a laser weapon's beam is magnified ten thousand times by the time it hits the retina.

English closed his own eyes. The mess was enough to make you want to retch.

He slammed Guiness's faceplate back down and stood up. The body was no longer somebody they'd lost in combat. Now it was a clear and present danger: "Listen up," he said, and he knew they could hear how harsh his voice was on all-com. "Fratricide problems are getting out of hand with this equipment. Guiness's countermeasures were fried and useless before he died. Or he wouldn't have died. So we killed him, girls. One of us. Some of us. Nobody in particular. No need for an investigation. Just keep in mind where your butts are, or we're going to lose more of us to our own weapons than to these fucking robots."

He went forward, taking off his helmet rebelliously. It was half-fucked, anyway. Ducking onto the flight deck, he saw Sawyer standing guard over the two angry, but now free to fly, Fleet pilots.

"Hi, fellas," English said as both heads turned his way. "You got something to say to me?" English still wore his kinetic kill pistol—always did. And as much as he hated killing humans, right now the two pilots who'd decided that saving their own asses was worth aborting English's mission with three of his men on an enemy hull in space weren't, to his mind, humans.

They were some lower form of life.

Something must have showed in his eyes. Both pilots turned around stiffly, without a word of complaint.

Sawyer said, "Hey, sir, you might want to get your messages."

"Just fucking tell me, okay, Sawyer? Whatever it is, it can't be so bad I need to hear it through this fritzy gear—it'll take me too long to find somethin' in this helmet that works the way it should."

"Yes, sir." Crisp. Taut. Cold as the space envelope around them.

As he really looked at Sawyer for the first time in hours, English caught a glimpse out the viewport of the planet called Khalia, below. Who'd have thought they'd be fighting to protect an alien stronghold? Nothing about this war made sense. . . .

"Sir—Toby, the *Haig* wants to know if we'll stop by the One-Twenty-first's ground coordinates on our way."

"Ain't on our way. Your gear must be in better shape than mine. Or do we not have wounded back there? I could have sworn—"

"Sir, Manning and TA went out there, to see what they could do for the One-Twenty-first. There was a big bang and now we've got a no-contact throughout a ten-klick area."

English leaned back against the wall. "Let's get there, Sawyer. You can brief me on the way."

He was filled with a weariness that was like something he'd felt before, only he'd never felt anything like this before. His gear was so heavy he had to put a hand on one of the pilot's couches.

And his heart felt it didn't want to beat. *No contact throughout a ten-klick area.*

Well, why the hell not? It was Saturday, wasn't it? English always hated to do dual missions on the weekend. He tried to remember what was the last thing he'd said to Cleary, and then gave up. He'd given her permission to do any damned thing she wanted.

With his blessing. He just hadn't figured she'd want to go try getting killed.

"How about casualty signs—sensoring readouts?" he managed to croak.

"Nothing. Some kind of backspill from the lobes of the non-nuclear EMP and TRE they were using. . . . The reflectivity of some source was enough to knock out everything in line of sight up to low orbit. We lost the overhead sensors in that area as well. We're lucky we didn't lose a manned spacecraft."

"Lucky," English murmured. That was nice to hear. It didn't matter how good you were, these days, if you weren't lucky.

When English's crippled outfit got to the coordinates of the 121st's distress signal and Manning and Cleary's subsequent rescue mission, English couldn't see any signs of life at first.

He kept coaxing his Delta Associate into some kind of delicate linkage with the *Haig* overhead, but they'd lost all the piggyback relays when they lost the geostationary comsat, and his Delta was full-up with mission data, still trying to self-repair all the damage its circuits had taken in the Syndicate engagement.

But the NOCM was plenty capable, yet. She was SERPA-spec, and when Sawyer booted the navy copilot out of his way and sat at the weapons officer's station, English realized how much his ER commandos had learned since they'd gone back to school.

And, English knew from the way his own body felt, you couldn't expect the results from an unconcerned navy pilot that you could from a Marine with a mission.

Sawyer and Manning had been an item since prehistory—way back when Sawyer was a sergeant and Toby was a lieutenant and they were collecting Weasel tails for their coup-coats.

"You go on aft, too," English told the navy pilot, who was glad enough to leave, since he was probably still expecting a 10mm slug in the back of the neck for trying to bug out while English had three men on that spaceborne LZ.

English had half a mind to do that still, the way he was

feeling. Just because the pilots weren't complaining yet didn't mean they wouldn't, later. But the mission was so successful, in Fleet terms, maybe you could let it go on faith. The Syndicate captive was parked at the *Haig* by now.

English had personally turned the Syndicate ship's control over to Jay's Operations Control as soon as Sawyer had briefed them. He'd had to do that before he could get an update on the 121st's situation.

Since he'd gotten it, everything that was happening to him was about a hundred kilometers away and badly attenuated. He knew Sawyer was in that same state, one you achieved only in certain kinds of combat when you were so overloaded that you either functioned at twice normal efficiency or half.

They were lucky, he and Sawyer, that they had some goddamn thing to do that seemed like it was going to help.

But since what they were doing was basically electro-reconnaissance and damage control, it only took the part of your brain that got used to interfacing intimately with special electronics.

English could feel his suit recalibrating itself to steal capability from the NOCM's undamaged circuitry, as if his Delta AI was telling him what it was doing.

As they swept down over the fire zone at last, electro-optics on full magnification and taking visual scans, English wasn't the least worried about getting shot at by whatever had blown this place to hell. There was enough residual damage that they had a good picture of what had happened.

It just wasn't a very survivable picture, if what they were guessing had been the case.

"Sawyer," he said softly, "all that rock and dirt and such might be our best hope."

Sawyer, his helmet on, visor up, trailing a lead into the console, turned his head. "You think they could have survived the planet-wrecker going off, huh?" Hopeful. A kid looked at him out of Sawyer's sick eyes.

"We got another, what, three klicks to overfly. The One-Twenty-first would have been in bunkers. When Manning and Cleary overflew low with a gigawatt of non-nuclear EMP beam and TRE management, my guess is they took out the threat that had the One-Twenty-first yelling for help."

"Yeah, and if the beam was on switchable, it went right down that straight-arrow excavation and tripped the interrupt circuit on the planet-wrecker. One booby trap, one hell of a subterranean explosion." Sawyer's blue jaw was bristling with hairs and shiny with sweat. It was so quiet on the flight deck that English could hear the sandpapery sound as Sawyer rubbed his callused palm over his chin to mask whatever expression he couldn't control.

They were a sorry pair, up here looking for their women and their friends and half hoping they weren't going to find their worst-case assessment.

"Sir, I can't see a way anybody could have lived through the transients of that blast. . . ."

"Nothin' shields like dirt and rock, Sawyer. So be prepared."

Dead was better than irradiated, at these power levels.

"The blowback crashed Manning and Cleary, that's for sure. And took out whatever coms the One-Twenty-first might have had a prayer of using, not to mention their weapons and any other damned thing they had."

So you didn't know if you were going to find lots of spectacularly dead bodies, or worse: lots of semi-destroyed but somewhat recognizable and sort-of sentient lumps of protoplasm that had once been Nick Kowacs's mighty Headhunters, the MRC that had been the 92nd's big-brother role model . . . and two of their own.

Two of their own. He'd had a bad feeling about this mission from before it started. He'd had a bad feeling about Cleary since the day she'd brought him her orders. He'd had a bad feeling about Sawyer and Manning ever since Grant from ISA found out that a sergeant was cleaning an officer's clock and used that information to blackmail the whole dumbass bunch of them into special ops because you couldn't say no to what you didn't understand was happening. . . .

English tried to rub his face with his hands and found his depolarized visor was in the way. "Delta One," he said quietly, "find me my people, you two-buck collection of chips, and I'll repair your ass rather than chuck you and start from scratch."

His Associate burbled at the edge of his hearing and English seduced the NOCM's nipples and sensors like he'd never had a chance to do to Cleary.

"I got somethin'," Sawyer said eventually in an absolutely flat voice.

By then English had it, too: a chewed-up chunk of ground that was a klick from the epicenter of the underground blast and glittering with fucked hardware.

"Get back there and see who wants to volunteer for this, Lieutenant."

Mentally, he was thinking he'd like Omega, Theta, and Alpha, Trask's three-team. They were all reasonably whole. . . .

Sawyer was unclipping the lead from his helmet to the console as he stood up and reached for his rifle and power-pack. "Wish we had ground packs."

They were thirty pounds lighter.

"We don't. I'm not expecting much resistance. Nothing electronic is sensing, let alone thinking, after the bath this place took. ETA five . . . four minutes."

Sawyer's visor was down as he headed aft.

English's dicey com sputtered to life in mono: "Captain, volunteers are Alpha, Theta, and . . ."

Everybody who was fit to fight wanted to join the party.

English took the team he'd hoped for, and left the rest to defend the NOCM. You could be wrong in this business. English and his 92nd were up and running here. The Syndicate could have brought in more hardware, sure that the Fleet wouldn't leave its casualties behind, and be lying in wait.

The first thing that everybody did when they hit the dirt was a wide sweep, recon rules, combat formations. The ground was littered with little robots, in some places as thick as grass seed in a plowed field.

You kept walking, trying to tell yourself you weren't afraid to see a hand or a foot with no body, just lying there somewhere. Telling yourself that was what you were here to find.

English had ported-in overhead from the NOCM, which was

a hundred feet above now and giving him everything from a synthetic-aperture alert-scan of the terrain for a hundred klicks in any direction, downloaded from some passing satellite, to micro-counts on the fried enemy hardware.

So he saw the worst of it first, through his helmet display.

And stopped for a minute, before he realized that nobody else on the ground could see what he was seeing, or would see it with such graphic clarity.

He called a grid square number and headed for it, banishing the real-time image of guys crawling over chunks of earth and stumbling blindly around and trying to dig each other out from under debris.

You set off a planet-wrecker a few klicks down, you move a lot of crust. It would have taken a couple hundred of those Syndicate bombs, maybe more, to have split open the planet totally, and this one was in that Alliance-excavated vertical shaft.

But it had done more damage to Toby English's heart than it would have if this whole side of Khalia was vaporized.

He wanted to look at this some way he could stand it. He couldn't tell from the visuals just who had whose arm over whose shoulder, or who was under what.

His Associate anticipated him and reformated the data so he got it as a nice, clean C&C grid: colored dots, moving across grid lines; blinking bars under them, awaiting identifying numbers.

You couldn't ask for a better buffer, and English's training responded to the mode of information transfer. He counted moving dots. When he got to seventy-four, he told Sawyer what he had.

There was ongoing, muted chatter in his com, because he wanted to hear live guys talking. He was running a semitransparent superimposition, so he could see his own men in his visual field, as well as the movement in the casualty grid, and his own guys' positions, fanned out over the area.

"Call them in, when ready, Sawyer."

Sawyer was looking for Manning's support craft, and English didn't have the heart to tell him he shouldn't. There was no way you wanted to push anybody, while you were doing this, to go any faster than that man could go.

There was just too much death here. English was trying to tell himself that as slow as they were going, it was faster than the Fleet, overburdened and still engaging the enemy out there in the space envelope, could have gone.

But he wasn't at all sure that somebody else couldn't have gotten here sooner or at least zeroed the problem sooner. Better.

He called the NOCM and told it to put down in the grid square where what was left of the 121st showed life signs. "And don't read me your fucking navy rule book. Patch me through to the *Haig*—Padova himself, SERPA authority."

He was going to get some medevac down here, or he was going to sit down here and crash every Fleet vehicle that came into the 92nd's line of sight, using the NOCM for booster power.

One thing about ER outfits was that on the ground or in space, you really didn't want to get one mad at you, if you were electronic or fiber-optic dependent.

"Delta Two, status report? Toby?" Captain Padova's voice was harried and full of static.

Jay Padova loved technological supremacy, so he loved Toby English's SERPA toys. The *Haig* had lots of similar experimental hardware because SERPA's ER commandos shipped in her.

English said laconically, "Status report: living casualties, at least seventy, in need of medevac, hours ago. What's the matter up there, Jay, you too busy to take care of your ground-pounders?"

"We didn't have any indications of life signs, Captain," said Padova stiffly. "At least, I didn't hear about it. And yes, we're somewhat overextended."

"Well, sir, I know that. Does the captain want to extend me a bird or two for the One-Twenty-first, since their own people seem to be too busy to give a shit, or am I staying out of the war until I ferry each of these guys up to their own ship, one at a time, personally?"

"Look, Captain," said Padova's voice, suddenly thick with

emotion. "I couldn't stop those women of yours. You gave them carte blanche to use your authority. Now, we'll have somebody down to you as soon as we can. Triage those wounded and get them—and yours—off the ground and back here as soon as you can. Forget protocol. We'll take care of the One-Twenty-first like they were our own."

A blast of static made all of English's visuals dump, then re-form. So Padova didn't hear him cursing the way no officer ought to curse a command chain.

When the static cleared, Padova was saying, "—and give Major Kowacs my compliments and best hopes, if he's alive down there."

"If he's alive down here, sir, I surely will. Delta Two out."

He punched at the manual cut circuit on his belt, but his Associate had broken the connection already.

Sawyer beat him to the fire zone. It looked like God had taken a handful of this alien earth and dropped it on the 121st for spite.

Alpha was already digging away at something that might have been a bunker. Artillery lay here and there. English's feet slipped on small robots that crunched underfoot like broken glass.

They were all over the place.

He retracted his visor and the smell of the fire zone was one of blood, new earth, feces, and fried flesh.

His ears heard an almost subliminal sobbing on a soft breeze. The 121st was a full company. He saw two guys with Headhunter patches pulling a third from a pile of rocks and dirt. Everybody was bareheaded, filthy, ripped to shit.

The first three faces he saw were badly burned. Then he saw a blind guy being fireman-carried by another Headhunter.

You just kept moving. His own all-com told him how hard this was for his people. He kept his visor open stubbornly: he was getting all the command and control he needed via audio.

His Delta Associate would tell him if he really should see anything more. Facing this carnage, he wasn't willing to screen it off with hardware-assists.

Every once in a while he said, "Sawyer?" just to make sure his lieutenant was still in the circuit.

Then Sawyer would say, "Still looking, sir."

He was glad he wasn't Sawyer, until he finally found Nick Kowacs and his big lady corporal.

Major Kowacs was propped up against a boulder. There was another, slightly smaller one, sitting on his left leg. He had Sie's hand in his lap. Her whole torso was shivering. Everything below her hips was under solid rock, and her face was bright red and yellow with flash burn.

English took off his helmet and laid it on the dirt beside his knee as he knelt down across from Kowacs. Could the major focus on him?

Kowacs had a communicator in his other hand, as if the damn thing might just start working. It was nonregulation, some little black job. One half of Kowacs's face was bright orange and suppurating. The other was greenish white.

At least they'd had pharmakits, English thought, until he realized that the pharmakits' electronics wouldn't have been dispensing, so whatever these guys got out of them was a matter of luck and no kind of measured doses.

When you manually tried to do anything in this fucking war, you screwed up.

Kowacs rolled his head, just slightly, as if he were aware that English—or somebody—was there.

English squinted at that face and couldn't tell if the swollen eyelids were protecting anything usable in the way of eyes, or if light could get past the lids. Kowacs's eyelashes were singed off.

"Hey, Nick," English said shakily. "It's me, Toby. S-sorry it took us so long."

Kowacs took a deep, ragged breath. "Toby. Sie'll be glad . . . you showed up. She . . . was sure . . ." Kowacs's blistered lips stopped trying to form words.

English reached out to touch his friend and then couldn't: he didn't know where to touch Kowacs that wouldn't hurt.

He said, "We'll get you guys out of here. Just sit tight." He thought he saw Sie move her head, so maybe she was still alive, but maybe not.

Anyway, alive was a relative term.

He wanted to get out of there, to turn his back and make himself useful somewhere else. So he didn't.

He sat down right there, legs crossed, rifle on his knees, to keep watch over Nick Kowacs and his Headhunter corporal until either they died or somehow the 92nd could get them free.

He put his helmet back on to try to figure how they were going to do that. It took a very long time.

And then, when they were doing it, Kowacs couldn't help but scream and English fled.

He broke and ran.

And ran. He pulled up short somewhere on the other side of one of the big rocks, head down, gulping air, leaning on the rock with a straight arm. He knew damned well they should have waited for the medevac, not tried freeing Kowacs and Sie on their own. . . .

Now he had to go back there, and face his own guys, who'd seen him cut and run.

But at least he wouldn't be seeing big Sie's mangled legs in his dreams forever.

The crying of the wind was the crying of the 121st, soft and muted, mixed and more like mourning or keening than guys in excruciating pain.

He took a deep breath and stood on his own, trudging back, eyes on the ground and on what his visor was showing for progress reports.

The medevac birds were ten minutes from being any use. When they got here, he'd find out whether strapping his own pharmakit on Kowacs had been the right thing to do or whether, because ER gear was calibrated and neuro-typed to the user, he'd just made a bad situation worse.

Sawyer said, "Hey, English, get your ass over here."

He'd forgotten all about Sawyer's hunt for the crashed support bird. He didn't need to ask where "here" was: it came up on his display, along with the best possible route.

His legs were rubber, and he couldn't bring himself to ask Sawyer what Sawyer had found.

Sawyer didn't volunteer anything, either. English had a rescue mission to run and they both knew it. That meant everybody was an equal priority.

It was bad enough to hike halfway to hell from the main fire zone before the medevac even set down. . . .

When he got there, Sawyer and his Theta team were just about finished cutting open the bird.

They'd punched out, both of them: no Manning, no TA Cleary. Their seats were gone, exploded out of the lost canopy, but you couldn't tell that until you got inside, because the bird had crashed on her back.

Sawyer looked up at him and wiped his arm across his mouth: "Now what?"

"Now we mark them down MIA and go back—or at least I do. I found Kowacs, alive, sort of; and Sie—less alive, sort of. I can't stay here—"

English's voice broke and Sawyer got off the wing he was sitting on, fast.

English didn't remember how Sawyer came to be holding him in a bear hug. He just stood there and shook until his lieutenant could let go.

English said, "You can stay here until you've satisfied yourself, or until you find something, or until I call you in. I call you in, you and Theta come, here? I don't need *you* MIA."

"Understood, Toby," said Sawyer. And: "We get the Observer, this time."

"Yeah," said English, slapping his Delta into ERASE, RERE-CORD. "We do." The Observer was Grant. If this rat fuck was anybody's fault, it was Grant's. The ISA honcho had had this coming for a long time. "Kowacs had what looked to me to be an A-Potential communicator—nonstandard for his outfit—in his hand." Only Grant could have given Kowacs SERPA-spec gear. "So whenever you're ready, Lieutenant Sawyer—"

"I hate MIAs."

"Yeah," said English. There was a part of his soul that was MIA, too.

He couldn't tell if they'd ever get any of the missing back. His body didn't think it needed a heart anymore, anyhow. It hadn't thought so for the last few hours.

He heard the medevac birds above and slammed down his visor. "Good luck, man," he told Sawyer, but he couldn't look at him.

They'd run out of luck, and both of them knew it. Next, they were going to run out of time. War doesn't stop just because you've misplaced a couple of people.

Even when you care too much about those people.

Caring about Kowacs and Sie and the poor fucked 121st was already more than English could handle. His helmet and his AI were beginning to seem like the only refuge he had in a world turned upside down and crazy.

He stayed in there, doing everything he could for everybody, but making sure that nobody was more than a colored set of number designators, until they had the entire 121st mede-vacked off the kill zone.

Then he had to go pick up Sawyer in the NOCM, and he couldn't say a damned word.

They hovered three feet off the ground, kicking up dust, until Sawyer and the Theta team came aboard empty-handed.

And finally, he was in a bird with no dead guys and no wounded guys: the medevac had taken the 92nd's own wounded to the *Haig*, as well as the 121st's.

English was secretly glad that he couldn't hear anybody crying or breathing with difficulty or groaning or moaning. Not in his com. Not in the belly of the personnel carrier. Not anywhere but in his memory.

The *Haig* seemed too empty to English, even though it was busy as hell with all the space combat units in the area that needed help from the leading-edge destroyer's special Intel-gathering capabilities.

MIAs made it empty. Missing In Action is the emptiest acronym the armed forces ever created. Your MIAs follow you around like personal ghosts, always there between you and what's happening in the real-time they may, or may not, be inhabiting.

Where *were* they, down there, Cleary and Manning? With all their electronics fried in the blast that crashed their ship, there just wasn't any way to find them. You could scan for life signs, if you had the entire ship's capabilities at your personal disposal. But not for a particular set of life signs. And there was plenty of life on Khalia. So it was a waste of time.

If they were slowly bleeding to death down there, English thought he'd be able to tell. If they were being eaten alive by renegade Khalians, Sawyer surely would have felt it. If they were already dead, the two men assured each other, then years of combat instinct would have let them know.

So they convinced themselves that Manning and Cleary were out there somewhere, trying to make it to an Alliance facility. It was what they wanted to believe.

And it was easier than thinking about the casualties they'd sent up, before the 92nd, to the *Haig*. Once they'd parked the NOCM and shepherded their own men through equipment check-in, after-action reports, combat refit, and ready-checks, there was nothing left but physicals.

Which meant you had to go up to the mededeck—where the 121st was. Where what was left of the 121st was.

The Headhunters had their own damned ward. English could have stayed out of there, if he were smarter than a piece of AI. But he'd been electro-research so long that he thought more like his Delta Associate than like a man.

Or so he told himself, as he used his officer's clout to browbeat his way past the orderlies and into the Headhunters' ward. He couldn't imagine what Sawyer's excuse was, for taking on all this additional punishment—or so he pretended.

But he did know. They'd lost their TA and the *Haig*'s Intel officer, and as far as they were concerned, they had some payback to do.

Big guys in full combat gear who had clearly just come through refit can look a little scary if you're in the lifesaving part of the war business. English's hardsuit was patched with shiny resurfaced places and inset with new, unburned electronic modules whose housings were smoked where the old ones had fried. His helmet didn't say his name on it, yet, since it was brand-new and he'd just ported his files and his ER micros into it wholesale.

He couldn't decide what was better: having his Delta One Associate running happily in a brand-new housing, or not having his name on his helmet. Next to the pharmakit slung at his waist was his kinetic pistol. It was the only piece of

equipment he had that didn't need a retrofit after this particular
Saturday afternoon.

A woman doctor came out of nowhere and planted herself
between English and Sawyer, and the oxy tent in which
Kowacs was lying, greased, patched, and hooked up to some
serious life-support.

English was still testing his helmet, so he had it on visor
down. He ran a WINTEL warning video display across the
front where she could see it: WARNING: INTELLIGENCE SOURCES
AND METHODS.

She gestured angrily at him, her mouth working. Somehow,
he didn't want to hear what she had to say, so he wasn't taking
audio. He put out a gloved hand, took her by the shoulder, and
moved her out of his way.

What right did she have to be up here giving him a hard time
when Manning and Cleary were MIA?

You got real quirky when things went this bad, this long.
"Sawyer, you want to stay here and deal with her?"

She wasn't going away. She was right back there in front of
him, seventy kilos of ministering angel. He tried to tell himself
that she was Kowacs's angel, so he shouldn't shoot her.

"Sir—Toby, if you're goin', go."

"Right."

He looked back once and saw the huge form of his ER
lieutenant looming, in full kit (including ELVIS pack), over the
woman, hands on his hips, apparently listening to whatever she
was saying.

English's gloved hand was shaking when he pulled the tent
seal open. He was taking full audio, so he heard the warning
beeper that said he'd disturbed something. Damn, he didn't
want to hurt Kowacs's chances. . . .

The man under all that medication wasn't looking any too
conscious. English went off line, flipped up his visor, and said,
"Nick, I need that communicator you had—the black one.
Nick, where is it? Can you hear me?"

Those painfully swollen eyelids quivered, as if eyes were
roving under them. Kowacs moved his fingers, and a sound
came from the 121st's major that English would never forget.

Animal pain that escapes despite your best intentions isn't

anything to be ashamed of, but Kowacs was trying to talk, not telegraph agony.

English leaned close. He could smell pus already, and burned soldier, and shit and worse. He wanted to close his eyes but he couldn't. He was coaxing, "Come on, Nick, remember the black box?" when Sawyer's voice in his com said, "I got it, Toby. Let him be. She says you're bringing germs he can't fight."

Great. What's a little more guilt? English got out of there, trying not to "touch anything, you dolt," the way the lady doctor ordered.

She slapped the black communicator down into his open hand as if she couldn't care less what she had there.

All war toys were the same to some of these folks, who cleaned up afterward.

"Is he going to be all right, Doctor?" English asked.

"That," said the woman with a face full of lines, "depends on your definition of 'all right.' Fit to fight, perhaps? I'm not sure. Maybe someday. But not all right, I don't think. Not ever. Let's hope we don't have to replace that much of you, sonny, in the near future: these Headhunters have about exhausted our store of kamikaze replacement parts."

"Are you threatening me?" he said very softly, through his bullhorn, as he polarized his faceplate flat black.

"No . . . Captain. I'm warning you. We're low on plasma, synthetic skin, and replacement organs—unless a few more of your friends here die and those haven't been microwaved so badly that their livers are medium well done. So don't bring us any more strays, *all right*? In case you need us. Do . . . you . . . copy . . . Captain?"

"Go fuck yourself," English suggested, waving a hand at her dismissively that, in other circumstances, might have lashed across her face.

"Sir, if you don't mind me saying so, you asked for that."

"And that's not all we're going to ask for," English said on the way out of there. They were up near the Intel decks. "Let's see if we can find out where this com box was tuned to send Nick's transmissions."

"Oh, man. You thinking what I'm thinking?"

"Take a look at it."

As they spoke, they were moving through the halls. Staffers up here didn't often see full-kit ground-pounders, but ER went where it wanted. This was the first time Toby English realized how much clout his SERPA ticket could deliver.

Sure, he could see Padova, anytime, and no regular Marine could do that. But his SERPA clout had them in the depths of the war room before he knew it. This was where TA should have been. If Cleary had stayed here, everything would have been okay. They'd have gotten to Nick's Headhunters anyhow. . . .

And then, finally, he admitted to himself that maybe there wouldn't have been any live Headhunters to get to, if Cleary and Manning hadn't gone in with their close-support weapons, and he nearly bumped into a console because he couldn't see straight for a minute.

MIA. Shit.

Sawyer was taking off his helmet. English stopped him. The war room was a wonder if you hadn't spent all that time on an electro-research station. Still, it was the best in the Fleet. And it was humming.

They stood around for a full five minutes before anybody bothered to ask them what they were doing there.

Then English said, "Friend of mine had this. We want to know how come, and who's receiving from it. SERPA requests immediate TS/SCI/RD response."

That moved asses. You had to learn the alphabet to succeed in this man's Fleet.

Somebody came back with a mini-message chip. "Here you are, sir. In your encoding. One copy only." Pale eyes tried to look past English's faceplate. No way, buddy: you're not going to know a damned thing about who I am or what I want; you couldn't get cleared for it if you lived to be a hundred. Eat your heart out.

On his dual-com, English said, "How about we go sit in the officers' lounge and see what happens when we send somebody a message on this?"

Sawyer said, "If it's the somebody I think you mean, do you want to see him in the officers' lounge?"

"Nope. But I want it clear where I was, at least some of the time tonight. After all, Saturday night, middle of a war—anything can happen."

Talking about killing Grant from ISA wasn't something you did with your gear up and running. There were too many ways to reconstitute wiped memory. And Eight Ball Command, Grant's outfit, knew every trick in the book. They wrote the book.

So the bar was a nice, loud, safe place to be, full of white noise and transients and neon. English cuddled up under a blinking beer logo that was putting out enough buzz to defeat any possible recording device except an AI-assisted lip-reader. He only talked when he had his beer mug to his lips.

They worked out what they wanted to do, and how. It didn't take long. After all, the two of them were experienced murderers, trained by Eight Ball Command and equipped for assassination of enemy infiltrators by the Interservice Support Activity.

Sawyer needed a shave. So did English. His eyes were bleary and his fingers stubbornly refused to find anything on that communicator that would tell him more than if you pushed TALK and talked, maybe something got sent somewhere. To somebody. The chip from the war room hadn't told him to whom, or where.

"We ought to take it back to the Ninety-second's tech bay and open it up, before we—"

"Here, Sawyer. Feel it," English suggested.

The com box was little, oblong, black as sin, and cold as hell. "You know APOT when you see it. This thing could be talking to the other end of the universe—but it's not. It's talking to someplace on the *Haig*. Otherwise, how would TA have gotten Kowacs's distress call?"

They *were* going to kill Grant, this time. But first they had to flush him. "You try," English suggested.

"Okay, sir." Sawyer's pupils were tiny black dots, despite the low light in here. "Ninety-second ER, Lieutenant Sawyer speaking. Request meet. Repeat, request one-on-one. *Haig* secure; request on-site. Sawyer out."

If English had had to hand/eye print his way into some

secure facility right now, he'd never have gotten past an AI screener looking for psychotic chemistries. He knew it. He just wasn't willing to do anything about it. Neither was Sawyer.

But they were smart enough to try making Grant come to them. After all, SERPA commandos had permission to jump echelon when they needed to.

The communicator didn't light up, answer, or do any damn thing except stay cold.

But along about closing time, somebody came in, looked around, and left without ordering anything.

"See that?" Sawyer said.

"Yep." Unconsciously, English checked the kinetic pistol on his hip.

"I told you," Sawyer said, drunk and sick at heart, sounding whiny, "they're not fools enough to give us a shot at the pig-bastard."

English had been to the bathroom twice, and nobody'd slithered out from under a urinal to fix a meeting.

"Let's go," he said, and got up.

If Grant wasn't going to come to him here, then they'd do it the hard way.

But as soon as they'd left the bar, two guys out of uniform closed in on them from either side, saying, "You're ER, right?"

"We're it," English affirmed. "What's it to you?"

"You've got a special mission briefing in twenty minutes on the Intel deck."

Bingo. "Why am I not surprised?" he said.

Sawyer said, "Redhorse isn't in any shape to deploy for at least forty-eight hours."

The two guys were clean-shaven, friendly looking, and unconcerned. "If you'll come with us . . ."

At least they didn't try disarming English. He wasn't in any mood for that.

Sawyer kept giving him looks. Their helmets were slung on their hips. English knew what Sawyer was thinking: they were throwing their lives away, trying this now, this way, on the Observer's terms.

But Grant had cost them way too much.

English had almost convinced himself that Grant wouldn't dare face them when they got to the Intel deck. Their escort stopped at an unmarked office door: "Here you go, sirs."

English, for one, didn't feel much like a "sir" right then.

Behind the door, Grant was waiting, sitting at a desk with his home-world haircut and that cat-and-mouse smile.

The Observer still had his tweaky red cord on his wrist.

English knew that if he let Grant start talking, he was lost.

Sawyer was already having second thoughts. Cold-blooded was lots harder than hot-blooded, and they'd had time to cool down.

Grant said, "I've got a mission for you boys that—"

English's kinetic pistol somehow leaped into his hand of its own accord. He never remembered making the decision. He never remembered sighting down its barrel.

He sure as hell never recalled squeezing the trigger gently, so gently, shooting one-handed at the big man in the suit behind the desk.

But then he remembered everything that happened in a rush: the men from the corridor outside pouring in, Sawyer's face, full of anguish and remorse, and Jay Padova's security people.

He saw a series of floors and walls and gun butts and fists. And then he saw a psychiatric counselor who told him, "You know, your timing was terrible, Captain English. The fighting has stopped."

He didn't know what that meant. He was too tired to care. He couldn't sleep for the MIAs in his dreams.

And nobody would let him see Sawyer. If he didn't want to talk to Sawyer so badly, he probably wouldn't have minded talking to so many guys he didn't want to talk to, including Grant.

And that was strange, because he was sure he'd shot Grant dead.

But the big home-world spook came into English's electro-restraint cell, sat down on the other side of the clear partition, and said, "If you're decompressed, Captain, maybe we can have a little talk. We still need you, and I'm willing to pretend this didn't happen if you are."

"You're the one with the fucking hole in you," English said

hoarsely. The big spook was too stiff when he moved not to be taped and stitched. One thing English knew by sight was a wounded man.

Forget this? His MIAs? Kowacs with that APOT communicator in his hand? How?

"English, I keep trying to teach you that I'm not your enemy."

"So, I'm a slow learner. Court-martial me. Let's pretend, like you said, that I believe you."

"Okay," said Grant, as smoothly as a newsreader giving a sanitized report of the Alliance's latest "victory." "SERPA wants you back in the field. So do I. But it's going to take some doing, this time, asshole."

"I don't care if I ever go back out. Didn't you get my message? I want to get some sleep, except I can't because some of my people are MIA. . . . Never mind. Fuck you. Go train another fool to use this freaky-ass gear. It makes you crazy. Or haven't you noticed?"

"We know. As I said, we're in a tight spot. Sawyer's agreed to take this deal. Why don't you?"

"What's the deal?"

"Back into combat, friend, no harm done. Nothing in your jacket. No questions asked or answered. Same venue. If you really want to shoot a human enemy, I may have the right person for you, in a little while. But right now, I'm considering this a misunderstanding between us, personally, and nothing to do with service records."

"Right, I've been in this hole for—" How long? He didn't know. Maybe not too long, if they needed him to put the 92nd back in the field. "—long enough to be missed, anyway, and *nothing happened*. Spooks." He shook his head.

"Is that a yes, English?"

"I dunno. How's Kowacs?"

"Yes or no, cowboy. We won't ask again. If I have to replace you, you're dogmeat. Come out of this, and you and I will go after the problem together. As I said, I'm willing to consider this whole episode just a misunderstanding."

Grant was one tough bastard, English thought grudgingly. "I thought the fighting had stopped."

"I can't talk to you until and unless you give me the answer I want to hear, Captain."

"You got it," said English with a deep sigh. It would be good to be able to move around freely. He missed Sawyer. He even missed his Delta Associate. But this was so weird, his hackles were up. "I got to tell you, I'm going to find my MIAs."

"I hope so, English. Now, if you want to ask me questions, I'll answer them."

Damn, you couldn't even screw up bad enough to get out of this fucking war. He didn't get it. But of course he did: the 92nd was too valuable to lose. It was nothing personal, as Grant said.

All of which made English not much more than nothing, himself. Next time he went hunting humans, he'd do better. But then he'd be hunting his MIAs.

Somewhere, Cleary and Manning were alive, he told himself. And so whatever he did to get to them had to be worth it. Nobody else would try to find them until there weren't any higher priorities.

He looked at the man he'd tried to kill and saw nothing but relief in Grant's clear, intelligent eyes. Then the mission briefing started, and Toby English realized that this was for real.

He was getting out of jail free, just like the card in his wallet said he could do. For the duration of the war, at least, *he* was too valuable to lose.

When he walked back into the Marine tech bay, he knew he'd only been in solitary for around forty-eight hours. He waved offhandedly to the non-coms working on their gear, and headed for his APOT suit.

In the helmet, hanging upside down on its hook, was a black communicator. Just like the one Kowacs had had. Maybe the same one Kowacs had had.

But this time he knew what to do with it.

Sawyer came up behind him and said, "Hey, sir. Nice rest, huh?"

He turned around and grinned at Sawyer bleakly. "Not really. Get staff together. I'll want to brief in forty minutes."

"Phew," said Sawyer. "Yes, sir."

English tried to assess Sawyer's damages as the lieutenant walked away. You couldn't see anything wrong in his lieutenant's walk or the set of his shoulders. It was all in the look of his eyes.

But everything was wrong in wartime, or else you wouldn't be out here fighting electro-intelligences in the first place.

Cleary, honey . . . Manning. This one's for you.

CALL TO CONQUEST
by Judith R. Conly

Lo! LONG WE linger and languish in lassitude,
vowed to vigilance in viewing the victory
of erstwhile invaders who, ending enmity,
forbade us to foray, fearless in friendship,
to blast to oblivion bare-skinned betrayers.

Solemn our study of swarms of swift ships
stalking silently, streaks across star screens,
while we watch, world-bound, like wilt-whiskered weaklings,
grasping at ghosts of gray-furred glory
from poets' patter of precious past pride.

But, brethren, behold! blood-bonded battle mates,
masters of mind and mechanical magic,
maneuvered by militant might from maintaining
positions prophetically planned for perfection,
falter before the fire-flood of foemen.

How can heroes huddle, heart-heavy and helpless,
while gold-greedy givers of grief gain ground?
Impossible! Peaceable pets seek permission;
warriors wait but for weapons to wield,
to limn lofty legends in laser-born lightning!

INTERLUDE

Articles of War
Article XXXVIII
All Papers, Charter-Parties, Bills of Lading, Passports, and other writings whatsoever that shall be taken, seized, or found aboard any ship or ships which shall be taken as Prize shall be duly preserved, and the Commanding Officer of the ship which shall take such a prize shall send the Originals entire and without Fraud to the Court of the Admiralty . . .

Article XXXIX
No Person subject to this Act shall take out of any Prize or Ship seized for Prize any money or goods, unless it shall be necessary for the better securing thereof, or for the necessary use and Service of any ships and Vessels of War . . .

From Khalia all the destruction and ruin was visible as no more than an occasional twinkling among the otherwise uncaring stars. As the fighting grew in intensity, streaks of light representing falling warships became more common.

Duane's attempt to pierce the Syndicate formation stalled, but forced the opposing admiral to commit his reserves. As the edges of the cone caught up to the dreadnoughts, the battle developed into a test of sheer attrition. Eventually the greater experience the Fleet personnel had gained fighting the Khalia began to give them an edge. Even so, the Syndicate ships continued to push forward until they were close enough to Khalia that several stray missiles actually exploded within the planet's atmosphere.

Then, even as Duane prepared to order the planet-based missiles into action, the Syndicate ships began to back slowly away from the planet.

RONIN
by S. N. Lewitt

IN THE MIDDLE of battle there was absolute silence. It brought back memories of other battles, other times. Bethesda and then Khalia itself, the ready hangar of the Screaming Eagles, the Scout Fast Attack Group. It had been lit just the same way and the waiting was just as hard.

Backlit schematics stained the darkness with nursery colors, far too innocent for the symbols on the main screens. On the tracking board ships did not die in a barrage of shrapnel and steel. They made fireworks in violet and tangerine, electrons that didn't record the reality of dying. Here in the bunker it was all perfectly still, impeccably clean.

A solitary human stood before the board. Even though he was surrounded by his own troops he was completely alone. His "men," as he thought of them, strained at their stations in the observation center, trying to emulate his rocklike immobility. They almost succeeded, although it was against their nature.

They did not have his reasons for standing so still, his need for something like prayer. Fixed on the board he interpreted the symbols as if he himself could see the battle that raged above.

They had all known that it was Khalia that the Syndicate wanted. Matsunaga could have told them that weeks ago, long before any recon reports had come back and before the Intelligence and Tactics Divisions had gotten hold of anything substantial. Matsunaga had known the same way he had known that the Khalia could be trusted and that the Syndicate was on the edge of breaking. He felt it in his gut.

An alien came up beside him. Matsunaga could smell the being, the raggy pelt and the rasping breath, and he turned slowly. It had taken him months to learn not to flinch from that smell.

"Shall we prepare now, sir?" the Khalian asked him. Only a few months ago he would have called the being a Weasel and his only conflict would have been should he aim for the head or the chest. Now this one was his most competent subcommander.

"Not yet, Asheko," Matsunaga answered softly. "Patience."

The Khalian growled and bared its teeth. Matsunaga looked away. Little children, that was the best they were. That, but terribly fierce. They were useful. He had to remind himself of that constantly, when the odor of wet fur and an undercurrent of disruptive growling became nearly unbearable.

Hadn't his ancestors been able to handle the unbearable when it was necessary? Hadn't it been one of their sources of pride, of propriety, to do so? And was his own duty and honor any the less because he lived now instead of then and his masters were the whole of the human race?

It helped to remember. He had already endured enough to make sure his plan worked. If it was needed. Part of him hoped that it would not be necessary. The other part, the larger, prayed that it would. Then he could finally prove his worth, his loyalty.

Again he thought of his very favorite story. When he was little his mother had told him about the forty-seven ronin every night for three years. Their lord murdered, these samurai had not followed him into the void. For three years they waited and endured insults. They were ronin, bandits, the lowest thing a samurai could become. And they let the stories about them grow, making people believe they had left honor and duty behind. They had waited for years, but eventually they had their revenge on the man who had murdered their lord. Then, their true duty done, they had chosen seppuku.

He had played at being one of the ronin, had imagined it when school lessons were boring, had known that there was no honor higher than those who had suffered to get their revenge. They had been his heroes, and Kazuo Matsunaga had always wanted to be a hero.

Then the Fleet had given him the chance.

He'd been one of the Screaming Eagles' top jocks, twenty-seven Weasel heads stenciled on his fighter's belly. Twenty-seven kills in vacuum combat and those Weasel raiders weren't wet behind the ears, either. Top of the line plasma cannon and homers on gyro tracers, all very state of the art.

There had been something magical about single combat with a raider. They were fast and good and turned like a dream. They could cut your tail at max and shoot smart goods at the same time. And, being built the way they were, the Khalia didn't have to worry so much about blacking out on high-speed turns and dives. They just went.

It had taken all his brain and all his ice-cold courage to fly those missions. Every one of them had been a surprise, doing escort duty for a bunch of whining indies who couldn't care from shit, out patrolling long hours in a hard seat with no toilet nearby, and then, all of a sudden, a Weasel appeared on the screen.

The first moments were vital. At long range the Fleet fighters held the edge. Their smart torps were faster with a better lock. No matter how the bandit flew the torp would get him once it pinned on target. But close in the torps were dangerous. He knew one guy who flew into one of his own ordnance in the middle of a fight. Talk about buying the farm the wrong way.

But escort patrols were so boring and long that sometimes it was easy to zone out and not notice the incursion in the first seconds, when a flyer could still squeeze the advantage, before the bandits closed in. He'd done that twice, and both times came closer to the void than he wanted. There wasn't any honor in being stupid. His *sensei* would have been horrified at his lack of concentration.

Which was how he got twenty-seven kills. Not just on smart torps, but on closing scissors on the gomer and slagging his wake down. The raiders might be faster than the Fleet fighters, but Matsunaga knew that his craft had the staying power, that he had the fuel to burn, and he could flush out an enemy and run him down like a wolf pack tiring its prey. Some lessons the old *sensei* taught were deeper than bone.

And the carrier was good, too. The *Jeanne d'Arc* held seventeen fighter groups on convoy duty and that was about all she did. The pilots knew each other like family and with convoy work, well, the indies might be a bunch of fat ingrates but they did lift over supplies every once in a while. Especially every time their asses got saved. And so the *Jeanne d'Arc* had the best wine cellar in the Fleet, the most recent entertainment tapes, the best-equipped rec deck in the entire history of human spaceflight.

And so life had been perfect, a thing that his ancestors would have found perfectly familiar and that Matsunaga found suited him better than any story could have. Go out and fight hard, clean, live or die. Then come back to wine, music, a long extra-hot bath, and a beautiful lady who was as dangerous in a fighter as any man. Heaven.

That had been before Bethesda had fallen. During the first skirmishes above Target there had been a glorious thrill in the clash, knowing that every strike brought humankind that much closer to freedom from the Weasels. Then they'd won and gone down to base. And found out they'd been lured out, decoyed, and this wasn't the Khalia home world at all. He'd been cheated. They'd all been ripped off of their victory.

Bethesda had been a nightmare then, and he'd been glad to be back sealed up in space again where he'd belonged. But the *Jeanne d'Arc* was no longer the pleasure cruise of the Fleet. Something happened in Bethesda, when they saw what the enemy could do. How ruthless and utterly inhuman the Weasels were. Somehow the indie-supplied luxury had gotten in the way of their mission, and after Bethesda the mission became paramount. No one missed the wine, the tapes, the delicacies of thirty-some worlds. This time they were going to hit the Weasels once and for all, exterminate them where they lived. That was all that mattered. It had all the marks of a good fight and Matsunaga had been ready, if not so eager as the first time. Hell, he wasn't a green kid anymore, anyway. A vet had to have some of the shine rubbed off.

The *Jeanne d'Arc* had been in the worst of it at Khalia. He'd been out, far from the pack and on to two hotshots at the same time when she'd been blown. He shouldn't have been that far away, should have stayed tight with the group. But damn, he wasn't Killean's wingman and Killean had this tendency to stay on the flight leader even when it wasn't the best tactics. So it wasn't really his fault that he'd been out.

There'd been that hunch, too, early in the day. Something about the carrier had seemed—unreal. He didn't know how to describe it. Just one of those hunches, one of those things that happens in a vet who survives, one of the things he learns never to question.

So he was way out gunning for these two raiders who were turning so fast on each other you'd swear they were dancing *Swan Lake*. Got both the bogies, too, but that didn't make up for the *Jeanne d'Arc*. She was gone and she'd been home, and all the people that had mattered since he'd left Seimpo had been on her.

He'd lost it then, and still didn't have enough memory to quite piece together what he'd done. Managed to cut through all the way down to the ground, gutting his plasma cannon till they were shooting dry. Wiped out a whole division of raiders sitting on their fannies waiting to lift when he'd flamed the fighter down. Got the Galactic Cross for it, too. Not that he cared.

No, Matsunaga had managed to keep most of that battle repressed in subconsciousness. The shrinks on the *Elizabeth* had done their best and then decided to leave him alone. He didn't do anything bizarre on the ward, played chess and acey-deucey with the other patients, joined the Thursday night crowd in the lounge for two hours of omni's best shows, complained about the food.

Maybe it was the complaints that convinced the staff that Kazuo Matsunaga was completely recovered, both body and wits, and discharged him. Only there was no unit to go back to, no Screaming Eagles with their own patches on their shoulders and their calligraphed headbands. The few survivors of the *Jeanne d'Arc* had been reassigned, spread into various units, given charity chores to keep them busy.

Matsunaga hadn't minded his job at first. Collecting up all the Khalian raiders, that had been worth something. Every time he came across one of those tiny one-seaters, all overburdened with guns and power and not enough control, he had wanted to celebrate. Just like getting them in the old days, only this time the tech boys stripped them down before the good guys got to torch them.

Lieutenant (j.g.) Kazuo Matsunaga had been in charge of confiscating even the shredded remains of Khalian raiders in sector seventeen. He had done his job happily at first, until his contact with the Khalia became more complex. He had to know more about them to understand where they might be hiding scrap and repair modules. He had to learn their language, at least the technical vocabulary, so that he could make his desires clear.

And the more he learned, the more he remembered his old lessons, the ones that the Screaming Eagles had all thought were so quaint and silly at the time. Things about the way a true warrior lives and acts, about how honor was not about acting out in a scout fighter because he'd been in a blind rage. The Galactic Cross had begun to leer at him in the mirror, knowing perfectly well that there had been nothing heroic in his actions at all.

The Khalia stirred a memory in him. It went deeper than his training, deep down into the race memory itself. They truly lived the way *sensei* had taught him a warrior lived. No turning away, no surrender, a willingness to live perfectly in the now. The now was all they had. Even the Khalian language was hazy on time in their verbs, and what was ancient and heroic and what was modern and well known and what was somehow only

real in the imagination were all woven together in their poets'
great sagas.

The language twisted and turned, mocked him with para-
doxes and simple truths that he had forgotten the same way he
had forgotten the flaming entry into Khalia's sky. The Fleet
xenopologists were not wrong; the Khalia did live for battle.
Death and life completed each other, halves of a perfectly
balanced whole. And the balanced and perfect moment of
being was neither life nor death, but the sword of honor that cut
through the fabric of both.

Slowly Matsunaga came to the conclusion that he understood the Khalia to the bottom of his soul. He still found their
faces unattractive and unreadable, their language unpleasant,
and their smell nearly unbearable, but there was something in
himself that he recognized every time he confronted them. The
Khalia did not live by greed alone. They were *bushi*, in a way
his old *sensei* had said no longer existed. They were *bushi* in
the way Kazuo Matsunaga had dreamed of being *bushi*,
following the way of the warrior like the true samurai of
ancient lost Japan.

He understood when human in the Khalia language shifted
from something that meant "hairless defenseless prey" to
"worthy opponent." There was no dishonor in being beaten by
a superior force. There was no dishonor in seeking to serve it.

This was not something Matsunaga's colleagues were about
to accept. Lieutenant Jarmon Reeves had told Matsunaga so
rather bluntly when they torched the last turned-in raider's
ship. "I don't like it when they turn stuff in," Reeves had said
thoughtfully. "I don't trust them. One of those is going to be
booby-trapped and blow from here to Tau Ceti. All this
'respect the worthy opponent' bullshit is just so we buy in,
that's it."

Matsunaga had kept quiet that time. He knew better. The
true warrior ethic of these people had spoken to his soul. It was
a thing Reeves could not understand. Jarmon Reeves had never
swept the archery garden because he had hit the target more
than the others, even when it was swinging, even when he was
blindfolded. Most of the Fleet didn't understand the strength of
being only and totally who you were, not the way the Khalia

did. They were berserkers who wrote poetry like the samurai of
old, and if they didn't have the refinement to fold the poems
into little paper boats with candles in them and float them down
the river under falling maple leaves, well, perhaps that was a
bit too much to want.

So he had played with the children in the school, teaching
them the first katas he had learned. What better way to make
contact than through their mutual warrior past? And what better
way to gain the confidence of the society than through the
children? He could come and sit and listen to their stories and
learn about these people the way they learned about themselves.

Then Matsunaga's cultural delicacy was rewarded. A
Khalian youngster, who had admired his discipline and courtesy along with his complete lack of tolerance for even the
slightest evasion of the law, had led him to the bunker.

The youngster was Asheko's younger brother, and the
bunker had been fully operational and utterly untouched. One
of the caches left by the Syndicate to insure their war of
attrition was waged to the very end, no doubt. The loyalty that
inspired such building, and that had turned it over to him, was
something he bowed before with respect. These beings,
however alien, had an intrinsic understanding of the fact that
only in serving something more than yourself could anyone
find true honor.

But he had been right and, dammit, Reeves had been wrong.
Once defeated, they were loyal. It was something the Fleet
didn't understand most of the time. Maybe that was why Ito
had left, come home to Seimpo. And to serve the victor, to love
it for its deadly elegance. It was pure, it was *bushi*, it was
something Matsunaga understood perfectly.

These aliens, they were primitive, and so they had the
advantages of the primitive. They believed and acted all at
once. It was a thing Matsunaga had always admired. It was
something he had studied and strove for and had missed every
time his arrow had hit the mark. He was still aiming, even
blindfolded. The arrow had always been an invasion when he
shot it, not the completion of the harmony of the target. It was
the essence of Zen, of *bushi*, of everything his throwback

imagination loved. It was the one thing he hadn't been able to achieve.

He should have brought back a Marine decontamination squad right then. But twenty-four perfectly armed little raiders, deadly and beautiful like the steel-tipped arrows of a bow, they were too perfect and useful to simply waste. Matsunaga looked at them and one of his hunches had overwhelmed him, clutching at his head and his belly and his knees. More than any order, more than any battle plan, he could see that to destroy these weapons would be more than criminal waste. It would be even worse than dangerous.

Someday the Fleet will need these things, he heard the voice of his *sensei* echo in his skull. Not because Matsunaga was psychic or even believed in telepathy, but because it was the kind of thing Ito would say. *Sensei* always, always insisted on paying attention to details, to using every advantage nature and their *kami* allowed, to figure every element into the balance so that the individual could achieve a perfect moment of *wa*, inner harmony. And it was this harmony that was the essence of battle, the heart of *bushido* itself.

His orders were to destroy, but a true warrior does not destroy wantonly. This bunker, who knew about them, he asked the young Khalian.

The boy had met his eyes fiercely. "My brother and his unit of the Home Defense," the child had rasped proudly. "Not even the Syndicate knows about this installation."

"They had to build it," Matsunaga had said patiently.

The boy had barked in what Matsunaga interpreted as a defiant laugh. "Our captives built it, and there are more like it, too. But I don't know about any others. The Home Defense was never invoked."

And a good thing, too, Matsunaga thought privately. Using the adolescents and elderly of the population as the very last line was something he respected the Khalia for planning. He was only glad that his own people hadn't had to fight these warriors backed against their own bedrock.

Matsunaga had kept their secret because he trusted these people, strange smelly people though they were. And because he understood their loyalty, and in the end because he could not resist the more personal loyalty the unit of Home Defense owed him. Kazuo Matsunaga was the commander of Khalia who would happily die under him. Who would fight for the glory of doing so.

"We do not like to wait," the Khalian rasped at his side. He had forgotten that the alien was there. "We like to attack."

Matsunaga nodded sagely. "We will attack when we are needed," he repeated. It was often necessary to repeat things to the Khalians. "There is more honor, more discipline, in doing what is needful rather than what appears noble at the time."

The Khalian grunted. Matsunaga hoped he didn't recognize the hokey lines off an omni special he had seen as a kid. Now he knew the line was bad and it thrilled him anyway, because it was true.

In the monitors he could see the damage, floating specks of light that faded and died. Sides looked nearly equal, the hot blue of the Fleet on the readout maybe a little more numerous, the screaming orange of the enemy concentrated in heavier ships. There was something there about the balance, something that made his gut give the warning. Something subliminal, maybe, about the positioning, something that no one in the battle itself could see.

The Syndicate was pulling back slowly, in a pattern that mimicked retreat but was not the real thing. It was a lure, he thought, drawing the Fleet fighters farther from their carriers, enticing the heavies at the tip of the formation farther into deep space.

Matsunaga wanted to swear. They were being led out, gently and expertly, but they were being led. They couldn't see it and he couldn't tell them. There wasn't anyone who would listen to him, except to shoot his head off. Mental-discharged ex-flyboy Matsunaga who wanted to trust the Khalia to guard their tail.

His throat was dry with anger, the tearless rage that threatened to erupt when he saw the shifts, the delicate-patterned interplay that most of the groundhogs at the Fleet Academy didn't know existed.

Oh, Matsunaga knew perfectly well enough. His *sensei* had told him, and *sensei* had been trained as a Fleet tactician there.

He'd been itching to refine the training he had had from the old man in the plain white dojo at home. Then he found out that the old man had known more than the entire General Staff together. It was only much later, when he was delicately given a medical/mental discharge, that he learned the old man had once been Fleet Admiral Ito.

No, that wasn't entirely true. There had been others. And Matsunaga knew that he was right, the way he'd always been right. That the feeling, the knowing, had never led him wrong. And they just hadn't been willing to listen . . . Maybe in Admiral Ito's day hunches were more respected. Or, more likely, maybe just Admiral Ito had been able to pull it off.

Overhead, the pattern was resolving itself on the big board. The lures were farther away now, and the whole shape of the battle had shifted. The cone was too long, too far from the planet, not heeding the readings indicating a deep reserve of enemy strength.

It had all the features of a pincer movement, only neither of the Syndicate flanks had moved. Matsunaga studied the schematic, willing Duane to see what was going on. He wanted to scream, to warn them, to explain. There was no chance, just the way there hadn't been any chance the times before. And he had learned his own lessons in patience much more painfully than the Khalians around him.

He waited. He counted very carefully to twenty in Khalian, a feat he had only mastered in the past month. And then he spoke. "Now. But don't move until I say so."

With that order Matsunaga left the command center. Khalians being who they were, they could not respect a leader who was not in front of them in battle. And Matsunaga being who he was couldn't resist the urge to take the fore and press the attack. More glory, always glory, alone and in front.

And so he did the checklist on the Khalian raider that he had commandeered as his personal fighter. It wasn't as graceful as the Fleet scouts, it wasn't as powerful as the ground defenses, but it was enough. The battle arrays responded to the test-check, the soft reassuring blue glow enveloping the whole board as the ship came alive.

"Number Seven, ready."

"Red Ball, ready."

"First Death, ready."

One by one the Khalians checked in, took their place in the hierarchy of the command by group and number, by experience and kills and pure and simple ardor. Still Matsunaga held them back. There was something else, a hunch starting to tighten like a fist of lead in his belly, a knowing that in the dark was some nasty surprise.

"Surprise is still the greatest weapon we have," Ito had told him when he was still a boy, brewing tea and sweeping the dojo floor. *More than your body, your training, your technology, even your intelligence, it is the creative artist who can defeat any odds or any technology. Surprise, elegance, patience. Battle is an exercise in harmony. If you are completely in the conflict, being and doing are the same, winning and losing are the same. Be perfectly empty. Let the arrow of being, of will, fly to the target. Be the arrow. Be the bow. Be the target.*

Be the target.

Space rippled around him, barren and cold, a Fleet lured out imperceptibly beyond the margins of decent rear cover. But the enemy was beyond, all their strength concentrated in the attack. Their flanks had not begun the long and deadly surround. Nor was there any reason to think that they could achieve that surround, not with the punishment they were taking.

Be the target.

If only they had listened to him before. That was a mistake, past, and the past did not exist. There was only now, and in the now were the twenty-four small raiders he had managed to salvage from the Fleet pacification plan.

Once he had decided to serve all humanity through the Fleet. The day he told Ito he had been accepted into officer candidate training, the old man had remained perfectly calm. "Drink your tea," the old man had told him. "If, someday, those you serve break your heart and are no longer worthy of your service, what will happen then?"

Matsunaga remembered being very confused. The Fleet couldn't possibly prove unworthy. They were the most perfect organization since the demise of the Shogunate. And so it had taken him some time to frame an answer, and longer to refine it. When he was ready to speak the teacup was empty.

"*Sensei*," he had said carefully, "my honor is how I do my duty, and not how I am used. And my duty is not to any one individual or even an institution, but to all of the human race, to any population that calls on us for aid."

The old man had only sighed. "That's a good answer, Kazuo," he had finally said. "But there's a long way to go between words and reality."

He hadn't said anything else. Matsunaga had poured another cup of tea and had left. Now, knowing that Ito had once been the great iconoclast of the General Staff, he could never return to the old man again and explain that he had followed his word. That reality had been very different from his dreams and that had not mattered. He had been publicly disgraced and used, eaten and spat out again by the system, but he still had his honor.

Matsunaga followed the computer voice tallying kills and misses. He didn't need the board to see it anymore. The pattern was already clear, and patterns were like all things set into motion, refusing to leave their trajectories until pushed by a greater force. And then, only if the force was rightly applied.

And suddenly he was no longer sitting in the cockpit of a Khalian raider, deep in a bunker he had given his good name and record with the Fleet to keep secret. Because he knew, even if they didn't, that this moment would come. It had always existed in the perfect and unending now.

There was nothing but the now. Nothing to want, nothing to hope for, nothing to lose. Only the moment and the movement in the pattern that was already set and perfect. Even Kazuo Matsunaga had ceased to exist as an entity and had taken his place in the dance.

He did not remember giving the order to launch, or what prompted it. He hadn't waited until the final word on the Syndicate group, returning from Target to appear between Khalia and the Fleet's defenders, cutting off their escape. There was no escape in space, anyway. Not that Matsunaga noticed.

But he was beyond all notice then, acting from instinct in the perfect circles of the perfected now. Without him, without his action, without his phalanx of Khalian raiders, the moment would not be complete. The painting would be missing those final strokes to make it perfect, the artist would be musing, meditating on where those last lines would go. And the arrow, released, was no longer in transit but already united to its goal.

Be the target.

He had said that to the Khalians so many times, but they were not capable of understanding the nuances of Ito's training. And so Matsunaga, in the whole perfection of the now, realized that they were his arrows, as the bunker had been his bow. They were honed and perfect weapons, ready to his hand, and he had spent a lifetime preparing to use them.

As no one else could. Even the Syndicate, who had known the Khalia for generations and had supplied them against the Fleet, even they had not truly appreciated the Khalia's heart. They were like steel, like the swords with a soul. Swords were simple in their beings, made only to kill and to win. The Khalia were simple, too, and sharp and clear.

The com was on when they launched. Matsunaga didn't need it, but the Khalians were silent. He had taught them that, too, and they had embraced his teaching like religion. He could feel them with him, that subtle energy shift that some engineers said was a function of combined energies in a multiple launch, but that Ito had taught him was the harnessing of wills to a single perfect point.

From the darkness deep below Khalia's surface they emerged into a flash of blue sky that deepened into indigo as they sped upward and free into space. A million stars replaced clouds in the canopy display. Far ahead he saw the glitter of the embattled ships, raiders, and heavies all mixed.

There was no scale here. They were far away, he knew, but they looked only like shiny unused toys. Closer up there would be dark spots and scars, the trimmings of war.

They were well trained and better chosen, these aliens whom he had selected for his personal command. They formed on him and waited, while he knew they must be tempted by the glitter-brights ahead. Not any real distance and some smart missile could take one or two down now. But they, like himself, were all unified in a single vision, a single thrust larger than any of them alone.

The Syndicate fighters didn't attack. Why should they? For so many years they had known the Khalians as their shock troops. Loyal reinforcements, more likely, since the Syndicate knew the Khalia's loyalty but not the creed that guided it.

Over the com, locked into passive, Matsunaga could hear enough of the Fleet communications to satisfy himself.

"Khalian raiders lifted, on vector two-oh-twelve. Right down our tail."

"Check your sixes, flyboys," came from one of the cruisers. Matsunaga knew because the boost was strong and the signal clearer than the other comments.

"Never trusted those Weasels," someone in a fighter griped.

The forty-seven ronin indeed. Obviously the Fleet had never learned history. Not Seimpo's version, anyway. Matsunaga wanted to turn off the passive and resisted. It was better for him to know. It was better that he follow their shortcut commands and have an idea where his twenty-four raiders could do the most damage—to the Syndicate flyers on the Fleet's tail.

Around him he could see the tiny Khalian raiders. He could feel the energy held back there. His men, his command, they were too well disciplined to fire before he gave the order. All their Khalian battle furor held in check against their nature, his men were waiting for him to choose the perfect moment, the best target.

As if there ever was any choice. Three big, fat Syndicate cruisers sat like bloated spiders in the middle of their pancake formation. Around them buzzed swarms of smaller craft, destroyers, scouts, fighters. All those ignored the Khalians rapidly penetrating their lines.

The Khalia had been allies for a very long time. Like the Fleet itself, the Syndicate didn't understand the very essence of *bushido* that could turn the whole population in their loyalty in only a few months' time. They, too, listened in on Fleet communication. They, too, believed the twenty-four raiders to be friends. But they would never regret their arrogant assumption of Khalian solidarity—Matsunaga was quite certain that they wouldn't live that long.

He held back. The energy behind him, inside him, built into a great and unstoppable wave. There was no choice now, no decision. There was no thought, either, only the complete and ineffable now, the moment, the paradox, the silence.

And in the silence Matsunaga knew himself to be the arrow and the bow, the bowman and the target, that all were united in this singularity. Battle crystallized reality, balanced it, and so to fight was to seek enlightenment. It was a thing he had never spoken of with his Khalian command. There had never been any need.

Matsunaga held back until he could read the painted numerals on the enemy hulls at visual range. And then, without a word to the group leaders of the flight under him, he opened up all cannon on a single point ahead.

The lead Khalians followed him, homing in on the other oversize cruisers in their sights. The heavies couldn't bring their guns around in time, or maybe they were afraid of mowing down their own fighter force, who were coming quickly around to destroy the traitors in their midst. "Why" did not exist. Only that the three cruisers blew before they could get off a shot between them, and they took their closest fighters with them to the void.

Only seventeen of the Khalian raiders were left when the blaze died. But those seventeen were jealous for the honor of the rest. They were not carefully overseen by tacticians, directing their fire to where it would be most useful. They did not spread out carefully and they did not venture past this single rearguard action.

No matter. It was a rout. The Syndicate ships, so confident of winning the day, were running before the Fleet fighters and ships of the line.

None of the Khalians returned. It would have been shameful for those who had, at least Matsunaga would have thought so. And Matsunaga himself, well, he hadn't even lived beyond the first blast.

Within the year, Master Tactician Ito, along with several young students from his dojo, and Jarmon Reeves had swept out the bunker and stripped it of all alien gear. They lay a wooden floor in the main hangar, and *bokkun* lined the walls. The main screens in the battle management center had gone silver-gray, their leads torn apart, and cushions had been placed around for daily practice of *zazen*, or sitting in meditation.

But the best place was undoubtedly the archery garden in a courtyard behind the main gate. There the targets were set on ropes over the garden wall and students practiced while the targets swung. Some of the students were blindfolded. Others were just learning to use the bow. And they were of every sentient race the Alliance had found. Mostly human to be sure, but there were others there. Even Khalians. Especially Khalians.

The Fleet had thought it was a waste of time and money, as well as a decent bunker, but the memory of Kazuo Matsunaga was too recent. And so there were several young officers there in Fleet uniforms, too, sighting down the arrows in the garden. Officers who would never forget the old, patient *sensei* who always said, "Be the target."

AFTERWORD

The Articles of War as reprinted in this volume are all taken, virtually word for word, from *An Act to make Provision for the Discipline of the Navy* as written for Queen Victoria in 1866, and was resurrected by Su Lin Allison almost intact for use by the Alliance Fleet. Which simply goes to show that some things never change.